REDEMPTION TIME

A novel

by Antony Johnson

About the Author

Antony Johnson, born into an Anglo Irish family, was educated at Wellington College. He was among the last few to be called up for National Service, serving with the 17th/21st Lancers in Germany. He persued an eclectic career, starting with spell in the City, followed by ten years in heavy industry, based in Manchester, all the while moonlighting as an amateur steeplechase jockey. Subsequently he became a professional racehorse trainer in Lambourn, sending out winners of races in the UK and France. A spell living in the Caribbean followed where he formed his own travel business.

Back in England he took this business to a higher level, visiting close on a hundred countries in each of the world's continents. This included riding a horse across Argentinian and Chilean Patagonia, a camel across the Tenere Desert in the Sahara and by various methods from St Petersburg to Siberia in Russia including the crossing of the frozen Lake Baikal, twenty six miles, in a horse drawn sleigh in temperatures of up to minus thirty degrees centigrade. In millennium year he competed and completed the London – Sydney Marathon rally, spaced over thirty two days through fifteen countries.

Previous publications include East Into The Sun, A Crack of the Whip and many travel related magazine articles.

Antony has three sons, Richard, Simon and Sam. His daughter, Jemima, a leading Three Day Event rider, was killed in a riding accident.

He lives in Dorset.

Acknowledgements

Many people have helped and encouraged me in writing this book. I am immensely grateful to everybody particularly when I'm thinking 'what the hell am I going to write next?'

If I may single out Sam Carter of Tandem Publishing who brilliantly saw me through with great professional skill my previous book, A Crack of the Whip, subsequently introducing me to my wonderful Literary Agent Susan Mears and her team including editor Jan Chapman.
To them all I owe a huge sense of gratitude.

To my publisher, Chris Day, founder of Filament, for his courage and support in taking me on.

To my very dear friend Grainne Kearns and her late husband Pat in Barbados a big thank you. During many years of living there they, and lots of others, became stalwart friends. Now Grainne keeps me up to speed with all that's going on there which has been most helpful in the writing of the book.

To my Godson, Henry Beeby, Chairman and CEO of Robert J Goff in Ireland for keeping me well informed and in touch with the Irish racing scene. Thanks also to him for introducing me to Nicky McDowell, the eminent Dublin Jeweller who gave me expert advice.

Candace and Reilly Travers in Zimbabwe were kind enough to permit me to 'send' a character in the book to their brilliant animal conservation farm which does so much for the rescue of injured endangered species and in breeding for release.

To my indefatigable friend and luckily near neighbour, Della Burke, my computer 'guru' who puts up ad infinitum with my typing tantrums and inability to understand more than 10% of what the computer is capable.

Lastly but very importantly my sons Simon and Sam plus their wives and families for their constant support and advice.

Published by
Filament Publishing Ltd
16, Croydon Road, Beddington
Croydon, Surrey CR0 4PA
www.filamentpublishing.com
+44(0)20 8688 2598

Antony Johnson
ISBN 978-1-915465-06-1
© 2022 Antony Johnson

Printed in the UK

Contents

CHAPTER 1

Will dropped his hands, allowing his horse to pull up. As they came to a halt, he turned to the lad on the horse upsides him.

"How was that, Joe?"

Joe, an experienced work rider and ex-jockey, muttered approval but said little. Will was in ecstasy; this was the first racing-pace piece of fast work that he'd ridden. Adam Platt, the trainer, rode across on his hack from his vantage point.

"Well, what do you think?"

"Absolutely amazing, just fabulous."

"I'm not talking about you, you idiot. I am asking about Commissar, the horse you are riding?"

"He was brilliant – fitter than I am. Didn't want to stop."

William Carpenter, 17 years old, in the early stages of his Easter holidays from school, in late spring following a severe winter, was in good spirits as they rode back to the yard, via a headland of a sown field, the crop just beginning to show above ground. He and Joe continued along a lane bordered by a tall hedge, with new leaves of pale virgin green glinting in the early morning sunlight. A chirpy song thrush sang merrily from its perch. Back in the yard he unsaddled his horse, rubbed him down and put on his rug. Adam Platt, a man in his mid-sixties, a former jockey himself, had won the Cheltenham Gold Cup many years before and was now a well-respected trainer, with some 40 National Hunt horses that he trained, mainly for farming friends and business people from Manchester and Liverpool. He came up to Will as he was heading for the tack room.

"That's what I needed to know. Races are won on the track, not the training gallops. I need them to want more, so well done."

Will smiled. "Thank you, Mr Platt," he said, mounting his bicycle to peddle off home a couple of miles away. He arrived just as his father, Angus, a rather sad-faced man, was leaving for his office in Liverpool in his elegant but elderly BMW. Will went inside where his mother, Mary, was busy cooking fried eggs and bacon for himself and his 13-year-old sister Joanna, already tucking into her cornflakes.

"All right, jockey, tell us all about it," she said, waving her spoon in the air like a whip.

Will hadn't come down off his cloud.

"It was brilliant," he exclaimed. "I couldn't believe how fast we were going."

"Oh, God, we'll never hear the end of this" she replied, head down back into the cornflakes.

Home was a medium-sized comfortable house at the end of a short drive off a B road near the old market town of Tarporley, Cheshire. It had previously been a Dower House. Their Dower House. But that was a long time ago in the 18th century when the family estate comprised several thousand acres.

Angus Carpenter had been properly brought up, took part in all countryside, social and equestrian activities, and he pleased his parents. Mickey, his father, with an eye to the family finances, decided to send him to Radley – then an upcoming public school with an enterprising headmaster and a fair bit less expensive than the likes of Eton or Harrow. This was followed by studying Estate Management at Cirencester. All was going well. In the mid-fifties, England won 3 successive Ashes series. In February 1960 the Prime Minister Harold Macmillan made his historically famous 'Winds of Change' speech in South Africa.

Post-war, Mickey's father Ralph paid little attention to social and rural affairs, though Mickey was a supporter of all country sports; rather more shooting than hunting. He ran a small family shoot at Welchmans, the family home, to which he invited his friends on a regular basis and headed off to Scotland and Yorkshire to shoot grouse in August and September.

The Cheshire Hunt Ball was held in those days at the derelict Peckforton Castle. Peckforton, a mock medieval castle built in 1844-50 by the eccentric John Tollemache, at that time the largest landowner in Cheshire, was perched on top of a conical hill about a mile away from another castle, the genuine 11th century Royal castle of Beeston. A complete folly, Peckforton was never properly lived in, it stood alone with marvellous views over the surrounding countryside. It had no facilities like electricity or water supply and was of solid sandstone construction. Teams of hunting volunteers spent a month each year cleaning the areas in the castle to be used, installing temporary lighting, heating, water, loos etc.

This particular year a fashionable band of the time, Confrey Phillips, was hired and the event took place in early November. Mickey and his wife, Molly, plus all the nobs of Cheshire society came and brought house parties, young, old, farmers, landowners, plus a few business people from Manchester and Liverpool. Angus had his own party of young people and the evening was a rip-roaring success. At about 3.30 a.m. Mickey and Molly left, tired but happy, to drive the few miles back home. At the same time, a milk tanker was making its usual round of dairy farms in the area. Coming out of the drive of one such farm close to a sharp right-hand bend in the lane, the driver, not looking left or right, pulled out, completely blocking the lane, just as Mickey approached. There was no possibility of escape; they hit the tanker broadside on and died instantly.

Will had the rest of the morning to himself. After lunch, he saddled up his own pony and hacked to the Cheshire polo ground for a Pony Club stick and ball session organised by a retired Army Colonel, Julian Shannon, who greeted him.

"Hello, young William. Good to see you back here. Home for the Easter holidays?"

"Yes Sir and glad to be. I rode a gallop for Mr. Platt this morning."

"Did you, by Jove; that must have been exciting."

"It certainly was. I couldn't believe we were going so fast."

"Well done. Now, let's see if you can remember from last summer how to hit a polo ball."

Will's elder brother, James, had introduced him to Col. Shannon. He had a few lessons, loved it and showed promise. James had been Head Boy at Harrow, captain of cricket and very popular. The brothers were very close, Will regarding James as his hero and mentor. A keen games player himself and an above-average student, he didn't consider himself in the same league as James, who was now at Cirencester Agricultural College on an Estate Management course.

The next morning's work at Adam Platt's was more routine. Will rode a nice young 4-year-old, that hadn't been in the yard long, in a steady canter. On his return home, he was surprised to see his father's car still in the garage, but as it was Friday he thought maybe he'd taken the day off. Both his mother and father were at the kitchen table when he walked in.

His father said, "Will, we have left Joanna to sleep in this morning. However, I need to talk to you."

Will poured himself a mug of coffee from the pot kept warm on the Aga and sat down.

"What's up, Dad? Is it my school report?"

Angus forced a little laugh and said, "No, it's a bit more serious than that. I rang James last night and asked him to come home for the weekend, he will be here later this afternoon. I have some extremely bad news that affects all of us and the family. I should have discussed it all with you before, but I've kept putting it off. I can no longer do so. We are in a very serious financial situation. You know that ever since your grandparents were killed in that horrendous crash, I have been running Carpenter & Cousin and taking care of the family finances. When I took on both jobs, I had no idea what a terrible mess awaited me.

First Carpenter & Cousin: your grandfather, I am afraid, paid little or no attention to the business and your great grandfather was killed aged only 23 in the Anglo-Zulu war in 1879. Actually, the business had been neglected since your ancestor Jack's time and he died in 1868 My father, Mickey, bless him, you can find excuses for: he was brought up in another era, life was different, free and easy for many of what you might call 'our sort of people'. We had just come out of the cataclysmic World War One and were facing the consequences in 1918 during which no family was unscathed by death or appalling wounds. Many thought this could never happen again so now let's get on and make up for lost time. Before we knew where we were it was World War Two. Your grandfather was a WW2 MC decorated hero; he helped save our country but at great personal and mental cost. When it was over and with one disastrous marriage behind him, plus a baby he never saw again, he couldn't settle down to life running a country estate and a, to him, boring office job in Liverpool. His second wife, my mother, was wonderful to and with him.

As you know, it was an unmitigated tragedy when they were

both killed in that terrible accident, heart-breaking for me. Picking up the pieces was very difficult but I have been lucky enough to have your mother, James, Joanna and you to come home to. Previously, following the enterprise, bravery and hard work of your ancestor, Benjamin, we were a very well-off family for many generations but financially it has been downhill for about the last hundred years. You can blame the two wars up to a point but really no member of this family has looked after the finances and fortunes for a very long time. They have just left it to others who have been both incompetent and lazy. After your great grandfather and grandfather died, the former still very young, huge amounts in death duties had to be paid. This meant Welchmans had to be sold. Actually, my father was in the process of selling it anyway at the time of his death, having received an unsolicited offer from the new owners to turn it into a smart country house hotel. The fact remains that the expenditure of successive generations of Carpenters for over the last century has far exceeded their income. Your great grandfather placed a large sum of money with Lloyds of London.

To fill you in, Lloyds is not a company, it is a collection of individual people or businesses that place money in their hands under the name of Lloyds to settle insurance claims. In 1686, a merchant, John Lloyd owned a Coffee House close to London Docks, where those involved mainly in maritime business, used to gather. Insurance was a new word in those days and it grew from there. In present-day terms to describe it as simply as possible, the business is now run by professional syndicates within the Lloyds network which place the business across the wide spectrum of industry, whatever it may be. The profit made by the syndicates is divided among those who have subscribed the money and paid annually by way of a dividend. It is possible, and in some cases obligatory, for the Names to have a Reserve account into which part of their dividend is paid with obvious tax advantages. However, the capital subscribed by each individual or business remains untouchable at Lloyds. It is only recoverable on receipt of notice that the Name wishes to withdraw from Lloyds and the period of such notice is three years.

In normal times Lloyds names can expect to draw a very handsome dividend from their participation but nevertheless, their capital is always at risk so the amount invested should be no more than what one is prepared to lose in case of a large claim or series of claims. What has happened to us is that a far higher proportion of our capital than should have been, was tied up in Lloyds. Recently, Lloyds has suffered probably the most traumatic period in its history, largely by way of utterly unexpected legal claims and awards in the USA for what is known as APH – Asbestos Pollution and Health hazard.

You may ask why did we not know about this and why was not something done about it? The short answer is that it was an area that has only recently come to light owing to the fact that massive claims have been paid out to individuals and organisations that have discovered that illnesses have been diagnosed as coming from being exposed to asbestos pollution 20 years previously. The cause of the original illness being unknown at the time.

The upshot is that my Lloyds liabilities exceeds my capital and I have no option other than to place our house on the market. I've heard it said that unlimited liability at Lloyds meant that they could take it all and leave you with 'an armchair and sixpence'. It breaks my heart and that of your mother to tell you this but there is no alternative. I spent the whole of yesterday with our financial advisers, lawyer and the bank, but no solution was found. I have arranged temporary finance of sufficient funds to tide us over, based on the value of this house and property, but life as we knew it has changed dramatically. I am afraid that you will have to leave Harrow, as I can no longer afford to pay the school fees."

Will sat in stunned silence and disbelief about what his father had told him. Then, rising, he went to his father and mother, clasped his arms around them giving them a huge hug and said, "Don't worry Dad, we'll manage somehow, let's see what James thinks."

Later, when James arrived, the scene was repeated. He, too, took the news in deep shock but in typical stalwart fashion, as elder brother and a born leader, stood resolutely with his family. He said that his course at Cirencester was coming to an end anyway, that he had made lots of friends and contacts, and would approach the change with courage and determination.

He ended up by saying, "I think we've all had enough for one day. Let's have a drink before we go to bed. Dad, you've had a terrible time fighting all this by yourself, although I think Mum knows more than she's letting on. I wish you'd brought at least me in on this a bit earlier; we're all your family, you know, and as a family, we stand together. You've done all you can, but from now on it's up to me and this young wannabe jockey here, to rally round and sort out what's best for us all."

As they were going upstairs he turned to Will and said, "We'll talk about this in the morning. I've got to leave before lunch."

Early next morning Will rang Adam Platt to say that he was very sorry, he couldn't come in that morning. James had come home late last night, but only briefly for the day, and there were some family things that he wanted to talk about. During a rather silent breakfast, James said that he had, indeed, to leave late morning though needed petrol in his car and went off to the local garage.

"I'll come with you – just in case, stranger, you get lost."

In the car, James said, "You know, I haven't said anything before, but something's been in my mind for a while that all was not well on the financial front. Probably, as Dad said, it was too late to do anything about it, but I wish he had brought it up, nevertheless. I'm very, very sorry for you, missing the best part of a Harrow education – I don't mean on the bloody educational front, but the fun and games in the last few terms at a public school like Harrow and its closeness to the fleshpots of London. But never mind, your time will come. Now, I've nearly done at Cirencester. Privately, between you and I, I don't know why Dad was so keen for me to go there, but he wanted me to, and I've enjoyed it, learnt a lot of things outside estate management similar to what I would have at Oxford. I've made what I am sure will be lifelong friends and had a lot of fun. Not a word to Dad and Mum but I have been looking at alternatives for a while and am seriously thinking about the army. It's reasonably well paid these days, there always seem to be places in the world where our troops are needed and it costs one nothing to be sent there. More importantly, I think it is absolutely vital that this country maintains a defence force that is considered worthy of the name to all those bastards who may harbour other thoughts. Yesterday's news has been the catalyst that has tipped the balance and I shall be starting to put my plans into action as of tomorrow."

CHAPTER 2

Outwardly, the weeks after the bombshell news passed with no apparent change for Will. He continued to ride out each day for Adam Platt and to learn to play polo under the tuition of Julian Shannon. Backstage, Angus went ahead with the agonizing task of placing all his remaining property and, indeed, his life on the market. James completed his Cirencester course, emerging with a highly commended diploma. During another visit home, he told Angus about his plan to join the army, explaining that many of his friends at Cirencester had army connections, which he had already started to follow up. He emphasised to his father that Cirencester had been very good for him, it had broadened his outlook on life considerably. "And, I quite fancy being in charge of a few blokes," he said.

For Will, the dream stopped at the end of the Easter holidays. He had to break the news to all his friends that he would not be going back to school. He was acutely aware of the sidelong glances in his direction and could only imagine what they were saying behind his back. He could also see that his father was distraught, however, all of them, his sister Joanna having been brought into the picture during a loving and tender mother and daughter scene, were wholly supportive of Will. In quiet moments on his own, he went over in his mind about what he knew regarding family history and that his father had reminded him about their ancestor Benjamin and the sugar plantation in Barbados. What must it have been like for Benjamin starting a new life in a far-off and strange land? All he knew about the West Indies was that they produced outstandingly good cricketers: the 3 Ws, Worrell, Walcott and Weekes, the legendary Gary Sobers and the army of fast bowlers: Hall & Griffiths, Holding, Roberts, Marshall, Walsh and Ambrose, to name but a few. Maybe he would go there one day. Then, *Hey, what's wrong with now? I've finished school, I've nothing to do except wonder how I'm going to make my fortune, so let's get started.* He thought about what James had said that day in his car and, *'right,*

I'll have a crack, too'. He remembered that one of his best friends at Harrow was a boy called Jimmy Van Duran, from an Anglo-Dutch family who had connections with a family that owned banana plantations in the West Indies, with a contract with a shipping company to bring their bananas to England. On the spur of the moment, he sat down and wrote a letter to his friend, Jimmy, setting out what had happened, his predicament, and why he had not come back to school. Would it be possible, he wrote, for Jimmy to ask his parents if there was any influence or introduction they could bring to bear, that would help him to get a job as a deckhand on one of the ships carrying the bananas? It was a very long shot, he knew, though nothing ventured, nothing gained, he thought.

A week or so later he received a very sympathetic reply from Jimmy saying how sorry he was and how much he was missed by all his friends at school. He also said that he would ask his parents to enquire whether there might be a possible opening for him with the shipping company. The next weekend Jimmy was out from school and at his home in London. He rang Will.

"I've broached the subject", he said. "It's a tricky one. My father has said that their cousins do have a contract with the shipping company and are very important customers, however, they cannot be seen to be exerting undue influence on matters of this nature. What they are prepared to do is to provide the address of the department responsible for engaging staff and the name of the manager. It would be up to you to apply for a position in the normal way and see how you get on. Between the lines, I get the feeling that it might be suggested to the manager that he grants you an interview, but from then on, it would be down to you."

"Thank you Jimmy; you're a star and I'll keep you posted. Let me have the name and address and I'll get on with it straight away."

Will wrote it down and considered his next step. He rang James who was staying with a friend in London while making enquiries about his future army career. He also spoke to his father. Between the three of them, they concocted a letter that they thought covered all the salient points, without sounding too much like a pleading or a begging letter. A reply came back in the form of a stereotyped letter enclosing an application form for a position in the company. The form itself was quite easy to complete with all standard questions, until the question *'why do you want to join the company and how do you think your contribution will be of use to the company?'*

The family 'board' got together again and the answer to the question ran thus: *'I am fit, healthy and, having achieved satisfactory exam results as detailed above, I consider myself intelligent. I am also ambitious, have a good team spirit and a desire to more than play my part. I am a good learner and am very keen to be a crew member on one of your ships.'*

Every day Will looked anxiously for the post to arrive and every day for what seemed an eternity, nothing came until one day, just as he had almost given up hope, a letter arrived from an address in Barry, South Wales which ran as follows:

'Dear Mr Carpenter,

We have received your application form for a position as deckhand and I should be pleased if you would present yourself for an interview at the above address as soon as you are able. Please telephone my secretary on the above number to make an appointment.

Yours sincerely,

Arthur Thomas

Personnel Manager.'

"Whoopee," he yelled, waving the letter.

The only person within earshot was Joanna, who came back with, "Oh, you're not the next James Bond are you?"

She also gave him a grin and a hug when Will showed her the letter.

He rang the number, spoke to the secretary, and made the appointment in a couple of days' time. On the day his mother took Will, dressed in his best, and only, suit to Crewe station for the journey to Barry, changing at Cardiff. The destination was a rather dingy building close to the docks. Will was shown into an equally dingy sparsely furnished waiting room with a few hard chairs; after a few minutes a bespectacled youngish man with close-cropped hair, dressed in an ill-fitting blue suit and brown shoes came in.

"William Carpenter?"

"Yes, Sir."

"Do come with me," leading Will into a small office lined with filing cabinets and other office paraphernalia.

A window with louvred panes looked out over the docks, though it did not provide enough light, which was the reason for the overhead strip lighting being permanently switched on.

Mr Thomas sat down behind his desk motioning Will to the cane-seated chair opposite him. He opened a file, smiled pleasantly at Will and said in a calm Welsh accent:

"Welcome to Barry and thank you for coming all this way. May I call you William?"

"Certainly though Will will do."

"Okay, Will. I've carefully read your application and the first thing that strikes me is why, with your upbringing and education, you want to be a deckhand?"

"Mr Thomas –"

"Do call me Arthur."

"– thank you, Arthur, I don't want to sound conceited or presumptuous in any way, but my feeling is that I am 18 years old, do not want to go to university, have no specific qualifications apart from five A levels, am not yet certain on a definite career to follow, though I have to start somewhere, and this chance, if it is offered to me, represents as good a start as any."

"Well, that sounds a pretty sensible outlook. Tell me something else: do you have a happy home life?"

"Yes, very. I have an elder brother and a younger sister, and both my parents still alive. We have had a financial setback, but we are a united family and as such, I am sure we will get through this and survive."

"What does your elder brother do?"

"He has recently completed a course at Cirencester Agricultural College and is now in the process of joining the army."

"Do you play or are you interested in any sports?"

"Yes, I am. I played rugby, cricket and tennis at school. I love horses and riding. I have a part-time job riding for a racehorse trainer and I follow most sports with interest."

After about ten minutes, Mr Thomas, to whom Will had warmed after being a bit hesitant to begin with, said, "We have a position coming vacant as a deckhand and cabin steward on one of our ships, The Star, she is called. She sails on a regular basis from Barry to the West Indies, calling at Barbados, St Lucia, sometimes St Vincent and Grenada, then directly back to Barry.

On the outward journey, the ship carries what we call general cargo, though from St Lucia onwards, on the return legs we bring bananas. The bananas are picked semi-ripe on the island plantations and placed in specially constructed containers on the ship, temperature regulated, so that the bananas fully ripen on board and are ready to be transported to supermarkets and other outlets to be sold to the public immediately upon arrival. So far, so good. Do you understand?"

"Yes, please continue."

"There is another side and source of revenue on board. We have about twelve passenger cabins on each ship. Generally speaking, these cabins are sold to and occupied by middle-aged to elderly passengers, who wish to take a month's cruise and cannot afford or don't want to travel on the enormous, fancy and very expensive specialist cruise liners. They do, however, expect to be well looked after and treated with respect. There is a bar and dining saloon which is shared between the ship's officers and the cruise passengers. In this way the passengers feel that they are part of the action, so to speak, and the officers are spread out on the table plan for meals with the passengers.

There are normally five or six deckhands on each ship, firstly to work manually under the supervision of a foreman or officer, on anything to do with the cargo, whatever it is. This is particularly relevant during loading and unloading times in the various ports. Secondly, each deckhand will be allotted two or possibly three cabins to look after during each section of the voyage. This entails making the beds each morning, cleaning and tidying the cabins, dealing with any laundry – not the actual washing, this is undertaken by the ship's housekeeping staff – and generally chatting up the passengers, looking after them and making sure they are having a good time. Additionally, you will be required to wait at tables in the dining saloon at all meal times and assist the barman with the serving of drinks etc.

Your accommodation is in a communal dormitory for all the deckhands, where you have your own curtained-off area. There is a common dining saloon for all the crew below officer level.

From what you have told me, I am prepared to offer you a position as described. I am not asking you for an immediate decision, but the offer is open to you for a period of forty-eight hours from now. So, if you have any questions, please fire away?"

Will thought for a moment and then said, "It sounds pretty good to me and I think I know what my answer will be; however, I would like to talk to my family about it as I think that is what they would like and expect me to do. Just one question - how long is each voyage?"

"I'm glad you've asked that; I should have told you. Roughly speaking, a month, depending on weather conditions, any problems with cargo loading or other unforeseeable delays. Again, generally, there is a space of about a week between voyages during which time you would be allowed time off for part of it."

The family board meeting was a short one. *'Well done you and go for it'* was the unanimous decision. Will put a call through to Arthur Thomas the next day to accept the offer. They had a brief conversation during which Thomas offered his congratulations; he said that a formal letter of appointment from the company would be sent during the next few days, but that Will would receive by telegram with the actual day that he was required to start work. Off the record he expected this to be in approximately two weeks' time.

Two days later the offer letter arrived confirming that Will was to be employed as a deckhand and cabin steward on the m.v. *Star* under the command of Captain Dickson for an initial period of one voyage from Barry to various ports of call in the West Indies and return to Barry, offer of further employment to be confirmed on return. Will was thrilled.

He called Jimmy van Duren, "Hi. Jimmy, guess what? I've heard back from the shipping company and they've given me a job as deckhand and cabin steward starting probably in two weeks' time. It's fabulous, I'm extremely excited, thank you so, so much."

"Great news, Will. I'm delighted for you."

"I'm going to write to your father to thank him for the introduction."

"Send me a postcard, will you, with a white sandy beach and a couple of dusky, bikini-clad maidens, and the best of luck!"

The next morning, Will told Adam Platt his news as soon as he arrived in the yard.

"I'm very pleased for you, Will. We'll miss you here, for sure."

"I haven't gone yet – won't be for another couple of weeks, I guess, and I'll be back in a month after that."

The lads in the yard had a reaction that was a little different, "What, off to the West fuckin' Indies, you jammy bugger, better watch out for the sharks, mate. Don't go dangling your toes in the water."

Julian Shannon took a more realistic view, "Very good opportunity for you, Will and I wish you well. They play polo in Barbados, so if you go on shore try to go to the polo ground. There's a chap I used to know called Keith Melville – had something to do with polo there. I went a couple of times with Mickey Moseley's Cheshire team. Really good fun it was."

The awaited telegram arrived saying that William Carpenter should report at 9 a.m. on 21st May to Captain Dickson on the m.v. *Star* at Barry Docks in preparation for departure the following day. He was told to bring his letter of engagement, passport and National Insurance Certificate. He had a week to finally prepare; to arrive at Barry docks at 9 a.m. meant that he would have to come the previous evening; his mother helped him find the nearest cheap hotel to the docks and to book him a room.

Two main pubs exist in the country town of Tarporley. The smarter of the two, The Swan, which, in addition to normal bar facilities, has an elegant dining room and restaurant. However, it is best known as the home of the Tarporley Hunt Club, the oldest of all such clubs in the land. Founded in 1762, the members consist of all the great and good in Cheshire society, the qualification of membership being that members, selected by invitation only and all men of course, should own a minimum of 500 acres in the Cheshire Hunt country. Inheritance played its part, as well; thus Angus was elected a member on the death of his father, Mickey, generations of Carpenters having been members since Benjamin acquired the land and built Welchmans in 1802.

The highlight of the club's social activities is a succession of dinners during the first week in November, to coincide with the start of the hunting season. Members, in Club dress of Scarlett Coat with Green Collar, Waistcoat, and Breeches, or Black Trousers, meet in the Club Room at the Swan Hotel. The Club invites hunting grandees from other hunts and have included, in the past, Captain Bay Middleton, the escort and lover of Empress Elizabeth of Austria, whose husband was Emperor Franz Josef. The Empress hunted with the Cheshire for several seasons in the 1880s, renting Combermere Abbey from Lord Combermere, though she often stayed as a guest of the Marquess of Cholmondeley (pronounced Chumley) at Cholmondeley Castle.

In more recent years the rules and membership of the Club have been more relaxed, resulting in members the likes of whom would not have been considered in pre-war days.

Terence Cuneo painted a brilliant portrait in the early 1960s of a Tarporley Hunt Club dinner in progress. Angus had a print copy hanging at home.

The pub at the other end of the town, is the Rising Sun, immensely popular with the younger crowd and farming community who meet up there regularly, especially on Saturdays. Will put the word about among his friends to come the next Saturday to celebrate his departure. This they did – in some style. Adam Platt turned up with his wife and three of the lads from the stables, plus many of the younger members of the polo and hunting crowd. Angus and Mary popped in for a short time bringing Joanna, who was now 14 and did not want to be left behind; they didn't stay for long, leaving the young people to get on with it. Serious hangovers abounded on Sunday morning.

Departure day arrived. Angus driving with Will beside him, Mary and Joanna in the back, they set off on the half-hour journey to Crewe station, where Will, clutching an old and rather battered suitcase, bid a tearful goodbye to his father, mother and sister on the platform when the train rolled in.

"We're very proud of you."

"Beats going back to school. See you in a month's time."

He was off on his life's first adventure.

"It's an ill wind that blows nobody any good," he muttered to himself, as the train chugged forward across a mixture of drab industrial and contrastingly beautiful English landscape glistening in the early summer's sunshine.

Changing trains at Cardiff, the taxi at Barry station took Will to his gloomy overnight hotel that had an overbearing smell of beer; he was handed a key to his room up one flight of linoleum-lined stairs.

"Kitchen closes at 8.30," he was told by the receptionist lady.

Dinner at a small round table was unmemorable and although it was still daylight outside, the light in the dining room needed to be on all the time.

The next morning, suitcase in hand, he approached the dock entrance in good time. The duty clerk stamped his passport and directed him to where the *Star* lay by the quayside. First impression was that she stood proud and imposing, the second being that the colour of white was somewhat *'off'* and he noted that the tell-tale rust marks round where the two forward anchors were stowed, told a story. Will made his way up the gangplank, where he was greeted by a smart, uniformed ship's petty officer.

"Name and reason you want to come on board?" he demanded.

"William Carpenter and here's my letter of employment," Will replied, politely.

The petty officer checked a list he had in a file, "Right, come with me".

He led Will along the deck, up a companion ladder, into the body of the ship and knocked at a door with the sign "PURSER".

"Come in," said a voice.

"William Carpenter, Sir," said the petty officer, ushering Will into the office.

The Purser, a well-built man dressed in a smart white shirt, dark tie and navel uniform, shook Will by the hand and said, "Welcome aboard the Star. I know that Mr Thomas will have told you about your duties on the ship, but I am going elaborate a little more. You are one of six deckhands, four of whom have been on previous cruises with the ship. The senior deckhand is Johnny Jones, with us a long time, he will give you day-to-day instructions. He knows his job backwards, is tough but fair, and it's best not to cross him. If you have any problems of whatever nature, I am the person you come to. All the ships' officers you will call Sir. The Captain's name is Captain Dickson, my name is Mr Enright and the petty officer who brought you here is the Chief Engineer, PO Jennings. Regarding your cabin steward and dining saloon duties, you will report to Mr Payne, the Chief Steward.

We have twelve double cabins on board and I shall be posting a list on the noticeboard with the cabin numbers, the names of the passengers occupying them, and which cabins each of you will be responsible for. In the mornings you will, as far as possible, clean your cabins and make the beds while the passengers are at breakfast. In the evenings you will repeat the exercise by tidying the cabins and turning down the beds. You are bound to come into contact with the passengers in your allocated cabins, and you will act accordingly with respect and politeness at all times, remembering that they are on a cruise and therefore a holiday, for which they are paying considerable sums of money. In the dining saloon you will help Brian O'Reilly, the barman, serve drinks before lunch and dinner, then wait at a table under the direction of Mr Payne. Any questions?"

"No, I don't think so, Sir."

"Right. Now I am going to take you to the housekeeping department to get you kitted out and then show you to your quarters."

"Thank you, Sir."

Enright rose and led Will through the door, locking it behind him; then down into the bowels of the ship, to a locked large storage compartment with fitted shelves and clothes hanging cupboards. Having glanced him up and down, Enright handed him two white shirts, two pairs of black trousers, one pair of waterproof trousers, yellow wellington boots, a heavy ship's anorak, a pair of black rubber-soled shoes and two t-shirts with 'Star' and the ship's emblem printed on them.

"Everything else, use your own, and be clean and tidy at all times."

Will piled his new kit on top of his suitcase and followed Enright to the junior crew's quarters, a long rectangular-shaped cabin with six curtained-off cubicles.

"Here, this one's yours."

Will plonked his stuff on the bed; a small cupboard with a fitted mirror and a wooden chair completed the furnishings. As he left, Enright told Will to sort himself out in his cubicle and to come back to his office at 12 o'clock, when he would give him and the other new crew member a quick tour of the ship.

Two of the other deckhands were unpacking their own things, too, Will introduced himself to one who was in the next cubicle.

"I'm Will," he said to a young man, probably a year or two older than himself with tousled fair hair, and a cheeky chappie look about him.

"Jake, you're new ain't yer, is this your first trip, or 'ave yer come from another ship?" in broad cockney.

"No, my first trip, and never been to sea before."

"You'll be okay. It's a good way to see the world. I have done three so far. Got to go but see yer later."

No sooner had he left when a much older, small, wizened man came bursting in, almost colliding with Will.

"Oh, you must be one of the new ones," he said, with a strong Welsh accent.

"Yes, I'm Will," he replied, holding out his hand, "Are you Johnny?"

Turning around, ignoring Will's outstretched hand, he said over his shoulder as he went, "That's what my friends call me."

The next to arrive was the other new boy, about Will's age, quite tall with dark hair who came in with the Purser, carrying his new kit, having had the same lecture as Will.

"This is David," said Enright. "If you two are ready, we might as well get the tour of the ship over now, so follow me."

They started up on the top deck with the bridge above them. The loading of the cargo had already started and much of the open space towards the bow had been taken up with containers lowered by giant cranes. The main cargo hold was at the stern end of the ship, where the decking was mechanically raised in two halves, to reveal a vast open space below, like the base of an amphitheatre, but with tiers of gallery-type layers on the sides on different levels. Here, containers were being lowered into the hold, directions to the crane operator up in the sky being given with hand signals by the foreman on the deck. A dozen or so crew hands stood by to remove the chains and lifting gear from around the containers. In the forward centre of the ship were the twelve passenger cabins. Actually, there were eleven standard cabins, plus one much larger, in the form of a suite. Enright took them into it.

Very smart, thought Will, like a small drawing room.

It had a sofa, two armchairs, views on three sides looking forward through large curtained windows, which can be fastened tight shut in bad weather, a bolted-down central table, a good-sized bedroom with two large bunk beds and a fixed table between them, fitted cupboards everywhere, a wardrobe with proper hanging space and plenty of coat hangers, fitted central and bedside lights, a fixed dressing table with chair and a pair of comfortable chairs fastened to the teak floor. A swing door led to a separate good-sized shower room with two washbasins and a loo, overhead lighting, shaver socket and mirror, towel hanging rails, plus all the goodies that go with a luxury hotel.

Lucky them who have this one. Do me fine – in my dreams.

The suite, more expensive than the other cabins, was referred to as The Owner's Suite. Apart from the sitting room, all the other cabins were similarly equipped. Enright said that the passengers would be arriving the next day by 4 o'clock at the latest and that departure was scheduled for 6 p.m.

He laid down that the bridge, approached by both an indoor staircase and outside companionway, was out of bounds to all, except for the Captain and the senior officers.

On the deck below, one deck down from the cabins were the officers' and passengers' bar and dining saloon as well as most of the officers' quarters.

The crew's accommodation, kitchens, communal showers, latrines etc, were on two separate levels further down.

Enright told them that on no account were they to go down to the hold but, at 2.30 p.m. Johnny Jones would collect all six deckhands from their quarters and explain their cargo hold duties to them. In the meantime, they were free to look around for themselves and get to know their way around.

Lunch, Will's first meal on board, was at 12.30 p.m. The crew canteen had a cafeteria system: piles of plates, cutlery etc, were stacked at the end of a long counter, into which were fitted hot cauldrons or cold dishes of meats, vegetables and desserts. Each crew member helped himself before proceeding to one of two long communal tables.

Back in their quarters, in addition to Jake and David, who

turned out to be a farmer's son from Somerset, appeared a dour-looking Scot, name of Rob McIntosh but known as Tosh, he was a bit older than the others, on his fourth voyage he said, made it clear that he did not want to go on another fucking tour of the fucking hold with Johnny fucking Jones. The sixth deckhand, and the last, was a black youth all the way from Tiger Bay in Cardiff, called Curly.

Will told Jake about his encounter with Johnny Jones, "Oh, don't worry about 'im. He's an old grumble pots; been doin' this job for far too long but 'is bark is far worse than 'is bite."

Just then, in came Jones, "Right, you lot. We're going to have a look at the shitty end of the ship but where most of the money is made. You'll be working in a roster made by me for all the time that you're not up in the fancy part of the ship. Down here your main task is to clear up all the shit and mess left around by others and there's plenty of it, mark my words, particularly during the loading and unloading periods in the various ports. Sorry, Curly, even though some of the gollywogs that come on board may be cousins of yours, I wish they had stayed swinging in their trees.

The other main job is more serious and here, if you value your lives, you will listen and do exactly what the charge hand or foreman tells you. We're in a floating warehouse that does not stay still when it's told. Most of this stuff is heavy, bloody heavy, and if it shifts around we're all off to Davy Jones, my uncle, and, if you think I'm nasty, I don't recommend that you meet *him*. But these guys in their overalls know what they are doing, have the right equipment to correct any shift in balance and know how to use it. So, do as you're fucking told."

With that, he led the little group through various hatchways down ladders into the vast hold of the ship. Sure enough, loading was in progress and all sorts of useless garbage was in evidence, including, broken pieces of heavy-duty cardboard, dustsheets, broken tarpaulin pieces and oily rags. It would have to be cleared after the shore dockers knocked off work and, again, the next day before the ship sailed.

Jones continued with his spiel, "Now, look all-round the sides of the ship and you'll see them safety cables and chains attached to electrically powered capstans. In an emergency, say, during a storm, these cables and chains have to be manually fastened to any cargo that has shifted, so that it can be hauled back into its correct position. Got it? Good; now we'll have a quick squint at how we get from A to B."

He led them to the far end of the hold, through a massively thick steel door, on the other side of which was a wide strong steel staircase that led down to a space about the same size as the inside of a village church. Two vast turbine engines were situated below them, the respective propeller shafts, each in diameter large enough for a grown man to crawl through, led to the stern of the ship and the propellers that the next day would be thrusting them into the Bristol Channel and out into the Atlantic.

Tour over, a somewhat chastened group, at least as far as the newcomers were concerned, were sent back to their quarters, told to put on their waterproofs and ship's anoraks and come back to clean up the hold, as the sign-off siren had just sounded.

Will spent a restless night holding his peace most of the time, listening and learning from what the older ones were saying and going through the events of what had been a tumultuous day.

The Purser had, indeed, pinned the passenger list on the notice board, beside which were the cabin numbers and the name of the steward allocated to each. Will had numbers 10 and 11. Number 10 was to be occupied by Dr and Mrs Evans and 11 by Mr and Mrs Mallory.

The team spent most of the morning of departure tidying up and clearing out the rubbish in the main hold, the majority of the loading having been completed. Will had time to go up to the passenger deck to check on his allocated cabins, where he was surprised to see that no. 11, to be occupied by Mr and Mrs Mallory, was the Owner's Suite. While up there he noticed that one, followed by another, very large wooden crates were being hoisted by a crane and lowered into a space that had been left clear next to the ship's rail on the foredeck, quite near to where he was standing. PO Jennings, the man who had checked Will's arrival the previous day, supervised the loading. Will was astonished to see that the wooden crates were stalls and that in each stall was a horse. The stalls had proper top and bottom doors, which had been fully closed while in transit on the crane, now opened by Jennings;

two pairs of bright, though wary eyes, under pricked ears were taking in their new surroundings.

Jennings saw Will standing near and said, "Know anything about horses, Will?"

"Yes sir, a bit. I am a work rider and stable lad for a racehorse trainer in Cheshire," he replied, giving himself a little promotion in title.

"Right, you've got yourself a job. I'll have a word with the Purser and see to it that Jones fixes up for you to look after our equine passengers during the trip. They're going as far as Barbados."

As they were talking, a smartly uniformed, well-built man with a round, pleasant face under a braided cap came up to them. Jennings stood to attention.

"Good morning, Sir." And to Will, "This is Captain Dickson."

"Good morning, Jennings. Everything all right with our horses?"

"Yes, Sir. This is William Carpenter, Sir. He is a new deckhand and has experience with horses, so I've told him to be in charge of looking after them as far as Barbados."

"Splendid. I'm sure he will."

He moved off, giving Will an encouraging smile as he did so.

Delighted, Will fastened back the top door of each stall, to allow both horses to poke their heads out. They would not be stepping outside during the whole trip. An iron-grey colt and a bay filly, quite young, Will judged them both to be three-year-olds. The bedding was sawdust and chippings; each had a half-full hay net hanging from a hook in their stall. Jennings told him that bales of bedding and hay would be stored in the foredeck hold. Will's job was to muck them out morning and night, to make sure their water buckets were kept topped up and ditto with the hay nets. Taking no exercise meant that they would require no extra food.

In a cupboard next to the kitchen, he found what passed as a body brush and 'borrowed' washing up towels, to enable him to groom the horses, thereby making them feel fresh and well. A kitchen fork sufficed to pick their feet out, though neither of them were shod.

The news of his new appointment soon got around his teammates, with him soon gaining the nickname, "Jockey", or just plain "Jock".

The passengers arrived in dribs and drabs during the late morning and afternoon, including a middle-aged English couple, who were on a one-way ticket as they were emigrating to sunny Barbados, having had enough of England. They had two very large containers holding their furniture and belongings, plus a car in which they'd arrived at the docks.

Of Will's charges, the doctor and his wife were the first to arrive. Dr Evans, a recently retired GP from a practice near Peterborough, the trip being a retirement present to themselves, which they had been planning and looking forward to for two years. Jolly and good-natured, they greeted Will enthusiastically and said how excited they were.

The other couple, Mr and Mrs Mallory, who arrived at about 3.30 p.m., were very different. Robert Mallory, late middle-aged, with iron-grey hair was reminiscent of a bulldozer, clearly one who was used to giving orders that he expected to be obeyed, rather than to receive them. His wife, Kathleen, was accustomed to being on the receiving end of orders, yet devoted and loyal to her husband. Will introduced himself, adding that he would do his best to help in any way that he could.

By 5 o'clock, all the passengers had arrived, the cargo loading was completed, and preparations for departure were in full swing. Captain Dickson broadcast technical instructions to the crew, as well as, a "Hello and Welcome" message to the passengers. At 5.45 p.m. the gangplank was rolled away and stowed. Bang on 6 o'clock, with a blast on the siren, the last of the mooring ropes were cast off from the quayside, coiled neatly on capstans on the foredeck, the Star inched away from the quay and slipped into the Bristol Channel on her way to the West Indies. A late May and lovely evening, Will could see the Welsh and English countryside, bathed in sunshine as they headed due west, the last of the light just fading as they hit the open sea.

After the passengers had done their unpacking, many of them went to the rail of the ship on the passenger deck to see the last sight of land before drifting along to the bar.

Mr. Payne, the chief steward, organised the deckhand team into sections: two to help Brian serving drinks, the other four to help in the officers' and passengers' kitchen, then serving dinner at tables of eight. The seating plans, which varied from day to day, listed the ship's officers including the Captain, intermingled with the passengers, to avoid them seeing the same people all the time. When the two on bar duty finished, they joined the others waiting at the tables.

The next morning Will mucked out, fed and watered his horses as his first job. They didn't seem to be in the least concerned or worried by the rolling motion of the ship, but in the mind of a horse, Will thought, there was precious little difference between a horsebox and a ship, except that on a ship they had a better view of what was going on. Will talked to them, as he would to a human being. He had learnt that the sound of a softly spoken human voice reassured horses, as well as giving them confidence in their handler or rider. In both cases, it is a two-way affair. That job done, he went to the passenger deck to deal with his human charges.

First to the doctor and his wife, who had been up early as they were too excited to sleep well: their cabin was left tidy with clothes neatly and carefully unpacked and folded away. Being a doctor, Geoffrey Evans was meticulous in keeping things in the right places. Neither he nor his wife were accustomed to having domestic staff, apart from a cleaner two or three times per week for a couple of hours each day.

Next, to the Mallory's, knocking on their cabin door first in case they had not gone down to breakfast. There was more to do here, like replacing the top of a toothpaste tube, night clothes left strewn around and towels on the floor. Most of the passengers were from a walk of life being elderly or retired, for whom a month-long cruise was a major highlight of their lives.

The Mallorys were different, obviously very well off, which Will could see from their quality of clothes, Kathleen's makeup, her husband's aftershave, ivory hairbrushes, and engraved gold cuff links. It did cross Will's mind as to why, in their position, were they travelling on this fairly modestly priced cruise, when they could have afforded one of the glitzy and expensive cruise ships that ply the world. The answer was provided a day or so later by Kathleen Mallory, who took Will on one side and explained that her husband, the owner of Supercar Ltd, a nationwide car rental business, had suffered a major heart attack not long before Christmas. Having been in intensive care and hospital for a considerable time, he was making steady progress, though he had been advised by his doctors that an extended holiday in quiet conditions with no distractions would be the best recuperation cure, however, he should not fly. The itinerary and content of this cruise ticked all the required boxes. Yes, he would be in trouble if he had another attack, though he had been in the care of the top heart surgeons in the country and assured that, as long as he did not over exert himself either mentally or physically, he would be okay.

In the evening of the first full day at sea, they began to see pods of dolphins circling around and keeping pace with the ship, rising with the waves, disappearing in the troughs, coming up with a leap at the top of the next one, giving a great display and enjoying themselves. Seabirds were still frequently seen and on the third day, they passed by the Azores Islands, close enough to be able to pick out some of the landscape details. Will wondered why one hears so little about these five Portuguese islands, he determined that later he would look them up on the map to learn more about them.

Will made good friends with his deckhand team, especially cockney Jake. His father was manager of a Coral's betting shop in Hackney and a small-time bookmaker in his own right at the Catford dog track, where Jake sometimes went to help him.

David, the farmer's son, was interested in seeing the horses; not a rider himself, he just loved all animals. His father had a large herd of Holstein Friesians on their farm in Somerset.

Curly from Cardiff, Mum and Dad from Grenada, was a hoot, had a hidden supply of spliffs, laughed off all the stick he received from Johnny Jones, calling him Taff the Gaff. Tosh the Scot couldn't stand him, though he didn't like anybody. Will had a run-in with him one morning, coming down below after his horse duties.

"Been playin' wit yer donkeys, yer fuckin' fandan?"

"Yes, and one has a thistle stuck up its arse."

The day before the *Star* was due to arrive in Barbados, Captain Dickson announced to the passengers at lunch that they would arrive at 6 o'clock in the morning but would only be in port until 7 p.m. that evening. He said that the Purser had details of various places to see, and excursions that could be arranged on the island. Taxis would be available and all the passengers had to do was take their passports, complete a landing form, and then they were free to go. The Purser would make any bookings or arrangements required prior to arrival. Will heard all this while serving drinks and waiting at tables during lunch. Johnny Jones had already told them all that shore leave would be granted to those who wanted it.

"Fancy a wander around?" he had suggested to Jake.

CHAPTER 3

The *Star* docked on time at the Deep Water Harbour, close to the capital, Bridgetown. Immediately the hustle, bustle, and noise of cranes swinging over the ship to unload the Barbados bound cargo, started. Will mucked out, fed the horses, and then he was giving them a quick rub over with his makeshift brush and tea towel, when the Captain appeared with a studious-looking man wearing glasses, dressed in a long-sleeved shirt and a tie.

"Morning Will," the Captain said. "I want you to meet Maxwell Geary, the owner of the horses. I've told him that you have done a good job looking after them."

"Thank you, Sir," replied Will, shaking Mr, Geary's outstretched hand. "It's been a real pleasure, Sir, to look after them. They are two very nice horses."

"The Captain says that you worked for a trainer in England," said Maxwell Geary, in a strong Barbadian accent.

"Yes, mainly with National Hunt horses, not flat horses."

"Ah, I see, the principle is the same though. Look, if the Captain will allow it, would you like to come ashore with me and see the horses' new home? I have a horse trailer here and you could come with me in my car."

"That would be absolutely fantastic," said Will, with a glance at the Captain, who nodded. "I do have a couple of jobs that I have to do, which will take about half an hour, but after that…?"

Captain Dickson said, "I'm sure that can be arranged and anyway it'll be at least another half hour before we have a crane available. You go, finish your work, and Mr Geary will see you on the other side of Immigration."

Will hurried off to complete his cabin duties for the Evans' and Mallory's, found Jake to tell him about the invitation from Maxwell Geary, and apologised for letting him down.

"Don't worry, mate, there'll be plenty of other opportunities," Jake said.

He had a quick change, grabbed his passport, ran down the gangplank, along the quay and into the near-deserted Immigration hall. He filled in the standard form, thrust it and his passport into the hands of the Immigration Officer, who stamped the passport, hardly looking at the form. He ran outside and there was Maxwell Geary standing by his car, behind which was a pickup truck with a horse trailer attached at the back.

"So sorry to keep you waiting," Will exclaimed.

"Don't worry – you haven't. We've only been here a couple of minutes. Now hop in and we'll go."

Leaving the dock area they turned right onto the wide Spring Garden Highway, soon taking a left turn past the famous Kensington Oval cricket ground, and wound their way through the urban area of Eagle Hall, then going uphill, leaving on the left the grand entrance to Government House, the Official residence of the Governor General, along Culloden Road, avoiding the centre of Bridgetown and coming onto, what looked to Will, like a park.

It was the Garrison Savannah, former HQ of the British West India Regiment in the 18th and 19th centuries, though since 1845, the racecourse.

On the way from the docks, Maxwell Geary told Will about the horses. Both were three-year-olds; the colt which had the slightly ominous name of May Go Twice, came from a trainer in Lambourn. His sire was a horse that had been trained by Jeremy Hindley in Newmarket called The Go-Between, a very useful two-year-old, winning seven races, including the Cornwallis Stakes at Ascot. May Go Twice had won a race as a two-year-old and was placed three times.

The filly, named Fawn Princess, was trained by another Lambourn trainer, Doug Marks, she had only run four times and had been placed in three of them. Both horses had been selected on behalf of Max Geary by an ex-army officer, Wellington educated bloodstock agent, Captain Tim Bulwer-Long, always known in racing circles as The Captain. He ran his own agency, Heron Bloodstock.

Max drove through the entrance gate acknowledging the wave of the security guard, signalling to him to allow the trailer behind to follow him to an area on the left of the race track that was surrounded by shade providing trees to rows of horse stalls. He pulled up in a wide open space, which included a small exercise ring and wash down area. It was past 9 o'clock in the morning, most of the training 'work' on the all-weather training track over for the day. Nevertheless, a lot of activity was still going on as stable lads and girls washed horses down, swept the stalls area, generally making the place look tidy. Small groups of people were discussing the morning's work and, one of them, on seeing Maxwell, moved towards him.

"Morning Peter," Max said to a thickset young man. "How did it go this morning?"

"Fine, Daddy. I'll run through it with you later, but what have we here?" he said, looking at the trailer, out of which the new horses were being unloaded.

"Wait. First, let me introduce you to this young man. Will, I want you to meet my son, Peter, who is also my trainer. Peter, this is Will Carpenter, who has been looking after the horses very well on the ship from England. He also has experience as a work rider and stable lad for a trainer in England."

"Very good to meet you, Will, thank you for doing a good job. You must tell me more in a minute, but now, Daddy, please can we take a look and see what you've brought here?"

The two horses were led up by grooms for inspection, the colt leading the filly.

"Here's the colt by The Go-Between; not very big, though neither was his sire. He's won a race and placed a couple of times. Looks the sort to go round here pretty well, and the filly by Realm – she was unlucky not to win, being placed second twice times, one by a short head and third once. She's a lovely looking filly and I hope she'll win a nice race here, she's sure to make a super brood mare. The good thing is that neither of them had too many races as two-year-olds. What do you think?"

"Pretty good to me. I like the look of both of them. I suggest we give them a bit of time to get over their journey and adjust to the climate change but, you know, they'll tell us when they're ready to do a bit more."

While this conversation had been going on, Will kept his distance away from them but became aware of a callow youth, scruffily dressed and clearly of different ethnic background, being sun brown, with non negroid features, standing beside him.

"What yo doin' here?" he asked, in an unfriendly tone.

Will, somewhat taken aback, said, "I'm just off a ship and have been looking after those two horses on board."

Maxwell Geary and his son Peter returned to where Will was standing. The callow youth disappeared as stealthily as he had arrived. Another very different looking man, who had been with Peter when Max and Will had arrived, now came up to them. Small, with a weather beaten face, wearing jodhpurs, a tight fitting long sleeved t-shirt and carrying a skullcap.

"Will, meet Challinor Jones, our champion jockey. Chally rides my horses whenever possible and we have had a lot of success between us."

Chally grinned and shook Will's hand, "Let's hope our luck continues with these two. They look the part to me."

After Chally had moved away, Will said, "Wow, is he really the Lester Piggott of Barbados?"

"Certainly is," was the reply.

A short while later Max Geary said that he must go to his office in the town, he asked Will if he would mind coming with him and waiting a short while before he took him back to the ship. Before leaving the Garrison, Will had a quick look at the track. A right-handed grass course, about six furlongs round, with the grandstand not far from where he was standing at the end of a short straight, a little over a furlong. So, a very tight track and on the turn for much of the way. The paddock is across the track in front of the stands.

On the way to Max's office, he asked Will for his first impressions of Barbados.

"It's fabulous, Mr Geary –"

"Max," he said. "Call me Max."

"– and it's wonderful for me to come here, so thank you very much. I'm especially grateful, I've always wanted to come here, as an ancestor of mine was one of the earlier settlers."

"Oh, what was his name?"

"Benjamin Carpenter."

Max let go of the steering wheel and stared at Will, "You're related to Ben Carpenter? Man, he was a legend in island folklore, a hero of the time. Had a sugar plantation in St John, a great man. Listen, how long are you here?"

"We leave tonight, I am afraid, but I think, if my job on the ship is still available, I'll be back in about a month's time."

"You let me know the date and I'll take you to see some of the island, including where your ancestor's plantation was. He made it the finest plantation of the time."

"That would be marvellous. I'll certainly let you know well in advance."

They arrived at Max's office on the ground floor of a smart-looking modern office building one block back from the main street of Bridgetown, Broad Street. Will followed Max through the wide glass doors. Max waved to the two reception girls, one black and the other a pretty white girl, went through another door and into his sumptuous suite of offices.

"I own the building but I kept this bit for myself," he said.

Will stayed in the ante room outside Max's private office, scanning through the two Barbadian daily newspapers, the Advocate and the Nation. Nearly all the news covered was local and included the arrival of the *Star*. On the sports pages, English football results were featured and tips for the next race day at the Garrison on the coming Saturday.

Max came out of his office a quarter of an hour later and said, "Will, I have something I have to deal with, would you mind if Lucille, one of my receptionists, took you back to your ship? I hope you don't mind and be sure to let me know about your next visit and when it'll be. Here's my card and I'll look forward to hearing from you."

"Thank you again and, of course, I'll give plenty of warning, though please don't put anything off on my account."

Max pressed the intercom button on the telephone, "Lucille, Will Carpenter is ready, please could you take him back to his ship now?"

Lucille, the white one, came in; Will smiled at her and followed her out of the door.

"Oh, and I'll give up an update on the horses when you come back," Max said, as they were going out.

Lucille led Will to the parking lot behind the office building and to a yellow mini moke.

"Is this your first visit to Barbados?" she asked.

"Yes, it is," replied Will.

"In that case, if you're not in too much of a hurry, I'll take you past some of the more interesting parts of the city."

Turning left onto Broad Street, they came to a square with a river forming the opposite side; in the centre of the square stood a high column with a statue on the top.

"Nelson's Column," she said. "Erected twenty-seven years before the one in Trafalgar Square."

On the left, she pointed out the Parliament buildings, and told him, "The second oldest to Westminster in the Commonwealth."

Turning to go round the square, she showed him St Michael's Cathedral then, having completed three sides with the river on their immediate left, she approached a bridge over the river. On the bridge, an enormous arch stood like a mini Arc de Triomphe.

"Completed in 1987, in celebration of the 21st year of Independence," said Lucille.

Driving on for about half a mile, Lucille stopped the car to show Will a fine sweeping view of Carlisle Bay.

"Until the Deep Water Harbour was completed in 1961, all ships, cargo and otherwise had to anchor, discharge passengers and unload cargo onto lighters in the bay, to be towed into the Careenage, which we'll see in a minute."

Turning back the way they had come and approaching the bridge, Lucille told Will to look to the left. The river became wider as it neared the open sea and formed a small harbour with reinforced banks on both sides. Shops, cafes and restaurants lined the roadsides on both banks.

"All those buildings used to be warehouses for the incoming cargo off the ships or to hold the cargo, mainly sugar in barrels, ready for placing in lighters to transfer onto the ships waiting in the bay. You can imagine the scene back in the old days of sugar being brought to the Careenage on horse or mule drawn carts from the plantations or sugar factories. No cranes in those days, everything manually handled."

Moving on, they came back into Broad Street.

"This is our Bond Street. All the best and most expensive shops are here, like the one we are just passing, Cave Shepherd. They have everything, fabulous jewellery, fancy clothes and leather wear, electrical appliances and probably the kitchen sink. A family run business with some partners, the senior one, Geoffrey Cave, is a good friend of my parents."

"Have you been to England?" asked Will.

"Yes, eighteen months back, I went on a secretarial course for three months in London."

"How did you like it?"

"Oh, it was good. I stayed as a PG with friends of my family in Putney; had a great time!"

By now they had reached the dock gates. Will got out of the moke, turned to Lucille, thanked her very much for bringing him back to the ship and for the tour of Bridgetown.

"It's been lovely meeting you and hope to see you the next time you come," she said.

"So do I," said Will, giving a cheery wave as he disappeared through the gate.

His own 'charges', the Evans and Mallorys returned in the late afternoon. Robert – he hated being called Bob – and Kathleen Mallory had broken doctors' orders and had gone for the day to the ultra-luxurious and expensive Sandy Lane hotel in the heart of the fashionable west coast of the island. Not surprisingly they retired to bed early, barely touching their dinner.

The Evans were rather more enterprising, taking a tour of the island, including the labyrinth of the brilliantly illuminated Harrisons Cave, where electrically powered road trains convey visitors into the depths of the caverns, showing amazing and beautiful galleries of stalactites and stalagmites, deep emerald coloured pools and waterfalls

Next stop St Lucia, departure time 7 p.m.

Early the next morning the *Star* nosed into the attractive natural harbour of Castries, St Lucia, dwarfed by a gigantic cruise liner already docked and discharging its thousands of tourist passengers, dressed in a variety of unbecoming flowery garments, which, in many cases, did not cover enough of their bodies. Boarding a fleet of buses, they dispersed to varying tourist destinations on the island, returning in the afternoon to be herded like flocks of sheep back on board. The ship left at dusk with a multitude of blasts on its siren.

St Lucia being a major exporter of bananas, the Star would stay for the best part of two days, the rest of that day and most of the next. During all the daylight hours truckloads of bananas were being brought to the quayside for loading. For the passengers, the routine was the same as in Barbados, though it was a very different island geographically and socially that awaited them.

Barbados is limestone based, whereas all the other larger islands in the Eastern Caribbean are volcanic. St Lucia is roughly oval in shape, very mountainous, spectacularly beautiful, and densely forested down to the water's edge. It is considerably larger than Barbados, yet less heavily populated. The best-known landmarks are the two conical Pitons, standing very close to each other, about three-quarters of the way down on the west coast.

The Mallorys came into their cabin just as Will was finishing mucking them out – he used that expression to himself, why not, he thought – and asked them what plans they had for the day.

"We're going some way down the coast to see the Pitons. The Purser says they are pretty amazing; there's a super beach right next door with a beach bar and restaurant to match, so that should sort us out for the day. What about you Will?"

"Don't think we'll get much shore leave. A lot of dirty stuff to do to get ready for the bananas to be loaded. Hope you have a really good day."

Will and Jake did manage an hour or so onshore in the vicinity of the very pretty harbour. Will remembered the old calypso, *The Banana Boat Song*, with the first line of "Hey, Mr Tally Man, tally me bananas", as they grabbed a couple of beers in a quayside café.

During the evening's 'turning down' cabin time, both his charges returned.

"Fantastic," said Mallory. "Pitons quite fabulous, coming straight out the water up to 2,500 feet. Restaurant and beach can't fault them. But, don't like all the black sand; not the same somehow. Of course, understand that it comes from volcanic lava, however, it makes the water seem very dark. Still very clear though, just a little off-putting."

The Evans' also said they had a good day. "Went up to Rodney Bay, lots of hotels, found one we liked at Gros Islet called Windjammer. Lovely white sandy beach – yes, had a lovely time. Last week there was an international Jazz Festival in the area. Jazz stars from many countries were performing, including Jimmy

Cliff from Jamaica, and Arturo Tappin, a brilliant saxophonist from Barbados, who has played twice at the Edinburgh Festival. Fabulous, we were told."

The next morning, The *Star* arrived in Georgetown, Grenada, just as the sun was rising over the eastern horizon. Georgetown harbour is even more attractive than Castries, with the fine buildings and waterfront cafes dotted around the natural semi-circular perimeter. Now a mostly quiet and peaceful island, Grenada has had its share of post-war problems.

From 1974 to 1979, unrest on the island and antagonism against the Prime Minister Eric Gairy caused an uprising. Maurice Bishop, a reactionary and Communist founder of the New Jewel Movement, overthrew Gairy and his government, and became Prime Minister. Bishop formed a good relationship with Fidel Castro, who promised help, Cuba being in bed with the Soviet Union at the time, resulting in Britain and the USA fearing further Soviet intervention in the Caribbean.

In 1982, Britain had just come out of the suppression of the Argentinian invasion of the Falklands. In 1983, President Reagan, supported by Margaret Thatcher, launched an American force to Grenada, with the help and support of Tom Adams, then Prime Minister of Barbados. The revolt was put down but on 19th October, Maurice Bishop was executed by supporters of a former colleague, Bernard Coard. Subsequently, the Governor General, Paul Scoon, was confirmed as temporary Prime Minister until, in a General Election in 1984, the Grenada National Party was elected, with Herbert Blaize as Prime Minister.

One positive outcome of the revolt was that Cuban forces sent by Castro started building a proper airport with a long runway, subsequently completed by US forces during their campaign to put down the revolution. This has been of great benefit to the tourism industry in Grenada; it is named The Maurice Bishop International airport, after the man regarded by many as a martyr and the saviour of Grenada.

In the deckhands' quarters, Curly woke early to prepare himself for his day back in his homeland, having obtained special shore leave after his morning cabin duties. He took off immediately after he was done with them, wearing his fancy short pants, a multicoloured t-shirt and a red bandanna.

Grabbing hold of Johnny Jones, who recoiled like a cornered tiger, he shouted, "Come wi' me Taff Gaff and see de light. I flyin' higher than dem banana trees all day!"

He bounded up the ladders and down the gangplank and could be seen dancing along the quayside accompanied by his friends and family.

"Fuckin' monkey, when did they cut his tail off? Come on, you buggers, there's work to be done," Jones barked out.

The established differing routines of the Evans and Mallorys continued, with Robert and Kathleen Mallory taking themselves off a short distance to the fashionable and delightful Calabash hotel, discreetly and efficiently owned and run, so they had been told, by an Englishman, Leo Garbutt, and his Grenadian born wife. It was situated on a lovely beach at the southern end of the island.

The more adventurous Dr and Mrs Evans took a car and trip inland to the very beautiful Grand Etang Lake in the crater of an extinct volcano, passing through lovely country among, not just banana plantations, but another important Grenadian export – nutmeg. Not for nothing is Grenada known as the Spice Island.

The next evening, The Star, now with its full complement of bananas and reunited with very red eyed Curly, set sail for the last leg of the voyage – the return to England.

"Got well stocked up?" Will asked Curly.

"Man, these are straight off de bush."

The second morning after leaving Grenada, Will was busy mucking out the Mallory suite, when Robert Mallory came back early from breakfast in advance of his wife.

"Shall I come back later, Sir?" Will asked.

"No," said Mallory. "I want to ask you something if you don't mind: why is an obviously well-educated young man like you, working as a deckhand/cabin steward on a ship like this?"

Will hesitated before replying. After all, he didn't really know Mallory, apart from what his wife had told him. On the other he liked his gruff manner and respected him as a successful man of business. He decided he had nothing to lose and so briefly outlined his and his family's situation in regard to the Lloyds crash. He made no reference to the ancestral connection with Barbados.

After a moment's silence, Mallory said, "What a horrible, sad story. I'm very sorry for you and your family. What are you going to do about it?"

"I don't know yet, Sir. It's all very new. I took this job as a way of seeing something of the world and to gain experience before deciding what's next. I've signed on for at least one more voyage."

The cabin door opened as Kathleen Mallory came in.

She said to her husband, "You are going on a strict diet from this moment on, both so far as solids and liquids – particularly of the alcoholic variety – are concerned. No messing – that's it. Definite."

They'd had a lovely day at the Calabash, hence Kathleen's displeasure.

"I've finished now, Sir, so I'll leave you in peace," Will said, shutting the door as he went below to see what Johnny Jones had next for him.

"He's a bright lad," Mallory said to his wife.

The next day Will was serving a drink to Kathleen Mallory in the bar.

She took him on one side and said, "My husband has taken a shine to you. Our son, Allan, was about your age when he died in a motorbike accident; it hit us both very badly, but perhaps my husband more than me. He was so looking forward to having him in the business. He's an old softie, you know, but he tries hard not to show it."

The *Star* docked at Barry almost to the day, a month after it left on the outward journey, in other words, just around midsummer's day. Both the Mallorys and the Doctor and his wife, bid a fond farewell to Will, thanked him for looking after them so well and handed him generous tips.

Robert Mallory also gave Will an envelope on the inside of which was not just money, but a card with his business and home telephone numbers, plus a message, which ran, *'Do keep in touch. if you want advice or help in any way, I expect to hear from you.'* It was signed Robert Mallory.

When the majority of the crew were discharged, they were instructed to report back in a week's time, including Will, who had been signed on for the next sailing. Of Will's team, Jake, Curly and Dave, the farmer's son had signed on, leaving only the surly Scot the Tosh to go on his own way.

Will rang home from the station to give his mother his arrival time.

"Sorry it's so late", he said.

Both his father and mother came to meet him, overjoyed to see him, eager to hear all his news and tales of what he had been doing and where. Deliberately Will did not ask about the home situation. That would come later.

CHAPTER 4

Joanna was in bed asleep when they got home and it was not until later the next day that Will noticed that his mother was playing an increasing role in bringing Will up to date.

On the positive side, the estate agent's valuation of the house and remaining twenty-five acres of land was reassuringly at the upper end of the scale but, conversely, so were other smaller properties that they were looking at. Neither of his parents wanted to move away from the area where they'd always lived, and especially at their time of life. Renting somewhere was therefore added to the equation – if 'somewhere' could be found. Although most of Will's friends were away at school, the week flew by. It was a quiet time at Adam Platt's with most of the horses having a summer holiday, although there were some young horses to bring on, so he rode out each morning.

He told Adam, "You know, there were two racehorses on the ship and I got the job of looking after them. They're crazy about racing in Barbados; the owner of the horses came to the ship and took me to the track, he showed me the stables where they are now living."

Polo was in full swing; Will spent every afternoon exercising the ponies, practising stick and ball arranged by Julian Shannon, and playing a few chukkas. At home he elaborated about his trip to Joanna and his parents with details about his crewmates, the horses, and how lucky he had been to have met Max Geary, who had spoken so highly about their ancestor, Ben Carpenter, referring to him as a "legend".

Will went to tell them about Robert Mallory and the kindness he had shown him. Angus had heard about Supercar and that it was a very reputable company; he advised Will to follow up on Mallory's offer to help. James' news was that after leaving Cirencester with a Highly Commended Diploma, at present he was staying with a friend in London, undertaking a series of interviews with army personnel.

First day home, Will sent off an airmail letter to Max Geary, thanking him again for all his kindness, giving him the date of the next arrival of the *Star* in Barbados and hoping it would fit in with Max's plans. He said how much he looked forward to seeing him again – and, as an afterthought, – his pretty receptionist.

In what seemed like no time, Will was back on the train to Barry, staying the night at the same dreary hotel as last time. When he went down to dinner, he saw another young man on his own and nodded to him. A moment later he heard the young man ask the waitress how far it was to the dock, so Will butted in telling him that he was going to the dock in the morning and would take him, saying that it was within easy walking distance. Further conversation revealed that he was joining the *Star*; obviously as the replacement for Tosh. Said his name was Chris from Liverpool. Will had already twigged that he was a Scouse, thinking that he sounded just like the comedian, Jimmy Tarbuck. He liked him and his sense of humour immediately.

They met up in the morning, Will took Chris to the ship, introduced him to PO Jennings, who was the duty officer again, at the top of the gangplank then taking him along to the Purser's office for his embarkation formalities.

"See you below later," he told him.

It was good to see his shipmates again, especially Jake, who he had become quite close to. He had also made it his business to be on good terms with Johnny Jones, as a method of not being allocated with all the dirtiest jobs.

The voyage followed the same course as the first one; no horses this time though. Will's charges were a retired solicitor from Swindon and his wife, plus two widowed sisters who shared a cabin, spending much of their late husbands' inheritances.

The day before their scheduled arrival in Barbados, the Captain made an important announcement to the passengers and crew on the ship's tannoy. He announced that a hurricane by the name of Gertrude had been tracked for the last two days and was seen as coming in the direction of St Lucia and possibly Barbados. It was a bit early, only 3rd July, in the hurricane season – the adage being "June too soon, July stand by, August a must, September remember, October all over".

Captain Dickson went on to say that in view of a possible hit by the hurricane, arrangements had been made for the ship to stay for an extra one or maybe two days in Barbados, meaning that the rest of the voyage would then be extended by the extra time spent.

Hurricanes start in the south Atlantic and graduate, gaining strength, as they proceed in a generally northwestern direction. Though they are easy to plot, they're not very easy to clearly define within a small longitudinal area. A small change of direction can make a big difference.

After passing the bulge of Brazil, they turn more sharply westwards into the Caribbean and towards the southern American states. Barbados, on the whole, has been pretty lucky; in 1979, they had a very near miss when David veered off at the last minute to cause havoc in Dominica, the last direct hit being Janet in 1955.

The *Star* docked on time at 6 a.m. the next morning. Soon after, Jones told Will there was a message for him in the Purser's office. Mr Enright handed him a telegraphed message from Max Geary, saying that a car and driver would be waiting for him from 9 o'clock onwards at the dock gates.

"I won't be ready by then," he gasped.

"Just do the best you can. As soon as your two lots of passengers have gone to breakfast, pile in there and fix up their cabins and then you can scarper. I won't be watching. Usually, passengers go down to breakfast quite early on port days and get busy with their shore trips."

Will drew some of his wages money from the Purser, prepared himself for his trip ashore and waited on the cabin deck until first the solicitor, John Darling and his wife Jennifer, came out and called out "Good Morning". As soon as they passed, he dived in. Leaving the cabin door open he heard and then saw the two old dears slowly leaving their cabin and going carefully along the deck to the stairs.

By 9.15 he was done, down the gangplank like a shot, into the immigration hall and out into the now familiar dock courtyard. There, instead of a saloon car and driver, stood the yellow mini moke. Will's heart leapt. He hadn't given huge thought to Lucille during the few weeks that had passed, except that he had liked what he had seen. Now excitement ran through his veins. She got out of the moke and held out her hand with a wide smile.

"Gosh, what a lovely surprise – I didn't expect to see you here," he exclaimed, taking her hand, holding onto it perhaps for a bit longer than he would normally.

"Good to see you, too. Max asked me to collect you and take you to the office. It's the same journey in reverse that we did last time, though we'll cut the City Tour this time. I believe he's going to take you on a bit of an island tour up to St John and beyond. We have a plantation in that area, which is where I live, so I expect you'll pass pretty close to it."

As she drove, Will looked at her from the passenger seat.

Yes, he thought, *she is very pretty; longish blonde hair, eyes set wide apart, a straight nose neither sharp nor bulbous, a wide mouth that showed all her front teeth when she smiled and a determined but not forceful chin.*

Allowing his glance to flit a bit lower, the rest didn't look too bad either.

Lucille Todd was the only child of her father, George and mother, Harriet. They lived at the Todd family plantation, Uplands, in the parish of St John, as had many previous generations of Todds. Educated privately at St Winifred's school, she was bright, forward thinking, and an active participant in school activities in and out of class, having played the part of Gwendolen in a school production of "The Importance of Being Earnest".

She was taught to ride by Sheila Griffiths, the British born wife of Barbados' leading orthopaedic surgeon, who ran a riding school at their property in St Thomas, competed in gymkhanas and Pony Club show jumping events. She had her own pony at home, which she rode all over the plantation.

School over, George and Harriet arranged for Lucille to stay with some friends in London to take a secretarial course, which would widen her experience outside of Barbados, make new friends and she'd learn a trade. All of these she did with enthusiasm, blossoming into an attractive and fun young lady.

Back in Barbados, she was able to exercise her secretarial and communicative skills, her father helped her to get the job as secretary and receptionist for his good friend, Max Geary.

Socially, she mixed and mingled with the young crowd and was well liked. Internally, she was not exactly worried; she was happy at home and with her job, though she knew that there was another life to be lived as well. She was intrigued, therefore, by this young man who she'd got to know a little when Max had asked her to take Will back to his ship and she was glad to see him again.

Lucille led Will into Max's office, knocking quietly on the door before going in. Max rose from his chair and extended a very warm welcome.

"I thought a change from me at the docks was a good idea; you'll be seeing more than enough of me for most of the day. If you're ready, let's go. I thought we'd have a check on the horses at the track on the way, I've arranged for Peter to be there. All horse work will have finished by now, so there shouldn't be many people about."

Lucille, back at her desk, raised her hand and smiled as they went past, "Have a good day," she said.

On the way to the track, Max told Will that the horses had settled down well and had started cantering. Chally Jones had had a sit on both of them and seemed pleased at their progress. He asked Will about the rest of his last trip and hoped all was well at home.

"Great to have you back," he said.

Peter met them in the stable block area of the Garrison; a groom led out first May Go Twice and then Fawn Princess. May Go Twice looked really fresh, well, and happy, giving a jump and a kick as he was led around the small enclosure. The filly, also, was fine, perhaps not quite as forward as the colt. It was good to see them both.

They didn't stay long, then before leaving, Peter said, "Look, a few of us are going to the local hot spot, Harbour Lights, tonight to see Barbados' best band, The Merrymen, play. They are fabulous; just wondered if you would like to come? I could pick you up from the docks?"

Will replied that he would love to, however, he wouldn't be free until at least about 8.30 p.m.

Peter said, "That's okay - we'll be meeting up a bit earlier for a drink, we could collect you after that. Things at Harbour Lights don't hot up until quite late anyway."

"Well, that would be marvellous."

Then Will, bearing in mind that he had stood Jake up on the

previous trip, asked, "Would it be okay if I asked a mate on the ship to come with us? I sort of owe him one?"

"Yes, I am sure we can squeeze him in. Bring some cash with you to get in and pay for drinks, etc. If you run short I can always sub you until the next time."

"Great. If I do run out, we will be staying here tomorrow, anyway, as there's a hurricane warning, I can repay you then."

"Oh, don't worry – and the hurricane warning has been downgraded with a change of direction towards Antigua."

"Fantastic – see you later then."

He got in the car with Max and they set off in a north-easterly direction, Max saying that he was not taking the most direct route to give Will the chance to take in a bit more of the island scenery. They went along the Tom Adams Highway, named after a former and highly respected Prime Minister, towards the Grantley Adams airport, after another Prime Minister and the father of Tom. Approaching Sam Lord's Castle, the home of an 18th-century rascal of that name.

Max asked, "You know about this fellow?"

"I've heard the name though do tell me more."

"A rogue, if ever there was one. About 300 yards off the beach below his house is a vicious long coral reef lurking just below the surface of the water. The old villain used to hang lanterns on the palm trees that lined his beach, misleading the captains and crew of sailing ships into thinking that they had arrived in Carlisle Bay and the Careenage a few miles further on. They foundered and were wrecked on the reef; he had his armed men ready to row out to the reef and plunder the ships of all their booty and treasure. The story is well told in the calypso, *The Legend of Sam Lord*. If you're going to Harbour Lights tonight, I expect The Merrymen will sing it."

Turning left soon after leaving Sam Lord's Castle, Max took the road up to the hamlet of Six Cross Roads.

"We are now coming into plantation country," he said, as they passed by an original plantation Great House called Sunbury, now restored as a tourist attraction.

"The interpretation 'Great House' reflects the Colonial Regency style of architecture at the time; wide covered verandas surrounding most of the house, protecting the inner ground floor rooms from the penetrating sun," Max said.

They made a slight detour for an outside view of Drax Hall, a forbidding-looking large plantation house still owned by the Drax family in England.

"Your ancestor would have been a frequent visitor," observed Max.

Soon after they entered the parish of St John.

"The beautiful and historic St John's Church is to our right, with incredible views over the east coast. In the cemetery is the tomb of Ferdinando Paleologus, a descendent of the brother of Emperor Constantine XI, who came to England in the 16th century, supported the Royalists, and fled to Barbados after the Battle of Naseby in 1645. He became a prominent sugar planter. He died in 1678."

Max stopped the car and opened a map.

"Look," he said, pointing to his right. "That's where Lucille and her family live, about a mile over there."

Putting his finger on the map he said, "This is where we are now and is about where Ben Carpenter's land began."

Max pointed to a sign saying "Wakefield".

"Is there somewhere called Welchmans anywhere near here?" asked Will.

Max looked up and said, "Yes, certainly. Welchmans Hall and Gully is one of the scenic viewpoints on the island. Why do you ask?"

"Because Welchmans Hall is the name of our old family home in England."

"That's amazing, Will, we'll be there soon. It's close to where the plantation boundary would have been."

Max drove on along a narrow road that eventually winds down to the bottom of a deep gully, alongside a flowing stream. Frangipani, heliconias, poinciana, anthurium, bougainvillaea, both travellers and cabbage palms, grew in profusion on both sides of the gully. Now and then, chattel houses could be seen with the sound of chattering children, mothers scolding them, and yapping dogs trying to join in with their daily tasks.

"Not a lot of change here in the last two hundred years, but look up there on the right," Max pointed to a large clump of untended land with palm trees, thick jungle plants and bushes, growing woven in with each other; looking closely, the ruins of coral and limestone walls could be picked out. "That's all that is left of Welchmans Hall."

They got out of the car for Will to have a proper look. He stood in silence for a short while, just taking it all in and letting his imagination run: two hundred years ago, this is where Benjamin Carpenter, actually lived, worked, created the plantation, brought up his two sons, George and Jack, made enough money to buy three thousand acres of Cheshire land, built Welchmans Hall, handy for the port of Liverpool where, with a cousin, he had set up Carpenter & Cousin, to handle the sale and distribution of the plantation's products in England and Ireland.

Max interrupted his reverie, "Come on, we'll leave the old world and enter the new one," he said, getting back into the car. "I'll take you down to the west coast, the playground of the rich and famous."

Down some narrow roads, through the hamlet of Rock Dundo, they came out at Gibbes Beach.

"I have to tell you that until thirty to forty years ago, sugar cane grew right down to the roadside from five miles to our right, and all along the coast to close on nine miles to our left, with very few gaps. There were just four hotels along all the West Coast – Paradise Beach, Coral Reef Club, Colony Club and Miramar. Now, as we go along, you will see little else apart from hotels, beach bars and smart houses on the right, and supermarkets, chattel houses and local shops, on your left, not to mention a world-class golf course and a polo ground."

"I play a bit of polo," Will said. "Well, actually, I'm learning to play and I love it."

"With the rescheduling of your ship, will you be here tomorrow? There's a polo match at Holders in the afternoon, so why not go?"

"That would be great. I'd love to."

"Okay, I can't go myself, but I'll have a word with Keith Melville, the Chairman of the Polo Club, he'll give you a visitor's pass. Introduce yourself as well to Tony Knowles, he's a good friend of mine, and he'll probably be playing. Go down to the polo lines and they'll all know him down there."

Not far down the road, they came to a high wall on their right with a gateway and closed gate in the middle. The word

"MADDOX" was sculpted into the wall.

"See that house," said Max. "That was the home of the famous English stage, film set and costume designer, Oliver Messel. He transformed an ordinary old Bajan farmhouse into a piece of theatrical magic. When he died in 1978, he left it to his nephew, Lord Snowdon, who was married to Princess Margaret; they often came to stay there."

"Who lives there now?" Will asked.

"Well, it remained empty for probably two years and was very neglected. You can't do that in this part of the world; you watch the weeds growing, the cultivated plants and bushes dying, as the termites are thinking it's Christmas every day. I was instrumental in helping an English fellow buy it, he spent a lot of money putting it to rights, as well as retaining all the old Messel features and architectural gems; he lived there for many years. They had some terrific parties – I went to some of them. Then there were marital problems; he sold it and went back to England. After that another Englishman bought it. I don't really know him, but I think he spends a fair amount of time there. I believe he was once a footballer."

Further along, they passed the entrance to Heron Bay, built in the style of an Italian Palazzo by Ronald Tree in 1947. Tree was one of Churchill's principle advisors during WW2.

"Now it is owned by Anthony, Lord Bamford, and his wife Carole," Max went on. "They have maintained and improved the house and huge gardens, bringing a lot of employment and benefit to the island."

Close by, they passed the entrance to Sandy Lane hotel.

"We're not going in there and I don't advise you to, not until you've made your next million," Max said, with a laugh.

Having passed many of the hotels and restaurants along the west coast that Max had been talking about, they were getting close to the harbour.

"The basic economy in Barbados is good," he said, as they drove into the entrance. "We have a parliamentary system based on Westminster, two political parties not that dissimilar in policies, and a strong manufacturing and distribution industry. All our politicians in both parties are black, as are the majority of the top names in the professions – lawyers, doctors, accountants etc. On the other hand, most of our larger businesses in the manufacturing and distribution sectors are owned or controlled by whites.

The sensible politician talks to the sensible businessman and vice versa; it works. But we rely, above everything else, on tourism now, as the key to our economy. Tourism is a new industry globally, in comparison with pre-WW2 days, with a far higher percentage of the world's population having a spendable income to travel. However, as it is very competitive, too, we have to keep ahead of the game. We are lucky to have an excellent communication system; it is possible to fly to any main destination worldwide with no more than one, or at the most two, stops. As I am sure you know, Concord comes in here twice a week from London in the winter months, and once a week at other times, the only other destination in the world it flies to, apart from New York."

Will said, "This has been a very emotional day for me – one I shall never forget, and I can't thank you enough. Great to see the horses looking so well, but to see where my ancestor pitched up over two hundred years ago and the actual land that he trod over, is just mind-blowing. You have been so kind and patient with me and I hope I can partly repay you somehow in the future."

"Have no fear; I have a feeling we have not seen the last of each other. You only have to call me. Now, enjoy your extra day here and I look forward to seeing you again in about a month's time."

Back on board, Will sought out Jake and told him about the plan for the evening.

"Cor blimey mate, that's a good one," he said. "Been for a bit of a mosey round this morning with Curly, could 'ardly understand what they was talking about, so glad 'e was there."

As business was slack in the dining saloon, all the passengers having gone on shore activities, Will and Jake had plenty of time to do their evening cabin duties. Dinner finished early with only a few of the officers there.

At 8.30 p.m. sharp, Will and Jake were outside waiting for Peter Geary and his team to show up. Soon a pick-up truck breezed in with Peter driving and Will was thrilled to see the blonde hair of the person next to him.

"Okay, pile in," Peter called, brief introductions all round followed, including Max Geary's other son, Philip, and another couple of girls.

Off they set, Peter driving, with Lucille and Philip in the cab, and the others squashed in the back with a few cushions to sit on. There was one person there who Will thought he recognized. It took him a while to work it out. Then, he remembered: it was the callow youth that had asked him, rather gruffly, what he was doing at the Garrison the day he had come with Max on his first trip to the island and they'd brought the horses off the *Star*.

The youth sat in a corner of the truck and seemed not to be joining in the general talk and chit-chat.

Instead, he was staring at Will, who looked straight back at him, smiled, and said, "I'm sure I've seen you before. Did you come up and speak to me on the racecourse about a month ago?"

"I see many people at de track," was all he got back.

End of conversation.

Driving through the centre of Bridgetown, Will showed Jake a few of the landmarks that Lucille had pointed out to him the day she brought him back to the ship last time. As they travelled on, a mile or more further down Bay Street, they came to a building on the sea side of the road. Neon flashing lights on the outside, with the sound of reggae music coming from within: it's the Harbour Lights club.

They went into a spacious area, open to the beach and sea on one side, with a long bar opposite on the other side; two steps down led to the dance floor and a bandstand mounted on a dais, on which a combo was playing a Bob Marley hit, *No Woman, no Cry*. The place was fairly full, split with about 70% being locals and 30% being tourists, Will thought. He recognised a few of the *Star's* crew were there, so Jake had some other people to talk to.

Peter Geary came up to Will and told him the Merrymen would be coming on in about ten minutes, "Had a good day with Dad, he tells me?"

"Fantastic in so many ways; we went through my ancestor's old plantation. He was so good to me. Great to see the horses, too, this morning, looking really good. Tell me about this band, The Merrymen?"

"They are brilliant; all local boys from old Bajan families. Just wait, you'll see; the lead singer, guitarist and main music arranger and composer is Emile Straker, Robin Hunte on banjo, Stephen Fields, guitar and Chris Gibbs, bass guitar, but they all harmonise the vocals."

Will saw Lucille talking among a small group. She beckoned him over.

"This is Will Carpenter," she told them. "He's on the *Star* ship and is a distant descendant of Benjamin Carpenter. My boss took him today to see where the old family plantation used to be."

"Yeah, it was fascinating and we passed by close to where you live."

The flood lights on the bandstand went out, there was a bit of scene shifting and when they came on again, there stood The Merrymen, five of them dressed in brightly coloured, flowery, loose-fitting trousers, with open-necked similar shirts, launching straight into their opening number, *Feeling Hot, Hot, Hot*. In an instant the dance floor was packed.

Seizing the opportunity, Will grabbed hold of Lucille and led her to the floor. He had a natural sense of rhythm, but this was something different.

Lucille stopped dancing, stood still for a second or two and said, "Just watch me for minute."

She slowly circled in front of him appearing to raise her hips slightly to the offbeat of the music, only moving her feet a little, yet gently swaying her body to the tune of the music in a mildly seductive manner.

"This method and movement can be adapted to whatever the tempo of the music," she said.

Will reached for her and soon they seemed to be coming close together like trees waving in the breeze. As song after song to different tempos continued, Will adapted himself to the mood, and became more adventurous, he was captivated not just by the music.

By the time Emile and the group played and sang the romantic, *Beautiful Barbados,* "Beautiful, beautiful Barbados, Gem of the Caribbean Sea", Lucille and Will were intertwined in each other's arms, like two joining clouds, oblivious to anything else, anywhere.

Still holding hands when they eventually came off the dance floor, Will said, "You know the ship's departure has been rescheduled by one day, so what are you doing tomorrow?"

"Whatever you are doing, if possible. It is a Saturday, you know."

"I should be able to get off the ship at about the same time as this morning."

"I'll be there waiting for you – and bring your swimmers."

"In the afternoon, could we go up to the polo ground? Max has arranged a visitor's pass for me, but I have to be back on the ship at 5 p.m."

"Of course we can. My parents are members anyway. Maybe they are coming – I don't know yet."

They kissed long and passionately on the outside deck overlooking the sea, before re-joining the others.

Later that night, Will was too excited and happy to sleep well, going over the whole evening, trying to remember every single moment.

In the morning he took a lot of stick from the others, stirred up by Jake, about his amorous exploits.

"Cor, where did you pull that gorgeous blonde from? A right bit of tip and run, you jammy bugger!" said Jake.

"Prin bird," came from Chris, the Scouse.

Will was late completing his chores in the morning, owing to the old widows being slow coming down to breakfast, but to his relief, luckily, all the passengers had booked out for lunch.

The yellow moke was there: this time Lucille got out and flung her arms round Will, kissing him firmly on the lips.

What a difference a day makes.

"Right," she said. "I've planned our day. After all the driving you did yesterday, we're going a short way up the west coast to a little beach just beyond Paynes Bay where the swimming is wonderful. There's a grassy beach bar there, where we can dump our stuff, have a swim, then come in for a drink and lunch. It's only a very short distance to Holders and the polo. I think my parents are probably coming, by the way."

Ten minutes later they turned off the main road by a tree from which hung a rickety board with 'Bamboo Beach Bar', painted on it, drove down a short track and parked in the shade. There were two or three other cars there, but not much going on inside, it being still quite early.

Lucille waved to a girl behind the bar who smiled back, "We're going for a swim and then will be back. Okay to leave all our stuff with you?"

"Sure. Just put it over there," she said, pointing to a corner where a couple of hooks were screwed into the wooden wall.

"There you are, Will. Change in there," Lucille said, looking at a door with a painting of a black man wearing Regency clothes.

"Where's yours then?"

"Over here," she said, indicating another door, with a lady in a bikini painted on it.

"That's more like it."

A minute or two later, out did come the lady in a bikini – and, *what a bikini,* Will thought. Yellow with two white spots in the right places on the top half and the same colour with a white chevron either side on both front and back, the two sections being held together with what seemed to Will to be no more than a silk thread, on the bottom half.

"You like yellow, don't you? And you must have a lot of confidence in your choice of material to hold it together."

They walked out onto and along the beach, arms wrapped round each other and then, waded into the crystal clear blue water until it was up to their knees, they dived through a little wave, swam a few strokes underwater, turning as they did so like dolphins and coming up to the surface face upwards to see the sun above them and each other with one slight turn of the head.

Will thought, *This is magic, it can't get much better than this.*

Meanwhile, Lucille thought, *I've waited a long time for this; please never let it end.*

They were both strong swimmers and struck out almost directly away from the shore, until Lucille beckoned Will to follow her a little to the right to where she knew was a patch of coral about ten feet below the surface. Even without masks, they could see a variety of multi-coloured fish darting about amongst the coral.

Coming back after a while to the shore, they sat on a sand bank under casuarina trees, drying themselves off under the sun and light breeze.

"What now, my love?"

"All I can tell you is that I've never been happier in my life, and that tomorrow and the days and weeks following will be sad ones, but with the silver lining that I'll be back in a month's time and hope you'll still be waiting for me."

"You can rest assured on that one. But what you are doing on the *Star* isn't going to last forever is it? What's on your mind?"

Will realised that they knew very little about each other – she less about him perhaps. As they sat there in peace, alone under the Caribbean sun, Will told her about his life so far and, in particular, about the last nine months.

"There, now you know you're sitting with a man with no prospects, no inheritance, and precious little money. I have a vision, of course, and the next few months will begin to charter the course of the vision. I can tell you that my next sailing on the *Star* will probably be my last, though I've already signed on, and by the time I see you next, I will be able to tell you more."

Lucille put her arm round him, leaned over and kissed him.

"Will, I am unbelievably happy to have met you, I've fallen for you hook, line and sinker. I can think of nothing more wonderful than being with you. We are living in the present and in hope for the future. Now, let's go and have a rum punch and some lunch, and gaze into each other's eyes while we can. Then we'll go up and meet the polo crowd."

A mixed bunch of people had gathered by now in the bar, which was open on all sides with a thatched roof. The tourists and locals, black and white, all looked happy as they made the best of their weekend. Lucille waved and said hello to a few of them, including a rather older man with reddish hair, a somewhat weather-beaten face, he was wearing a coloured shirt over a pair of blue shorts. One hand was firmly clasped round the waist of an attractive and much younger lady, his other hand held a half-empty glass.

"You may not believe it, but that man is probably the most successful lawyer on the island and one of the richest men. He is also a serial womaniser and can drink anyone of either sex under the table. He is somebody not to get on the wrong side of. Name of Nile Winters."

"Tell me about Max Geary," Will asked. "He's been unbelievably good to me."

"Max is amazing. He is a master tactician, has a finger in so many pies – real estate, community matters, tourism, industrial affairs – you name it, he's probably there. He sits on the board of some of the biggest companies on the island; there is nobody who is anybody that Max doesn't know. And he loves his racing and is a leading light of the Turf Club. He and his wife, Eileen, are good friends of my parents. They are immensely popular among most of what you might call the social and business community. I'm not sure how long his family have been here or where they originated, though I think it was Ireland, three or four generations ago."

They finished their drink, had a quick lunch of flying fish, coleslaw and salad – about the cheapest on the menu.

As they were leaving, Nile Winters put out an arm, "Hi Lucille, where you goin' and who's your friend?"

"His name is Will Carpenter, he's a budding polo player, so we're going up to the match at Holders and that, Nile, is all you need to know," she said, flashing him a big smile.

"Give my best to your parents," he laughed.

On the way to polo, Lucille explained that the ground forms part of Holders original plantation, which was bought post-war by Janet Kidd, the daughter of the first Lord Beaverbrook, the Canadian-born newspaper magnate, and a principal adviser and aide to Churchill during WW2. Janet Kidd converted the plantation house to suit herself and her family, though the large area of flat land just below the house, she lent and, subsequently, gave to the Club, to make it into a ground for the emerging sport of polo in Barbados.

The match wasn't due to start until 3.15 p.m., it would consist of four chukkas of seven minutes each, with an interval between each, which meant they wouldn't have time to stay for the whole game. Parking close to the Clubhouse, Will said to a girl on the doorway that there should be a visitor's pass for him.

"Are you William Carpenter?"

"Yes, I am," he answered.

"Right," she said. "Mr Melville asked me to give you this and that he hoped to meet you inside."

To Lucille, she said, "Hi Lucille, lovely to see you. Are your parents coming today?"

"I think so, Cheryl, and good to see you, too."

They went through the Clubhouse and onto the ground.

"As we have plenty of time, can we go down to the pony lines? Max has given me the name of someone he would like me to meet."

"Who's that?"

"Tony Knowles."

"Oh, I know Tony; he's a good chap and lives not far from here."

"Is there anyone that you don't know?" said Will, with a laugh and a hug.

The lines, about a hundred yards away from the Clubhouse, were full of activity, as ponies were being unloaded from trailers, grooms were doing the same with kit, and players were milling around getting organised.

"There's Tony," said Lucille, pointing him out and beckoning to the tall youngish man of about thirty, who's wearing white polo breeches, boots, and a blue team shirt.

"Hi Tony, I've brought someone you should meet."

"Hi, Lucille, I know, I know. You must be Will Carpenter. Max has been singing your praises."

"That's very kind of him, though I don't deserve them. I'm only a novice player but I love it."

"Will's only here for today off his ship, the *Star* which leaves this evening."

"That's a shame, have a good look round and let me know what you think of polo in faraway Barbados."

"Well, if it's anything like what I've seen so far, it will be fantastic. I expect to be back here in about another month, maybe I'll see you again then."

"That would be good. Look, if you've got time, let me know, and perhaps you could come up here, or to my place, and have a ride on one of my ponies. Depending, there may even be a practice chukka going."

Lucille said, "I'll be making his plans and if he has enough time off the ship, I'll get him to wherever you are. I'll let you know."

"Yes, ma'am," replied Tony, with a wink in Will's direction.

Tony hurried off to check on his ponies; Will and Lucille were just starting to walk back to the Clubhouse, when a voice coming from close behind them, said, "I watchin' yo, Gringo."

Will turned around only to see the same callow youth, who he'd seen at the Garrison, and also last night in the pick-up truck on the way to Harbour Lights. He was slinking away now, with his back turned.

"Who is that fellow? I have now seen him three times and each time he makes remarks like that."

"He's a redleg and an oddball. Been knocking around the racecourse and here for a while now. You know what a redleg is?"

"No, I don't."

"A redleg was the slang name for an indentured servant. These were people imported into Barbados, and other islands, during the final years of slavery, when it was clear that slavery was to be terminated. Plantation owners brought them in, not as slaves, but to do the work of slaves under different conditions: they were not 'owned' by their masters, they were provided with homes – chattel houses – to live in and with subsistence, i.e. basic furniture, food and clothing but paid a pittance. Their indenture – similar to the more up-to-date apprentices or interns – lasted a fixed time of, say, five years, after which the 'servant' was entitled either to stay with his employer, or seek employment elsewhere. Almost, without exception, they came from poverty-stricken areas and many of them were petty criminals or worse, who regarded being shipped abroad was better than jail. They were allowed to bring their wives and children. Many of them were from Scotland. Generally, they did not settle well, the blacks didn't like them and the whites didn't trust them; they kept themselves to themselves, mainly in an area of St Lucy referred to locally as Scotland, intermarrying with increasing frequency, resulting in incestuous relationships. That boy's name is Frank, don't know his surname. Peter Geary has tried to be kind to him and to include him with others, like he did last night."

"I tried to talk to him in the pick-up," Will said, "But he wasn't having it. Don't know what happened to him later, but he wasn't on the return trip."

They had got back to near the Clubhouse where there were many more people about.

"Watch out, here come the parents!" Lucille said quietly, giving Will's hand a squeeze.

George and Harriet Todd having spotted their daughter moved towards them. George, tall and thin, wearing his regulation light grey trousers, and slight darker tropical jacket, a pink shirt and tie, and a Panama hat. Harriet, also quite thin, with a lovely open face, wears a flowery dress. Coming up to them, both kissed their daughter, George removing his Panama, to reveal his grey, receding hair, before turning to face Will. Lucille made the introductions. Will shook both parents by the hand and said how wonderful it was to be in Barbados and how kind Lucille was being showing him around.

"How did you meet?" asked her mother.

"In Max Geary's office," replied Will.

"Yes, the last time he was here, Max asked me to take Will back to his ship from the office."

"Oh, you're here on business then?"

"Well, if you call looking after a couple of racehorses as a deckhand on a ship business, yes, I suppose I was."

"He's underplaying himself, Mum. He's a very competent rider, rides for a racehorse trainer in England and plays polo."

"There is a semblance, but only a semblance of truth in what Lucille is saying, particularly as regards to polo. I am only learning."

"Well, hope you enjoy the game today. I'm quite thirsty, would you like to have a drink before it starts?"

"Sounds like a great idea."

They went into the bar, now pretty crowded. Will had a Banks beer, both parents have a vodka and tonic and Lucille has a lemonade. As they were talking, a man wearing a smart suit, not very tall, with frameless glasses on, and eyes that twinkled, came up. He kissed Harriet, said hello to George, and put his arm around Lucille.

"Now, who do we have here? You must be William Carpenter."

"Yes," said Will, looking at Lucille for help.

"Keith Melville. So glad you've got your pass and welcome to the Club and to Barbados."

"Keith is Chairman of the Club and a very good friend," interposed George.

Will said, "Thank you so much for the pass and I have a message of good wishes for you from Julian Shannon, who is my polo coach and mentor in England."

"Oh my God – yes I remember Julian; he used to come with Mickey Moseley's Cheshire team. Lovely man and a good player, too. Please pass on all my best wishes to him, too. What's he doing now?"

"He retired from the army and doesn't play much polo anymore, though he's still very involved with Cheshire polo and is coach to the young players."

"You couldn't have anybody better. Now, as the game is about to start, I had better go and watch."

Lucille, her parents and Will went up into the small stand

together, Will particularly keen to keep an eye on Tony Knowles and his ponies.

Sadly, when the match was only halfway over, Lucille told her parents that they had to leave and that she'd be back home in time for dinner. Slowly they drove past the Bamboo Beach bar, on past Paynes Bay, and all too soon were back at the dockyard. It was too public to show the emotion that they both were holding back. They had both said all that there was to say and the looks between them said it all over again.

A tight squeeze of hands, a kiss, and then Will said, "Don't cry, darling one. I'll be back soon."

With that, he was out of the car and through the gate in a flash, with a disappearing wave.

CHAPTER 5

In St Lucia the next day, Will went to the central Post Office in Castries, where he mailed by Express Delivery two letters. One was to Max Geary in Barbados, expressing all he had already told him verbally, going on to tell him the date of the *Star's* next arrival, which he saw was a Saturday and hoped it might be a race day.

The other letter was to Robert Mallory. In it, he said that, while he was most grateful for the experience he was gaining on the *Star*, he thought that it was time to look for something more challenging. He asked that if Max was serious in his offer of help and advice, could he possibly come to see him when he arrived back in England in just over a week's time. He told Mallory that he was committed for the next voyage, which he planned to be his last. He gave Mallory his home address and telephone number.

He also sent a "LOVE YOU" postcard, which he placed in an envelope to Lucille, and a saucy one with no envelope to Jimmy van Duran.

The rest of the voyage was uneventful – certainly in comparison. Will went about his tasks in a proper manner, though his mind was elsewhere.

During the Christmas holidays of the previous year and before he went back to school for what turned out to be his last term at Harrow, he had had a crush on the daughter of one of the playing members of the Cheshire polo club, having seen a lot of her at local Christmas parties. Having recently passed his driving test, he borrowed his mother's Volkswagen and took the girl, Judy, for supper in a pub and to the cinema in Chester. Afterwards, he drove her home, both of them being aware that her parents were out at a dinner party.

The relationship was consummated, eagerly, a little clumsily, but with plenty of enthusiasm. It was also somewhat hurried for fear of the impending arrival home of her parents. There then followed an agonising two weeks of worry before she was able to tell Will that "all was okay". Soon afterwards, she went off for a gap year with another girl travelling around South America, arranged by an Argentinian polo player friend of Judy's father. Will's feelings for Lucille were in a completely different zone.

Arrival at Barry followed the same procedure as before, except that Will and Scouse took the same journey together as far as Crewe, with Scouse going on to Liverpool. Scouse was a cheery bloke like a lot of Liverpudlians with a good sense of humour. He told Will that his father was a taxi driver, so with any luck, he wouldn't have to pay to get home from the station. They fixed up to come back on the same train next week.

Again, both Will's parents came to collect him. News gushed forth from each side: first, very good news that James had been accepted into his regiment, depending on him passing his officer's training course, which he had already started at Sandhurst. Will filled them in on what he had been doing. Apart from the ship routine which they already knew about, he added that there was nothing special about the passengers or the cargo on this trip; however, he emphasised what a brilliant time he had during his shore leave in Barbados. He did not tell them about Lucille at this stage, he just spoke about Max Geary mostly, and the people that he'd met through him, also the extra day he spent in Barbados due to the hurricane scare.

His parents gave him the home news. Their friends, John and Helen Blackford, who lived on, and farmed, a sizeable amount of land, much of which had been part of the Carpenters' Welchman Estate, had recently taken back in hand a farm that had been let to a tenant, which meant that the actual farmhouse had become empty. They had offered to let it to Angus.

"That's very much in the air at the moment," his father said, changing the subject.

Next day, in the post, a typewritten envelope addressed to Will arrived. Inside, on Supercar headed writing paper with an address in Solihull, it ran:

'Dear Will,

Thank you for contacting me.

Please telephone my secretary to arrange an appointment to come and see me, as soon as possible.

Yours sincerely,

Robert Mallory.'

After Will showed the letter to his parents, he dashed to the telephone and dialled the number and asked for Mr Mallory's secretary. He was asked for his name and put through.

A voice answered, "Agnes White."

"Hello, my name is William Carpenter and I've had a letter from Mr Mallory asking me to contact you."

"Yes, thank you for calling," she said in a Brummie accent. "Mr Mallory is in a meeting at the moment but has asked me to arrange a time for you to come to see him so … let me have a look. He's very busy this week, but if you could come at 12 o'clock, midday, tomorrow, he could see you then."

"That's great; I'm only in England for a week so that would be marvellous."

"Right; ask for me when you arrive. Goodbye."

Will put down the telephone and looked at his mother standing by his side.

"Well done, Will; that's encouraging."

They looked up train times and discovered that it was possible to go from Crewe to Solihull with a change of trains at Birmingham, Moor Street, arriving at Solihull in time for his meeting,

"Now then, Mum, what's all this about the Blackfords? Dad seemed reluctant to talk about it in the car last night."

"Yes, the farmhouse is called Ayshford…"

"I know where that is."

"I'm sure you do. It is a good, old-fashioned farmhouse, big enough for us, though it probably needs a bit of a makeover having been occupied by a tenant farmer for very many years. Evidently, he's retiring and has no sons willing to take it on. Could be ideal, but Dad has a mental block in that it is on Welchman's land, even though it has not been owned by a Carpenter since before WW1. Also, he doesn't like the idea of accepting charity from a friend."

"Does James know the score?"

"Yes, but he's not easy to get hold of at the moment as he's flat out on the course. I hope he'll ring while you are here."

"It's kind of the Blackfords to offer. In principle, I think it could be a goer and you should take it seriously. Why don't you and Dad go and have a look, see what kind of a state it's in. There are probably a lot of things that need putting right after having been occupied by a tenant farmer for so long."

"Yes, we should do that; I'll work on it with Dad."

"I'll have a word with him as soon as I get an opening and, in any case, before I leave."

Supercar Head Office was not opulent and a far cry from Max Geary's in Bridgetown. A large red-bricked Victorian building in the heart of the Black Country. Only a short taxi ride from the station, Will entered through a heavy, grey-painted, formidable door with four heavy duty glass panels. Inside, behind a reception desk on a tiled floor, sat a lady who could not have been more opposite in shape or form to Lucille. To her right was a stone staircase leading to the second floor.

"I am William Carpenter and I have an appointment with Mr Mallory's secretary."

The receptionist picked up her telephone, "There's a Mr Carpenter to see you, Aggers," she said, in heavy Brummie. "She'll be down in any minute. Please take a seat."

Will wondered where he was supposed to take the seat to and decided just to sit on it. "Aggers", a well-rounded lady with pleasant enough features, although looking that she was well capable of taking care of herself in tricky situations, soon appeared.

"Welcome Will, do come with me; Mr Mallory will see you now," she told Will.

She led him up the stairs, along a corridor, then into a very large room, furnished in a modern way, though it had tall Georgian-type windows in contrast to the Victorian building. In the centre stood a huge mahogany table with matching chairs. The room clearly doubled up as the boardroom, as well as Mallory's private office. Mallory rose from behind his desk in front of which were two chairs. In another corner were a sofa, a round table and two armchairs.

"Well, Will, how very good to see you," he said, holding out his hand and signalling Will to one of the comfortable armchairs.

"Not quite the *Star*, but the best I can offer you. Would you like a cup of tea or coffee?"

"No thank you, Sir, but I'd love a glass of water."

Mallory nodded to Aggers who left, returning almost immediately with the glass of water.

"I am so glad that you have come. In fact, I would have been very disappointed had you not. But let me tell you that all I can offer you is the opportunity for you to fulfil the chance I intend to give you, and to build on the opportunity. I started this business on money that I had borrowed from a friend and benefactor. I am not lending you any money so you have nothing to pay back. Your contribution will be to the business of Supercar and thereby to your own financial advantage. It's a tough world out there, there are winners and losers. I've seen enough of you to believe that you could be a winner though it will be up to you to prove my belief to be correct."

"Yes, Sir, I understand. If you offer me a position with your company I promise you I will do my utmost to justify the faith that you are putting into me. I have signed up for one more voyage on the Star, though I would be available from 1st September."

"Good. Any more questions?"

"No, Sir."

Mallory got up, went across to his desk and pressed an intercom button, "Aggers, ask Jim Briscoe to pop in, would you? Jim Briscoe is the personnel manager; he will be responsible for all your training period, which could last for one to three months. If, after the three month period, either he or I decide that you are not for us, it will be Goodbye, with no hard feelings. After one month has elapsed, he will report to me on your progress. He has my complete confidence but you will report to him, not me. You probably won't even see me. One thing – this is for your own good and mine, too – do not discuss or mention to anybody that you have had any previous connection with me."

Jim Briscoe knocked on the door but came straight in. A tall bespectacled man of medium build, he walked over to where Mallory and Will were standing.

"Jim, this is William Carpenter, but call him Will. I've offered him a junior position with us, subject to the usual provisos and to him making the grade. I've told him that you will go through all the employment details with him and arrange a period of training. He will be available to start on 1st September by which time his present job will have terminated."

He held out his hand to Will saying, "You go with Jim now. Good luck to you and I hope you make it."

"Thank you, Sir – I'll do my best."

"Right, young man, please come with me," Briscoe said, leading the way out of Mallory's office, along a passage and into his own glass partitioned office in a row with other similar ones, it was furnished with a desk, two chairs and several filing cabinets.

Pulling out a form, he started filling it in, "Name, address, telephone number?"

Will told him.

"Age and date of birth?"

Again, Will told him.

"Present occupation?"

"Deckhand and cabin steward on board ship."

"What do you know about the company and what attracts you to Supercar?"

"Not very much except what I have heard and seen advertised. It appeals as a youngish company in a growing field. I am very fortunate to have the opportunity of joining the company. Maybe you could tell me bit more, Sir?"

"You may call me Jim. Mr Mallory founded the company in the early fifties believing that the fledgling car rental business could only grow with the increase in worldwide and domestic travel and that the major existing rental companies were mostly all foreign owned. He saw that there was a niche opening. He was right; we are now close on the heels in the domestic market behind our foreign competitors. The business is owned and under the control of the Mallory family, but Mr Mallory launched a scheme a couple of years ago that a percentage of the shares are made available at a discounted rate to employees who, in the opinion of the board of directors, have deserved them. Such allotted shares can only be held by employees of the company. In other words, if a holder of such shares leaves the company, he or she must relinquish them at market value. This scheme is separate from the company pension scheme. Do you understand?"

"Seems pretty good to me," Will replied.

"I will send you a contract of employment which you must sign in the presence of a non-family professional person and return it to me before 1st September. Your initial period of training will be here, probably for about a month, during which time you will be attached to people working in the various administrative departments, and you will learn from them the basics of how the company works.

You will be expected to find your own accommodation though I will provide you with a list of local hotels, boarding or guest houses that you can contact directly. How does that sound to you and please ask any questions that come to your mind?"

"Nothing comes to mind right now, but I'm sure I will have. Please could you let me have the list of accommodation addresses? I've only got a few days to get that sorted before I'm off on my ship again."

Briscoe reached into a drawer and handed Will a sheet of paper with all the names, addresses and telephone numbers.

"Here you are. All the very best to you and I look forward to seeing you again on 1st September at 8.30 a.m. sharp please. Ask for me on arrival."

Will rose, shook Briscoe's hand, thanked him and left his office. Downstairs he asked the non-Lucille looking receptionist the way to the nearest bus stop.

At Crewe train station later, his mother, Mary Carpenter picked Will up on her own.

"I've got a job!" he called out to her.

"That's marvellous, darling – terrific news. Well done."

Will filled her in on the events of the day though he could tell that something was on her mind.

"I'm worried about Dad," she said eventually. "He's just not himself."

"Yes, I know we discussed this yesterday. I promise I'll pick a moment tomorrow."

Will was up early next morning to ride out at Adam Platt's; he was put on a new arrival in the yard, a four-year-old that Platt had recently bought for a lot of money in Ireland for a Manchester business patron. It had won a point to point and big things were expected. They were only doing steady cantering work but Will was delighted with him.

"... pulling my arms out," he said, as he came back to the yard.

He told Adam about his new job starting in September in Solihull and said that he hoped to be home most weekends, which meant he would be able to ride out on Saturdays.

After breakfast, he found his father mulling over some papers in his study.

"I think it is really good of the Blackfords to have offered to rent out Ayshford Farmhouse to us, Dad. Ayshford's a super house, just the right size, no near neighbours – just the job."

Angus looked up, "I don't want it to appear that I've had to go, cap in hand, to a friend asking to rent a property that used to belong to the family."

"Look, Dad, it's not like that, and it's not what people will think. To start with, I gather that the house has only become vacant as the tenant has decided to retire, which left John Blackford with a substantial empty property. What's he going to do with it? He owns the land all round it; he wouldn't want to sell it, would he? Or have people he doesn't know all over the place? They might be motorbike fanatics: think of the noise they would make! It would bugger up the shooting, too; the pheasants, let alone the keepers, wouldn't like it much.

If you sell a property, you have no control over what they would do and, what's more, even less control if they sold it on to somebody else. No, from his point of view, renting it out is the best option and to rent it to a friend like you is even better; he would be sure that the place would be properly looked after by people he could trust.

Of course, it would all depend on the terms of the lease but that's what your agents and solicitors are there for – to be sure that it is a level playing field. Regarding the past, we've done all we can on that front and it must be put behind us. We are a united family - you, Mum, James, Joanna and me. I know James would agree with me so why don't you ring John Blackford, thank him for the offer, say that you and Mum would like to meet him at the house, go over it, see what needs to be done by him to put it in order and discuss things that you might want to do with or without his help. If there is an agreement in principle, tell him that you accept and hand it over to the professionals on both sides to sort it all out. You're doing him a favour, for heavens' sake, just as much as the other way round."

"Hmm, I hear what you say – it makes a lot of sense. I'll think it over again and let you know when I've made a decision."

"Okay, but don't hang about. You don't want him thinking you're not interested and he offers it to someone else."

"I take your point. In the meantime, the estate agents seem quite optimistic that we'll get a decent price for the Dower House and will have all the particulars, sales brochure etc ready within the next few days."

"That's good, Dad. Remember the song in the Monty Python film, *Always Look on the Bright Side of Life*."

Apart from very brief hellos and goodbyes, Will felt guilty that he had hardly seen his sister Joanna. It had been late when he got home on his first night, then he had been away in Solihull the whole of one day and Joanna had been out with a friend in between the two days. That afternoon, after his talk with his father, Will took Joanna for a long walk across country and along lanes. The spring had not been brilliant, haymaking was late and not of good quality, however, the corn was now ripening and harvesting was just around the corner. In the hedgerows, it looked as if the better summer that followed the wet spring was going to provide a bumper blackberry crop in a few weeks' time.

"It's been a tough time for us JoJo – as much for you as for the rest of us, but as the saying goes, *life is not always a bed of roses.* There are always a few pricks and thorns along the way. With any luck, the pair of us still have a long way to go."

"Yes, and we are lucky that we are a happy family together, despite the barbed arrows that sometimes fly."

"Gosh, that's a very grown-up remark. How's school going?"

"Pretty good really. Bit of a culture shock; I was nervous and shaky to start with though I'm much better now and it's great to be able to come home every night. Mum is being fantastic, a real brick, it's just sad to see poor Dad so down in the dumps."

"Yes, the problem for Dad is that he's seen this coming for too long and is cross with himself for not being able to come up with an answer. He feels that he is letting us down, which is bullshit. But don't let's be gloomy. We'll have to start thinking about what's best for you quite soon. Any ideas? I'm starting my new job with Supercar in September and I'm really looking forward to it, and there's the big move to Ayshford coming up, that will be good for all."

Determined to make the most of his last few days at home, Will called Julian Shannon and fixed up to exercise some ponies the next afternoon.

"I'm off on my next trip on the banana boat in a couple of

days, which will be the last, as I've got a new job here, starting in September," he told Julian. "I'm hoping though to have a day on land in Barbados as on my last trip there I met a chap on the polo ground called Tony Knowles, who said he knows you. Oh and I met Keith Melville, too, he sends his best regards to you."

"Good, please return them if you see him again. I remember Knowles; he was just out of the junior ranks then, though he looked like a promising player. Bloody good fun, those Moseley trips were – not just the polo. Good news about your new job, what is it?"

"I'm joining a firm called Supercar Ltd, a rising star, I honestly believe, in the car rental business. I'm going for a month's training at their HQ in Solihull but goodness knows where I'll be posted after that; with any luck, I'll be able to come home at least on some weekends. If it's okay with you, I hope I'll be able to keep on with the polo."

At breakfast after his last day riding out for Adam Platt, the post arrived and Joanna pounced on a letter with a Barbados stamp, it's addressed to Will.

"Will, what's this strange letter addressed to you? It's obviously not a business letter as it's not typewritten, so what are all these funny little signs plastered all over the back of the envelope? And who is L. Todd?"

"Give that to me," Will said, snatching it out of her hand.

"Well, aren't you going to open it – it might be important?"

"Piss off and eat your cornflakes before nanny comes to take you off for potty time."

"Ooh, it must be important. I think it is a "LOVE LETTER"."

"That's enough, you two," Mary said, blowing an imaginary referee's whistle.

Will shoved the letter into his pocket, gobbled his breakfast up and shot upstairs.

It was, indeed, a love letter, telling Will all he wanted to know: the Saturday of his arrival was a race day and there was a chance that May Go Twice might be running. Also, her parents told Lucille that she could ask Will to stay the night with them, if she wanted him to, and if he could get overnight leave off this ship.

'I DO want you to and you MUST get leave. Tell the Captain I said so', she had written.

Lucille went on to say that she had arranged with Tony Knowles to go straight to his place when she collected him off the ship. He could then have a ride on at least one of Tony's ponies.

Then they would have time for a quick swim and lunch before going on to the races.

He dashed off a quick, loving reply, making sure that Joanna didn't see it before taking it to the post office.

CHAPTER 6

Frank Doune was indeed a Redleg or Poor White – another description of the indentured servants that had arrived in Barbados in the early nineteenth century. They were called redlegs locally as they'd come from very poor areas in Great Britain, and they'd travelled in appalling conditions on the ships bringing them over. They were totally unaccustomed to a tropical climate and hot sun, plus they wore completely unsuitable clothing; they suffered badly from sunburn. Most of them were illiterate, many had no birth certificate and took their surname from where they lived.

Frank's family came from Doune, a small town or village in those days, near Dunblane, in Scotland.

Frank's father was a typical 4th generation redleg descendent, a short and thin, bad-tempered drunk, who made his meagre ends meet by taking menial, casual work from anyone who would pay him. He'd clear water culverts on cane fields, cut back encroaching vegetation on plantation tracks, or any other unskilled work that he could find, in the parish of St Lucy. His wife was of similar but more robust build than her husband, she helped on an hourly basis as a cleaner at the local school.

Their only child, Frank, was a throwback, born in 1982, with an outsize tree trunk on both shoulders. From his earliest days, Frank knew that he was different. Intelligent, always inquisitive, ultra-canny, he did well at school, though he did not make friends, except when he could make use of them. He was willing to learn but showed no respect for those who were teaching him, nor for his parents.

It was not a happy home; any money his father earned went on Banks beer, the cheapest local rum and spliffs. He was foul-tempered, violent or morose when drunk, which was most of the time. In appearance, Frank bore no resemblance to either of his parents. On the small side, gangly and skinny, with a sallow complexion and straight black hair.

When he was eleven years old, he graduated from a primary to a secondary school in Speightstown, the main town in the north of the island, leaving home at Benthams, St Lucy, on the school bus at 6 o'clock in the morning.

It was in Speightstown that he saw for the first time, another side of life. Not only the smart shops and restaurants but discreet nameplates on elegant buildings conveying such information as Accountants, Lawyers, and even larger buildings, Banks. Well-dressed people, black and white in suits and ties, walking purposefully in one direction or another and then, another sort of community consisting almost entirely of white people, wearing coloured open-necked shirts and shorts. He watched them go into shops and emerge carrying smart coloured bags, emblazoned with the shop's logo. A look in the shop windows told Frank the cost of the goods displayed.

Frank's school hours ended at 3 p.m. He had homework to do though that was relatively easy and could wait. He had been watching one particular café and bar that seemed to have a high turnover of patrons. One day, after school, he walked into the cafe and straight up to the person he knew from his own observation to be the manager and said, "Yo want help washin', cleanin'?"

"How old you?"

"Thirteen," he lied. "I come 3 hours, 3 to 6 at night."

Night in Barbados language can start any time in the afternoon.

"Wait round the back. I come."

A few minutes later the manager came out of the kitchen door.

"Okay, I give you $1.50 per hour, 3 to 6, start tomorrow."

The Barbados dollar was tied to the US dollar, but at half the value. So Bds $1.50 = US$0.75.

Frank went home and said nothing to his parents.

Two days later he said to the manager, "Weekends, I come longer. 6 hours okay?"

It was and he did. And during the school holidays as well.

This was another world, a world away from his miserable life in St Lucy, a world of which he should be a part. He scouted the coastline from Six Mens Bay in the north to as far south as Holetown, halfway down the coast using his student bus card, taking in all the opulence, without even a thought of how it came about. Along the beaches he watched water ski boats with ladies in skimpy bikinis and athletic-looking men zooming backwards and forwards, crisscrossing the wakes of their boats; jet ski riders skimming along doing figures of eight in the surf, the mock pirate ships packed with glass waving tourists, dancing on the deck to the music of a steel band.

One morning he watched a jet ski rider coming in from the open sea to a small slipway in Speightstown. Closer observation showed two more jet skis in a shed on the slipway and a ski boat moored close by. A young man, a little older than Frank, fastened the jet ski to a post on the slipway.

Frank approached him, "How yo' ride that?"

"Easy, man. Go talk to Walton," he said, indicating a tall, handsome and smooth-looking black man wearing a bandana tied around his head, he is tinkering with one of the other machines.

He repeated his question.

"By taking a lesson. Fifteen bucks to Ervin over there and away you go."

Frank had never spent anything on himself but something made him say, "Ain't got fifteen bucks, pay tomorrow?"

"If you don't, they'll miss you in church next Sunday. What's your name?"

"Frank."

"Ervin," he called out. "Give young Frank here a fifteen minuter. No longer."

Ervin came over, "You ride a bike?"

"Yeah," he hadn't, only a push bike.

"All the same, 'cept you stand. Watch."

Stepping onto the machine he sped away, did a U-turn and came back to the slipway.

"Steer like a bike, starter and throttle in your right hand, keep your head up looking in the direction you wanna go and don't look down. If you fall, the machine stop automatic."

Frank slipped off his shoes, and mounted the machine, which moved slowly forward. He lost his balance and fell straight in.

"I tell you look up. Give more throttle, you must be de boss like riding a horse."

Next time he was better but still fell. The third time he completed a circle of the little harbour, realising that adjusting his position and relaxing his leg muscles in tune with the movement of the sea beneath him was the clue. Something else clicked in his calculating mind.

That evening he raided his money box for the first time. The next day he gave Walton $15.

"You want help cleanin' machines, boats? I come evenin's, weekends?"

"No, but if you come and I need you, we'll see."

He began to spend time after his stint at the café, going round to see if there were any jobs he could do. It worked; Walton let him hose down the jet skis and the two water ski boats that he operated with minor maintenance and repairs. He didn't pay him but he allowed Ervin to give him a couple of lessons. Walton Dailing operated two ski boats and four jet skis along the west coast, either under contract, or arrangement with various hotels, or by freelancing along the beaches, being hailed like a taxi by tourist holiday makers. Walton and his main assistant drove and gave lessons to the guests. It didn't take Frank long to be skilled on a jet ski and after a matter of weeks, Walton considered him capable enough to send him out on his own.

He told Frank, "Your job is to go to a beach, do a fancy couple of turns to attract attention, go to the shore and interest people to have a try. Some will have done it before, others you will have to teach, the same way as I have taught you. You charge $15 for 20 minutes, either for them riding the jet ski or for a lesson. Be very sure to watch the time and don't go over twenty minutes. At the end of each day you will bring the money that you have taken back to me. I will take $10 per ride and the rest is yours."

Frank soon worked out that being a jet ski operator and instructor was more lucrative than working as a washer up/cleaner at the café – especially when he devised his own plan, which was that for every four 20-minute lessons or rides he would give Walton $10 each for three of them, keeping the fourth entirely for himself. He still worked the evening shift at the café.

He never told his parents what he was doing. Not that they would have cared anyway. Home was merely somewhere to lay his head. His mother provided what little food there was and his father, he saw only infrequently. If he returned home at night, he was drunk and asleep when Frank left in the morning; often he didn't come home at all and sometimes remained away, sleeping rough somewhere for several days. Frank kept all the money that he made from the café and subsequently from his jet ski 'earnings' with Walton Dailing in a metal box; he kept it in a secret trap he had constructed under the floorboards in the chattel house.

Walton's driver/ski instructor on his other boat was a happy go lucky character appropriately so, named, Lucky. Frank made it his business to make friends with Lucky for another reason. Lucky, in turn, had a friend called Ned, calling himself Natty Ned, a Rasta, who painted Rasta Caribbean scenes on blank t-shirts that he sold to tourists. Lucky went into 'business' with him, selling the t-shirts to his water and jet ski clients, then dividing the spoils. But Ned had another side-line which interested Frank; he lived, literally, up a tree in no more than a shelter he had constructed himself on a tiny plot of land in the hamlet of Rock Dundo, on the first ridge up from the sea. On this quarter of an acre plot that no more belonged to Ned than to the man in the moon, he planted and grew a few vegetables and small bushes for sale; these, however, served as nothing more than camouflage for the main crop, marijuana, which was hidden behind the bushes. The t-shirts sold for $20 each and samples of the "main crop" were discreetly available to Lucky and, now to Frank as well. Below and to the right of Ned's plot lay another small area of unoccupied scrub land at a slightly lower level. On Frank's instigation, Ned planted an irregular-shaped pyracantha hedge, over five feet high and impenetrable, behind which he doubled his marijuana crop.

Frank's day job fitted in with his overall life plan; to become a 'have' rather than a 'have not' by whatever means. He saw Walton being on good social ground with hotel managers and their tourist clients. This really irritated him because he knew his own character failings. Answer? Somehow he must change. Who were they, after all, why and how were they so fabulously rich? What did they have in common? A dominator that he noticed time and time again, particularly among the English and Irish, was an animal. The Horse. The horse in two guises, both competitive: racing and polo.

Frank was 16 now; left school having played truant for most of his last term. The answer to his own question was simple: he would have to learn to ride. What was it Ervin had said about riding a jet ski? *'You must be the boss, like riding a horse'*. He had heard of a woman, Mrs Griffiths, who ran a riding school at her property in St. Thomas.

In typical Frank style, he made several reconnaissance trips to the property at different times, watching the pupils, all of them white, being taught the various disciplines, walking, trotting and cantering around a circular enclosure. The more advanced pupils were also given lessons in jumping over specially constructed poles that could be adjusted in height set between two uprights. Frank checked on Mrs Griffiths' normal routine, the most likely times that she left the property, where did she go and when did she usually return. He memorised the registration number of her car. He discounted walking up to her front door, thinking that that placed him at a disadvantage.

One afternoon, when Sheila Griffiths came out of Holetown post office, Frank walked up to her and said, "Mrs Griffiths, yo' teach me to ride?"

Sheila looked him up and down and said, "I shouldn't think so, but I can try."

"What time I come?"

"Ten o'clock tomorrow morning, you know where to come?"

"Yes."

"Right. What's your name?"

"Frank."

Sheila was just coming with a class when Frank arrived the next morning. He noticed a few girls and one boy waiting like himself.

"Right, Frank, come with me. Have you ever ridden before?"

"No," he said, deciding not to mention the few times he had ridden the plantation ponies.

"I will give you a course of three lessons, which will cost you $75. By then I will know if I am wasting my time and your money. I have three other beginners so let's go."

Frank handed her $75; she rounded up the other three and led them to a row of pony stalls.

"The first thing you need to know is that your horse or pony is your friend. As such, you must treat each other accordingly and on no account appear nervous."

The first part of the lesson was spent teaching them how to prepare the pony, brushing it over including its mane, tail and forelock, picking its feet out, all the while talking to the pony and making it feel at ease. Next, she taught them how to put on the bridle and saddle. When all this had been done to her satisfaction, she called four senior pupils to come and show each beginner how to mount their pony. All aboard they were led out into the arena, or ménage, as it is known, to walk around one behind the other. At the end of the lesson, they were taught how to dismount and to ensure that each pony had water and hay in their stalls.

Sheila Griffiths admitted grudgingly to herself towards the end of the third lesson that Frank had the talent and ability to ride well. He was the best in her novice class. She signed him on for another six lessons for $20 per lesson. At the end of the course, he was cantering with confidence and had popped a number of ponies over low show jumps in the arena.

Sheila Griffiths kept her word. She taught Frank to ride and ride well, but received no show of gratitude or appreciation from her pupil. She had had enough; she didn't like Frank or the disruptive way he behaved to other pupils, particularly to those who showed promise, as if he was jealous of any form of success by others. He was no fun to have around and she didn't need him; it was as though he was jealous of any form of success.

One match day at Holders she was chatting to Tony Knowles who she knew was looking for extra grooms for his ponies and said to him, "I've got this redleg boy who I've taught to ride from scratch. He's doing some yard jobs as well so knows his way round a stable. He's a surly bugger with an outsized chip and probably a loner, but he can ride well and has no fear. He has mentioned to me that he would like to get into polo. He's got no money that I'm aware of and lives up in St Lucy, but if you're looking for someone he may suit you, as long as you don't stand any nonsense."

"Thanks, Sheila – send him to see me and I'll have a look at him."

"I've done all I can for you, Frank and it's time for you to move on. If you are interested in polo, Mr Knowles, who is a member of the Barbados polo team, will grant you an interview. He will be at the ground tomorrow evening exercising his ponies. I've told him about you so you may introduce yourself. He will be expecting you."

"I go tomorrow," was all he said.

Sheila also knew most of the trainers at the Garrison and that Peter Geary might be looking for an extra lad, so she mentioned this to Frank as well.

At Holders the following evening, Frank, who had been watching the activities on the field for an hour from the shelter of the trees on the far side of the ground, went up to Tony as he dismounted from his pony, "You want help with ponies?"

"What's your name?"

"Frank."

"Yes, Mrs Griffiths has spoken to me about you. She taught you to ride, I believe. You are a very lucky boy. Mrs Griffiths is a brilliant teacher and knows more about horses and ponies than pretty well anybody else on the island. How old are you?"

"Sixteen."

"Get on this pony, walk round the outside of the ground and then take it on a collected canter for one circuit."

Sheila Griffiths was right, he said to himself, as he watched Frank do exactly what he had been told. He could see that he had good, soft hands and that this normally highly-strung pony was calm and relaxed.

"Come to my place at Glendale at 7 o'clock tomorrow morning," he said to Frank. "I'll show you the setup and we can discuss matters then."

Polo in Barbados is an amateur sport. All players have their own day jobs or businesses, Tony Knowles being no exception, having his own construction company that he had built up over a number of years, operating it from a site in Warrens Industrial Park. He lived with his wife and family at Glendale, St Thomas, where he kept his polo ponies.

At 6.30 the next morning Frank was in the vicinity of the Knowles smallholding at Glendale, at a vantage point on a slight rise looking down at the house and stable yard, standing back on the other side of a narrow road. He watched Knowles come out of the house and walk across to the stables, dressed in his working clothes of light-coloured trousers and an open-neck shirt. Then he saw first one and then two boys turn into the property on their push bikes. On the dot of 7 o'clock, he walked along the short drive, just as Knowles was coming back from the stables.

"Good morning Frank," Knowles greeted him. "I'm glad you've made it on time."

"Morning," replied Frank.

"Based on what Mrs Griffiths has told me, I'm prepared to offer you a job here, but before I do so, I must tell you that you will treat me, my wife, family, the other staff and the ponies with respect and politeness. Do you understand?"

"Yes, Mr Knowles."

"Right, your job will be to be here at 7 a.m., muck out and dress over the ponies, give them their food as directed by Joel, my headman, exercise the ponies, again as directed by Joel. Your morning work will usually finish at approximately 10 o'clock. At 4 p.m. you will report here again and follow Joel's instructions. One or two evenings per week in the polo playing season you will accompany the ponies to Holders and look after them during the stick and ball practice exercise. On match days, almost always at weekends, you will come with the ponies and look after them between chukkas during the matches and take them back home afterwards, bed them down and feed them, as instructed by Joel. Is that clear?"

"Yes, Mr Knowles."

"You will be paid $150 per week for a trial period. Any questions?"

"No, Mr Knowles, I would like the job."

"Right. You can start now. Joel!" he shouted.

Joel, middle-aged, short and wiry with bandy legs, came over.

"Joel, this is Frank, He rides well but has no experience with polo, so please help him where necessary. He is ready to start now."

"Okay, boss. Come with me Frank."

CHAPTER 7

Scouse lent out of the train window as it was drawing into Crewe station, waving like mad to Will as he saw him coming along the platform with a middle-aged lady, whom he correctly took to be his mother.

"Look, somebody's waving, looks as if to you."

"Yes, that's my friend Scouse; he's on the ship with me. A great guy from Liverpool, a proper Liverpudlian, terrific sense of humour, you'd love him. His father's a taxi driver."

They hugged closely. Mary hated to see him go.

"Don't worry Mum. I'll be back in a month. I'm really glad Ayshford looks like being a goer. Everything will be alright. Love you so much Mum –and Dad, and Joanna. Thanks for everything Mum and look after yourself."

He climbed onto the train and into the seat that Scouse had kept for him, waving again to his mother as the train pulled out of the station. In conversation, it turned out that Scouse's father wasn't just a taxi driver. Scouse's surname was Knabb and his father called his business Knabbs Cabs, consisting of himself plus two other drivers. Knabb senior specialised on long distance work to airports, business meetings and conferences, theatres, parties, sporting events and the like, leaving most of the local stuff to the other two. Useful to know, Will thought, Liverpool being not too far away from where he lived.

The first thing next morning, back on the *Star*, Will went to the Purser's office to say that he had been offered and accepted a very good and permanent position with a UK company, so sadly this would have to be his last voyage on the *Star*.

"I've really enjoyed and appreciated my time with the company, Sir," he added.

"Sorry to hear that, Will, but glad for you," Enright said. "You've done a good job with us and I'll certainly see to it that you will have a favourable reference."

"Thank you, Sir – there's just one more thing. Remember those horses I looked after on my first trip? Well, one of the horses may be running in a race on the day we arrive at Bridgetown and the owner has asked to come to the races and stay overnight, Sir. Would that be alright, Sir? Jake and Scouse have very kindly offered to stand in for me for my cabin duties."

"Oh, all right Will. It's against the rules but I'll look the other way and pretend I don't know."

"Thank you very much, Sir."

The passengers occupying Will's two cabins were a rather dull, elderly retired couple from Harrogate, and in his other cabin he had a young couple who had chosen the trip for their honeymoon, named Simon and Camilla Richardson; they were married the previous day at the bride's home near Stroud in Gloucestershire. Both seemed very friendly and eager to talk about life on the ship and about where they were going. Simon Richardson said he was a partner in a venture capital business in the City and his new wife worked for a firm of interior designers in Chelsea. Will did his best to fill them in on what he had learned on his first two trips.

"Can you give us a few tips on what to do on shore on each island?"

"It depends really what you want to do. In Barbados, for instance, swim and lunch on a beautiful beach, take a trip to see fabulous scenery, go to Harrison's Cave which the Purser will speak about, or a visit to an old plantation house; there are many good alternatives. Personally, I'm going to the races."

"The races?" Simon exclaimed. "Do you mean they have a racecourse in Barbados?"

"Certainly," Will replied. "Two trips ago I looked after two racehorses shipped out here from England on this very ship."

"Camilla and I love racing; we often go on Saturdays to courses within range of London and we have a number of friends involved with the sport."

"Is the racecourse far from the docks and how do we get there?"

"That's easy. Just tell your taxi driver to take you to the track; it's only twenty minutes or so. Tell him when you want picking up and that you'll pay him on return to the ship. He'll probably give you a tip or two, probably best ignored, but you could look out for a horse called May Go Twice. Racing is very popular in Barbados."

Six o'clock next morning the *Star* was at the quayside at the Deep Water Harbour. Will packed all he needed into a plastic bag so that when he had finished mucking out both cabins, all he had to do was to put on his smartest trousers, clean white shirt, grab his passport and make his well-practised run out to the entrance courtyard. There, sure enough, was the open-topped yellow moke, out of which stepped Lucille wearing a flowered skirt, her blonde hair streaming behind her as she ran to greet him, flinging herself into his arms, then hardly saying a word until they were back in the moke. Then a torrent, both interrupting each other, hands still clasped together.

Lucille said when they had calmed down a little, "Now, have I got an action-packed day for you. Actually, you know most of it already – thanks, by the way, for your lovely letter…"

Will interrupted, "Speaking of letters – and I adored yours, of course – but my wretched sister got hold of it and gave me such stick about all the diagrams and capital letters signs on the envelope… "

"She didn't open it?"

"No, of course not, but I was teased to death."

Lucille laughed, "Anyway, we're on our way now to Tony Knowles' home where he keeps his ponies… Oh, I can't tell you how wonderful, wonderful it is to see you…"

"Ditto, my lovely sweetheart – the old ship seemed to be going so slowly this time, but please let time stand still now."

Tony and Susan Knowles' house at Glendale was in open country, not too far from Tony's business site in Warrens Industrial Park.

Nearing the house, "I should tell you that I've heard that oddball Frank chap may have got a job at Tony's. Evidently, he needed an extra groom and Sheila Griffiths recommended that he went to see him. Peter Geary told me that he'd been sniffing around the Garrison as well. If he is there, it's no big deal anyway as Tony will kick him out if he's any problem. When you've had your ride, shall we go to the Bamboo Beach Bar like we did last time?"

"Yes, my lovely, anywhere as long as you come, too. I'm on the highest and most beautiful cloud ever."

Tony saw them coming and came out of the yard to meet them, saying, 'Hi', to Lucille and planting a kiss on both cheeks and holding out his hand to Will. "Very good to see you again. Wow, a month has flown by. Your tour leader here tells me you have a busy day in front of you, but come and see what we've got here and if you fancy having a sit on one, that would be fine."

"I'd just love to. I've been riding a few during my week at home plus some racehorses, so I'm not completely out of practice. I've got a pair of scruffy trousers and a t-shirt with me but nothing else in the way of riding kit, I'm afraid."

"Have a look in the tack room over there. There may be a pair of boots that fit you."

Will slipped out of his smart trousers and shirt, hung them on a hook, put on his dirty and found boots that fitted okay.

Tony called out, "Joel, where are you? Can you bring out the new Argy for this young man to have a sit on?"

"Yes, boss."

Joel appeared out of one stall, went into another and brought out, tacked up, the "new Argy".

Will mounted him, Tony handed him a polo stick and said, "I'll chuck a ball out there for you to have a hit, but make yourself comfortable on him, take him into that field over there, walk and trot him round in circles and then give him on steady canter round the outside of the field doing the odd twists and turns, nothing too sharp though."

Will did exactly what he had been told and was exhilarated. The pony had been so well trained, felt like Rolls Royce beneath him, light as a feather and beautifully balanced. On his way back he caught sight of Frank looking at him from behind the row of pony stalls.

"That was fantastic. Can't wait to tell them back home in Cheshire that I've sat on such an amazing pony."

"Did you say Cheshire?" said Tony. "Man, you come from Cheshire? You must have known Mickey Moseley. He used to bring a team from Cheshire out here for many, many years. What a man and apart from being a very good player, could he drink? He kept all the rum distilleries in business all the time he was here."

"Sadly I never met him, though all the stories that I've heard bear out what you say. My mentor, Julian Shannon, knew him well."

"I remember meeting Julian, he came out at least once, maybe twice. Mickey used to take a little wooden house on the east coast, near Bathsheba, and you needed two days under a cold compress after his lunch parties."

Lucille appeared by their side, "Well, if you two have finished reminiscing, please can I have my friend back? We're off for a swim and then to the Garrison. One of Max's horses Will looked after on his ship is running this afternoon and we mustn't miss it."

Tony said, "You ride as well as she seems to think you look. That fellow would have had you on the deck otherwise. Any time you are here you got to tell me."

"Thank you very, very much. I loved it and I will…"

Fifteen minutes later they were at the Bamboo Beach bar and in the sea reprising their last visit, both of them having been longing for it from opposite sides of the Atlantic ocean. Will answered his own original question to himself with, *No, this is even better.*

During lunch, he asked how the invitation for him to stay the night came about.

"That was easy. I did nothing; I was going to ask but hadn't worked out how to do so, then they brought it up themselves. They must have taken a shine to you when they met you the last time. I said I would ask you," she said, with a giggle.

She continued, "We'd better get going soon; I think May Go Twice is in the second or third race. I haven't had time to tell you but he had his first run last Saturday and finished a good third; Chally was delighted with him and thinks he has a great chance today but there is a hotpot owned by Tom Canon, the boss of one of our biggest food and drink distributors, which will certainly start favourite. Max did say that, not just because you are coming, he might let Fawn Princess have a quiet first run. Peter will make the final decision, though I think that Max would like you to see her in action."

A huge crowd was gathering at the Garrison. As Lucille deftly weaved her way into the main car park; a man dashed out, "Afternoon, Miss Lucille."

"Afternoon Kel – here you are," she said, getting out of the moke, signalling Will to do the same. "This is my friend, Mr Carpenter. Will, this is Kelvin, but take no notice of his tips. He'll park the car."

"Oh, Miss Lucille – dat not so and Mr Geary's new horse – he win today."

"I hope so," said Will. "I looked after him on the ship over."

May Go Twice was in the third race over 1,000 metres, roughly five furlongs, with Fawn Princess down to run in a later race. The crowd was milling around, full of chatter and good humour, the jockeys on their way out of the weighing room for the first race and across the track to the paddock directly opposite the grandstand. The Barbados Turf Club had its own partitioned-off section of the stand with its own entrance staircase, guarded by an official. Will noticed that all members of the club were smartly dressed in suits and wearing ties, with the ladies also smartly attired, some even wearing hats. Not quite Ascot, more Goodwood style.

Lucille and Will mingled with the crowd, Lucille showing Will off and introducing him to her friends. The first race, over seven furlongs got underway amongst much excitement in the crowd, jumping and shouting rising to a crescendo as the runners flashed past the winning post. After the next race, Will spotted Max Geary coming down off the Turf Club stand; he and Lucille intercepted him.

"Will, welcome back to the Garrison," he said, with a grin. "I see you have your chauffeuse with you. A little bird told me you would not be alone. I hope May Go Twice will do you proud, though we'll be hard-pressed to beat the favourite. The filly has come on so well recently that Peter has decided to let her have a little introductory run today as well."

Just then Will saw Simon and Camilla Richardson approaching them.

"We took your advice to come to the races," Simon said.

It was Will's turn to do the introductions, "Max, this is Simon and Camilla Richardson: Max Geary. I am their cabin boy on the Star."

Simon asked, "Well, so what about this horse May Go Twice that you told me about?"

"You had better ask Max: he's the owner."

"Good to meet you; I was just saying to Will – hope he'll go well, though it's only his second race since he arrived here. See you later, I hope; I'm off now to have a look at my horse."

Will said, "All I can tell you is that I believe that he is quietly fancied."

The jockeys came out; Will could see Chally Jones talking to Max in the paddock. He dashed over to see him and May Go Twice came out onto the track on his way to the start. He looked magnificent; a horse ready to race. Going over to the tote booths,

Will plonked Bds$20, all that he could afford, on him. In a five furlong race at The Garrison, if you don't get a good start you might just as well have stayed at home, but Chally jumped him out well, took a pull and settled in third or fourth place, close up behind the leaders. Turning for home, the favourite stole a two-length lead and looked all over the winner, then Chally got to work and came with a beautifully timed run with his horse producing a good turn of foot, getting up close to the line and winning by a neck going away at the finish. Although Will could hardly hear because of his own shouting and cheering, the noise of the crowd was deafening and he caught sight of Lucille beside him jumping up and down and yelling, 'Come on May Go' at the top of her voice.

They dashed over to see Max Geary lead in his winner and congratulate Chally Jones. Then, spotting Will and Lucille, he grabbed them both and invited them to come up to the Turf Club stand for a celebratory drink, where they were joined by many of Max's friends including Tom Canon, the owner of the favourite, who had finished second.

"Where did you find that one from?" he asked.

Max laughed and said, "Never mind where he came from, this young man here," as he indicated towards Will, "looked after him so well on the ship that he came on from England, that he was bound to win."

Max introduced Will to his wife, Eileen, an ample bosomed lady who bubbled with excitement and bonhomie, "Max has told me so much about you and how you looked after his two horses on the way here."

And then to Lucille, "Lovely to see you, my dear. Your parents not here today…?"

Before Lucille could reply, Eileen had been dragged away by somebody else.

When all the excitement had died down a little, Lucille whispered quietly to Will "I know you would like to see Max's other horse run, but perhaps we should leave after that. I want you so much on your own."

"My thoughts entirely," agreed Will.

He went off to the tote booth to collect his winnings of $100 – $80 for winning plus his stake back of $20.

Chally Jones employed completely different tactics on Fawn

Princess, not bouncing her out of the stalls, but allowing her to run at her own pace towards the rear, before threading his way past tiring horses to finish a respectable fifth and hardly knowing she had had a race. A real confidence booster. Will and Lucille slipped quietly away. Kelvin, the car park attendant, was full of the joys, having lined his pockets with dollars on May Go Twice's win, but Will and Lucille now only had eyes for each other.

Leaving the racecourse they made the half-hour journey to Uplands Plantation, Lucille explaining on the way that her family had emigrated from Scotland in the 19th century, her great grandfather having been a second son. Not wanting to be a soldier or a clergyman, but knowing somebody who knew somebody, who knew the Governor of the day in Barbados – She said with a smile, "As I am sure my father will tell you. He would certainly have known the Carpenters of the day."

At Four Cross Roads Lucille turned left; about half a mile later a driveway and sign read UPLANDS PLANTATION. A mahogany-lined avenue on a gravelled drive went straight until around a bend the Great House appeared seventy-five yards in front of them. Not huge by any means, though an imposing two-storey coral stone house with a wide veranda all-round the ground floor, with the upstairs rooms set back from the veranda's roof. Tall doors, the full height of the ground floor opened into the inner rooms, all with jalousie-type window frames of Georgian style.

"Hello, you two, very good to see you again, Will. Welcome to Uplands, I hope you've had a good day at the races," George said, coming out to meet them.

Lucille kissed both parents, then, "We've had a terrific day. Max's horse, which Will looked after on the *Star* two trips ago, won, would you believe it? It was so exciting, he beat the favourite, a horse of Tom Canon's, by a neck."

They entered through the veranda into the hall leading to a most elegantly furnished drawing room with two sofas and several armchairs placed in sections of the room; floor to ceiling bookcases lined one wall, a mahogany round table partly covered by magazines including *The Spectator,* recent copies of the air mail edition of *The Daily Telegraph* and that day's *Advocate,* one of Barbados' two daily papers. From another table, Harriet poured tea from a silver teapot and offered milk from a silver jug and sugar from a silver caddie.

We could be in England, Will thought.

"Was this your first experience of the Garrison?" George asked.

"I've been there a couple of times to see the horses in the mornings but, yeah, it was fabulous and a great feeling about it. Until recently I had no idea that racing was so popular here."

"That's terrific and well done you. We know Max and Eileen very well; they are such good friends. Nothing happens in Barbados that Max doesn't know about. Now, I gather from Lucille that you have another connection with Barbados?"

"Well, yes, I suppose so, although it is from a very long time ago. My ancestor, Benjamin Carpenter was one of the early settlers here in about 1780, but for a variety of reasons the family connection has died out. However, it's fascinating for me to be lucky enough to come here and see it for myself. It is so kind of you to ask me to stay tonight."

George said, "Ben Carpenter arrived here about forty years before my great grandfather, Francis, but my grandfather, Percy, would have known Ben's sons George and Jack."

"I think Ben died in 1834 so your great grandfather might well have known him, too."

"Never mind all this historical stuff," Harriet interrupted. "You can talk about that later. I'm sure Will would like to dump his stuff and know where he is sleeping, Lucille, why don't you show him? We are quite early birds, just come down when you are ready. We'll have a drink and dinner will be at about 7.15."

"Yes, of course I will, Mum. Come with me, Will."

She took him up a wide mahogany staircase, along a corridor to a bedroom at the end with views on two sides. Will flung his bag onto a chair and turned into Lucille's waiting arms.

She whispered, "Not now, my lovely, as Mum said, they go to bed quite early but we'll give them time to go to sleep and then I'll come to you. It's better that way; I know every inch of this house in the dark and where every floorboard creaks. For tomorrow I've prepared a picnic to take you somewhere you won't forget. Just the two of us."

She showed him the bathroom just across the corridor and left him.

Gazing out of the bedroom window in the fading light, the cooing of the doves and fluttering of the yellow birds in the trees being replaced by a chorus of cicadas and the high-pitched croaking of tree frogs, while a family of monkeys chatting and arguing flittered from tree to tree, Will let his mind wander like he did at Welchmans: here in the still quiet of a landscape, not too difficult to imagine his great, great grandfather, two-hundred years ago on his land, only a few miles from where he was standing. *Come on, Will, you've got a beautiful girl waiting for you downstairs, it's all up to you now: if Benjamin Carpenter could do it, so can you.*

He had been a bit worried that the conversation downstairs might be a bit stilted, though he need not have been. A middle-aged man wearing black trousers and a white shirt asked what he would like to drink.

Just then George appeared saying, "Ah, I see that you've been intercepted by Horace, but why don't you try an Uplands Special, distilled from own cane with a twist of our own mangos, not too lethal I can assure you. Horace, here, doubles up as plantation foreman, driver on occasions, and comes in to help whenever needed in the evenings. Sherry, his wife, works in the house and helps Greta, the cook, in the evenings."

"Thanks, I'd love one of your specials," Will said, just as Lucille and her mother came into the room.

Dinner of lightly grilled fresh barracuda was served by Sherry and Horace who dispensed a good bottle of Chilean wine.

During dinner, George outlined the activities of work on the two-hundred-acre plantation, "Sugar production in Barbados is on the wane and has been for some time: we can't compete with fully mechanised open spaces of five-hundred acres plus in Florida and other areas. Here, to find ten acres of flat land is rare. So we have had to adapt; most of our products now are in the form of vegetables for the local and other Caribbean markets and fruit. Most of the fruit is harvested unripe but ready for export by sea and air. You will have had experience of this on your ship. Barbados has become much more industrialised and tourism is now the largest industry with over 400,000 visitors coming to our island every year. This figure includes cruise ships which, in my opinion, do us few favours and bring very little to the island by way of revenue as so many of the passengers' activities are prepaid to the cruise shipping lines."

Dinner over, it was not long before George and Harriet said that it was, "All very well for you young, but we're off to bed. Please help yourselves with anything else you need."

"I've been up since before dawn myself, preparing for the docking routine plus an exciting day at the races, so I'm pretty tired, too," Will said.

He followed his hosts, thanking them profusely for dinner, giving Lucille a quick peck on her cheek as he did so.

An hour later, his bedroom door opened; a ghostly figure glided towards the bed shedding a silky white robe as she did so, sliding into bed with him. They reached for each other, arms intertwined, their bodies drawn together as one. Will cast off the single sheet that was covering them and gently turned Lucille over onto her back. The very nearly full moon cast its magic beam through the open window onto their naked bodies. They kissed passionately, their tongues playing together, Will holding, then stroking, then kissing her breasts, first one nipple and then the other, flicking his tongue, making them rise perkily to his touch; with his left hand, he reached for her ankles and very slowly travelled up to her knees, to her inner thighs gradually extending to the moist junction where one leg joins the other.

"I want you now," she whispered into his ear, her own hand guiding him to where they joined into one being.

Slowly, very slowly they made true love to each other, whispering all the while, kissing, gazing into each other's eyes to the abandonment of everything and anything else.

As he rose and fell inside her, their combined mounting ecstasy coincided with her saying, "Now, fill me now, now, I can't wait any longer – yessss, oh yes."

They lay, clasped to one another, breathing untold happiness and joy into what they were sharing. A long time later, he was aware of the same ghostly figure slipping away as silently as she had come.

When Will came down soon after 7 o'clock, breakfast laid out neatly on the dining room table, Lucille and her parents already there.

"Sorry I'm late but good morning," he said.

"You're not a bit late," replied Harriet. "We're always up with the lark as they say in England, though we have only just come in. I hope you had a good night's sleep."

"Couldn't have been any better," said Will, resisting with difficulty any glance in Lucille's direction.

When they had finished Lucille said, "Will has to be back on his ship at 5 o'clock this afternoon. We'd better be leaving quite soon to make the most of the day. I've sort of got the picnic ready, we're off to Harrismith."

"That'll be an experience for you Will, so I won't spoil it for you," George said.

"I've put a bottle of wine and a sample of Uplands Special in your cooler," he added.

Everything for a seaside picnic – rugs, a couple of folding chairs, towels and the all-important cooler – were loaded into the moke.

"It's been a real pleasure seeing you here and both of us hope you'll come again the next time you are in Barbados," George and Harriet, talking almost in unison, as they waved goodbye.

"I hope so, too," said Will, as they drove away down the drive, taking an easterly route towards Culpepper island, where they turned right onto the coast road going south across the rather bare and windswept countryside.

Fifteen minutes later, Lucille pulled off the main road onto a dirt track before coming to a halt by the side of a forbidding-looking ruined and roofless mansion house, on the edge of a cliff.

"Here we are. This is Harrismith," she said.

Will got out of the moke and walked a few yards to the edge of the cliff, looking down onto the most perfect half-moon shaped two-hundred yard sandy beach onto which crashed large waves, coming, as it were, straight from Africa. This indeed was the most easterly point of Barbados. Will wondered if the large rectangular shell of the house had ever been welcoming.

A narrow path and uneven steps led down to the beach which was completely deserted. A few stunted palm trees, bent against the prevailing wind, provided minimum shelter, but on the right-hand end of the beach some overhanging rocks did offer shade from the sun; this is where they were heading.

Dumping the picnic and holding hands, they tore off their outer clothing, ran down to the sea and dived through the first big wave. They were not surfing waves, but big crashers that slammed down from a height of six to eight feet. Both strong swimmers, even so, Lucille advised not to venture much further than twenty yards from the shoreline. Fifteen minutes later, exhilarated, exhausted and in love, they emerged from the sea. Back at their place by the overhanging rocks, they stripped off, brushed the sand from their bodies with towels, spread the rugs on the sand side by side and lay down.

"You are as beautiful to see in the light of day as you are to feel at night," Will murmured, as they explored each other's bodies once again, stroking and kissing everywhere.

"Tastes salty," Lucille said, looking up at Will, who responded by gently pushing her back a little, parting her legs as he did so.

Taking their time they climaxed together; they didn't want their love-making to end. Tears of happiness welled in Lucille's eyes while they lay soaking it all in, knowing that nothing else in the world mattered; they were together. Without bothering to put on any clothes, they put lumps of ice cubes into the glasses and filled them with Uplands Special, spread out their picnic of barbecued baby chicken breasts, a delicious salad and mangos straight off the tree, all of which they could eat with their hands, taking their time before dashing back into the surf.

It was then that the first tinge of sadness crept in. They both knew that their following final slow, beautiful, rhythmic lovemaking when they emerged from the sea for the second time, would be their last until neither knew when and in two hours' time they would be parted. Carefully, they packed up the remains of their picnic making sure that no trace of them having been there was left. Different thoughts crossed their minds as they turned away from their love spot: Will's that he wondered if he would ever see it again, and Lucille's that, although she knew that she would, as it was a favourite place for a family picnic, the magic of today would never leave her.

They meandered their way through the parishes of St. Philip and St. George. In a farm gateway in the last bit of country that they passed through, Lucille stopped the car for their last long, passionate kiss; soon they crossed over the main highway, passed close to Government House then the Kensington Oval and all too soon they were at the gates of the Deep Water Harbour, both close to tears.

They had said all that there was to say and promise so the final moments were the same as a month before. A quick kiss – on the lips this time – and a final wave at the gate and he was gone. Lucille turned the little yellow moke round, felt the empty but warm seat beside her and let her emotions flow, bursting into floods of tears that lasted all the way back to Uplands.

For Will, it was different. His emotions were just as strong as Lucille's but he had to contain them, being back on board the ship surrounded by shipmates and passengers returning and with all preparations for departure well underway.

Jake was in the deckhands' quarters when Will came in.

"How did it go then, mate, get yer leg over did yer? Me, Scouse and Curly went to Harbour Lights again where that band of yours was playin'. Cor, bloody marvellous they was. Been all over the world they have, y'know, Carnegie Hall in New York, big stadium in Toronto, even the Albert Hall in London. Curly was 'aving a ball wiv all them other chalkies."

"Chalkies?"

"Yeah, chalkies. Y'know: chalky whites, blacks."

Will told him to piss off but thanked him again for standing in for him.

Up on the passenger deck, he was preparing the Richardson's' cabin when they came in.

"Well, what have we here? Not just a cabin boy but an aspiring jockey, polo player and Miss Barbados as a girlfriend! Your friend Max Geary, who you kindly introduced us to, asked us up to the Turf Club bar after racing and was singing your praises. We didn't leave until 7 o'clock. Are you going to do the same for us in St Lucia and Grenada?"

Will grinned sheepishly and muttered something like, 'You should be so lucky'.

Simon continued, "We had a marvellous day today, too. We spent much of it at Cobblers Cove hotel owned by the Godsal family from England. Had a wonderful swim on their beach, drank too many rum punches and then had a fabulous lunch."

The *Star* departed on schedule but by the time Will had finished his evening duties in the dining saloon it was 9.30 and after 10 o'clock by the time he climbed into his bunk and recounted to himself everything that had happened during that tumultuous and blissfully happy two days. He was also very tired so sleep came easily and welcome to him.

Back at Barry, following the scheduled stops in St Lucia and Grenada as before, it was a round of farewells; first to the disembarking passengers, to Mr and Mrs Harrogate and especially to the Richardsons, though not before he had asked them how they had heard about the cruise.

"Really, through my parents, who are very good friends of a family with Dutch connections, who have connections with the shipping line."

"They wouldn't be called Van Duren, by any chance?"

"Why, yes! How the hell did you guess that?" Will laughed, while he explained that it was his old school friend, Jimmy Van Duren, who had been instrumental in Will getting his job.

"It's a small world," exclaimed Simon Richardson, giving Will an envelope.

"Our address is inside," he said, as he shook Will by the hand.

"Very good luck to you and let's hope that our paths will cross again."

Next to his crew mates, all of whom he had got on very well, even the tough softy Johnny Jones, "I'll miss you", was all he said, but with kindness and a rare smile.

Then to Jake, swapping addresses, "Not heard the last of yer, mate."

"Ditto, my friend."

To Dave, the quiet farmer's son, Scouse he would be seeing on the train home, and to Curly, he with the sense of humour, spliffs and good nature.

Finally, to the ship's officers. Captain Dickson who said that he would provide a very good reference for Will, if ever required; the Chief Engineer PO Jennings; and the Purser, Gavin Enright, who had turned a blind eye at a critical moment. Lastly, to the ship herself; Will turned around gazing upwards as he descended the gangplank for the last time, battered suitcase in hand, and again as he stepped onto dry land raising his hand in salute and a silent Goodbye and Thanks. Then it was off to the station with Scouse and to telephone his parents telling them of his arrival time at

Crewe. The train journey was poignantly sad for him this time. He would not be making it again. Like the closing of a door; Lucille seemed even further away. The almost physical pain that he felt, made worse because it had not been possible to make any plans for their next meeting.

When a door closes, another one opens: the start of a new phase in his life that he knew would take up all his time and energy. If he had any anxiety that Lucille felt the same, he need not have worried; she was going through the same heartaches and for the same reasons. They had resolved to resort to loving letters, the first of which from her would be waiting for him at home; he had been able to send letters to her from St Lucia and Grenada. Telephone calls to and from Barbados in those days were very expensive and had to be booked several hours beforehand and even then were unreliable.

"You okay, mate?" Scouse asked.

"Yeah, sorry, just a bit preoccupied."

"It's that bird ain't it?"

"Yeah, s'ppose so."

"Come to Liverpool, mate; soon find yer anovver one."

Will laughed.

"That's better."

Coming into Crewe, Will said, "You're a good friend Scouse. Our paths will cross, I'll see to that."

As usual, it was Will's mother who met him at Crewe, throwing her arms around him and making all the right noises that mothers make to returning offspring. In reply to Will's questions, she filled him in on all the home news: contracts had been signed for the sale of the Dower House at the top end of the agent's valuation and another contract had been agreed for the rental of Ayshford Farmhouse from the Blackfords, at a rent considered by Angus' agent as fair and reasonable. They had already started to move some things with the big move scheduled in two weeks' time. News from James was encouraging he had completed two-thirds of his officer training course with highly commendable written reports. That was the good news. On the negative front, Angus' mental condition was deteriorating. He was permanently listless and depressed despite all that Mary, Joanna, and his close friends could do. His doctor had prescribed anti-depressant pills which were only partially working as Angus himself had a phobia about taking them for fear of forming an addiction.

Will had only a very few days before he was off to Solihull to start his new job so, forewarned about all the above, as soon as he and Mary had arrived home, he dashed into the house to find his father sitting hunched up in his chair in the study.

"Hello Dad – it's wonderful to be home and to see you. You look fine and Mum's been telling me all the good news about Ayshford, which I'm delighted about. So glad it's all signed and sealed and that you'll be moving very soon. You can now put all the horrid trauma of the past year behind you and I promise you all the family are behind you and are so happy about what you've been able to achieve. For my part, I've really enjoyed what I've been doing for the past four months; it's been a tremendous experience and an eye opener, and now I've got a proper job to look forward to."

Angus smiled, got up and embraced his son, "Well done, Will, you must tell Mum and me all about your adventures and the new job."

Which, at dinner later that evening, he did, with particular reference to the time he had spent in Barbados.

"Ben Carpenter was quite a hero and is a legend, you know Dad. I crossed over the land of the plantation and saw the ruins of the original Welchmans Hall."

"All right, Smartarse, cut the Christopher Columbus cackle and tell us about L. Todd," interjected Joanna.

"Lucille Todd is a very nice young lady who happens to work for Max Geary. I met her a couple of times, among several other people, who were very kind to me in Barbados but wait, I haven't told you the exciting news. Remember, I said last time that I had looked after a couple of horses on my first trip? Well, one of them was running on the day we arrived in Barbados this time. Max very kindly asked me to the races and, guess what, the horse won and I had $20 on him," Will said, anxious to steer the conversation away from Lucille.

"Oh, and was Miss Todd at the races?"

"Her parents are members of the Turf Club and she came, I believe, with them."

"How very convenient."

"Now, stop all this, you two; that's enough," Mary Carpenter interrupted.

"Yes, back in your box," Will echoed.

"Now then, a bit of really good news," said Mary, "James rang an hour ago to say that he's got thirty-six hours leave and is coming home tomorrow."

Will went to meet James at the station where they greeted each other with a big brotherly hug. On the way home, they filled each other in with their news. Will told James about his three cruises on the Star, his meeting with Max Geary, and how kind he had been, taking him to the old plantation and that he was in love with Lucille.

"Not a word about this to Joanna; she's giving me enough shit about it as it is," though he did add that it was serious and how much he was missing her. "She's very special, you know."

"They are all special," said James. "Lucky both of you to have found each other and I look forward to meeting her."

For his part, James told how much he was enjoying his course and how very tough physically and mentally it was.

"Only another six weeks to go and then, after a bit of leave I'll join the regiment – as long as I pass," he concluded.

The regiment was based at Tidworth but he was awaiting news of a posting quite soon.

"Where to?" queried Will.

"Don't know, could be Northern Ireland, Afghanistan or any of the other hot spots."

Will briefly summed up the home situation.

"Mum's okay with it all, but Dad isn't. See what you think and then let's have a chat about it. You've only got a day at home and I leave to start my new job the day after you go, so we haven't got long."

One of the first of his friends that Will had contacted on his return was Jimmy van Duran to tell him the story of him meeting the Richardsons.

"Oh, yes," Jimmy had replied. "What an amazing coincidence. They are very good friends of my parents, although quite a bit younger. He's quite a city whiz kid. I'll tell my parents about you meeting them. By the way, when can we see each other? Why don't you come up to London? You can stay with me and we'll attack the town."

"That's a brilliant idea and I'd love to, however, I've landed what I hope is a great job with the firm of Supercar, you know, the car hire people and I start next week. I'll tell you about it when I see you."

They went on chatting about this and that, including Will saying that he was lovesick about a girl he'd met in Barbados; they agreed to meet up as soon as possible.

The only other time the brothers could talk privately was when Will took James back to catch his train at the end of his leave.

"We've got to keep a watching brief on the situation", James said. "Luckily we are both in England for now. Presumably, you will be able to come home on some weekends and I will do also when I have my leave at the end of my course. I don't think Dad is ever going to be like his old self again, though Mum is strong and when everything is sorted at Ayshford, he will be able to take things easily with not too many worries. Joanna may be a concern when she is a little older, but you never know, and we can both keep an eye open and give her and Mum all the support that we possibly can."

Another brotherly hug on the platform as the train rolled in.

"I'm very proud of you brother James," Will said.

"You, too, young 'un; you've done so well getting this job and I'm right behind you."

Before leaving on his last trip on the Star, Will had selected lodgings with a Mrs Fitzgerald, walking distance from the Supercar office. He was offered a decent-sized bedroom with a nearby, but not necessarily private, bathroom. Breakfast was included in the rent and a light supper would be provided at an extra cost, as long as she was told before leaving in the morning. Mrs Fitzgerald, who spoke with an Irish accent, said she had a total of four rooms which she let out in her house. There was a pay telephone, though incoming calls were not accepted, however, would be possible on her private line, only in an emergency.

CHAPTER 8

At 8.30 a.m. on 1st September, Will entered the door of Supercar Head Office and asked to see Mr Briscoe. He had travelled down the previous afternoon clutching the same battered suitcase that he had taken on all the *Star* voyages, now packed slightly differently.

On arrival at New Street station, he bought a street map at W.H. Smith's and caught a bus to Solihull, then used his map to find his way to Mrs Fitzgerald's street and house. A late middle-aged, well-preserved lady with hair turning grey, she welcomed Will in her soft southern Irish accent, that was kind but business-like, and showed him to his room. He had a single bed with a bedside table and light, a chest of drawers covered with a lace mat and a couple of china ornaments, a hanging wardrobe with a large bottom drawer, a hard desk type chair and another what might be called an 'easy' chair, plus a washstand and basin with a mirror above. The curtained sash window overlooked a small garden at the back of the house. Across the corridor, the bathroom with a bath and incorporated shower. Next door, a separate loo.

Mrs Fitzgerald explained that he would share the bathroom with one other guest, a young man training to be a solicitor. There were two other rooms, one of which was taken by a typist who also worked for Supercar with the fourth room presently unoccupied. She said that she guessed that Will would like some supper; it would cost £5 if he wanted it. He thanked her and accepted; neither of the other residents were present and Mrs Fitzgerald did not sit down to eat with him. He unpacked and went to bed quite early.

Office hours were 8.30 to 5.30, Monday to Friday. Jim Briscoe told him he would be attached to experienced operators, covering different aspects of the business, spending one week with each of them. At the end of the month, he would be expected to answer written questions covering all sections that he had learned so far.

Will took stock of his situation; he was missing Lucille as she was him, containing matters with long, loving letters. Yes, his situation and that of his whole family had changed, yet he was not in the least bitter. He reflected on how many nineteen-year-olds had the opportunity to do as he had done in the last six months, at no cost to his family; how lucky he had been in making the connection with Robert Mallory and how he was bloody well not going to let Mallory or himself down. During that month of basic training and learning about Mallory's company, he worked hard and studiously, taking notes in an exercise book, both during the day and in the evening, noting any questions that he wasn't sure about that would require answers the next day.

He sailed through the test paper at the end of the month that Jim Briscoe sent for him.

"You've passed, Will. Congratulations; now go home for the weekend and I'll talk to you again on Monday."

What he did not say was the comment he had written at the end of the report he had sent to Mallory:

'This young man has exceptional talent. All those with whom he has worked during the last month have been highly impressed. I recommend a posting to a senior manager for further training.'

On Monday there was a message waiting for him from Briscoe asking him to come to his office.

"Good morning, Will; hope you had a good weekend. Come with me, please," said Briscoe and led Will straight along the corridor to Mallory's office, knocking at the door and leading Will in.

"I've brought Will Carpenter to see you, Mr Mallory."

"Good morning, Will," Mallory said.

"Good morning, Sir," replied Will.

"I've been reading Jim Briscoe's report on your first month with us. It seems that he is satisfied so far. As you now know, we have a number of subsidiary or branch offices, dotted round the country. My policy has always been that while we must have desks and booths at all major airports, our main offices and collection depots are situated in the less smart areas of main cities; witness here our HQ, well out of the centre of Birmingham. Therefore, it is of vital importance to have expert and immediate communication between the airport desk, the area office and the collection point. At the airport, we only keep spaces for cars for which we have orders. One of our main sources of business outside the London area is Ringway, Manchester's airport; our main office and collection point is in Altrincham, just outside Manchester's conurbation, it's within easy reach of the airport. We have a vacancy for someone to work directly under and report to the Depot and Area Manager, Fred Ogden. I am offering you this position, noting at the same time that it is within range of where you ordinarily live. As you will be making very frequent journeys between the depot and the airport you will need to have the use of a Supercar, but your fuel allowance will be minimal. In other words, if you choose to live at home, your commuting expense will not be covered. What do you say?"

"I think it is a very good offer, Sir, and I accept with pleasure and gratitude."

"Okay, Jim will you sort out all the details – oh and by the way – Good luck, Will."

"Thank you, Sir."

Fred Ogden, the Supercar Area Manager for the Manchester depot, was a tough, fortyish, stockily built Lancastrian; a bachelor for no other reason than he preferred his own company and saw no reason to, in the words of Henry Higgins in *My Fair Lady,* to "let a woman in my life", and certainly didn't want any screaming children around the place. He could do all he wanted when he wanted – and with whom he wanted. He was also very good at his job, intensely loyal to Robert Mallory and his company. He welcomed Will, having read the glowing report sent to him by Jim Briscoe.

"Now, lad," he said to Will on his first morning. "I am the boss here; you'll work with me, do as I say, but any ideas or suggestions that you have, bring them to me and we'll get on fine."

Will had learned and studied all the locations of the Supercar network around the country; he was delighted to come to Manchester. Not only could he live at home which suited him and the family for personal reasons, but he also realised that Manchester was a very important area for Supercar with Ringway airport on their doorstep.

Most of his first couple of weeks were spent at the desk at the airport, which operated on a 24-hour shift basis, with a rota of two staff per shift. Fred's area included Liverpool airport, sea ferries from Liverpool and Holyhead to Ireland, and Leeds/Bradford airport, plus a small tourist office in Chester.

At home, the move to Ayshford completed, Mary Carpenter was very pleased to have Will living at home; so was Angus, although he was only a shadow of his former self, placing more of a burden on Mary.

James had been home on leave on and off for a couple of weeks, having passed his training course with distinction, he was now back with his regiment at Tidworth. The rumour was that they were going to Afghanistan. It was duly confirmed in early December that the regiment would leave immediately after Christmas.

With James home on leave for Christmas, all the family were together in their new home. On Christmas Day, Will called Lucille in Barbados, a happy/sad conversation for both of them; happy to be able to speak, sad because they were not together with no immediate prospects of being so. Will had three weeks of holiday entitlement each year, though having only held the job for four months, most of which was spent in training, now was not the time to think about holidays and anyway, he could not afford to fly out to Barbados.

No polo in the winter, however, he still rode out for Adam Platt on Saturdays and went racing with him sometimes when he had runners at local meetings, such as Bangor-on-Dee, Uttoxeter, Ludlow or Haydock Park.

Socially, Will met up with the usual gang at the Rising Sun and had a few days hunting with the Cheshire Hounds, when, mounted by Richard Tomkinson, the Master, he stood in for the second whipper in, who had broken an arm in a fall.

In March, he organised a party for his friends to go to the Grand National at the end of the month. He asked Jimmy van Duren and his current girlfriend to come up and stay for the weekend, and he kept his word with Scouse by asking him to provide transport in the form of a minibus to take them to Aintree and, more importantly, to bring them home again.

Scouse had now started to work for his father; Will was delighted to see the Knabbs Cabs minibus with Scouse at the wheel coming down the drive at Ayshford. On Grand National Night he booked the private room at The Rising Sun for the whole party for dinner; he would have liked to have had the party at Ayshford but Angus was not too keen on this idea.

James' news from Afghanistan was that he and the regiment

had settled down well in Helmand Province; obviously, he could not go into any details. He gave an official address that all the family could use for correspondence,

Will got on very well with Fred, he found himself taking on more responsibility when Fred was visiting other areas within his domain or attended the Area Management meeting at HQ. The feeling was mutual, Fred liking and admiring this young man who had come into his business life with such enthusiasm; he enjoyed bringing him on and into management matters; sometimes they went together to meet customers and suppliers. Working as a team, the two of them improved the turnover and profitability in their area, stretching the boundaries into uncovered sections, and making deals in large seaside hotels for their guests.

Once, when an evening meeting looked like being a late one, Fred suggested that Will stayed the night with him to save him from a very late journey home. He lived in a very smart two-bedroom flat between Altrincham and Hale, furnished bachelor style and very tidy, his spare room immaculate with its own bathroom. Will discovered that Fred's main hobby outside the business was traditional jazz. He had an amazing collection of old records and CDs, featuring all the famous jazz kings, Louis Armstrong, Sydney Bechet, Dizzy Gillespie, Duke Ellington and the rest. British stars such as Humphrey Lyttleton, Chris Barber, Ronnie Scott, Johnny Dankworth plus, although not really jazz, Acker Bilk on clarinet playing *Stranger on the Shore*. When in London, Fred always ended up at Ronnie Scott's. Most of his holidays were built to coincide with Jazz Festivals around the world; he told Will that he once went to Chicago, purely for a concert featuring the brilliant drummer, Buddy Rich.

They established a strong business rapport. This was good for both of them: Fred's parents had died several years ago, he had no brothers or sisters, was happy with his bachelor state, a keen golfer and a prominent member of his club, he had many social friends and therefore was a good 'spare' man. He loved women for fun and company and could hold his own in any form of conversation.

Will had positive thoughts and feelings, *I've got something going here for which I can count my lucky stars, missing Lucille like hell but this is a proper job in the real world, with a mentor I can laugh with, as well as work with. Perhaps not play as I'm not going to start playing golf and Fred would look f'ing stupid on a horse, never mind a polo pony.*

As spring moved into summer, polo took up all Will's recreational time. Helped and encouraged by Julian Shannon, he was turning into a more than useful young player. He had attracted the attention of Robby Huxtable, the father of Will's erstwhile girlfriend, who fortunately was unaware that his daughter and Will had forfeited their virginity jointly on the sofa in his drawing room.

Robby was the very well-off Managing Director of a major industrial company in Manchester, as well as being a pillar of Cheshire Polo Club. He wanted to form a junior polo team that could play against similar teams from other Clubs and was prepared to invest a large sum to support the plan. Two other members joined in, provided their own sons could play. Poor Angus, of course, could not contribute, however, between the other three, there was enough money produced to buy or lease ponies, and to provide admin cash to support the operation.

Will was the best of the young players, therefore an automatic selection for the team. The Club had two grounds on which to play; during the summer, half a dozen matches were played by the young team, either in practice among the eight or so men and girls considered to be good enough or as a selected team against other clubs within a day's reach. The experiment was a success, with Will being recognized as the best player both by home and opposition teams.

On a Monday morning towards the end of September, as he was driving to Manchester, Will realised that it was over a year since he had started working for Supercar, and nearly a year since he joined Fred in Manchester, therefore thirteen months since he and Lucille had kissed goodbye at the gates of the Deep Water Harbour in Bridgetown. His love for her had not diminished and, judging from her letters to him, neither had hers for him. But there was something nagging in his mind that needed attention. Will had not looked at or even wanted to look at any other girl since and he had this amazing job and opportunity that he put it first in his life. Was it fair to Lucille and what was she really thinking? They were both still young with most of their lives in front of them. Supposing they managed to have a week together either in

Barbados or in England, and then have to go through the terrible parting again with the Atlantic ocean between them?

Will decided that he must take the lead and put all these things to Lucille; he hated the thought that she might be holding onto him lust because she was too lovely and kind to let him down. Come what may, he didn't want anything to come between them ever; what they had could never be taken away, however, it was he who had come into her life in her country, then gone away again. He must do something about it for her good and for his, too.

He wrote a loving letter in which he listed all these points in as kind and delicate a way that he could. He emphasised how much he loved her and always would do, but that also he was tied to the fabulous job that he had obtained and intended to make his career and that he was not in a position to ask her to drop everything and come to England at this stage. He ended up by saying that if she wanted to throw his letter in the waste paper basket and continue as now, he would be thrilled but said, *'please think carefully about your future life, as I don't want you to lose out because of me, I will understand and continue to love you until I die.'*

He looked at the letter for two days, making the odd alteration here and there before taking the final step of letting it drop in the letterbox.

The next few days were unhappy ones. Had he done the right thing? Will she think I'm trying to break it up? All sorts of other worrying thoughts continually flashed through his mind. But she's not here anyway so what difference does it make? Come on Will, pull yourself together; you've got a brilliant, challenging job so get on with it.

At last the letter he had been waiting for, arrived. Luckily Joanna had left for school before the post arrived. Mary hid it from her, putting it in Will's room for him to see when he returned from his office.

He got himself a drink, sat down and opened it.

'My Darling, Darling Will,

Your last letter is the most beautiful, loving, lovely, sweetest and probably saddest letter I have ever received. I have read it over and over again. It is typical of you to be so kind, thoughtful, understanding and farsighted. I love you from the bottom of my heart and always will. But you also write with such sense about us and our situation. If you were here, or I was there, I am certain that we would be together and busy making plans for the future. But we're not and there's the rub.

Don't think that I have not thought along the same sort of lines as you, but you are the one who has had the courage to take the initiative. As you say, it's been a year now since that dreadful parting after such a fabulous couple of days. I am writing this upstairs in the room where we spent most of the happiest night of my life. It is our room and will remain so, as long as I live in this house.

Many things have happened to you during the past year; I am so proud of you getting this fantastic job and making such a success of it – and don't say you are not because I know that you are.

I have just been here, trying to carry on as normal, but pining for you all the time, going round with my friends, to the races occasionally with my parents, with the gang to the likes of Harbour Lights from time to time, though with you firmly fixed in my heart. I've tried not to show it, although I think my parents have an idea of how I feel. Perhaps, now, I should open up a bit more with them.

Of course, you're right; we have to live our own lives. I have not looked or wanted to look at anyone else and shall not start doing so now, but who knows what will happen; que sera, sera. All I do know is no one ever, ever will take your place in my heart and that when we meet again – and we will – and in whatever capacity, my love for you will be still there, always.

Now, on other things: as you know I am still working for Max Geary, rather more as a sort of PA these days. May Go Twice has won a couple more races and been placed a number of times. He is very consistent and always does his best; however, Max has asked me to say, if I am in touch with you (!!), that Fawn Princess has come on in leaps and bounds; she won a valuable open race, (that is open to all comers from other islands and imports from England and the USA, recently over a mile (1600 metres) and will make a fantastic broodmare when she has finished racing.

All I can say now Will, my darling, is that paradoxically nothing has changed but maybe a little different. If ever anything does change, I can promise you that you will be the first to know and I also know that you would do the same to me.

In the meantime, please don't stop writing. You are my Guardian Angel.

Your ever, ever loving,
Lucille'

Will sat there in his chair for a long time. He didn't know whether he should be happy or sad. In fact, he was both; he was happy with the realisation that Lucille still loved him and that he had been correct to write in the way that he did, though sad for them both, at the same time. But at least one thing was clear: neither of them should need to feel any guilt about how they should go about their day-to-day lives.

Christmas came and went. All the family were together, except James, who had sent as Christmassy a message as possible, communication not being easy due to the normal security measures. Mary and Joanna made pretty Christmas decorations, hung mistletoe from a balcony over the stairs into the hall below and both of them, plus Will in the evenings, erected and decorated the Christmas tree. He spent ages with the Christmas tree lights, which, when finally found in a twisted, mangled mess in the bottom of a trunk failed to raise even a flicker after he had done a jigsaw puzzle job on them, so it was off to the toy shop to buy new all singing and dancing new ones with 'gears' that you could change the display, formation, and even the colour, at the flick of a switch.

"These have got to last for at least the next ten years," he informed the assembled family.

The highlight for Will was telephoning Lucille at Uplands on Christmas Day and hearing her voice and news. Harriet Todd had answered the telephone, and had a few words with Will, wishing him a happy Christmas, before handing him over to Lucille. Will found it easier to enquire about what she had been doing and asking about the horses etc, because he knew about the scene and scenery there, whereas Lucille knew nothing about Will's surroundings and home.

The army had arranged for all officers and men to record their family Christmas greetings and for these to be made available in time for Christmas. Heavily censored, of course. James had also sent a family Christmas card by army mail. Will suggested, and Angus and Mary agreed, that James' recorded message should be played to the family at 2.55, five minutes before the Queen's Christmas Day broadcast.

CHAPTER 9

One day in late January, Will enquired, "Fred, you said early on that I should come to you with any ideas etc, that I might have. Well, I have a question and, for that matter, an idea. Why is it that Supercar, a well-established and highly successful company, has no overseas branches like the other big names in the business?"

"The old man won't have it," Fred replied. "I've suggested it to him many times but he just won't wear it. Says we're doing fine as we are, so what's the point in going abroad? I think he believes it is more than he can handle and is worried about making the step. He had a major heart attack two years ago, you know. But if you want to do an analysis on the subject and then submit it to me, I will make sure that it gets into the old man's hands – and it will be in your name."

During the next few weeks, Will set about compiling such a report. He listed where the car rental international companies had branches worldwide and made another list in more detail showing only the European branches. Finally, he made an analysis and proposal, showing estimated costings of setting up a trial operation in Ireland, including Northern Ireland, with a head depot in the Dublin area and sub depots to cover the likes of Shannon and the south west. In the preliminary section of the report, he included figures obtained from the Bureau of National Statistics and showed how much the volume of tourist and business traffic had increased annually since the end of WW2. Will finished his report at the end of March, submitting it to Fred just after another very successful Grand National weekend, which he had organised. By this time, he had been working with Fred in Manchester for eighteen months.

"We'll see what, if any, difference a report like this from the younger generation makes," Fred said, after having read it. "It's very good, by the way."

A week later, Fred called Will into his office.

"The boss wants to see you," he said with a smile. "And I should make it pretty quick, if I were you, before he changes his mind."

Will put the call through to Aggers straight away.

"Hello, Will," she said. "I've been expecting your call. Mr Mallory will see you at 11 o'clock tomorrow morning – that is, if you've got nothing better to do!"

"I'll be there."

When he got home that evening he told his parents about the report he had written and that he had been called to see Mallory the next day.

"Maybe I won't have a job by tomorrow evening," he said, half-jokingly.

Aggers met him when he arrived in Solihull the next morning and took him straight to Mallory's office.

"Good morning, Will," he said, from behind his desk with the report laid out in front of him.

"Good morning, Sir."

"If I've told that stubborn old Lancastrian bugger Ogden once, I've told him ten times that we stick to within our own shores and now you, you young whipper snapper, with all of a year and a half's experience, have come up with a similar daft proposal that will drive us to bankruptcy in no time. Having said that, over a long time I've very sensibly conserved a considerable reserve fund in case of any serious emergency that might hit us. Therefore, I'm going to put the essence of your proposal to the Board at the next meeting for discussion. I hope and expect, however, that I will be overruled by the other Board members, who will put it down to my taking the first steps into senility. In the meantime, I will reply to Ogden, but not a word to anyone by either of you."

Getting up from his desk, he led Will over to the more comfortable side of the office, sat down and invited Will to do likewise.

"Well done, boy. I am very pleased with you, but your work has only just started. There is a long road ahead for you, which I shall be watching carefully."

Will drove home happy, but keeping his fingers firmly crossed.

In the office the next day, Fred showed Will the letter he had received from Mallory containing all that he had told him the previous day.

"We want to be very careful about this one, lad, for your own good and mine. If this scheme is approved by the Board, it is their decision and nothing to do with you or me – at least for the time being."

"You're a wise old owl, Fred."

"Aye, lad; there's plenty of knockers out there, as you'll no doubt find out."

A few days later on a bright, sunny spring evening, after a good though long day in the office, Will drove home, having hoped to stop off at the polo ground for a bit of practice, but he was running too late for that. He was in good form; the crops were sprouting and the trees and hedges were brightening with the beautiful virgin green of spring, as the brilliant yellow of the rapeseed fields stood out in profusion against the setting sun; each evening the shape of the dairy cattle could be seen more clearly as they made their way back after milking.

Will drove through the gates of Ayshford; he could see his mother standing close to the house. She didn't look right. Something was the matter. She had been crying. In her hand, she held a piece of paper. Will got out of his car; she handed it to him.

It was a telegram; it read:

'IT IS WITH PROFOUND SADNESS AND REGRET THAT I HAVE TO INFORM YOU THAT 2nd LIEUTENANT JAMES CARPENTER HAS BEEN KILLED IN ACTION IN AFGHANISTAN. HE WAS TRAVELLING ON AN ASSIGNMENT WHEN HIS ARMOURED VEHICLE WAS HIT BY A LAND MINE. ALL FIVE MEMBERS OF THE CREW UNDER THE COMMAND OF LT CARPENTER DIED INSTANTLY.'

It was signed by a Col. Irving and included full contact details. Will hugged his mother, both of them overcome by their emotions.

"Your father has taken it very badly and is inconsolable."

Will went in to see him, he was just slumped in his chair behind his desk, unable to speak. Joanna came in, in floods of tears; Will wrapped his arms around her as they wept together, holding each other very tightly. A while later Will picked up the telephone, dialled Fred's home number and told him the news.

"I'm so sorry, lad," he said. "Just take your time."

Will, grieving his heart out, took command of the situation. He loved and admired his brother and had always looked up to him, but realised that he, now, was de facto head of the family and must act accordingly.

Will called Col. Irving on the number given in the telegram. The Colonel, deeply understanding and sympathetic, said that the RAF Hercules transport plane bringing the bodies of all five crew members back, would be arriving at RAF Brize Norton in two to three days' time and that he would let Will know precise details as soon as he had them.

Will contacted a local firm of undertakers that he knew about, advising them of what had happened and arranged for them to bring James home from Brize Norton as and when. He also contacted the vicar of Tarporley, David Hatch, who he knew slightly, to make provisional funeral arrangements. David immediately offered to come and see the family, and Will explained that his father was the one who needed all the help that the vicar could give him. He promised to come that very day.

Col. Irving telephoned to say that the plane would arrive at Brize Norton at approximately 11 a.m. on Thursday 22nd April. On the day, Will drove his mother, father and sister to Brize Norton, leaving home early in the morning. A reception party met them and took them to a long, low building with large windows facing the runway. They were shown into a comfortably furnished room with armchairs, sofas, and a few tables and chairs. They were served with coffee, tea and biscuits. Family members of all the deceased crew gradually accumulated in the room and either stood or sat in uncomfortable silence. Col. Irving moved from group to group offering comfort and sympathy all around.

They all watched in silence as the giant aircraft landed and slowly taxied to no more than seventy-five yards from the building. A platoon of soldiers headed by Col. Irving as they marched smartly out to the plane, and then they stood at attention. A military band played sombre music as the huge loading ramp at the rear of the plane slowly lowered onto the tarmac. A detachment of the platoon moved forward to receive the first of the five coffins, each one draped in a Union Jack flag and capped with wreaths. Four other detachments followed and when they were ready, the five coffins, first James' and then his four crew members, were slow marched to an area close to where the families were watching.

Five hearses were waiting to receive them and take them to the respective family homes. Each family were called forward individually to see the coffins loaded into the hearses. Will had arranged for James to be taken straight home where he would lie until the day of the funeral. Angus had said that he wanted James to be laid on his desk, which he had covered with a deep purple table cloth.

The funeral took place at St. Helen's Church, Tarporley, four days later on 25th April, ten days after James' death. The church was packed not only with family, friends and relatives, but there were also many young people, including old school friends of James. One of them was Jimmy Van Duren, in age halfway between James and Will, who had now joined a firm of stockbrokers in the City of which his father was a senior partner. Student friends from Cirencester and so many others also attended, James had met and befriended them in the army and elsewhere.

A detachment from his regiment acted as pallbearers. A bugler from the regiment played *The Last Post* at the conclusion of the service.

Afterwards, a very pretty, tall girl, on the arm of her parents, came up to Will, introduced herself as Sarah Whatcombe and said, "I loved him so much; he was so special."

This reminded Will of James' words to him about Lucille, "*They are all special*", that he had told him once.

To Will's surprise, Robert and Kathleen Mallory came, "We never met him," Robert said. "Though if he was anything like you, I wanted to be here."

Likewise from Fred Ogden, "I'm with you, lad," was all he needed to say.

During the service, Will recalled that the last time he and the family had heard James' voice, was on the last Christmas Day.

Among the hundreds of letters received by the family was one from James' Commanding Officer, in which he included the words:

'*... in the comparatively short time that James was with us, he had shown exemplary skills as an officer of outstanding ability. He was much admired and respected by his brother officers and his men. His loss is devastating, not only to his family and friends but to the Army and his Country.*'

He received a heartrending letter from Lucille; when it arrived he took it straight to his room before opening it and reading all that she said, overcome with emotion for several reasons apart from his own personal grief; one, that she cared so much for him and his grief, two, that they couldn't console each other verbally, and, three, that they were so far apart.

At home and for the first few days after the funeral, Will did his best to console his father and look after his mother and sister, as well as undertaking all the admin matters that occur at such times. He kept in constant touch with Fred. He rode out a couple of times at Adam Platt's and had one stick and ball practise on his own on the polo ground. A week, including a weekend, after the funeral, he went back to work, getting stuck in, checking what had happened in his absence and catching up with all matters in his domain.

A week or so later, Fred, who had been away for a couple of days in other parts of his area, called Will into his office.

"It was the Supercar board meeting yesterday," he stated. "And the old man called me at the Wolverhampton office asking me to come to see him in the afternoon."

He paused, looking at Will and enjoying keeping the young man waiting on tenterhooks.

"The proposal to open an office and extend Supercar business into Ireland has been approved in general by the Board."

He caught Will's gleaming eyes and wide grin.

"That's the good news. The bad news for me is that the crafty old bugger has asked me to be overall manager i.e. extend my area, but that you will be in charge as my deputy, in other words, do all the work. I have agreed in principle, as long as I can relinquish some of my outlying areas here. So what do you think about that?"

"Bloody marvellous, that's what I think," replied Will.

"Thought you would. You'd have to go and live there, of course; in other words, relocate."

"That can be arranged," said Will, briefly flicking his mind over what that entailed.

"It's my own bloody fault," grumbled Fred. "Never should have suggested it to the old fart in the first place. Takes no notice of me and then you come along and he thinks it's all your fucking idea."

There was a suspicion of a grin on the older man's urban features.

"So, when do we start?" questioned Will.

"Yesterday," was the muttered reply.

CHAPTER 10

Will sat at his desk in the Head Office of Supercar (Ireland) Ltd, in the north Dublin suburb of Santry, only a few miles from Dublin airport. He had spent the best part of six months making a recce of southern Ireland, concentrating first on Dublin for the HQ and then deciding between Cork and Limerick for a sub-office. He made all the preliminary searches on his own, before calling Fred in to advise and adjudicate.

For Dublin, the site in Santry came out best; only a short distance from the airport, a good lease on a building in a business park, with enough total space and good access. The ferry port of Dun Laoghaire was a bit farther away to the southeast though perfectly manageable from Santry.

The choice between Cork and Limerick went Limerick's way for three main reasons; one, it was closer to Shannon airport than Cork; two, it was a lesser distance to Dublin; and, three, the feeling was that the business in and around Cork, Killarney and Kinsale, all major tourist areas, could be handled from Limerick.

Mallory had been kept in the loop, and been very supportive in agreeing that all the legal, lease negotiating and administrative arrangements could be handled by the team at Solihull.

The family had been thrilled when he had first told them about the go ahead though his mother was more than a little worried about how she was going to cope with Angus without Will living at home.

"Don't worry Mum. I'm always at the end of a telephone and I'll be home as many weekends as I can. I'm only going to Ireland, you know, not Australia!"

He had been living in and out of hotels for the whole six-month period, though he did get home most weekends, taking a Friday evening flight to Ringway, and the same in reverse on Sunday evenings. At least this way he got his washing done. He played several polo matches at junior level, and gained a place in a couple of matches on the home ground with the Cheshire team.

Will settled upon a base for himself in a manor house just

outside Dunboyne, Co Meath, that had been converted into flats. Ideal for his needs, only twenty minutes or so from Santry and not too far from Dublin. In 1798, Dunboyne had been a rebel stronghold in the fight against British rule, and in 1921 it was an important IRA command post. He took a ground floor furnished, one-bedroom flat, with its own private entrance.

He and Fred had engaged the services of a well-known recruiting agency in Dublin for all the staff that they needed, both at Santry and the very small number needed in Limerick, where they had secured a temporary office with limited space for the small fleet of cars that they estimated would be needed there for day to day business.

Will recruited a young Dubliner, Patrick Byrne, as his deputy and assistant; a good school record, keen rugby player, father office manager for a firm of accountants in Dublin and had completed a course at Trinity College Business School. Will liked him and sent him over to Solihull for a month's training, exactly as he had done.

Right, they were up and running.

Mallory's team and publicity department had put out an extensive advertising campaign in the UK and especially in Ireland. Invitations went out for the opening party to all Irish travel agents, individual journalists specialising in travel and finance for national and regional newspapers, regional directors of British Airways, Aer Lingus, EasyJet and Ryanair, and managers of all the leading hotels in the Dublin area with a Press Release on the day.

Fred came over a few days before the opening and Will was delighted that Mallory agreed to perform the official opening, bringing Kathleen with him. Will arranged a giant marquee in the parking area with sample cars of all ranges displayed. The heated marquee was equipped with subtle lighting, floral decorations, an audio system and a dais with a microphone. Behind the dais, an enormous banner proclaiming: "WELCOME TO SUPERCAR (IRELAND) LTD", provided an impressive backdrop. The caterers had attractive girls serving champagne, white wine or soft drinks to guests on arrival and a wide range of canapés to be handed around throughout.

At the appropriate time, Will stepped forward to the microphone, unannounced and simply said, pointing to the banner, "Ladies and Gentlemen, Welcome to Supercar Ireland and to the man who started it all, the founder, Chairman and Managing Director – Robert Mallory."

Mallory made an excellent, brief speech in which he emphasised that this was the first venture of the company outside the UK and where possibly better could it be, other than in Ireland. He took great trouble to introduce by name, Fred Ogden, and Will Carpenter, who were in charge of the whole operation and that it was Will who would be running the day-to-day side of the business. He concluded by thanking everybody for coming.

The evening was a success – no doubt about it.

Afterwards, Will had arranged dinner in a private room in the best hotel in Santry, where the Mallorys were staying, for Robert, Kathleen, Fred plus Jim Briscoe, and the chief PR man at Supercar, Paul Offley, and himself. Mallory, moved and happy, offered congratulations to *the boys,* as he called Fred and Will, wishing them all the luck which, as he put it, "they bloody well need, to pay for this evening's party."

He turned to Kathleen as they entered their bedroom at the hotel, "The boy done well – so far."

The next time Fred came over, the two of them drove down to Limerick to put the final touches to the small office and depot there. Having Fred around was a great help; the conversations between them included the Irish mentality and way of life, about which Fred knew very little and understood less.

Will told Fred the old joke about the English tourist couple who, coming out of Dublin, stopped a passer-by to ask if he could direct them to the right road to Galway, only to receive the reply, "Well, I wouldn't be starting from here."

He also told him about an actual conversation that he had heard walking to work early one morning, during his training month in Solihull, between two Irish navvies arguing while working on a building site, one from Limerick and the other from Tipperary. "There's only one road in Tipperary," said the Limerick man, "and that's the road out!"

He drew Fred's attention to the beautiful countryside through which they passed from the five-thousand acre, wide open space, of The Curragh in Co. Kildare, an area smothered in old Irish myths and leprechauns, though better known as the home of Irish racing; further south, through the rural county of Laois with farmland, many castles and mansion houses that had been owned by the Irish gentry of the 18th and 19th centuries, lots of them now having been turned into county house hotels and golf courses.

"Come on Fred, you're a golfer," said Will. "Bring your clubs and you can combine business with pleasure at weekends in this area and where we'll be very shortly – Tipperary, although this might suit me better than you with some of the best hunting country in Ireland. By the way, did you know there is a famous jazz festival in Limerick each year? You must come to that."

"Yes, when is it then?"

"About a fortnight ago."

"Now, you bloody tell me."

"Don't worry, Fred, I can fix it all up for you next year."

He told Fred that, way back, his family came from Co. Galway, a bit further north and west to where they were at that time, and that one ancestor had volunteered to join General Lord Cornwallis with 2,500 Irishmen in 1755 to fight for England in the War of American Independence.

"Oh, and what happened?" asked Fred.

"They lost."

He went on to say that his ancestor never came back to Ireland, he had ended up in Barbados, where he started and farmed a sugar plantation.

"How is it that your family came to live in Cheshire?"

"Oh, that's a long story. Maybe I'll tell you one day."

It was now deep into autumn, the evenings were drawing in, polo was finished for the year, and winter was just round the corner. Outside his business life, Will thought, he mustn't just sit around in the dark, waiting for something to happen. Obviously, he must go home to the family for Christmas and the New Year; he wanted to anyway, particularly as it would be the first Christmas without James. But maybe he should lessen his weekend trips home and find things to do in Ireland.

An idea struck him, at home the next weekend, when he rode a really nice new horse, recently arrived from Ireland, on Saturday morning. In the yard afterwards, Adam and he were discussing the horse's performance and the morning's work in general.

Will said, "Adam, it looks as though I'll be based in Ireland for quite a while; I was just wondering if you might be able to give me the odd contact in the horse world over there? I've rented this flat just outside Dunboyne and if there was any chance of being able to ride out on a Saturday, say, and to meet a few people outside my business life, that would be great."

"Of course, I can and will. I'm dashing off to Haydock now but this evening I'll come up with some ideas. There's this fellow Fergal Lynch - he found the horse you've just been riding – he lives somewhere up there north of Dublin and I'm sure he'd help with an idea or two. I must rush now, I'll write your Irish address and telephone number down and leave it in the office, and I'll give it some thought when I get back."

Will saw his old girlfriend, Judy Huxtable, that evening along with several of the young crowd in the Rising Sun, she was back from her year in South America and now working in London. They had a catch up – Judy said that she was so desperately sorry about James and that she'd heard that the family had moved. She told him about the fabulous time she'd spent mainly in Argentina and Chile. Will talked to her about his work, first as deckhand on a ship going backwards and forwards to the West Indies, what a great time he'd had in Barbados and the other islands, then, about the job he'd got with Supercar in Manchester, and how he had just been appointed to open a branch in Ireland. It was lovely to see her and to catch up, though he felt no urge to take matters any further.

On Sunday, he had a good talk with his mother and sister. Joanna was still at the stroppy teenager stage though finally growing out of it, Will thought. She was becoming more responsible and helpful to her mother, and at her day school where she'd made a number of good friends and done well academically, as well as on the games field. Soon it will be time for her to move on, which he needed to talk to their mother about.

"Mum," he said later. "I've got to go quite soon to catch my plane, but there are a few things we should talk about. I've got this amazing job and have been given the responsibility of setting up a whole new branch of the company in a foreign country. Now, I know you and I don't think of Ireland as a foreign land, yet even though it is just a hop, step and jump flight across the water, it is, strictly speaking, abroad. I am in charge there and I must make my project work. What I'm trying to say is that I may be coming home less frequently. The business doesn't just shut up shop at weekends, far from it. I should be there more often than not. Also, I have a life to lead and hope to meet friends that are not just colleagues. Adam Platt has kindly said that he will put me in touch with friends and contacts in the horse world, that's why you may be seeing a bit less of me during the winter. Out of sight is not out of mind though, the telephone is always there and I will be there, too, either in person or at the end of a message.

The other thing I wanted to touch on is what's next for Joanna? She can't go on for too much longer at her present school, she will need to spread her wings. She will soon be a very attractive young lady; we must prepare her for the pleasures and pitfalls to come. We are not in a position to send her off on an all-expenses-paid gap year, however, there are many opportunities for girls like her to travel to wonderful foreign lands – for instance, Zimbabwe or Kenya – she could work with respectable families caring for endangered species of animals, those that have survived poaching acts. Also, sooner or later, she must enlarge her circle of friends. Of course, she already has good friends here at home, but in another year or so, she should have some sort of semi-educational course in London – cooking, secretarial, artistic, design, fashion or otherwise. Doing any of these, she is bound to meet birds of a feather, girls – and boys – of similar background with whom she can form possible lifelong friendships. There will be boys, suitable or not suitable, with whom she'll want to play or fend off. Food for thought."

"Will, darling – you are growing up aren't you? You're quite right; I shall miss you terribly but, as you say, it is not as if you are in Seoul or some other godforsaken place. I do rely on you very much now that Dad is not his old self and we no longer have our darling James. And you are also right and farsighted about Jo. She's a lovely girl and we must keep her that way. I will talk to Dad."

As if to emphasise what he had been saying to his mother, back in his office on Monday morning, Pat Byrne reported to him that there had been a problem at the airport on Saturday. A family had booked a large car for a week's holiday to take them all down the west coast from Connemara, all the way down to Tralee. Killarney, Bantry and on to Clonmel, Waterford, and back along the east coast for their last night in Dublin; however, the order was mistakenly transposed to a small compact car, with no car large enough for them and their luggage being available for a swop. They were furious, demanding to see the manager. Pat spoke to them on the telephone, the best he could offer was two small cars at no extra cost, which did not satisfy the customers who set off still in a rage.

Luckily, the airport staff had details of their itinerary; Will reached them on the telephone at a B & B near Ennis, offered profuse apologies and told them that he was arranging for a luxury 7/8 seater car to be delivered to the hotel where they were due to stay in Adare, near Limerick, that evening at no extra cost for the rest of the trip. Next, he called the Limerick office to arrange the delivery of the car and to collect the two small ones. As a final gesture, he arranged with the Adare hotel that their overnight stay was to be complimentary to the guests and to send the bill to Supercar Ltd at Santry.

Their trip ended the following Saturday morning. He went to the airport to meet them to apologise in person for the error at the start of their trip. They turned out to be a very pleasant family from near Ripon in Yorkshire and were most appreciative of the action Will had taken. He gave them his Supercar card and asked them to contact him personally for any future requirements, which they promised to do.

Fairyhouse Racecourse, only about fifteen miles north of Dublin, is one of Ireland's premier courses, the home of the Irish Grand National that runs each year during the Easter weekend; a dual purpose course with both National Hunt races in the winter and flat racing in the summer. When Will saw in the paper that there was racing at Fairyhouse that Saturday, he decided to go. He bought a badge to the members' enclosure and mingled his way around, getting the feel of the place before the first race. Not that he expected to, he didn't know a soul. After the race he went into the bar to buy a sandwich and a pint of Guinness; turning away from the bar, glass in one hand and sandwich in the other, he was cannoned into by a stoutish man wearing a Husky jacket and a cloth cap. Much of his Guinness tipped onto the sandwich, the rest onto his overcoat and thence to the floor.

"Oh, by jeez, I'm so terribly sorry," expostulated the man, pulling out a not totally clean handkerchief and rubbing it against

Will's coat, which had the opposite effect to what was needed. "Let me fetch you a drink and whatever you had in your other hand."

"Don't worry," said Will. "It was an accident."

"No, I insist. I was rushing to buy some drinks and shouldn't have bumped into you," he said as he hailed the well-endowed, genial barmaid and asked her for three double Irish whiskeys and a brandy, all with sodas.

He added, "And a pint of Guinness for this young man."

"This is very kind of you," Will said to him. "But honestly, there's no need."

"Nonsense, it was my fault." Then, after a pause, "Are you on your own?"

"Yes, I am actually. It's my first time here."

"Oh, you're from across the water, then?"

"Yes, but I love horses and racing."

The barmaid produced a tray with the Husky man's order on it.

"Come with me and I'll introduce you to my friends. Careful, now as you go; we don't want any more accidents – my name's Tom by the way."

He led the way to a corner of the bar where a group of similarly clad men stood discussing the result of the race.

Approaching them Tom said, "What's your name?"

"Will."

"Here we are, lads, Sorry I've been so long; had a bit of a problem and sent this young man's lunch for six. His name's Will."

There was a round of helloes and grunts as the others helped themselves to their drinks.

Tom said, "Will's from England and it's his first time here."

"And what brings you here?" asked one of the others.

"I've just been setting up a branch of the car rental company, Supercar, the first one out of England."

"Oh, yes I heard about that. How's it going?"

"Well. Okay so far but it's very early days."

"You like racing then?"

"Yes, love it and anything to do with horses. When I'm in England I have a part-time job riding out for an English trainer."

"And who's that now?"

"He's called Adam Platt."

It was time for more drink to be spilled. One of the group, glass halfway to his mouth, put it down again dislodging most of the contents.

"Did I not have Adam Platt on the phone only two nights ago? Are you Will Carpenter?"

"Yes, I am."

"Fergal Lynch," he said, reaching out his hand to Will. "I was to call you but now this bumbling old fool here has beaten me to it."

"Less of the bumbling old fool, Fergy. Your round next."

"Very good to meet you. Tom here has done me a favour, even if it was by mistake. Adam has told me a lot about you and all the horses that you have found for him over the years."

"Yes, we've had some successes, though some disasters too. How's that one I sent over recently, North West Passage, coming along?"

"He's a really nice horse. I rode a bit of work on him last Saturday and he nearly pulled my arms out; should be ready for a run in the New Year."

Drinks finished, they all moved away to see the runners for the next race but arranged to meet up later in the day.

It was a typical cold and damp Irish November day, with the bar offering the only warmth and comfort available. Will bought the drinks without spilling them after the main race of the day, a valuable three-mile steeplechase won by the favourite, trained by Willie Moore.

Fergy Lynch turned to Will, "Adam said on the phone that maybe you'd like to ride out over here, maybe at weekends. Where are you living?"

"I've a rented flat just out of Dunboyne."

"Me and Tom been chatting; there's a young man, good family connections, rode a few winners as an amateur, done a stint as pupil assistant with Willie Moore and set up as a trainer a year back, near Trim. I know he could do with a bit of help. The name's Harry Kennedy and I have his number if you want to call him. It would be no more than twenty-five minutes from Dunboyne."

Will took the number and said, "Yeah, sounds really good; I'll give him a call and see what we can work out. Thanks very much."

Next morning, Sunday, about midday he called Harry Kennedy's number.

A lady answered, Will asked, "Could I speak to Harry Kennedy please?"

A male voice came on the telephone, "Harry Kennedy."

"Hello, my name's Will Carpenter. I was talking to Fergal Lynch at Fairyhouse yesterday and he said you might want a bit of part-time help riding out?"

"Yes and hello. He called me too; tells me you ride out for Adam Platt in England and you're now working here in Ireland but not in racing. What is it you do here?"

Will told him about the job and that it was a full-time, but he might be able to come on some Saturday mornings. Harry said that would be fine and how about the following Saturday.

"We pull out first lot at 7.30, so could you be here around 7.15?"

"Certainly," Will said.

Harry gave him directions, it was fixed.

The following Saturday, Will left his flat in the pitch dark and drizzling rain, though Harry Kennedy's directions were good. A mile or so outside of Trim he turned into a gateway marked 'Lostock Stables', leading down a short newly gravelled drive. Ahead, in the half-light, he could see the shape of a house on his right, distinguished only by lights shining in two downstairs rooms. Past the house an open high metal gate led towards a quadrangle of brick-built boxes that faced onto a gravelled walkway, circling a grassed lawn in the centre of which stood, in the gloomy light, an unidentifiable obelisk. Will parked by the metal gate.

A young man wearing jodhpurs, a strong weatherproof anorak and riding helmet, came towards him.

"You Will Carpenter?"

"Yes," said Will.

"Harry Kennedy; glad you could come and you obviously found your way okay. Bloody awful morning but it is late November. We won't be doing anything too serious this morning unless it clears up later. I've put you on a nice young horse, a four-year-old called Forge Lane. He's had a couple of runs over hurdles showing promise – came third last time, so should win a hurdle race, though I think his future will be most likely over fences. I'll be coming out with you and the others so just follow me or my head lad, Ronan, over there. Do come in and have breakfast with us afterwards."

An hour and a half later, coming in cold and wet, to the warm kitchen, Harry and Will were greeted by a good-looking girl wearing jeans, natty-looking furry slippers and a heavy winter sweater.

"My sister, Siobhan," said Harry. "She's also my housekeeper, cook, secretary and general gofer."

Breakfast of eggs, bacon, sausage, and tomatoes, resting on top of the Aga with toast and marmalade already on the table laid for three, coffee pot on the hotplate, prompted Will to say, "If she can do all the other tasks you've listed, as well as this, you've got a winner without needing a judge."

With a laugh and a swish of a tea cloth she sat down and they all tucked in.

"So you bumped into that old rascal Fergy Lynch did you?"

"Well 'bumped' is pretty close to the mark," said Will, going on to explain what had happened the weekend before.

"Fergy and Tom Kearns are old buddies. Tom's more of a hunting man than racing. Hunts with the Ward Union and a great man to hounds; he was out on the day – and this might be interesting to you – back in the 70s, a hunted stag ran across the runway at Dublin airport, the hounds and much of the field close behind. The Master told the huntsman to cut the wire fence and off they went across the runway, cheered on by the airport staff. Could never happen now, I suppose. Fergy's a great judge of a young horse, he's had a lot of success on both sides of the Irish Sea. I don't know Adam Platt though I've heard a lot of good things about him. How did you get involved there?"

"His place is very near to our home in Cheshire and I started riding out for him in the school holidays when I was fifteen. Sort of graduated from Pony Club stuff, which I had got a bit bored with. After leaving school it's been a bit hit and miss. Until I came over here I was working for Supercar in Manchester and I was living at home with my parents, so it has been mainly just Saturdays or any time off that I had. Adam's a great guy, a former jockey, won the Cheltenham Gold Cup in about 1937, I think."

"Did he really? Do you want to go out second lot?"

"Yeah, sure if you want me to."

"I've got a good old 'chaser you can ride. Has won a few races, and belongs to my father who kindly transferred him to me when we came here a year ago. Takes a bit of a grip though he knows his way round here backwards. Was going to ride him myself but there's a young one I want to have a sit on, so let's go."

Will stood up and picked up his plate and coffee cup to take to the sink.

"Don't worry about all that," said Siobhan. "Fanny from the town will be here in a minute." She swapped her natty slippers for riding boots lying in a corner.

"Good God, you don't ride as well do you?" he said.

"And what would I be doing here if I didn't ride?" she said, putting on her windcheater and helmet with a knitted bobble hat over it.

The weather had improved, the rain had stopped and a fresh breeze sent scudding clouds with glimpses of the sun in the cloud breaks.

"We bought this place nearly two years ago," Harry said, as they walked towards the stable yard, "or rather the bank and my father did. It had been a dairy farm of about three hundred acres. A typical Irish farmhouse with not too many mod cons and a range of farm buildings in dilapidated condition. We put a bulldozer through the lot of them and built a modern stable yard which can accommodate sixty horses which you can now see, equipped with all you need – tack rooms, feed house with connecting food storage lofts, hay and straw barns out the back, staff resting rooms with lads and girls loos and a small canteen – the lot. At the moment we have forty horses, so room for a few more. The house we touched up a bit, making it warm and weatherproof, with not too many frills. That will have to wait."

Harry called out to Ronan, "Ro, Mr Carpenter will ride Spring Garden, I'll ride Mr Kerrigan's new one."

Siobhan went off to find hers.

"Usually, we do most of our faster work first lot, however, it was so ghastly and murky this morning that I decided to change things round a little. Also, I'm frequently off to the races by mid to late morning, particularly on Saturdays, though we've no runners today. Last Saturday I was at Ballinrobe, near Lough Mask, where we had a winner."

Harry took Will to Spring Garden's box.

"What I want you to do when we come to the bottom of the gallops, is to set off in front which will be no problem – it's where he likes to be – but don't go mad. Me and two others will be behind you and when we come up sides of you, take a pull and let us go on. He won't like it but it's all I want him to do. He hates soft ground and is more of a spring and autumn horse so is on the relatively easy list at the moment. The gallop will be over seven furlongs, okay?"

"Sure, I'll let him run on behind you when you come to me."

In the bad light of early dawn and rain of the first lot, Will didn't get much of an idea of his surroundings; now as he and fourteen others headed out along a track, he could see undulating land with a gradual slope away from them. Most of the string, including Siobhan, separated soon for walking, trotting and routine canters but Harry, Will, Ronan, and a couple of other work riders, kept on the track until they reached a point where Will, looking round, could see the outline of the stable block way behind and above them. Close by, a purpose constructed all-weather track, easily wide enough for three horses to gallop upsides with racecourse rails on either side, pointed in a slightly uphill direction away from them as far as the eye could see.

"We'll come back to this in minute, first we'll have a pipe opener."

Through a gap in the hedge, they went into an open ten-acre field with a less sophisticated hard sand track around the outside.

"We'll do one circuit, nice and steady now," Harry said, setting off in the lead.

Will very soon understood what Harry had said about his horse *'taking a bit of a grip'* meant. Spring Garden had no desire to be either nice or steady; Will had trouble in getting him stuck up the backside of the horse in front of him with nowhere to go, however, constantly talking to him softly, got him to settle.

In the gallop proper which followed, it was a different story. Will jumped his horse off smartly as he had been told to do Spring Garden, keen yet happy sped along at a sensible pace in the lead; after about three and a half furlongs, Will could sense the other three closing on him as he eased Spring Garden over to his left to give the others room to come by him.

Immediately he felt them coming Spring Garden picked up his bit, changed gear and was off, "Oh no you don't or not today anyway," Will called out to him, taking a very firm pull on his reins.

The others passed by and when they had gone eight to ten lengths clear, Spring Garden dropped his bit, accepted the situation and lolloped along quietly to where the others had pulled up.

"Everybody happy?" asked Harry.

Mutterings of approval all around followed, with general chit-chatting on their way back to the yard.

"You were right," said Will. "He didn't like being overtaken."

"He's a grand old horse and loves the sun on his back. The trouble is that he gets allotted such big weights in handicaps nowadays due to all his success that he's difficult to place and not getting any younger. We usually succeed in finding one or two for him, so we'll just have to wait and see when the spring comes. I'll probably give him a run or two in soft ground to try to outwit the handicapper, but he hates it so much that I feel sorry for him. He loves his racing on the top of the ground and the poor old bugger doesn't realise that we're doing our best for him. This was nothing serious for him this morning, it just kept him on his toes and I'm glad that you said he was enjoying himself; from what I could see, it looked so."

Back in the yard, Harry said, "Thank you for coming. Now that you've seen the setup would you like to come again? I'd be happy for you to whenever you have any spare time."

"Yeah, I'd really like to. Really enjoyed this morning. I could make it a regular on Saturdays, at least most of them. Depends if there are any work problems; some Saturdays I may only be able to come for first lot. If I do have any other time, perhaps I could give you a call? Going back home for Christmas though I'm not sure of actual dates yet."

"Okay, that's fine, see you next Saturday."

"Look forward to it and thanks to your super cook for breakfast."

Will had two messages on his answering machine in his flat; one from Fred saying don't call back until the evening as he was out playing golf, and the other from his mother.

He rang her, "Hello Mum."

"Hello, darling, I hoped it might be you. Just checking on your Christmas plans and movements. I thought it might be nice if we asked a few local people who've been so kind to us over the past couple of years, to come for a bit of a Christmas party, either lunch or early evening. What do you think?"

"I think it is an absolutely smashing idea. What does Dad think?"

"I haven't really discussed it with him very much, though he'll go along with it – worrying about the cost, of course."

"Come on, Mum, we only live once and I can chip in for a bit if you like. How many were you thinking about asking?"

"Oh, I don't know – about twenty-five to thirty, I suppose."

"What about the catering?"

"Joanna has a school friend whose mother does this sort of thing and would arrange it. Who would you like to put on the guest list?"

"Let me think off-hand, Julian Shannon and his wife, the Platts, oh and the Huxtable family, the Tomkinsons, and, of course, the Blackfords."

"Ah – yes I think you quite fancy Miss Huxtable."

"Mum, that was a long time ago. Would Dad be able to arrange the booze?"

"Yes, I think so."

"Well, go ahead and keep me posted. There could be one or two of my young polo players to bring the average age down a bit."

"Right, I'll go ahead then. What have you been doing today and how's business going?"

"Answer question two, okay, thank you. Quite a good week. Question one, been riding out for a trainer near Trim."

"That's exciting. How did you manage that?"

"Tell you when I see you. Love you, Mum. Speak again soon. Let me know about the party date. Christmas Day's on a Monday. I should be able to come on the previous Friday, but not sure if I can stay all the time until New Year. Might have to make two trips."

"Okay, will do, bye, darling."

In the evening he called Fred, "Okay Tiger, how many little birdies did you catch today? Or are they bogeys, in which case, kindly blow your nose."

"Piss off, cheeky. Listen, lad, I may have some business for us both. My golf club wants to organise a long weekend next spring, say late April or early May, in one of those fancy hotels with golf courses that you showed me when we drove down to Limerick. Could you check if the manager came to our opening party and if not chat him up over accommodation and golf. I think there would fifteen to twenty players, with or without their WAGS. They were thinking of hiring a coach but I'm trying to persuade them to hire cars from us to give them more freedom to the countryside etc if they have their own individual transport. We'll give them a good deal, of course, and would be looking for one from the hotel as well."

"Wow, that could be a goodie. I'll get cracking on it on Monday. As you know, I'm a world expert on golf but if you could find out any preferences that they might have, it would help. In the meantime, I'll get my spies on the job."

"Okay, lad, enjoy the rest of the weekend. Bye."

"Ditto and play well. Talk to you on Monday."

On Monday, Will called Pat Byrne into his office, "Pat, any of your family play golf?"

"Yes, my father does and so does his brother, my uncle Colin, or Con as he's known. My father won't admit it but Con's the better golfer. Why do you ask?"

"Fred called me over the weekend. He wants to bring a group of players from his club near Manchester for a hooley long weekend next spring and has asked us to fix it up for him. Wants a fancy hotel on a smart golf course, somewhere south of Dublin. Any ideas? And could you check on our guest list for the opening party to see if any golfing hotel managers came to the party?"

"I'll check the list and ask my Dad about golfing hotels. He's sure to know."

Next day Pat said, "I took home the list of hotels that sent either managers or representatives to the party and showed them to my Dad. He picked out one or two but it depends on how much Fred's mob want to pay. There's a wide disparity. Both he and Con think that two that should be considered are Mount Juliet in Thomastown, Co Kilkenny, and Kilkea Castle in Castledermot, Kildare. They are both pretty pricy at the top end of the range. Mount Juliet is the old home of the McCalmont family in a fabulous location with a golf course designed by Jack Nicklaus, about one and a half hours' drive from the airport. Kilkea is a bit nearer. If he wants to do further down the scale, there are plenty more to look at. Kilkea sent a rep to the party but we did not include Mount

Juliet on the list as it's a bit too far. Probably packages would be cheaper midweek than at weekends. Would you like me to make some preliminary enquiries?"

"Yeah, go ahead and get some ideas and prices, then I'll discuss them with Fred."

Will was not unhappy about progress with bookings picking up well for the Christmas holiday time.

Saturday came and so did Will at Lostock Stables at 7.15 on a much better morning than the previous week. Still quite dark and cold with a touch of frost, however, it was clear with the glow of sunlight coming brighter from the east.

"Morning Will, thanks for coming again; quite busy this morning. I'm off to Thurles later – we've a couple of runners there, I want to get as much done first lot as possible. I want you to ride Small Talk, the one I rode last week and then a second contingent will be waiting at the bottom of the gallop and we'll come up again. My tractor driver will be waiting for us at the finish of the first bit of work to take us back to the start. A lad will be waiting to take Small Talk back to the yard."

The fifteen-strong string set off, separating as before with the routine canterers going one way, as Harry and Will, with two others, going the other, repeating the preliminary canter as before.

This time, at the bottom of the gallop proper, Harry said, "I want to find out a bit more about the horse you're riding. I know the ability of mine so will be watching yours closely, please stay right upsides me. If your horse shows signs of distress or feels tired, shout to me. I don't want to disappoint him; in fact, I want him to win and be happy about it, so if he is still going well, I shall take a pull so that you can finish in front. Don't worry about the other two; they are experienced and are just here for company."

They jumped off at a good pace, Harry dictating it, Will right upsides him. Small Talk, taking a firm hold yet well within himself and keen to go on, was clearly going the better of the two. Near the end of the gallop, Harry and the others dropped away and Will finished two lengths in front. His horse had a good blow but looked around, ears pricked and happy. Harry was well pleased.

"I'll tell you when you can have a bob or two on this one," he said.

They dismounted; a lad and a girl got out of the waiting Land Rover and took charge of Harry and Will's horses, setting off for home with the other two in the gallop. Mick, the driver, took them back to the start.

"Mick's the farmer here," Harry said. "He harrows the all-weather gallop every day before 7.30, sometimes twice if needed, looks after the fencing, keeps the land and ditch drains clear and tends the garden in his spare time. Isn't that right, Mick?"

"It is, it is. But, you've forgotten about milkin' the cow."

"The cow! What cow?" exclaimed Harry.

"Oh, you didn't know about the cow? Well then, there's no need to be telling you now."

Ronan, the head lad, on one horse, with a lad and a girl on two others, were down at the start. The two juniors dismounted, Harry indicating to Will to take the girl's horse and mounting the other one himself.

"These are all four-year-olds, turning five on the 1st of January. They've each had a run-in a point-to-point and been hacked around during the summer. Done plenty of cantering work though this is their first time on the gallops. The one you're on has come via Fergy Lynch as did Small Talk by the way; he saw it run in its point to point, went to see it at the owner's farm near Rathkeale, and bought it for an owner of mine. Probably paid too much for it, though these horse-producing farmers are as sharp as Swiss Army penknives. They keep the horses in shabby dilapidated buildings to make you think they've no money, that's before you see them driving away in their swish BMWs. He's called Not Me Too – the horse, that is. Daft name. We'll give them a nice half-speed gallop – we call it half-speed – which it isn't, of course, but just take it from me or Ro. Okay. Let's go."

At the top, Harry said, "What do you think of that?"

"I should think okay for a first effort. Ran a bit green, looking about and not sure what to do next. I thought yours and Ro's were both going a bit better than mine."

Back in the yard, Harry said, "A pretty good morning's work, I thought. Very pleased with Small Talk. Hope you can ride him next time. Let's go and have breakfast."

In the kitchen, Siobhan, wearing a different pair of jeans with the same natty slippers, said, "Breakfast's ready. Good morning

Will, you've survived another episode of Lostock Force Ten."

"It's been good. Really, I mean it."

"Got to leave in half an hour," Harry said. "I told Ro that you'd ride one second lot Will. Is that okay?"

"Yeah, sure."

"What you've seen so far here is only stage one of our long-term plan. One of the reasons we bought the place which had not been a racing stable before, as I mentioned, is because it had been a dairy farm with little or no cereal production, therefore virtually none of the land has been ploughed for generations. You probably haven't noticed that we have laid out plans and markers for a grass gallop, making gaps in hedges, installing land drains, and all sorts of other stuff. This was on the advice of the top guy who maintains the gallops on the Curragh and he should know what he's talking about. He designed and supervised the construction of the all weather, at huge expense, I might add. The grass gallop will be fantastic when it's completed though won't be usable for at least another year or maybe more, depending on what kind of spring and summer we have next year."

Then he gobbled his breakfast.

"I must dash and quickly change," he said, rising from his chair.

"Wait a moment. Are we going to the pub tonight?" asked Siobhan, glancing over at Will. "Because, if so, why doesn't Will come with us if he's got nothing better to do?"

"Why not; how about it, Will?"

"I've got no plans, so I'd love to."

Will and Siobhan walked down to the yard.

"Thurles is a good two and half hours' drive from here. We've just got the two runners, both with maybe an each way chance but no more than that. Joe Maguire, our stable jockey, rides them both. He lives near Kildare but usually, depending on where the racing is, comes here at least once a week to ride work and schooling, sometimes staying the night. You probably haven't seen them – the string of schooling fences and hurdles in the middle of the farm."

Ronan was waiting for them, "Miss Siobhan, you're on Nagaland, Mr Carpenter, come with me and I'll show you yours. She's a mare, Miss Canada, six year old so going on seven, quite a light framed chestnut, doesn't need a lot of work. She won a moderate hurdle race at the back end of last season. I think she needs the sun on her back and better ground so we're not doing too much with her at the moment."

The string pulled out along the drive and onto the road this time, turning right, trotted a mile, then off along a farm track and back through a gate onto Lostock land, a routine canter of two circuits and back home after an hour and a half. Siobhan said, "If you would like a bite of lunch, do stay and watch the racing on the telly if you like?"

"Thanks very much Siobhan, but I've got a few things I must do so better get back; it would be great to come to the pub tonight though. Probably best to meet you there, so tell me where and I'll see you there."

"Okay, it's The Bounty Bar, near the castle, it's easy to find. Sort of 7.15/7.30 ish?"

Will actually didn't have that much to do, he just thought it was pushing it a bit to stay on. He checked with his office, no dramas there, he grabbed a sandwich and a pint in his local and went home. He switched on his own television as one of the two races in which the Kennedy horses were running was shown on national television. The horse, Thurlwood Prince, showed up well for most of the race though he ran out of steam approaching the last fence and was just beaten out of third place on the line.

"Well done with Gold Streak," said Siobhan on Harry's return, "I watched it on the racing channel. Fantastic. What a clever brother, I've got. I asked Will to stay and watch, but he had other things to do; he'll meet us at the pub later."

"Yes, thanks. Thurlwood ran well, too; I think he'll come on for the race. That Will rides well, you know, and gives good feedback without any bullshit. Could be useful to us. I think you quite fancy him."

"Fuck off! But yes I do a little, don't you dare tell him so."

"A good-looking chap like him, sure to have a girlfriend tucked away in England," said Harry.

Following Siobhan's directions, Will found his way to the Bounty Bar in Trim without any difficulty. A quaint little inn with a pool table in the bar, a small restaurant and log fires in both rooms. A few guest rooms upstairs. Harry and Siobhan had just sat down when Will arrived.

"Guess what, Gold Streak won," Siobhan said, raising her hands in glee.

"Shit and I missed it. His race wasn't on the box, but well done, fantastic."

"You're right, it wasn't on national TV, I watched in on the racing channel which we subscribe to, it covers all races. He won well with a bit in hand," Harry said. "Come on, let's have a drink, what would you like, Will?"

"I'm happy to stick to wine," he said.

"Okay let's have a bottle of their quite drinkable white to kick off with."

He turned and called out to the barmaid, "Flo, we've had a winner, please bring us a bottle of your white stuff and three glasses."

They ordered dinner, pork chops for Harry and Will, chicken Kiev for Siobhan, plus a bottle of Merlot chosen by Harry.

"Now, Will tell us about your Christmas plans. You live in Cheshire, you said, with your family?"

"Yes, my father, mother and younger sister. I have to tell you that we had a family tragedy nine months ago. My elder brother, James, who was in the army, was killed in Afghanistan."

Harry and Siobhan held up their hands in sorrow and horror.

"Oh, Will, I – we, are so sorry and sad for you. How awful I am so sorry again; poor you and your family." It was Siobhan talking, though Harry joined in putting out his hands in sympathy.

"Yes, it was terrible, terrible, but we just have to get over these things and I thought you should know. It makes it all the more important that I get home for Christmas this year. My father, in particular, has taken it very badly. He's had a rotten couple of years in various ways and needs family support. Luckily my mother can provide this and is bearing up very well. My little sister, Joanna, is growing up fast and I think will be a knockout in a year or two's time and we'll have plenty of trouble there, I expect. Anyway, enough about me, what are your plans?"

"Well, our father is primarily a financial businessman with an office in Dublin and a lovely family home on the banks of the river Liffey, near Sallins in Co Kildare. He sits on a number of company boards and is a serious whiz kid or wizard as we tease him constantly. Siobhan and I are the only siblings; our mother died of breast cancer three years ago, so my father is alone though by no means lonely. They were devoted to each other in most ways but we are pretty sure that father had a few bits on the side and we have no reason to believe that situation has changed. Although it was never actually discussed, it is our understanding that mother accepted the situation and, as I said, they were devoted in all other ways and there was never any question of divorce. I think father will come here for Christmas. He was heartbroken when she died as, naturally, were we."

"That's quite a story and well done the pair of them for sorting everything out together. What else can one say?" said Will.

"Enough of this morbid talk. Have you got a girlfriend, Will?" asked Harry.

"Yes and no is the answer. My last job before joining Supercar was a deckhand on a banana boat to and from the West Indies. We took out general cargo and brought back ripening bananas. In Barbados I met this gorgeous girl; she works for a businessman I met, who sounds very like your father. She and I hit it off big time and are still corresponding though it's been two years now since we've seen each other."

"I'm going to volunteer to be your stand-in lover on this side of the Atlantic," said Siobhan.

"Sis, you can't say that. Will might not even fancy you."

"I just did say it and it's up to him to say whether he does or doesn't."

Will hid his face with his napkin in embarrassment.

Then he stood up, bowed and said, "Madam, I accept your proposal with pleasure but, as they say in the sales brochures, you have forty-eight hours to change your mind. Shall we continue with dinner?"

All three of them burst into raucous laughter, causing the other diners in the room to put down their knives and forks and stare at them.

Harry said, "I'm terribly sorry, we've had a winner today – maybe two it seems, so we are having a little celebration. I do apologise."

Harry picked up the tab for dinner, despite protests from Will.

"I'm doing this and no arguing. Apart from anything else, I

appreciate your helpful comments on the horses that you have ridden. It's good having you around and I hope you'll continue coming so thank you."

"I like it too, very much. Just what I was hoping to do. I can come next Saturday but that will probably be the last one before Christmas. As for you, Madam," he said, as he turned to Siobhan. "Your forty-eight hours expires on Wednesday so, if you have not changed your mind, please will you do me the honour of allowing me to take you to Dublin where you can show me the delights of your wonderful city and do me the further honour of giving you dinner. Maybe we could confirm one way or the other by telephone on Wednesday morning?"

Leaving the restaurant Siobhan said, "I shall not be changing my mind but let's talk anyway," giving Will a full-blown kiss on his lips as she got into Harry's car to go home.

CHAPTER 11

What am I going to do now and how am I going to break it to Lucille? were Will's thoughts as he drove back to his flat. *I suppose it was inevitable.* Everything churned away in his mind. *I'll sleep on it,* he told himself.

Sunday morning, he woke with a half plan. He would talk to his mother, *That's what parents are there for – to act as one's greatest friends and advisors in matters such as this. Discretion can be guaranteed and advice given if not impartially but with the best instincts of their offspring at heart.* He decided that his mother rather than his father was the best option.

He called her, "Mum, hello it's me. What are you doing today?"

"Hello, Will darling, lovely to hear you; what have you been up to? All fine here, slowly getting into the Christmas spirit and looking forward to seeing you soon. The party invitations have gone out – not formal ones, you know, just postcards and some by telephone."

"Good, that's fine and can't wait to be coming the week after next I think it is. I'll probably come on Friday 22nd, maybe the afternoon of the 23rd. Work's okay, I'm popping into the office today and then to the airport just to show my face to the duty staff, a bit of morale boosting. Mum, there's something that I want to talk to you about, not now, when would be a good time for you? It's a bit private."

"Oh dear, darling – nothing too serious I hope? Maybe best if I call you as you are more likely to be on your own than I am. Would around 5 o'clock be okay for you?"

"I can make it any time today to suit you so fine, 5 o'clock then. I'll be here."

Five o'clock, she rang, "Now, darling, what's the matter?"

"Well, Mum it's woman trouble – actually girl trouble, not really trouble but problems. You know how very much I fell in love with my beautiful Lucille in Barbados and her with me. That state of affairs still exists but it's well over two years since we've seen each other and I've taken a fancy to a girl over here and have an important date with her this coming Wednesday. I've no idea how it will work out, though Lucille and I have promised each other that each would tell the other if anyone else came into our lives. I don't know what to do."

"You poor darling; I do understand. Affairs of the heart are frequently possessed with problems. Yours is one of honour, which is highly commendable. There are those who would flit from one to another without a thought. My advice to you, knowing nothing apart from what you have told me, is that you should go ahead with your date on Wednesday, see how it goes and we can talk more about it when you come for Christmas, have further thoughts and talks about what, if anything, you should do next, over Christmas. After all, it will only be another ten days or so before you come. I see no point in you communicating with Lucille on the matter and causing her any concern until you are sure about your longer-term feelings for the new girl. You must tell me more about her when you're here."

"Thanks, Mum, That's very sound advice. You can mention it to Dad if you want to, but not a word to Joanna."

"No, I promise."

In the office on Monday morning, Pat Byrne said, "I've had replies from Mount Juliet and Kilkea Castle for Fred's golfing bonanza. There's not a lot between them but, as I suspected, mid-week packages come cheaper by roughly 10% at weekends, but I guess Fred's lot would rather come at a weekend."

"Probably. Can you fax them off to Fred and I'll have a word with him on the telephone. Christmas bookings seem to be warming up and New Year even more so. You better check with Limerick to make sure they've enough vehicles or if we need to send any extra ones down there."

"Bloody hell, they must think we're all fucking millionaires," Fred said on the line to Will, having received the golfing costs.

"Come on, Fred, these are top of the range places, you know, and quite used to having the odd millionaire around."

"I doubt my lot will pay that much. I'll circulate it all and get back to you – probably after Christmas now."

"Listen, about Christmas, My Mum and Dad are planning a little party on the evening of the 27th. We'd love it if you could come? It won't be a late affair – 6.30 ish, drinks and a few light goodies to eat, I hope you can make it?"

"The 27th? Thanks, lad, let's have a look. Aye, that would be really nice, I'd love to do that and meet your Mum and Dad."

"Wonderful, I'll tell them. We'll talk again soon."

At 9.30 on Wednesday morning, knowing that it would be between first and second lot time, Will called the Kennedy number. Harry answered.

"Hello, Will, all well with you?"

"Yes, I think so. Thank you very much for dinner on Saturday. Great fun and I think we all got a bit carried away. I had better have a word with your lovely sister if she's around?"

"She's right here."

"Hello, lover to be…"

"Hang on, You're not still floating around on that cloud of winners with silvery linings are you?"

"I'm right down to earth having been dumped on my bum first lot this morning but everything else is in the right place including my mind so what's the plan 007?"

"Okay, okay, clause one of the contract is for you to report to HQ at 1830 hours today. Further operational plans will then be revealed. In other words, pitch up at my place at about half past six and we'll go from there."

After work, Will stopped at the off licence on his way to the flat to buy a bottle of champagne and some nibbles. He also bought a candle. *Well*, he thought, *It's close to Christmas, why not.*

Home in good time, he lit his log fire, had a bath, dressed in clean clothes, a quick glance in the mirror, then into his sitting room, puffed up the cushions, drew the curtains and lit the candle, having found a candleholder. He retrieved the bottle of champagne from the fridge, opened it and poured himself a glass.

Headlights penetrated through the curtains. Will went to his front door, and opened it in time to see Siobhan switch off the lights of her car and climb out. He took her hand and kissed her as firmly as she had done to him leaving the pub last Saturday.

"Do come in," he said.

"Thank you," she responded.

She was wearing a woolly type stole over her shoulders, which

Will removed, revealing a three-quarter length, emerald green, close-fitting dress with matching high-heeled shoes.

"Welcome, madam," he said.

"Thank you, Sir," she replied.

"Okay, let's cut the cackle and have a drink."

He poured her a glass of champagne.

"I hope you like this stuff. I thought we'd start as we plan to continue."

"I love it. Come here; my turn."

She put down her glass, placed both arms around his neck and kissed him, her tongue probing the inside of his mouth. Will felt his body reacting to the feel of her pressing against him.

He led her to the sofa and took a severe pull of his glass, "I've booked a table at the Trocadero in St Andrew's Street at 8 o'clock. Heard it's good; do you know it?"

"Certainly I do, I think my father practically lives there. It's where a lot of theatre people go, you know, actors and the like. What a great choice, couldn't be better. It'll take a good half hour to get there, though we've plenty of time."

"If somebody, a week ago, had offered me a bet at 500 to 1, that I would be sitting here a week later with a lovely, sexy girl, just think how rich I would be."

"You're the sexy one: you ooze it."

"Thanks, pussy cat. Come on, let's finish the bottle and get on our way. We don't want to rush; I don't know what the traffic will be like and you'll have to direct me, I've no idea of the way."

"Sure I will. I'm ready when you are but must have a pee."

Glasses and bottle empty, Will showed Siobhan the bathroom, blew out the candle, stoked up the fire putting a guard around it, picked up Siobhan's stole and collected his own overcoat from the cupboard in the little hall.

"Okay?"

"Very."

Will drove, following Siobhan's directions. He hadn't gone much into the centre of Dublin in daylight, never mind in the dark. As they closed on the centre, he picked out a few landmarks along O'Connell Street, across the Liffey in the direction of St Stephen's Green before turning off into St Andrew's Street. The restaurant's name in bold illuminated letters shone above the entrance. A uniformed concierge checked Will's reservation, handed their coats to an attendant and then showed them to their table in the medium-sized dining room, next to the wall. Lined above the dado rail were photos of internationally known actors and actresses. White tablecloths with cutlery already laid and discreet shaded lamps decorated each table; they sat down in the comfortable chairs lined with red velvet that matched the colour of the walls.

A waiter brought them a glass of white wine while they ordered; Siobhan, a delicate prawn and sambuca risotto to start with, followed by duck breast; Will, chicken liver pate and a very underdone fillet steak – the main speciality of the house, the waiter told him. Will ordered a bottle of Louis Jadot Macon. They talked – almost non-stop. Siobhan adored her brother, five years older than her. She had always been a tomboy, climbing trees, riding since she was three, chasing after her brother whenever possible, skiing holidays during the Christmas or Easter holidays, a cooking course in London, and a stint as a receptionist at an estate agents' office, arranged by her father, though she didn't like it.

One day her boss called her in when she had arrived late for the umpteenth time, saying, "Siobhan, you seem to regard your employment here as a spare time occupation, so I suggest you take your undoubted talents elsewhere."

She continued, "Harry was horse mad from year dot. Pony Club, gymkhanas, hunting with the Kildare, West Meath and Galway Blazers, though racing has always been his favourite. He liked riding in point to points, yet he always wanted to be a trainer. Dad got him an introduction to Willie Moore, which resulted in him being taken on as a pupil assistant; it helped that Dad had two horses in training with Moore. He rode well and learned his trade. Moore rewarded him by giving him rides as an amateur and he rode half a dozen winners. When the opportunity came up, after four years with Moore, to buy Lostock, Harry and father jumped at it. And the rest you already know," she concluded. "I knew what I wanted, which was to come with him. Luckily he agreed."

She took a sip of the wine.

"Will, I am loving this evening and being with you. It is so exciting; I want to know all about you, not all at once but when we have, I hope, more time together. I was very naughty, wasn't I, to say what I did on Saturday? Got a right ticking off from Harry and I'm not going back on a word."

She put her hands on the table; Will picked one up, stroked it, kissed it and put it back again. Then, the same with the other one.

"What would you like for pudding?"

"Just you, please. Can we go?"

"What about Harry's love life? Has he got a girlfriend?"

"Strings of them. I lose count and forget the names. They seem to come and go. I think the main one at the moment is away in London, I'm not sure. He hasn't found one yet that he wants to marry. I suppose when he does, I'll be out of a job."

Will put logs on the smouldering remains of the fire; flames soon took hold, a flickering light casting dark shadows in the room. In his bedroom, he switched on the bedside light. Siobhan, in the sitting room, cast off her stole; Will reached for her; with his arms around her back, he unzipped her dress allowing it to fall to the floor. As she stepped out of it, he unclipped her bra strap and led her into his bedroom, holding her hand and allowing her to fall gently onto the bed. Looking into her brown eyes, he leant forward, and ran his arms down both sides of her body reaching the elastic of her tights and knickers. She raised her body enough for him to draw them down over her bent knees and thence to the floor.

She sat up. "My turn now," she murmured, undoing his tie and slowly each button of his shirt, jettisoning it to join the collection on the floor. She fiddled with the trouser fastenings, slowly eased down the zip until they slipped to the floor, revealing a distinct swelling under a pair of red patterned underpants. With one brisk tug, off they came.

"Hello willie, I want you," she said, giving it a little kiss and falling back on the bed. Will straddled over her, stroking and kissing her forehead, lips and each breast in turn, then moving lower to the furry brown mound, which he kissed and played with before straightening and sliding gently and easily inside her.

With a little gasp, she said, "Don't hurry."

"There isn't a hurry. I don't want this ever to end."

They gazed at each other, their bodies in perfect rhythmic movement.

"This is so fabulous, kiss me again," she whispered.

In complete unison, the final climax came. They remained where they lay for how long neither was aware, silent now in words, but not in thought. At last, Will moved to one side, pulled up the sheet and duvet cover, and cuddled up to her, allowing them to fall into a deep sleep clasped to one another.

At six thirty Will stirred; looking to his left at Siobhan's breasts rising and falling in sleep, the faint vestige of a smile on her oval-shaped face and the light brown hair in dishevelled ringlets reaching to her shoulders, he gave a gentle touch and planted a kiss on her lips. She opened her eyes.

"Hello 007."

Another day had started, though not yet dawned.

"It'll be cold, wait here while I go and put the heating on full blast."

"I've got my day kit in the car."

"Ah, so you came all prepared did you? I'll go and get it for you."

"Well, it wouldn't look good in a racing stable for the Guvnor's sister to be running about in her ball gown at 7 o'clock in the morning. Never mind what they'd think, it's what they'd be saying."

Will stoked up the fire, turned up the heating, seized his overcoat and went out to retrieve Siobhan's bag from her car.

"There now, no one would ever know," Siobhan said, coming out of the bathroom in jeans, a roll-top sweater, her hair neat and tidy. The only things missing were her natty slippers. Instead, she wore a pair of flat outdoor shoes.

"I don't know if I'll be riding out first lot – I rather hope not," she said, gulping a mug of coffee that Will had made for her.

"Thank you for the best night of my life," she said hugging him. "You're coming on Saturday aren't you, so why don't you come after work on Friday and stay at Lostock? I don't know if we have any runners at the weekend, I will as soon as I get home; if we do maybe we could all go to the races."

"Sounds wonderful, though I don't want to push my luck or upset Harry. What would he think about me staying?"

"Don't be daft, I told you he's had a string of girls who've stayed over. Anyway, he likes you. He's told me so more than once – of course I'll check with him and the racing plans for the weekend, it'll give me an excuse to talk to you. It's Thursday now, so we're talking about tomorrow evening, you know."

Coffee finished, Siobhan bundled her last night's clothes into her bag, another hug and kiss for Will, off through the door, into her car and away.

In the office, Will called Fred, "Fred, listen, I've been thinking about your golf package and before I plead for a discount from the hotels, I've had an idea you could put to the old man. Golf is big business; why don't you suggest that Supercar sponsors a weekend golf competition, open to any organisation, company etc that places X amount of business with us."

"That's a great idea, lad, although we are still new in Ireland and need to make more of a mark first. Walk before we can run, okay? Definitely something to think about for the future, though I dare not put it to the old man at this stage. We've only been going a few months. Which day are you coming over?"

"Yes, you may be right. I got a bit carried away with the idea, I'll put it to bed for this year. I'll carry on with your club plan. Probably a week tomorrow, the 22nd. Not sure if I'll stay until the New Year. I might come back here for a couple of days as things are hotting up for New Year and I don't want any dramas. See you on the 27th anyway."

He put down the telephone and immediately it rang again.

The switchboard girl said, "Will, there's a Miss Kennedy on the line for you. Shall I put her through?"

"Yes, okay."

"Will, it's me, Absolutely fine for tomorrow. Harry's delighted and even quite pleased for me too, I think. Pitch up when you can. We've one, maybe two, going to Roscommon on Saturday, and we don't have to decide right now. Harry's happy for us to come if we want to. It's only an hour's drive which means you can ride first lot and probably second as well if you like. By the way – missing you like crazy. Work hard and see you tomorrow."

"Ditto and I will. I'll call you when I'm leaving here."

Next, Will called his mother, "Hello, Mum, how are the party plans going and how many do you think we'll be?"

"Going okay, I think we're up to twenty-five, with just a few don't knows in addition, so, around thirty max. Why do you ask?"

"Well, you know my man Fred Ogden, he was my boss in

Manchester and is still, technically, my boss over here? He did come to James' funeral though I don't think you met him. He's a real good egg, a stubborn Lancastrian, a bachelor with no close family, but lots of friends and a great sense of humour. I speak to him most days and he comes over here quite often to check and advise on what we are doing. I thought it would be kind, if you didn't mind, to ask him to the party. I need to see him anyway while I'm over; he'll get on with anybody and lives between Altrincham and Hale, so not too far to come."

"Yes, darling, of course, if you want to and are sure he won't feel out of place."

"Thanks, Mum. I'll be coming on the evening of the 22nd though I must be back here on the 29th or 30th and I won't be with you for New Year. My young deputy will be in charge here over Christmas and I must let him have some time off for New Year. We're getting quite busy."

"That's a shame about New Year, but I quite understand. How was the date last night."

"Tell you when I see you."

Will tucked himself up in bed early that night. Under his pillow, he found a crumpled piece of paper with a scrawled note, *'Goodnight 007'* it read.

A busy day on Friday with a lot of bookings, mainly for New Year, a high proportion from Americans flying into Shannon to break in the New Year in "the old country". It was good business; Will and his distribution team worked hard to arrange a flow of extra cars from Santry at regular intervals to go to the few spaces that they had available in Limerick and Shannon. He called Siobhan at 6.15 to say that he was on his way.

"Am I flattering myself," he said on arrival. "Or are you the cat expecting the cream?"

"I don't like cats, I was just expecting you, lover boy."

"I'm glad about that because I'm not mad about cats either, here's a foretaste," he said planting a big kiss. "Oh and here's a little house present, not really for you – it's for your brother. Where is he?"

"I think he went upstairs for a bath, but he'll be down in a minute. Come with me, I'll show you where we are."

Siobhan's comfortably furnished yet not over large bedroom is on a corner of the house on the first floor, it had two Georgian sash windows with long curtains down to the floor. Will put his battered suitcase on the floor and bounced on the bed, where he was joined by Siobhan.

"Just an aperitif," she said. "Come on I'll show you the bathroom and then we must go down."

"Hi. Will, you okay? Good to have you here properly," Harry said, as they came down.

"Very kind of you to have me, Here, this is for you," he said, giving Harry the bottle of champagne he had put on the kitchen table.

"Don't open it now – keep it for your next winner."

"Gosh, thanks so much. Might have to wait a long time though. Siobhan, where are you and what's for dinner? It's kitchen supper tonight Will, but let's have a drink. I've got a whiskey and soda – Irish, of course."

"I'll have the same if I may. I'm weaning myself onto the Irish and liking it."

Harry said, "Now, before I forget and talking about winners which I wasn't, you remember that horse that you rode a week or so back, Small Talk? Joe Maguire was here the other day and schooled him over our hurdles. He jumped like a stag. Joe was thrilled with him. I've put you on him first lot in the morning and we'll try him with a decent horse with good winning form, which either I or Ronan will ride and we'll see what happens."

"Right, you two, grubs up. Cottage pie and peas, straight from the supermarket," said Siobhan, extracting hot plates from the Aga. "Help yourselves. Chilli sauce on the table if you want to jazz it up a bit."

Harry opened a bottle of red wine.

"Let's get the boring bit over," he said, getting stuck into the cottage pie. "We've just the one runner at Roscommon tomorrow. I did think of running Spring Garden, my father's horse that you rode on your first visit, but he's got top weight, they've had a lot of rain up there, the ground is officially 'soft' and my guess is that it's more likely to be 'heavy'; he would hate it and it's just not fair on the old horse, that's why I've pulled him out. I may run him in a better class race at the Leopardstown New Year meeting. He won't win though I hope the handicapper will take note and drop him a few pounds. I think father would prefer to have a runner at Leopardstown than flogging all the way up to Roscommon."

"If you're going and would like a bit of company, I'd love to come with you," said Will.

"That would be great. Let's see what the morning brings. Now, remind me of your Christmas plans?"

"I'm going home to England on the 22nd, back on the 29th or 30th, not sure which yet."

"Well, if you're back in time, the Leopardstown meeting is on the Friday, Saturday and Sunday so, if you and Siobhan are still on speaking terms by then, do come with us. It's always great gas and I hope we'll have a few runners."

"Sounds terrific; I will be on call from my office but fingers crossed there'll be no dramas."

"How's your Supercar thing going?"

"Still early days, though it's going quite well, I think. We've just got the two depots, the main one at Santry and a smaller one in Limerick that takes care of Shannon and the south. We're getting really busy, morale is high so, yeah, I'm reasonably optimistic."

"If we're not speaking by Leopardstown time, it'll be his fault, not mine and you'll have a sister dressed in black from top to toe," said Siobhan, taking a deep gulp from her wine glass.

"Go on with you, Sis, I was only pulling your leg."

"For your information, Miss Kennedy, I have every intention of returning after Christmas and not only for the benefit of Supercar."

Not much later, with everything stacked in the dishwasher under Siobhan's supervision, the two lovers were upstairs. The somewhat inadequate heating system only took the chill off the cold so getting undressed, in and out of the bathroom and into bed didn't take long. Once there, the urgency stopped, their bodies warming by being wrapped together, still in the exploration stage, and the excitement of their lovemaking.

Will found a scar high on Siobhan's left leg, "What's that?" he asked, running his hand over the mark.

"It's where I fell out of a tree; landed on a big stone. I must have been about five; had stitches in it."

She twisted down the bed and took him in her mouth, licking and kissing.

"Now, please put it in its proper place," she said.

Will moved on top of her; she gave a little gasp as he entered her, reaching under her body with both arms as he thrust forward. Changing position several times, she achieved orgasm after orgasm until the ultimate for them both when she could feel the flow of love passing from him to her.

"This is the most beautiful happening ever for me. Just you and me. You have the most sensational body, so firm and athletic. Please can we do this over and over again."

Siobhan's alarm went off at 6.30. They struggled awake, hot water in the bathroom took an age to come which made Will's shaving rather touch and go. Nevertheless, they were downstairs, Siobhan in her natty slippers, by 7 o'clock. Harry was already down.

"God, I thought you two lovebirds would never get up. Didn't dare come and call you. Thought I might have been interrupting something."

"Hark who's talking. Please be telling me how many times it's been the other way round."

Grabbing a quick cup of coffee, Harry and Will made their way down to the yard, leaving Siobhan to prepare breakfast. Ronan was waiting for them; Harry confirmed the plan for first lot, Will to ride Small Talk, Harry on Pelican Point, a three-time winner, the last of which had been a decent class race at Fairyhouse and Ronan on Spring Garden to act as lead horse in the gallop. As usual, the string split into two sections, Harry, Will and Ronan taking the route to the main gallop and the rest, routine canterers going the other way.

At the start of the gallop, after the preliminary canter, Harry said, "Right, Ro you set a good half-speed pace, Will, you stay upsides me. When I go to overtake Ro, come right with me. Ro, you drop out then; I don't want the old horse to do any more at the moment. Will, if you can stay with me or go on, do so. Don't hit him but you can wave your stick at him as long as he is enjoying himself. This is a serious gallop. All understood? okay, let's go."

Ronan set a strong pace, Harry and Will two lengths behind. At halfway, Harry moved up, Will right with him; Ro fell away. Will, full of horse beneath him, glanced right at Harry crouching a little lower and giving his horse a tap down the shoulder. With two furlongs to go, Will let out a couple of inches of rain; Small Talk leapt forward. Harry struggled to keep up. Will never picked up his whip and finished three lengths clear of Harry's horse.

"I think we may have a racehorse," Harry said as they pulled up together.

Ronan joined them, "That was a very smart piece of work," he said.

"God, Ro, if you say that, it must be special."

Small Talk had a good blow, but no more than that, as they walked round in a circle.

"I'm not as experienced as you two, though all the time I've been riding work for the last three or four years, I've never sat on a horse that had given me that sort of feel," Will said.

"Now Ro, no gossiping please. You know the policy: if we have a good one all the lads and girls will have a bonus if it comes off. I don't want the whole of Trim to know."

Breakfast had a special feel all of its own that morning. Harry, ecstatically happy as was Siobhan, equally for herself and her brother, and Will with the thought that he'd ridden two winners in the past eight hours – something which was happy to pass on to Siobhan when they were alone.

"Well, at least I was one of them," she said. "And that it was only a horse I was sharing you with."

"What about Roscommon?" Harry said, "Our race isn't until 3 o'clock though as it's a good hour and three-quarters drive, I think we'll have to skip second lot."

"Why don't you and Will go together?" said Siobhan, "I've plenty of secretarial stuff to do and I'm a bit behind with it. You should be back around sixish unless you get led astray."

"That might be difficult in Roscommon."

"Okay with me," said Will. "Please let me take you both to the pub we went to last Saturday, or somewhere else if you prefer. It was such fun and who knows what further propositions might be forthcoming. Can you fix that Siobhan?"

"No, I don't see…"

"No buts, Harry and no messing."

"Roscommon, not top of my pops," Harry said in the car. "Though I was advised from a young age about racing, that one should keep one's horses in the worst company and one's women in the highest. Good advice don't you think, Will?"

"As you will have observed, I'm doing my best to follow that advice, at least so far as the latter is concerned."

"I'm very happy that you and Siobhan have hit it off. She's my sister and I'm devoted to her. We are very close indeed and have the perfect brother and sister relationship."

"That's obvious. She has told me how much she worships you and the only thing she wanted, when you set up at Lostock, was to come with you."

"She's a headstrong tomboy of a girl. Always has been. Made a few mistakes along the way, and had to learn the hard way sometimes; she has a heart of gold. I'll bet that you've never had or will have again a proposition put to you like hers last Saturday!"

"I couldn't believe my ears," Will said. "All I can say is that it saved me the trouble of having to do it myself with the usual 95% chance of rejection."

"In hindsight, it looks as though you would have been lucky. Getting back to Small Talk, I'm going ask Joe Maguire today to come next week for another schooling session. If that goes well, I will enter him in a race early in the New Year at a minor meeting and we'll have a crack. My horses don't usually win the first time out though this one might be different; we may be unlucky and find another hot one in the race. I'll go through all the known form of the others very carefully. The owner, Tim Kerrigan, is a good friend. I met him when I was at Moores; this is the second horse he's sent me; the first one wasn't much good, let's hope for better things this time. The plan will be to beat the bookmakers: with no previous form to work on, he should be a long price in the betting forecast; we want to keep it that way. Tim will want a good bet, as will I. I'll organise a stable bet, including Tim's and mine, which will include an amount that I shall allocate for the lads and girls in the yard. If you want to participate, that would be fine. The bets will be placed in small quantities in betting shops round the country quite close to the scheduled time of the race, with no money being bet by us on the track. The bets in the shops will be at the prices shown on their boards at the time. This should be at around 20 to 25, to 1."

"Could I have 100 euros on him?" asked Will.

"Yes, that would be fine; after all, you are a key player in the plot. Don't give it to me now – and I hope you won't have to at all."

They were approaching Roscommon, a pretty, right-handed country course.

"This horse today, Golden Dandy, is a bit slow and loves soft ground, staying well. I suppose he has an each way chance. Joe will be up with the pace all the way to make his stamina pay. The owner, a farmer, John Flynn, lives near Castlerea and Roscommon is his local track. Golden Dandy is his only horse and he is coming."

Harry gave Will his spare trainer's badge and went off to the weighing room to check on the horse's safe arrival and declaration, reuniting in the bar, where Will had ordered them both a Guinness and sandwich each.

"Well now look what we have here, a trainer and his new assistant," Fergal Lynch announced himself.

"God, what the hell brings you here? Not your normal scouting patch?"

"Just been to see a local guy with a horse he was trying to sell."

"And what did he show you?"

"He showed me the door when I told him what it was worth. And how is this young man getting on with you? Must be okay if you've brought him all the way up here and how's that young horse I found for you – what do you call it, Small Talk or something?"

Will felt a sharp pain as something hit his ankle.

"He's going on okay. He'll probably be ready for a run somewhere in the New Year. Will, here, rode him a routine canter this morning."

"What did you think of him, Will?"

"It was the first time I've ridden him. He seems a nice young horse. We were just in the middle of the string, you know."

"Pop in to see us soon Fergy and a happy Christmas to you. I must be off to find my owner. I've got one in the next but one race – each way chance, I suppose."

Will said, "I'm going home to England for Christmas next week and will be seeing Adam Platt. I think he's coming to a small Christmas party my parents are giving."

"Give him my best and I'm glad you made contact with Harry. "See you again soon, I hope," and with that, Fergy walked off.

Will looked at Harry, about to ask him why his friend had kicked his ankle.

Harry apologised, "Sorry about your ankle Will, but if you'd said a word, the whole of bloody Ireland would have known about it."

"Don't worry, I wasn't born quite yesterday and my lips were already sealed."

"If we go ahead as planned, I may include Fergy, though these guys take shed loads of commission."

They were walking over towards the weighing room when Harry spotted his owner, John Flynn, a red-faced, jovial-looking man, wearing a heavy overcoat that covered most of his ample frame, on his head was a deerstalker-type hat.

"Hello there, Harry, thanks for coming all this way and how's the Dandy today?"

"Hi John, good to see you; meet Will Carpenter who's helping me out riding some of the horses at weekends. The Dandy's fine and in good form. I hope he'll give a good account of himself; he'll certainly like the ground and must have a chance as long as he doesn't find one or two that will do him for speed at the end. I think we should tell Joe to go on or at least be in the front group to ensure a strong pace. I'm just off to collect the saddle, I'll see you in the paddock."

In the collecting covered area of the weighing room, Joe Maguire having weighed out, waited for Harry to come for the saddle. Joe, 29 years old, a top-flight Irish jockey for several years now, had been Harry's choice of jockey ever since he started up on his own. He had two other rides today, one in the first race in which he found himself on the deck but undamaged and another in a later race.

"Afternoon, Joe," said Harry. "I want you to meet Will Carpenter. Will has been coming to us for a few weeks now to ride out – and ride work – for us on Saturdays. We had a bit of excitement this morning. I'll give you more detail on the telephone but that horse you schooled this week…"

"Jeez, the new one, you mean that nearly jumped over the moon?"

"… yes, Small Talk. Will, here, rode him in full gallop with me on Pelican Point and Ro on Spring Garden this morning. He beat us pointless. Now, not a word to anyone, understand, as I want you to come and school him again next week and then we'll form a plan for a race for him in the New Year."

"Never heard a word of that. I'll see you whenever you say.

What about this fellow today? Better to keep well up there, don't you think, to make the most of his stamina?"

"Absolutely. The owner is here, I'll see you in the paddock shortly."

In the paddock Will watched Harry talking to John Flynn and Joe and, a few moments later, the lad leading the horse out onto the course proper where Joe cantered him down to the start. He had a tenner each way at 8 to 1. Joe set off in front ensuring a good gallop for the three-mile steeplechase, staying in the leading group in the field of twelve. With three fences to go Joe made his move and had a two-length lead approaching the last.

"Go on Joe," Will shouted.

Then he could see another horse, Single Bid, making up ground fast. The winning post came too late for Golden Dandy, Single Bid getting up to win by half a length.

On the way home, Harry said, "I am afraid he's one of those 'nearly' horses. He's won a couple and we thought he'd go on to win more, but he's been placed 2nd or 3rd so many times. He just lacks that bit of speed that makes all the difference."

The race struck a chord in Will's mind: the result of today's race was the same in reverse of May Go Twice's win that day at the Garrison. Was it really two and a half years ago?

A little later, Harry said, "Will, have you ever thought of taking out a license to ride yourself?"

"Yes, I have on occasions though I decided against it for a number of reasons. First, I can't afford to have a horse of my own in training and don't have a parent who could buy one for me. Second, I have a good job for which I am starting to be reasonably well paid; I am well aware that riding in steeplechases is a hazardous occupation. I'm no use to my employers if I'm wandering round with a sore head or hobbling on crutches. Another reason is that I have another equine interest."

"Oh, what's that?"

"I play polo."

"Polo?"

"Yes, P O L O. I played at pony club level since my early teens and more recently with the Cheshire Polo Club as a junior, coached by a retired army officer. Last season I had a few games with the senior team. I really love racing as well and what I'm doing with you, though I know I can go on playing polo to a much older age than I could race as a jockey."

"You're probably right there. I know some of the guys at Phoenix Park Polo Club and could get you an introduction if you want."

"Yes, I do want; that would be fabulous if you could. I have a handicap of -1 at the moment, though I am told it won't last long. I don't know how long I'll be based here, I guess at least another year."

"I've booked the pub as you asked," said Siobhan, when they arrived back. "No exciting news here except Dad called wanting to know what we're doing for Christmas, in other words, could he come here. Must be having a quiet day. I told him we were expecting him. I gather you just got touched off today."

"Yes, the same old story with this horse, I'm afraid, but we mustn't be disappointed. Second is better than third and a long way better than last."

"And how's my knight in shining armour?" she said, wrapping her arms around Will, hugging him.

"Careful Sis, don't break his bloody neck, we need him here."

In the Bounty, they were greeted by Flo, the barmaid, "Welcome back; how are you going to entertain us tonight? Last Saturday's other guests said that they were bringing a big party to see the second act and how the drama unfolded."

"Tell them they're too late and that everybody lived happily ever after," Harry said.

Conversation brought them together. They were no longer strangers, having to make an effort. Talk between them went over the past few weeks, of the connection of Adam Platt to Fergal Lynch to Will to Harry and the chemistry that sprang between Will and Siobhan. It was as if they'd known each other an infinite amount of time. Harry asked Will how the connection with the West Indies came about. Will, speaking with open candour recalled the day when his father told him the money had run out and why.

"I was totally stunned," he said. "Suddenly the lives of my mother, James, Joanna and myself had disintegrated. My poor father was worst hit as he had known it was coming for a while, though he was searching fruitlessly for a non-existing escape clause, without having to let down his family. To this day, he holds himself to blame, frankly, if blame has to be apportioned, it lies with previous generations. I was not yet eighteen at the time and I knew that my ancestor had, under extraordinary circumstances, found himself in the West Indies towards the end of the 18th century and he had done very well there.

With no job or prospects, I got a job as a deckhand on a banana boat working my passage, so to speak, to see what it was like. On the ship, I got the job of looking after a couple of racehorses being shipped to Barbados. On arrival there the ship's Captain introduced me to the owner of the horses. He sort of took me under his wing and on my next trip, took me to see where my ancestor's plantation used to be and what he had achieved in those days, which was not only for himself and his family, it also was of financial benefit for the island of Barbados and many of its inhabitants. Again, purely by coincidence, part of my job on the ship was to look after a passenger recovering from a heart attack, who subsequently offered me the basis of the job I have now. So now you see why I can't afford to be a jockey."

"That's quite a story, Will, thank you for telling us. Never been out there myself but a lot of the flat boys go to Barbados every winter; the Coolmore gang, you know, the Magniers, Phonsie O'Brien et al. Robert Sangster has a lovely house there where they all congregate like bees round a honey pot. I believe he sponsors a big pro-am golf tournament each year."

Later, in bed, Siobhan said, "What you told us in the pub, made me feel even closer to you. I want to know every single thing about you. I really wanted to come with you today as I feel that all time not spent with you is time wasted, I just thought it was a good opportunity for you and Harry to go off on your own. I know, because he told me so, that he likes you very much and is so happy for me to have met you. Please tell me about your girlfriend in Barbados and how you met her?"

"Yes, my beautiful one, I will sometime. Right now I want to hold, see, and love you in the knowledge that our lives are becoming inextricably linked."

It was Sunday. Siobhan had not set her alarm. Will woke; they were cuddled together like spoons in a kitchen drawer, Will's left arm under Siobhan's pillow. With his right arm, he stroked her, gently running his hand down her body and over her bottom. How smooth and silky. He could feel her moving slightly and pressing harder against him. Gently pushing his hand between her legs, he manoeuvred himself into position and slipped inside her. Her right arm stretched across to his own bottom, her hand pulling him to her, urging him on. Not a word had been spoken until a little while later, she moved her head enough to look into his eyes.

"Good morning," she said.

Harry came in from the yard while Siobhan prepared breakfast in her dressing gown and natty slippers. Will, washed and shaved, came down at the same time.

"It's all right for you two, some people have work to do," Harry grumbled.

"Will you please be remembering the times you've been banging away upstairs with Nicky, Maggie, Helen of Troy, and even Joan of Arc, while I've been your Sunday breakfast slave down here."

"Hmm – I can tell you something about your boyfriend that I bet he hasn't told you."

"And, what's that?"

"He's a polo player and quite a useful one, I believe."

"Shit, is there anything you can't do, Will?"

"Cook."

Breakfast over, Harry retired to his office for routine Sunday morning trainers' stuff, telephoning owners, making race entries and his normal call to Joe Maguire.

"Come on, Will, let's take a little exercise, we'll have a walk round the farm from ground level to places you haven't seen yet. I'll find you a pair of wellies."

"You can take mine," called out Harry. "We must be about the same size."

Cold but dry, they had a good walk, including inspecting the row of schooling fences and hurdles situated in lines next to each other on a slightly uphill slope. Four fences made from regulation birch, tightly bound, fitted into timber frames, a little lower than on the courses themselves though strong enough to do the job; the last fence being an open ditch with the raised guard rail two and a half feet short of the fence proper.

"Will you be able to stay tonight?" Siobhan asked. "I do hope so."

"I think I really ought to go back to get ready for tomorrow and have a change of clothing," Will replied.

"Don't be daft, let me wash your office shirt. It'll be dry later and I'll iron it for you. There's nothing else you need; I'll wash your knickers when we go to bed tonight so they'll be dry in the morning. If we get up at 6.30 which I do anyway, you can leave at 7 and be in your office by 8, so what's wrong with that?"

"Come here, naughty; give me a wintry, cold kiss. I can't fault your plan."

"There's something else. I've an appointment in Dublin on Wednesday afternoon and my car might feel like taking a slight detour in the Dunboyne area on the way home."

"And would your car be thinking that it might have gone far enough in one day?"

"You cotton on quickly, don't you?"

"Consider its parking place reserved."

They were on their way homewards.

"What's your appointment in Dublin, if I may be so bold as to ask?"

"Oh, it's nothing much. Just a routine check-up. You remember I told you that my mother died of breast cancer? Well, I have been told by her oncologist that, just to be on the safe side, I should have once per year check-ups and that's what I'm doing. Nothing to worry about."

Siobhan had put a joint in the Aga before their walk; that, with some heated up vegetables, boiled new potatoes, a bottle of wine, and a glass of boys' port with their cheese, was lunch. A log fire in the cosy sitting room and the Sunday newspapers sent all three of them into a snooze. Around 5 o'clock Harry and Will went down to the yard; Harry didn't have a formal evening stable inspection on Sundays, just checked over Golden Dandy, who was okay though quiet and very tired after his hard race the previous day, and then they checked the likely runners for the next few days.

A snacky television supper followed by an early night completed the day.

Seven o'clock on Monday morning Siobhan waved her man off in his clean white shirt and knickers. She had woken before Will; although still dark she could make out his form lying next to her and could feel and hear his deep breathing.

I am so happy, she said to herself, *please God, let nothing take him away.*

Will was glad to get to his office in good time for his last week before Christmas. Pat Byrne had spent a day in the Limerick depot the previous week, so Will went through everything with Jim McDonald, the depot manager, on the telephone. He had poached Jim, experienced and keen, from Hertz. During the long call, he was satisfied with Jim's assurance that he had all the cars he either needed or had coming in the pipeline.

Will told him that he was away for Christmas and Pat would be in charge, "You have Pat's home number in emergency and I'll be back in good time for New Year in case you have any problems."

Mid-morning he spent a couple of hours at the airport desk, checking and double-checking all bookings, staff rosters and having a few words with customers as they collected or returned their cars.

No call from Fred, so he decided to leave that one until he saw him at Ayshford.

Will called Siobhan, "Listen, Sweet Pea, what sort of time will you be through with your quack in Dublin tomorrow?"

"Probably around 4 o'clock. Why?"

"Well, unless you've got nothing else to do, you'll be at the flat before me."

"When does a girl ever have nothing else to do when there are shops, hairdressers and…"

"Okay, never mind, just trying to say that I'll leave the key under a hideous empty stone flower pot by the door. I might not be there till about 6 o'clock."

"I'll be there, pining my heart out."

"Don't do that. I want it."

"You've already got it, stupid."

Will stopped to do a quick shop on his way home, making it a little after 6 when he arrived, he was happy to see Siobhan's car parked outside. She looked wonderful in a dark red winter skirt, knee boots and a red and white checked jacket over a blouse to match the skirt. Her winter coat hung on the hook by the door.

"Hello and welcome. Do come in lover boy, my heart's desire.

I've turned the heating on and lit the fire to make us nice and cosy, please may I have a kiss now?"

"Happy to oblige," said Will, gathering her to him holding her head, pressing their lips together, not letting go for a long time.

"Phew, that's better," she said. "Can we have a drink now?"

Will got a bottle of wine out of the fridge in the kitchen, two glasses off the shelf and poured out the wine.

Sitting together on the sofa, he said, "Now tell me what the quack said?"

"I think I'll live for another year until I see him again," she said with a laugh. "He just prodded around and took some X-rays, he seemed quite happy though."

"So he bloody well should be, prodding you around."

"Don't be so silly. That's what us girls have to put up with all the time with doctors."

"I thought we'd go up the road to Slevins, a pub-cum-restaurant on Main Street in the town, I've been once or twice and it's okay."

"Will, my lovely, I'll go anywhere, as long as it's with you."

"Right – here, let's have another glass of this, then we'll go."

They had a good table in a corner. Pepper steak for Will, lamb chops for Siobhan, and a bottle of house red.

"Any Christmas news?" Will asked.

"Not really, Dad's coming on Christmas Eve. He'll probably stay for a couple of nights. We've got possible runners on Boxing Day at Fairyhouse and Limerick, but I hope that you'll be back in time for the New Year Leopardstown meeting. That's always fun and I'm sure we'll have runners there. What about you?"

"I'm going over on Friday as you know. It'll be the first Christmas without James which will be quite difficult, but we're having a small party on the day after Boxing Day for local friends who were so supportive when he was killed. I'll be back on the 29th, not sure which plane yet - we'll talk about all that while I'm there."

"I hope we can talk every day. I shall miss you so much."

"I shall miss you, too, but we mustn't be sad. It's not for long. You asked me to tell you about Lucille."

"Yes," she said.

"It all stemmed from the racehorses. I told you about them. The owner is this chap, Max Geary, Barbados' equivalent, I suspect, of your father. Lucille is Max's receptionist and secretary. I met her in Max's office when he asked her to take me back to the ship. I met up with her on my next trip and we fell for each other in a big way. On my last trip, she asked me to stay the night at her parents' plantation and took me for a picnic on a fabulous deserted beach the next day. Then back to the ship. It was the last time I saw her, two and a half years ago."

"Oh, Will, what a sweet and lovely story. I'm so glad you've told me. Did you sleep with her?"

"Yes and we made love on a deserted beach."

"Have you stayed in touch?"

"Yes, two telephone calls and a multitude of letters, although they seem to be becoming less frequent from her and maybe from me, too."

"Have you told her about me?"

"No."

"Are you going to?"

"Yes."

"When?"

"I've been trying to work this out. The two telephone calls I mentioned have both been on Christmas Day and I shall probably call her again this time, though a telephone call on Christmas Day is not the right time for me to say what's needed to be said. She may have a new boyfriend, I don't know, she hasn't said anything about it. The plan running through my mind is to wait until about mid-January, then write to her. We have said in our letters that something like this may well happen to either of us and we undertook to tell each other so that is what I'm going to do."

As they were getting into bed, Siobhan said, "I'm glad that you're going away as I'm due to be off games for a few days quite soon, so your absence will take the temptation away. I'm alright for now, though…"

CHAPTER 12

It was snowing at Manchester's Ringway airport when Will's Aer Lingus plane landed soon after 7 o'clock. Saying a quick hello to the Supercar desk staff, he picked up the keys for the car waiting for him and got on his way. Luckily, the snow flurry didn't last long, still it was well after 8 when he arrived at Ayshford.

When Mary saw the headlights, she dashed to the door to welcome him.

"Hello, Darling, welcome home," she said putting her arms around him. "Come in quickly, out of the cold."

Grabbing the old battered suitcase, he followed her inside.

"Sorry, I'm a bit late – it's all looking marvellous Mum, Christmas cards all over the place, lovely Christmas decorations everywhere and the tree, but what about the lights?"

"Thought we'd leave that to you; we're sure to have ballsed it up."

He hadn't noticed that his father and Joanna had come into the hall behind them.

He gripped his father in a bear hug, "Hello, Dad fantastic to see you – and JoJo, my, just look at you, young lady, give us a kiss. I can't tell you how wonderful it is to be back again. Now, is it a dry house or is there a drink for a working man?"

Will ran upstairs, threw his case on his bed, swopped his jacket for a cardigan, had a pee and was down again to take a gulp out of the whisky and soda thrust into his hands.

"Now, tell us all your Irish news," said Mary, when they had sat down to a happy family dinner, laid by Joanna, cooked by Mary, supplied mostly by Angus, and Will in attendance, "How's it going and what have you been up to?"

"Where to start?" said Will. "First and most important, the business side which, after all, is what I'm there for. It's performing in excess of expectations and has improved considerably since I was last home. We are the new kids on the block now, thanks to the good publicity and advertising arranged by the company HQ, together with having done our homework and taken time to recruit good staff, we are ahead of schedule. But we have to be very much on our guard not to become one-night wonders. Our competitors will be and are very keen to make any possible dents in our armour that they can, which is what we've done to them. That's one reason I must get back before New Year. We have a double fistful of bookings from Americans coming into Shannon and our small operation in Limerick will be stretched to the limit. I'm having to arrange for a convoy of cars from Santry to be sent down there, it's all quite exciting."

"Your spell in Manchester must have been a very good education for your new job," said Angus. "And it helped you to be selected for the Irish job."

"Yes, very much so; I've been hugely helped and still am being, by Fred Ogden, who I am very glad to say is coming to the party next Wednesday. Not to blow my own trumpet, but I did sell the idea of a branch in Ireland to the MD in the first place."

"I don't suppose you've had much time to make many friends outside your business?" asked Mary.

"That's also true or was to start with, however, I've had a great introduction recently via Adam Platt. He told his Irish agent about me and put me in touch with a young trainer, Harry Kennedy, near Trim. I've been going there to ride out for the last few Saturdays. I actually went racing with him last Saturday to Roscommon after riding work in the morning. He told me the other day that he knows quite a few of the local polo club people. With any luck, I may get a chance to play a bit of polo next spring and summer. That's enough. What's the gossip round here? JoJo, you're the gossip queen, what's been going on?"

"Nothing, that's what's been going on."

"Come on Jo, darling, that's not true. You've been very helpful to me ever since the end of term getting the house ready for Christmas, helping with the party invitations and with your friend Kate and her mother, sorting out party eats and stuff."

"Boring."

"It's not boring. It's what people have to do to run a house and entertain friends. You can't expect to be asked to parties, and other exciting things, if you don't do your own bit. We haven't been able to have a proper party for some time, due to the move and everything, we just want to make it fun for people, particularly at Christmas."

"Okay, sorry Mum. At least we've got Will back, You'll make it exciting, won't you Will?"

"Yes, I'll dress up as Father Christmas and come and tickle your toes."

Next day, Will got busy on the tree decorations after breakfast. He found the lights which he had carefully packed away in the original box the previous year.

"Come on JoJo, you can help me with this. Hold the stepladder still while I climb up – no, not like that, you goon – how can I go up the ladder with you standing in front of the bloody thing. Hold it by the side."

He draped the lights in a way that they cascaded down the tree like a stream flowing down the rocky contours of a mountainside.

"There, how about that? Now you can hand me up all the little angels, pieces of fake snow, Snow White and her chums, baubles, bangles and beads, for me to fasten the top ones and you can get cracking on the ones lower down."

An hour later, "Okay, all we need now is the tinsel. Where is it?"

"I don't know."

"You must know, you live here! Go and ask Mum."

Mum appeared.

"Where's the tinsel?" Will asked.

"Oh, darling, yes I think I know, it's in a different shaped box to all the other things, you know – long and flattish, I put it somewhere, now where? Wait a minute."

She disappeared, returning a few minutes later with a flat box wrapped in a dust sheet. "There," she said. "I knew it was important – that's why I put it in the cleaning cupboard."

"The cleaning cupboard? Why did you put tinsel in the cleaning cupboard?"

"Because I thought it had something to do with the hoover, you know to clean out the underneath bit that sucks up all the dust and everything."

"Mum, oh dear, I thought you were the brains of the family. Here, Sis, give it to me and hold the side of the ladder."

Later, Will found his mother preparing lunch in the kitchen. Angus was tucked away in his study where he had been all morning and Joanna was nowhere to be seen, assumed to be tidying her room.

"We must do something about Jo," he said. "She's wandering about like a lost soul. She's probably had all there is to be had at her present school and is marking time. Are there any of her age, schoolfriends or whatever, coming to the party?"

"Yes, you are right. I have discussed this with Dad, though as you know, it's so difficult to get any form of decisions out of him these days, and I hate badgering him. She's asked Kate to come to the party and the Tomkinsons are bringing their eighteen-year-old son, Jason. We could ask Judy Huxtable to bring her young brother, can't remember his name, he must be about sixteen. Would you like to ring her and ask?"

"I'd much rather you asked her parents," Will replied.

"Okay, I will. Now, what about you and your lady friend problems?"

"Yes, Mum I do want to talk about it. It's two and half years since Lucille and I said goodbye at the dockside in Bridgetown, not knowing when we would see each other again. We loved each other and were heartbroken to be parted. In letters, we promised one another to tell the other if anybody important entered our lives. Recently, letters from her have been coming less frequently, I suppose the same could be said about my letters to her. I have now met someone; she is the sister of the young trainer I am riding for and she is called Siobhan – she's the one I've told you about. She and her brother live together and have done ever since he set up as a trainer two years ago. She acts as his housekeeper and secretary; the system works very well for them both; they are very close. Their mother died of breast cancer three years or so ago and their father lives in considerable style an hour out of Dublin. Siobhan is different to Lucille in some ways, but similar in others; a tomboy as a child, headstrong, outgoing, and very attractive. She is also intensely loyal and devoted to her brother.

We are very smitten; I feel that I must keep my promise to Lucille and tell her. The question is - how and when? As you know, we've spoken on the telephone on each of the last two Christmases and I feel it would be unfair if I didn't call her this year; though it would be unkind if I ruined her Christmas by telling her then. What do you think?"

"Oh, Will, I don't know. Provided Lucille still thinks the same about you, you're in a no-win situation whatever you do. I agree that Christmas Day is a bad choice. Let me ask you a question: how sure are you about Siobhan? You say that she is headstrong and outgoing; fine but who's making the running in this contest, her or you? Are you sure she's not taking hold of you as a young, good-looking, fun guy, who's a good rider with an important day job? After all, you've only known her for a few weeks. My advice to you is to hold off saying anything to Lucille for now. Maybe something will happen that will prove to you that Siobhan is as loyal to you as she is to her brother. I also think that this situation cannot go on for long; I suggest that you make a deadline of, say, one month and if you feel the same then as you do now, you should write to Lucille and tell her."

"Thanks, Mum, that's very sound advice and I'll think about it. Now, back to Joanna. Remember, a while ago, I suggested some alternative ideas that we should, perhaps, think about. I'm not certain that she's ready to be cast adrift in London; I can see bad influences creeping in there before she is ready and her being led astray. I think she needs to broaden her mind and gain experience with other young people but under adult guidance rather than supervision. I have an idea that might work, I know of a farm, now more of an institution, in Zimbabwe that is a ten thousand acre game conservancy. Founded as a cattle, maize and tobacco farm by a man called Norman Travers, it branched into game conservancy about fifteen years ago and has had tremendous success in rescuing poached black rhinos and other species, including elephants. They now have a rhino breeding and release operation which is proving very successful. Called Imire, it is about a hundred miles from Harare – down the road in African distance terms – and is run by the Travers family, with dedicated Zimbabwean staff and changing teams of young volunteers, girls and boys over the age of eighteen. Volunteers are housed in comfortable rondavel-type houses, all food on board is provided for them and there are plenty of opportunities for organised trips to be made to places such as Victoria Falls. Of course, it doesn't come for free but the costs are way, way less than, for instance, safaris or trips organised by commercial travel companies. Talk to Dad about it and if you think it might be a goer, I'll find out the costs etc."

Garech Kennedy drove his Bentley as near to the front door

at Lostock as he could in the pouring rain on Christmas Eve afternoon.

"Is anyone at home?" he called out, coming through the door.

"Hello Dad," came from two directions, Harry from his office and Siobhan from the kitchen.

"Let me give you a hand," said Harry, taking his father's suitcase.

"God, what a bloody day, at least the traffic isn't bad."

Garech, a man of a little over medium height with plenty of grey hair, horn-rimmed glasses, square-shaped head, reddish complexion showing a bit of wear, nodded at his son and kissed his daughter. Dressed in corduroy trousers, a rough check shirt and red socks running into brown Gucci shoes.

"I see you are not expecting to go for an appetising walk," said Harry.

"Bloody well not, but I've got boots in the car and a schoffel coat if I'm not too late for evening stables."

Later, during dinner, Harry said, "Guess what, your daughter has a new boyfriend."

"What, another one? What kind of a fool wants to take her on?"

"Don't be so horrid, Dad. I haven't had a proper boyfriend for a long time and I'm very choosy these days."

"Who is he, where does he live and is he employed?"

"William Carpenter, in England and yes."

"An Englishman; when were you last in England?"

"I wasn't. He works here, he is the manager of the new Supercar operation in Ireland."

"Oh, I heard about that. In fact, I was asked to the opening party but didn't go. How did you meet him?"

"I can answer that one," Harry broke in. "I introduced him to Siobhan."

"You did? At some party I suppose?"

"No, exactly where you are sitting now."

"What here? What the blazes was he doing here? Renting you a car or something?"

"No, he was riding work for me. He's the best young work jockey that I've come across."

Mary Carpenter rose early on Christmas morning. Although it would be only the four of them for Christmas lunch, she wanted to make it extra special. She and Angus had tossed whether to have goose or turkey – heads goose, tails turkey: tails came up so turkey won. By the time Joanna came down, Mary had prepared it ready for the oven. She and Joanna laid the table for lunch and arranged breakfast in the kitchen. Wrapped presents lay under the tree. Will appeared.

"Gosh, I'm sorry I'm late."

"You're not and anyway this is holiday time for you. Happy Christmas, darling."

"And a very happy Christmas to you Mum and to you, darling Sister."

David Hatch, who had conducted James' funeral, the vicar of St Helen's for the past ten years, presided over Christmas morning service at 11. Will followed his father and mother into the church with Joanna at his side, the first time he had been since the funeral.

Angus, a regular but not doctrinal churchgoer, liked to sit in the 3rd or 4th pew on the right of the church, to where he led his family. Nodding heads, smiles, mouthed Happy Christmases all around; the congregation, occupying about three-quarters of the church, sang *Once In Royal David's City,* amend the prayers, did their best in the psalms, heard some of the lessons while trying to remember if they had put the turkey in the correct oven. They joined in lustily singing *Hark the Herald Angels Sing,* hoped the vicar wouldn't go on too long in his sermon – he didn't, though he made a humorous remark about overcooked turkeys.

After the sermon, the congregation put away the hymn sheets, pretending they knew *O Come All Ye Faithful* off by heart, knelt like sprinters on their blocks through the Blessing, and joined in the unseemly fast shuffle towards the door to be high in the queue to shake hands with the vicar, "Oh, what lovely service, vicar", and had a race so as not to get stuck in the car park.

Family Carpenter took their time. Will's thoughts – and prayers – during the service, first for James, his brother never to be seen again – *What would James have done,* was now a frequent question that Will asked himself – to his family – to Siobhan, imagining the scene at Lostock – to the sun having only just risen over the Uplands Plantation – *What is Lucille thinking today?*

David Hatch greeted them, Will thought, with extreme kindness, he knew where their thoughts as a family lay that day. A good man of God. Will wiped away a few tears as he walked back to the car.

The Kennedys are an Irish Protestant family. At breakfast, after Happy Christmases all round, Harry said, "We'd better leave at 10 o'clock; the service at St. Patrick's is at 10.30…"

A loud knock on the front door interrupted him, "Who the hell is that, banging on the door on Christmas morning?"

"I'll go," said Siobhan.

She returned a minute or so later.

"Look," she said smiling. "I've been bunched!"

She was holding up a bunch of twenty-four bright red roses, clutching a card in her hand, which read, *'Happy Christmas, Princess, 007.'*

"Will I have a chance of meeting your young man sometime soon?" enquired Garech Kennedy.

"I hope he will be able to come to Leopardstown during the New Year meeting," Harry said. "So you'll meet him there."

"He's lovely, Dad, took me to dinner at the Trocadero."

"Oh, so it was you! Louis, the maitre d', said he thought he saw you having dinner with a young man recently. I told him I doubted it, as you didn't know anyone rich enough to take you there, except for your brother and that he certainly wouldn't be doing that."

Angus, Mary, Will and Joanna were back at Ayshford in good time for Mary in charge, helped by Will and Joanna to put the finishing touches, light candles, put the crackers on the table and generally fuss around. Will fetched the champagne from the fridge, then he said quietly to his mother, "I'm off to the telephone for a minute."

He dialled Lostock.

Siobhan answered, "Darling, lovely, sweet Will, Happy Christmas and thank you, thank you so much for my wonderful, heavenly roses. Such a fabulous and beautiful surprise, I can't thank you enough."

"Good, glad they arrived; a bit worried no one would deliver on Christmas morning, though the nice lady in the florist's assured me that it would be okay. How are you, Sweet Pea and how's it all going there?"

"It's fine. Dad's here. Very suspicious about you, until Harry told him about the riding. It was so funny: Harry told him that you and I met here, and Dad thought you must have come to try and rent him a car! Tell me about you."

"We're okay, just back from church. Won't do presents etc until after lunch, so haven't opened the little parcel I found at the bottom of my case. Let's talk again later. I'll call you."

Before they went into lunch, Will said, "I don't want this to be a sad moment, so no blubbing please, but this time last year, just before the Queen, we played James' recorded message. This year, I would just like us to raise our glasses and say, 'James, sorry you are no longer with us. We miss you. To James.'"

Frank Doune hated Christmas. Shops and supermarkets decorated with stupid chains of brightly coloured paper, stretched across ceilings and round windows, pictures of an old man with a white beard dressed in heavy red robes, wearing a silly hat with a bauble on the end, carrying a sack containing goodness knows what on his back, often riding on a cart over snow, pulled by a spindly cow with spiky horns: what the hell's snow anyway? Looks cold and we don't want it here. Silly people, black and white singing the same stupid songs in overflowing churches, praising someone who's dead and probably never lived anyway. Haven't they got anything better to do?

Lunch over, Mary very happy with it, Angus quiet but chipping in now and then, Will holding it all together despite thoughts straying elsewhere and Joanna, happy with her family though insecure in her mind.

The drawing room fire lit, and they settled down to watch the Queen. Marvellous as always, what a Rock, and what an example to the rest of us.

Then, present time; from Will a litre bottle of Irish whiskey for his father, a lovely big silk scarf for his mother, and a decorative charm bracelet for his sister, for which she squealed in delight, putting it on and waving her arm about immediately. The family had combined for a large, well wrapped present for Will. He opened it while saying to his mother that she shouldn't have spent so much money on the Christmas wrapping paper, "Never mind,

I'll fold it up so you can use it again."

Inside he found a very smart and expensive suitcase-cum-holdall with different compartments, one of which could be separated and used as an overnight bag.

"This is wonderful and thank you so much," he said, gripping his father's hand and kissing his mother and sister.

"I couldn't bear for a man of your importance and stature going round with that battered old thing any longer," Mary said.

"Thank you again. I shall take this everywhere but for sentimental reasons, I can't bear to throw the old one away." Lastly, he turned to the small square parcel he had retrieved from his old case. Opening it, he found a black leather box about four inches square and two inches deep. Inscribed in gold on the bottom right of the box were the letters WC. On the inside of the lid, a small silver plaque let into the fabric; on it, a loo seat with the numerals 007 was engraved in the middle. Will picked up a square card out of the box, *'You see what a girl can do while she's waiting for her man'*.

It was time for Will's second call of the day. Automatic calls to Barbados had only recently become available; Will dialled straight through to Uplands.

Harriet Todd answered, "Hello Mrs Todd, it's Will speaking. Happy Christmas to you."

"Oh, hello Will and a very happy Christmas to you, too. Are you in Ireland or England?"

"I'm with my family in England and envying you in the sunshine."

"Well, yes it's lovely, so I'm not complaining. I'll give Lucille a shout, I know she'd love to talk to you, just hold on, I'll find her."

A short pause, then the familiar, soft voice, "Hello, Will, it's lovely to hear your voice and happy Christmas."

"And to you, Lucille. How are you?"

"Oh, fine. Where are you?"

"In England with my family. Just had lunch; we'll probably go out for a walk before it gets dark."

"I hoped you would call. I think about you a lot, but when we speak I forget all the things I wanted to say."

"Same here. I'm going back to Ireland on the 29th and will write again, as soon as I can. Very busy with my job there and glad to say it's going quite well. Doing some riding for a trainer over there in my spare time."

"That's good. I'll write too, with news of the horses etc."

"Okay, Lucille. Lots of love to you. Please say happy Christmas to your parents."

"I will, bye bye Will. Big kiss."

"Bye Lucille and same to you."

Lucille put down the telephone.

"He still means a lot to you, doesn't he?" said Harriet.

"Yes, he does, but we've both got our lives to live. Maybe I should move on. I've seen quite a lot of Josh recently, as you know. I like him, though I don't know if it will turn into anything else. Why do I feel so sad after speaking to Will?"

Will felt sad, too. Couldn't put his finger on it.

He told himself, *Listen, there's an ocean between us, we must get on with our lives. I have the gut feeling that she may be thinking the same, and rightly so'.*

He called Siobhan again. Harry answered this time, "Hi, Will, she loves her roses, your girlfriend – happy Christmas by the way – she pinned one on her coat to take to church this morning; hang on, she's right here jumping up and down like a two-year-old about to be loaded into the stalls."

"Hi, lover boy…"

"Sweet Pea, your box and all that goes with it, is just pure magic, sensational, and my new favourite possession. Furthermore, it really is just what I wanted. I didn't have a box like that to put nick knacks, cuff links and the like in. Thanks a million and I love the inscription."

"Well, having made a close inspection of your bedroom a few times now, I thought it might fill the bill. Any other news since this morning?"

"No, not really. I expect we'll collapse in front of the telly until we can find the energy to climb the stairs to bed. What about you?"

"Probably about the same. We've three runners tomorrow; Harry thinks the inappropriately named Island in the Sun has a chance, though the other two, no more than each way hopes. I think Harry and Dad will go, but I probably won't. Hope to talk to you instead."

"It will be my main feature of the day, I assure you. I shall be tuned in to watch King George at Kempton and I don't suppose they'll give the Irish results and I'll be relying on you to tell me."

"Okay, sweet dreams – I hope of me. Bye."

"I hope so, too – bye."

Boxing Day dawned, cold but bright, with an overnight frost. As most of the shops were closed, the last-minute things for tomorrow's party would have to wait. However, newspaper shops never seem to close, that's why Will drove into Tarporley to collect theirs, taking Joanna with him. Corals betting shop was also open.

"Bet you've never been in one of these, have you JoJo? Come with me for a piece of further education."

Inside the dingy shop, walls lined with rows of racing pages from the sporting press, Will looked for the Irish section and saw that Harry Kennedy's horse, Island in the Sun, was the second favourite in a race at 3 o'clock.

Taking Jo by the hand, he produced a £10 note, took it to a counter at the end of the shop and wrote the name of the horse and the £10 bet on a slip of paper and presented both to a tired-looking man behind the counter who nodded, stamped the slip, took the £10 and gave the duplicate copy back to Will. They left the shop; no word having been spoken.

"That wasn't very exciting," said Jo.

"Learning is not always exciting. It's what you do with the knowledge of what you have learnt, that sometimes becomes exciting. JoJo, you are growing up into a lovely, pretty girl to whom I am devoted as your brother and lifelong best friend, I hope.

We must now think about what's next in line for you and what direction career-wise you wish to follow. I will help you as much as I can with whatever, but I need input from you to enable me to do that."

"I do enjoy cooking. I don't want to be a schoolmistress or to sit all day in an office. I like being outside and I love nature and animals. I would like to ride more though am not sure if I'm brave enough."

"Well, that's a start. I'll talk to Mum and Dad, though you

are now old enough and responsible enough to take part in any discussions about your own future."

"Dad doesn't like talking about this sort of thing."

"Well, talk to me or Mum, so that we can help Dad to help you."

Will called Siobhan about midday, "Hello, my lovely one, how were the dreams?"

"Awful, my knight in shining armour galloped up to me and fell off. I couldn't help him because his armour was too heavy."

"Listen, sweetheart, my plane arrives at midday on Friday. I'm not sure what your plans are but I'm nervous about going to Leopardstown at the weekend, particularly as it's the New Year and we have a very heavy workload. Pat Byrne is in charge while I'm away, with strict instructions to call me here in an emergency, though I am due to take over from him when I get back and therefore will be on call. I should be able to arrange cover for me on Friday afternoon, after that, I really must be within range of a telephone, that's why I don't feel I can come on Saturday."

"Oh, Will, I was really looking forward to showing you off at Leopardstown and Dad is longing to meet you."

"I'm very disappointed, too, but my conscience is pricking me big time. It would look terrible if something happened and I was at the races. I really must be in my office or at least available on Saturday."

"Yes, of course, I understand. Supposing I came to you on Friday lunchtime, we could go on to the races together, come back here, you stay Friday night, ride out first lot on Saturday and then go to the office?"

"That might work if I can fix it with Pat. I could give the office the Lostock number for Friday afternoon and night. Will there be anybody there in the afternoon?"

"No, but we have an arrangement to divert calls to Ronan's number."

"Let's try for that then. I'm so sorry, it's very disappointing for me, too. Will your father be at the races on Friday?"

"I don't know, I'll have to ask him. I'm off now to put my head in a bucket of water. If I survive, please can we talk later?"

"Mum, did you and Dad have any more thoughts about the

Zimbabwe idea for Jo? It's only that I had a chat with her this morning, asking her what she would like to do next. She really does need to put her mind into gear; it's in neutral at the moment; she's coasting and this can't be allowed to continue or she's going to be left behind in life. She's the same age now as I was when I became a deckhand."

"I did but got nowhere. Look, find out the rough cost and I'll tackle it again."

"Okay. I'll do that. We've got to crack on with this one."

"I agree, darling. It's lovely having you here. You breathe new life into the place. Sometimes I get a bit low; I don't want to complain but it is difficult. Sometimes your father hardly speaks all day, just shuts himself away in his study. We are really lucky this place came up; I don't think I could have coped with buying and moving into a new house and possibly a new area. I do hope Dad will come out of his shell for the party tomorrow and chat to his old friends. With any luck, it may rekindle his spirit a bit."

"I know, Mum, you are being wonderful. I must ring you more often, even if I've got nothing in particular to say. Jo did mention cooking; you know there is a fabulous cooking school in Ireland called Ballymaloe, but I believe it's fiendishly expensive. I'll ask Siobhan about it. She did a cooking course in London actually, I'll ask her about that, too."

He called Siobhan again.

"What news, Pussy Cat?"

"He won, Island in the Sun at 11/4."

"Brilliant, please congratulate the trainer. I had a tenner on him. Please will you come with me?"

"Where to?"

"The island in the sun, stupid."

"Just try to go without me."

"I wouldn't dare."

Next morning at breakfast, Will asked his sister, "Jo, can you come and help me in Tarporley again. Mum's given me list a mile long for the party."

They set off after they'd eaten. In town, they stopped outside Coral's.

"A bit more further education for you, Jo. Here, take this piece of paper, go inside, hand it to the man at the counter. He will give you £37.50. Count it to check that is the amount he has given you."

Will followed a few feet behind. The counter man took the betting slip, looked at Joanna, then up at Will standing behind, who nodded, counted out £37.50 – £10 at 11/4, plus the stake – and gave the money to Joanna, who, following instructions checked it, put it in her pocket, turned round and left the shop, Will having already done so. Again, not a word had been spoken.

"JoJo, what you have achieved is an example of using knowledge of something learnt. I learnt that the horse, Island in the Sun, stood a very good chance of winning the race and, acting upon this knowledge, I invested £10 on it. I am not inviting you to be a gambler; you learn through experience. I happen to know and ride for the trainer of the horse in Ireland and decided to act upon his advice. Now, as a reward for listening to me, please give me my original stake of £10 from your pocket and put the remainder in your money box."

Fred Ogden arrived among the first at the party. Greeted by Mary and Angus, saying how glad they were to meet him, having heard from Will how much he liked working with him and for all the help he had and continued to give to their son. Will and Fred had a quick business chat before joining the party proper.

The Party was a success. Angus came out of his shell, much cheered up by seeing many of his old friends as they talked and reminisced about things past.

Will made an excellent host, introducing Fred around to everyone, including Richard Tomkinson, the Master of the Cheshire Hounds, with the comment, "I can't think of anything you two have in common, except you're both my Master, so have a go."

He saw Joanna having a good chat with Tomkinson junior, Richard's son, Jason; it pleased him and he had a passing word with his former girlfriend, Judy Huxtable, "I hear you're working in Ireland. How's the love life?"

"Tip top, Jude – and yours?"

"Pretty cocked up, thanks."

His friend, Adam Platt said, "My spies tell me you're to be seen all over Ireland, even as far as Roscommon."

"I know where that piece of information came from. Thanks so much for the Fergy Lynch connection; I'm riding out at weekends for a lovely guy called Harry Kennedy, suggested by Fergy."

Gradually, people started to drift away. By 9 o'clock they had all gone except for Joanna's friend, Kate, who had been helping her mother, plus a young man, Ken, who had been drafted in as barman. They all helped to clear up most of the mess and then they left, too, leaving the family to sit down in the kitchen to eat supper, which consisted of the party leftovers, some bangers Mary had kept in the warming oven, and to have a party post mortem.

"Well done, Mum and Dad," said Will. "I thought that went off very well, thanks to your organisation and planning."

"Hey, what about me?" piped up Joanna.

"Sorry Jo, I didn't mean to leave you out. I know you did your bit; I apologise. Saw you chatting away to young Tomkinson."

"Yeah, he's a bit dreamy. Liked him."

"My plane's at 11 tomorrow morning," Will announced at breakfast. "Siobhan's meeting me at lunchtime and we're going racing at Leopardstown in the afternoon. I'm on call over the weekend and will be in the office on Saturday, which is a pity as the stable will have runners at Leopardstown, some of which I've been riding."

"Who is Siobhan?" asked Joanna.

"She is Harry Kennedy's sister who lives and works with him. She is kindly picking me up and giving me a lift to the races."

"What's wrong with your own car?"

"I've never been to Leopardstown and am not sure of the best way to get there."

"How will you get home again if you have no car?"

"I knew that sometime we'd find a use for that old dog kennel outside the back door, so get in it."

CHAPTER 13

Siobhan was there at the flat waiting, when he arrived, out of her car in a flash, running to him.

"Oh God, I hope you've not been here long in the cold," he said, holding her tightly in his arms. "I must get another key cut for you."

"I'd wait for you until the ice melted; Will, Will, I've missed you so much! Tell me everything you've been doing."

"All in good time, my lovely one; you know most of it anyway. Let's go in now. Time for a quick change and then we must be off. I want all your news, too."

She watched him change, "Hey, what's that smart suitcase?"

"Present from the family; fabulous, isn't it. Look there's an attachment I can use as an overnight bag. Stick my riding gear for tomorrow in it, would you. I'll do the rest."

Ten minutes later they were off.

"It's about 20 miles from here, but we have to go all round Dublin to avoid going through the centre, it'll take a little short of an hour. We've two runners today, Joe rides both of them; one is Dad's horse, Spring Garden in a two and a half mile chase – Dad's coming by the way. He won't win as he's no good on softish ground, which we have today."

"Yes, I know the horse and have ridden him. Harry told me he planned to give him a run here more, in the hope that the handicapper might drop him in the weights. What's the other horse?"

"This is the interesting one: Pelican Point in the main hurdle race. He's a goodish horse; Harry thinks he has a fair chance."

"It's interesting in more ways than one. Pelican Point is the horse that we tried Small Talk within the gallop three weeks ago. If he wins or runs well, it is a good pointer."

The racecourse at Leopardstown, a village very close to the port town of Dun Laoghaire, is left-handed; definitely one of Ireland's premier courses, hosting both flat and jump racing of a high order.

"Dad's got a table in the Owner's and Trainer's dining room," Siobhan said.

He and Harry had already started their lunch when Harry saw them coming.

"Over here," he shouted, waving at them. "Sorry, we had to start."

"Don't worry, we got here as soon as we could, Will's plane didn't land until after twelve. Dad, this is Will."

"You've done well," said Garech, getting to his feet and shaking Will by the hand. "Glad to meet you at last. I've been hearing that you have other attributes than a car salesman."

"He's not a car salesman Dad. He has a very important job when he's not riding Harry's horses and he's my lover."

"I said he had other attributes; they seem pretty full-time ones."

"How do you do Mr Kennedy, extremely glad to meet you, too."

"Do call me Garech, you already seem to be very much part of the family set-up."

Siobhan and Will sat down to order lunch, while Harry and Garech finished theirs.

"Not being rude," Harry said. "But, Dad and I are going to push on and check on the horses and leave you two lovebirds to finish your lunch. Spring Garden's race is the one after the next. Come down to the saddling boxes and give me a hand if you like."

Dad and son left.

"First impressions favourable," Garech said to his son, on their way down from the dining room.

"I think he's a very good fellow, level-headed and good fun. He's also a bloody good rider. His firm must think highly of him to have sent him over here to start up a new branch of the business at his young age. A pity, he would have made a top-flight jockey."

In the dining room, Siobhan said to Will, "I'm so sad about tomorrow, Will, but I'm also very proud of you doing what is right for you, don't worry, there'll be plenty of other opportunities. I might even come and sit in your office doing my knitting."

"Don't be silly. Come here, help Harry and enjoy yourself. Let's finish lunch and get down to the action."

Spring Garden performed as expected. Being a hard puller, Joe Maguire let him go off in front and enjoy himself until he got tired, starting to flounder in the ground. Joe just kept him going, let him coast home at his own pace, finishing nearer last than first, a good eighty yards behind the winner. Will and Siobhan were not left on their own; Fergal Lynch with Tom Kearns in tow, plus a couple of the Fairyhouse team, centred on them.

"Is there anyone left at Lostock Stables?" asked Fergy. "The whole Kennedy string seem to be here - father, son, daughter and new work jockey who has hotfooted it from Cheshire, where I happen to know he was whooping it up yesterday."

"Your idea of whooping may not be the same as mine, Fergy, but who needs a tic tac man with you around?" said Will.

"What about Pelican Point today?" he asked.

"Fergy, I've just stepped off a plane having been whooping it up, remember, so how should I know? He must have an each way chance, I suppose."

Pelican Point looked magnificent walking round in the paddock, head held high, taking in all his surroundings. Already the winner of three races, the last of them on soft ground, Harry thought he was still on the upgrade, though there were three or four others with similar form, as was to be expected in a race of this quality at the Leopardstown Christmas Festival meeting. In the betting ring, most bookmakers had him chalked up at around 6 to 1. The jockeys filed their way out of the weighing room, into the paddock, grouping around their respective trainers and owners.

Harry said, "Joe, you know the horse, ride the race as you find it. I hope they go a decent gallop and I am sure he'll stay. He's got a turn of foot as we know, ideally, don't try to hit the front too soon."

Will went over to the bookmakers and had E25 each way at 13/2, joining Siobhan, Harry and Garech in the stands. In the race, Pelican Point took a good, firm hold, however, Joe had no problem in settling him down in mid-division about six or seven lengths off a good pace set by one of the favourites, Freshwater Bay. With three flights of hurdles left, Joe moved up a place or two.

"Steady Joe, not yet, that's okay, he's still nicely on the bridle. Keep him like that, no hurry yet," Harry muttered, his binoculars focussed on the race leaders.

Two to go, "Yes, great jump."

He was now third, but there were four or five still in with a chance of closing in on the leader, Freshwater Bay. Between the last two flights, Close In came with a run and challenged the leader, jockeys hard at work, Pelican Point still third. Both leaders rose at the last together. Pelican Point a length away with Lysander closing fast. Joe got a tremendous leap from Pelican Point and landed practically level with Freshwater Bay and Close In. He sat down and rode for all he was worth; with a hundred yards to go he hit the front, but Lysander, only half a length behind, going hell for leather. On the line, he held on to win by a neck.

Joe raised his whip in the air in triumph, Lysander was second, and Close In, third. The Kennedy clan, Will included, hoarse with shouting and joy, grasped hold of each other, slowly allowing the adrenalin to subside. Stevie, Pelican Point's lad, led him and a grinning Joe Maguire into the winners' enclosure amidst a cheering crowd.

"It looked close; you know, but I had a bit in hand. Provided he jumped I knew I was going to win from two out," Joe said. "This is a decent horse; he knew the other one was there but kept pulling out a bit more. He was going away from him on the line and he'll stay a bit further."

Will collected his winnings and joined the others in the bar, who were already stuck into the first of two bottles of champagne ordered by Garech.

"Harry tells me that you have some ancestral connection with the West Indies," Garech said to Will.

"Yes, two hundred and odd years ago, an ancestor ended up in Barbados. He had fought in the American Independence war, and caught the eye of his CO, Lord Cornwallis, who had a word his boss, George III, who granted my ancestor three hundred acres of land on Barbados, on which he planted sugar. He was an Irishman, actually, the second son of a landowner in Co. Galway."

"Fascinating story. Have you still got the plantation?"

"Good Heaven's no, but I have seen where it once was."

"So you've been out there?"

"As a deckhand on a banana boat."

"Hmm. My late wife and I went to Barbados quite a few times and loved it. Stayed at Cobblers Cove hotel."

"I've driven past it though I've never been inside."

"Oh, so you got around the island a bit then?"

"It's an odd story and you may not believe it, but on one of my trips on the banana boat, I got the job of looking after two racehorses that were being shipped out there. On the deck, landing in Barbados, I was introduced to the owner of the horses. To cut the story short, evidently, my ancestor was quite a bigwig at the time, made a lot of money on his plantation and put a great deal back into the island in philanthropic ways. On my next trip, this chap kindly took me round the island and showed me where my ancestor's plantation used to be."

"You must tell me more. Are you coming tomorrow?

"Sadly not. I am on call all weekend so shall be in and out of my office. I'm going back to Lostock tonight though with Siobhan, ride a bit of work for Harry first lot in the morning, then buzz off to the office."

Back at Lostock later, Harry said, "Saw you making a hit with the old man, Will."

"I don't know about that. I was just answering the interrogation."

"No, you did fine, I can tell."

They were all still on a high after Pelican Point's win.

"I must look seriously for a race for Small Talk. He's about ready, I think. You can ride him in the morning, Will; see what you think."

"It's been a long day, and such a happy one," Will said to Siobhan, on their way up to bed.

"It's going to stay happy for a while yet," she replied, "I've been waiting for this for nearly two weeks."

Conor O'Neill had an early start that Saturday. He kissed his wife goodbye, leaving his house soon after 5 o'clock. He was due at the Supercar depot in Santry at 6 to drive a car down to the Limerick depot. It was the third time in four days that he had made this trip; *business must be good,* he thought to himself. He picked up the ring road round Dublin before hitting the M7, which would take him nearly all the way. Tuning in to Radio Eireann's early morning programme, listening to the banter, the snippets of news and light pop music, he was happy. He had the next day, New Year's Eve, off, plus the following two days to recover. Something to look forward to.

The heavy articulated lorry he was about to overtake then lurched violently left. Conor could see shreds of rubber flying off two wheels of the nearside rear section of the trailer. It half straightened as the driver fought to regain control then slewed again, right this time. Conor saw the side of the trailer overturning in slow motion on top of his car. Then, the lights went out.

Half an hour earlier, Will pulled up Small Talk at the top end of the gallop.

Down at the start, Harry had said, "Will, this time, don't jump him off: give Ro and I a good six lengths or so start. Keep him behind for the first two furlongs, then make up your ground, come by us and let him stride on if he's good enough, as fast as he wants to. Don't ride him out or hit him."

Will did what he was told, however, Small Talk did not like being left behind expending a lot of energy fighting for his head. As soon as he came up on the heels of the other two, he settled. When Will asked him to go on he shot past them, finishing six to eight lengths clear. He made a mental note to advise Harry not to repeat these tactics, and to let him settle in the company of others.

Over the hill, while still pulling up, he saw the Land Rover coming fast in their direction, Siobhan driving.

She jumped out, leaving the door open, "Will, come quickly; there's been an accident. Your office has been on the line. Give me the horse, take the Land Rover, and go and ring them urgently."

"There's been a bad accident," the duty desk manager at the airport, Kevin Flynn, said, "It's one of our drivers, Conor O'Neill, they think he's dead."

"I'll be at Santry in an hour, get there yourself and arrange for a replacement at the desk if you need one."

"That won't be necessary, Bernice, here, is very responsible and we've no scheduled bookings for the next couple of hours."

Siobhan came in breathless, as he put down the phone, "Will, my poor darling, what's happened?"

"Don't know any details yet, but it's very bad. I think one of our drivers has been killed. I'm rushing to change – could you fix me a mug of coffee?"

He dashed upstairs.

Harry appeared, "So sorry, Will. Siobhan will fill me in."

Siobhan came up with his coffee, "You'll let me know what's

happened as soon as you know, won't you? If you are going straight to your office, give me the flat key. I'll go there and wait for news from you."

"Don't change your plans just because of me. I must rush now, talk to you later."

"Give me the key or I'll be sitting outside in the cold."

"Bless you Princess, here you are."

He arrived at the office near on 8.30.

Kevin Flynn, the duty airport desk manager was already there, "I don't know a lot. The Garda called at 7.20 to say that there had been an accident on the M7, near Roscrea, between a heavy goods vehicle and a car. They identified the car as being the property of Supercar from the registration number. They think the driver of the car was fatally injured."

Will picked up his telephone, "Get me the Garda station in Roscrea," he asked the receptionist.

"My name is William Carpenter; I am the manager of Supercar Ireland Ltd, speaking from my office in Santry. I am enquiring about an accident this morning on the M7, near Roscrea, involving one of our vehicles."

"One moment please, I'll put you through …"

Another voice came on the line, "You are Mr Carpenter from Supercar?

"Yes."

"I regret to inform you that the driver of your car has been pronounced dead at the scene of the accident. Our officers are at the scene, along with medical support and ambulances. The body of the driver, who has not been formally identified, is currently being taken to Nenagh General Hospital. I understand that the other vehicle involved was a heavy goods vehicle, which sustained multiple burst tyres at the rear. I also understand that the driver of the goods vehicle sustained only minor injuries."

"Thank you very much for this information. I can tell you that the name of the driver of our car is Mr Conor O'Neill. He was an employee of our company on an authorised routine journey taking a car from our Santry depot to the one in Limerick. Please will you keep me informed of all information that you obtain and also what we need to do at our end concerning this terrible accident.

Mr O'Neill was married and I need to know the process regarding informing his widow and the identification of his body."

"Yes, I certainly will be doing all that. We will call you as soon as ever possible."

"What a horrible and tragic thing to have happened," Will said to Kevin Flynn, "Is your shift finished now or are you going back to the airport?"

"It's about finished, but I'll go back anyway to see Bernice and tell Tom Bright, who will be taking over from me, what's happened. God, his poor wife, who's going to tell her?"

"I'll see what the Garda say, though it may have to be me."

Will called Fred at his home number, "Hello, lad, what's up?"

Will told him.

When he had finished, Fred said, "What can I say, lad, simply awful. Shall I come over?"

"No, Fred. Very good of you to offer, though I must deal with this myself. I think you should tell the old man and maybe it would be good for the company's image if you came over for the funeral, whenever it is."

"Yes, I'll do both those things."

"It's breaking the news to his widow, that I'm dreading. I'll see what the Garda say. The other thing that I was thinking is that I hope the Garda will make a very thorough inspection of the artic, particularly the tyres. It seems very strange for a 'multiple' – their word – bursts to have happened."

"Yes, certainly in England the police would do that."

"Thanks Fred, if you don't mind I'll keep in close contact with you on this one."

"There's a call for you, Will. The Garda from Roscrea."

"Okay, put them through…"

"Mr Carpenter? – Michael Keegan here, the Garda, Roscrea. Shocking accident this morning; all of us are very sad and upset about the death of your Mr O'Neill. He has been confirmed dead by the head medic at Nenagh General. Death would have been instantaneous; he was grossly disfigured. Makes identification even more difficult. I want to talk to you about how to proceed; he did have identification on him so we have his address in Stillorgan. I can telephone his wife and/or send an officer, or you can make arrangements to do this. Speed is of the essence; we don't want the news to leak out to a third party. I should say that if at all possible we should avoid his wife having to identify his body. The medics can clean and repair him as much as possible, but it's not a pretty sight. Do you know him or his family personally?"

"No, I don't, nor do I know his family. He has only been working for us for a few months but was a careful and conscientious driver. Under the circumstances, I think it would be best if I broke the news to her and endeavour to find a close relative to do the physical examination. What about the other vehicle? I assume your experts will be making a report; it seems strange for there to have been a multiple blow out of tyres."

"Yes, of course there will be a detailed examination. The vehicle is and will remain in custody of the Garda until this is carried out."

Now for it, Will thought.

"Please can you let me have Conor O'Neill's home telephone number?" he asked his operator. "Don't call the number, just let me have it."

He wrote the number down, picked up his telephone and dialled it.

"Hello," a lady's voice said.

"Is that Mrs O'Neill?"

"Yes, it is and what can I do for you today?"

"My name is William Carpenter. I am the manager of Supercar. I am very deeply sorry to have to tell you that your husband, through no fault of his own, has been involved in a serious accident this morning on his way to Limerick and has been fatally injured..."

Silence the other end, then, "Fatally injured... Do you mean he's dead?"

"I am afraid so – yes."

Another long silence followed by sounds of crying and, "Oh no, oh no, not my treasured Conor."

"Mrs O'Neill, please may I come to see you. I could be there in forty-five minutes?"

"What am I to do, what am I to do?"

"I will help you as much as I can and will be with you very soon."

He put down the telephone.

It rang immediately, "Miss Kennedy is here to see you."

Siobhan came into his office.

Will hugged her and said. "Can you face coming with me? I've just put the telephone down from telling a poor lady that her husband has been killed. I'm on my way to see her in Stillorgan."

"Of course. Let's go."

In the car, Will filled her in on everything. Siobhan knew the quickest way to Stillorgan, formally a quiet country village that is now a suburb of Dublin. Will gave her a piece of paper with the O'Neill address. They were there in under half an hour. Will knocked on the door. A distraught-looking man of about forty opened it.

"I'm William Carpenter and this is my friend, Siobhan Kennedy."

"Come in please. My sister is upstairs, she'll be down in a minute. Thank you for coming; please tell me quickly before she comes down. She is totally devastated; there are two children who, luckily, went out for the day earlier with my wife and children, when you rang. My name is Liam Brophy."

He led Will into a small sitting room. Will told him as much as he could, and Conor's wife came in. She had washed her face, removed her makeup and brushed her hair, though that did not hide her overwhelming grief.

"I'm Nora," she said.

Will introduced himself and Siobhan. Siobhan went to her, took her in her arms, and led her to a chair where she collapsed, tears running down her cheeks, her body shaking and wracked with pain and anger.

"Why Conor? Why me? Who has done this to us? What are we going to do?"

"Mrs O'Neill, this is terrible for you and your family. We are here to try to help you as much as possible," Will said.

He signalled to Liam to come out of the room with him, leaving Siobhan with Nora.

"We have to go through the ghastly business of formal identification," he said, "I have been advised by the senior Garda inspector on the case that, if possible, your sister should not do this. Conor was horribly disfigured in the accident; it has to be a close relative or recognized professional person who confirms the identity."

"It's best that I do it," Liam said, "I don't need to tell her about it do I?"

"No," said Will, "if you would like me to, I will take you to Nenagh and bring you back."

"That's very good of you. Thank you. When should this be done?"

"As soon as possible. How about tomorrow?"

"Okay. There are arrangements I'll have to make here. My own wife does not know yet so there's all that to be done. I will try to get Nora and the two boys of nine and seven to come to our house. It'll be a squash but we'll manage somehow, we live only ten minutes away."

They exchanged telephone numbers and went back into the room.

"Mrs O'Neill, we should leave you and Liam now, but I've told him that we are here to help. He knows how to contact us and I assure you that we'll do everything we can to support you and your family."

"Thank you; I can't believe it all. Tell me it's a dream?"

Back in the office, there was a string of messages for Will. Fred, Robert Mallory and journalists from some of the national newspapers: the *Independent, Irish Times, Irish Mirror, Sun* and the *Corkman,* were among them.

He looked at his watch. It was still only midday.

Siobhan said, "Have you had anything to eat today?"

"Not yet, I haven't," Will replied.

"I'm popping out to get you a sandwich now which I'll bring you. Then I'm going to do a quick shop for us later. I noticed when I went to the flat on my way here that the larder was a bit bare."

"You are my Star in the East and Sun overhead."

"You do things for the one you love."

His first call was to Michael Keegan of the Garda, Roscrea, "I've been to see Mrs O'Neill; she's is in a terrible state, poor lady. Luckily her brother, Liam Brophy, lives only ten minutes away and he was there when I arrived. I've arranged for him to do the formal identification and to bring him down myself to Nenagh tomorrow, probably in the morning. Will this be okay?"

"Yes, I think so. He'll be the brother-in-law of the deceased?"

"Yes. Lives nearby and clearly much involved with the family."

"Okay, I'll fix it, Let me know the approx time. Both vehicles have been lifted from the scene of the accident and are in Garda custody, pending examination. This will not take place until after the New Year holiday, but I or my deputy will keep you informed about all this."

Next Will drafted a Press Statement:

'*The Management of Supercar (Ireland) Ltd regret to announce that a vehicle driven by their employee, Mr Conor O'Neill, on an authorised journey, was involved in an accident with a heavy goods vehicle early today on the M7 near to Roscrea, in which Mr O'Neill sustained fatal injuries. The details and cause of the accident are under examination and scrutiny of the Garda, as is the condition of both vehicles.*

The company requests that the privacy of Mr O'Neill's family should be respected and that no disruption to this privacy by members of the press or public should be made at this difficult and sad time.

No further statement from the company will be issued until the results of the above mentioned examinations have been completed.'

Will rang Fred and read out the draft Press statement.

"Aye, lad, that sums it up fine like. Put it out. I've spoken to the old man, he's very sad and sorry, says he'll call you."

"Yes, there's a message that he called. I'll ring him back soon. I've been to see the widow; very bad scene there but met her brother and am taking him to the hospital at Nenagh tomorrow for him to make the formal identification."

"Bloody hell, you poor bugger, but well done."

Will called Robert Mallory, "Very sorry to hear about all this, Will. Terrible business; Fred has filled me in. Can you tell me about the family? We'll have to see what we can do for them."

"Fred probably hasn't been able to tell you yet that I was with them when you called earlier. Conor's wife, poor thing, is in a bad state. I met her brother and am taking him to identify the body at Nenagh hospital tomorrow. He seems a level-headed sort of guy and lives close by. There are two children, both boys aged nine and seven. That's about all I know at this stage."

"I am sure our car was in proper mechanical order, but what

about the artic lorry? Have you any information about that?"

"Not yet, though I've spoken to the Garda superintendent in charge of the case. He told me that both vehicles are in the custody of the Garda and will be subjected to rigorous examinations. It seems strange to me that there should have been multiple burst tyres at the same time, I'm sure it will all come out in the wash."

Will got back to his flat at about 5.30. Inside, the curtains had been drawn, the heating on and a log fire burning in the grate in his sitting room. Siobhan came out of the kitchen wearing an apron over her jeans, hugged him to her and planted a kiss on his lips.

"Will, my darling one, you've had a hard, gruelling day and I'm immensely proud of you. You've handled everything with bravery, skill and common sense. I've done a little shopping and am about to cook us a cosy dinner together. And I've got something else for you: here please take it."

She handed back his front door key, producing another one from the pocket of her jeans, "See, I've got the key of the door, now."

Will collected Liam Brophy at 9 o'clock the next morning. He was waiting outside his front door.

"My poor sister's in a very bad way. She and my wife are doing their best to comfort the boys. I've arranged with my doctor for a counselling lady to come round later."

"Rest assured, Liam, that I and my company realise the trauma that you are all going through. I have spoken to my Managing Director, who has authorised me to do everything we can to support your family."

At Nenagh General, Will did not go into the hospital, he waited outside in the car. It had only taken half an hour for the form filling and actual identification to take place, but the poor man was in a dreadful state when he came out.

"It was him alright, though almost impossible to recognize. He had been literally crushed like the meat of a sandwich, though I could see the wedding ring on his finger was his. Thanks be to God Nora didn't come. I had a hell of a job stopping her."

"Come on, you need a drink," Will told him.

They stopped at a pub. Liam had two pints of Guinness and a cold pork pie. Will had a drink of water and joined Liam in a pie.

Liam slept most of the way home.

Next Friday, 5th January, Will arrived at Lostock after work. Harry came out of his office to greet him.

"I've found a race for Small Talk," he said, "at Limerick, a week tomorrow. The race is confined to novice horses that have never won a race; just the job. It's at the new course, just outside Patrickswell, only opened a year or so back. There's always been racing at Limerick but the old course at Greenpark was closed a few years ago; this is the first purpose-built course in Ireland for yonks."

"Sounds perfect," said Will.

"Joe schooled him again while you were away. He was delighted with him; jumped like a buck. You can ride him in the morning; he won't need much."

Siobhan appeared, "Hi, lover boy, how's yourself?"

"A bit knackered, but all systems go otherwise. Great that Harry's found a race for Small Talk."

It had been a tough week. The family had arranged the funeral at the Roman Catholic Church of the Sacred Heart at 2.30 in the afternoon of Tuesday 9th January.

Will called Fred to tell him.

Fred said, "That's okay, lad, I'll come over in the morning."

"Fine, I'll meet you, we can have a bit of lunch, then we'll go on to the service. Why don't you stay the night, put in a couple of hours in the office next morning and go back in the afternoon? I am ordering a wreath from the company and liaising with Liam Brophy, Conor's sister, about arrangements with the undertakers. Do you think we should pay for this?"

"Aye, I do. I think it's only right."

"I agree. I'll confirm this with Liam and book you a room at the Dunboyne Castle."

The accident and matters related to it occupied much of Will's time. In off the record conversations with the Garda, it was looking like there were problems with the artic, though Will decided to keep them to himself until he received the official report. While talking to his mother, really to thank her for all the Christmas festivities, he told her about the accident. She was horrified.

No stable runners that Saturday after the successes at

Leopardstown. Will rode out two lots in the morning, first as planned on Small Talk.

"I'm going to let him come up on his own this morning," Harry said. "Just let him enjoy himself."

Harry was right, he didn't need company; he knew what he was about to do within forty yards of the start of the gallop, jig jogging, giving little bucks and feeling full of himself.

Will spoke to him in a quiet voice, "Okay, just hang on a moment, wait, quiet now... okay, let's go."

He took off, not going mad or running away, though settled at a strong pace, head down, having a great time, loving it all the way.

He knew he had to stop as soon as Will took a pull and said, "That's enough now."

In racing parlance, he wouldn't have blown a candle out.

Harry, who had watched from a position a furlong short of the finish, rode up to Will, "So?"

"He could have done it again and probably again. He was just loving it."

His other ride was on a young horse, just turned four. Only broken in as a three-year-old, six months before, he had been spotted with others in a field by Fergy Lynch, who bought him from his former owner for a new client of Harry's. Named Kloof, Will rode him no more than a strong exercise canter alongside Siobhan, on a promising horse called Camogie, who had won a race the previous year, though he had suffered a tendon injury. His comeback was only just starting; he was well and pulled up sound.

"Just thinking ahead about next weekend," Harry said at lunch. "I've had a word with Tim Kerrigan about the POA for our proposed little coup at Limerick. I've also forewarned Joe to make sure he doesn't take any rides elsewhere. As I've said, all our combined bets will be placed off course on the morning of the race by me. I expect most of the other horses will have run more than once – in fact, the more races in which they've run the better. Bookmakers will make their book based on the individual form of each horse. Small Talk has no form, never having run in a race and unless we have a hidden mole in our midst, no information about his ability. My guess is that he will be chalked up at 20/1 or higher; we can expect some of the money to find its way back to the track and the price to contract. That shouldn't worry us as our money will be placed at the bookmakers' opening prices, and I've told Tim and Dad not to go anywhere near the bookies on the course. You'll come, won't you?"

Will looked at Siobhan, and said, "Wild horses – sorry for the pun – wouldn't keep me away though I was just thinking as you were speaking, that as I'm due to visit our small depot in Limerick it could suit me to do some work there on Friday, then stay over for the races on Saturday. I'm thinking out loud now, wondering if your secretary might be allowed a day off to come with me? We have Conor O'Neill's funeral on Tuesday and I expect some of our boys down there as well as from Santry will want to come. It was to the depot in Limerick that Conor was driving last week. Not written in stone; just an idea."

"And not a bad one either. I won't come on Friday, though maybe I can stay over after racing on Saturday. I think Georgie will be back from some exotic place and …"

"Georgie?" asked Siobhan.

"Yes Siobhan, Georgie - remember?"

"No. I thought it was Jenny from Kilkenny?"

"Do catch up. You're way out of date."

Will met Fred off the plane at 12 o'clock on Tuesday.

"I've got a little surprise for you; I've fixed up a little lunch for us at my place; saves us having to go to a pub. You haven't seen where I am living, have you?"

"No, I don't think so. That's kind of you, lad."

Will opened the door and ushered Fred indoors. Siobhan, with an apron over her black dress greeted him.

"This is my other surprise," Will said. "Fred, meet Siobhan Kennedy."

Fred took half a step back, "Well, er yes, it is a surprise and a very pleasant one – hello young lady, I am most pleased to meet you."

Then, turning to Will, "You young devil, you never told me about this one."

Siobhan said, "That may well be, but Will has told me so much about you and how you've helped him that I almost knew you before meeting you, so come in, have a drink and I'll just go and sort out a bit of lunch."

"She's a cracker," Fred said.

Will, Fred and Siobhan took their places towards the rear of the Church of the Sacred Heart. A pleasant-looking young man of about twenty handed them a service sheet on entering the church.

"I'm Connor's cousin," he said.

The coffin, laden with wreaths, stood in the nave. Soon Nora, heavily veiled, escorted by Liam Brophy, followed by her two young sons, immaculately turned out in black suits and ties, hair carefully brushed, moved slowly up the aisle to their places in the front pew, where other close family members, including Liam's wife, were already seated.

Will observed and was pleased that several Supercar staff members from Santry and Limerick were present.

The priest conducted the service in a quiet yet encouraging manner, constantly turning towards the family as if to assure them that Connor, although no longer with them, was in God's good hands.

After the service and burial, during which Nora could no longer hold back her tears, her body shaking with outpouring grief, Will introduced Fred to Liam Brophy.

Liam thanked him and Will for all that the management of Supercar had done; Fred replied on behalf of the company saying how sorry he was but, "We will continue to help and support you and the family in the weeks and months to come."

It was time for them to depart, to leave the family to mourn.

Will said, "Fred why don't we have bit of a chat and show our faces at the office, then I'll take you to your hotel."

"Sounds like a good idea, lad," Fred replied. "This evening, the two of you can have dinner with me at the hotel, unless you have other plans?"

"No Fred, that would be great. We'd love that."

Siobhan said, "Could you drop me off at the flat, Will, I'd like to tidy up lunch and you can come back for me later?"

"Good plan."

"Thanks for coming, Fred," Will said on the way to the airport next morning. "And for dinner last night."

"Aye, a terrible thing for that poor family; you will keep me posted won't you? She's a smashing bird, that one of yours, a right good lass and such fun. I should hang onto that one."

"I'll do my best and thanks as always for your advice. Now, I know you're not a racing man, Fred, but have you ever been to a betting shop?"

"No, can't say I 'ave."

"Okay. Next Saturday, find one, go inside, ignore everybody except the man or girl behind the counter, take a slip of paper from him or her and write on it '£5 to win on Small Talk at Limerick. First show.' Give in the piece of paper and a five pound note in exchange for a duplicate of the slip and leave the shop. Do NOT, on any account, mention to any of your golfing pals or anybody else for that matter about this. Ring me in the office on Monday and I'll tell you what to do next."

Next morning, Wednesday, Siobhan called Will in his office, "It's all right for you, lover boy, sitting in your lovely warm office. Just been riding out and it's brass monkey bloody cold here. Plans more or less finalised for the weekend. I'll come to you tomorrow evening, then we can go down to Limerick together on Friday morning. Drop me off somewhere in Limerick – I'll find plenty to do, don't worry – while you spend as much time as you need at your office. You can pick me up at Perry's hotel and we can go on from there. Harry and, yes it is Georgie, will go straight to the course on Saturday. Tim Kerrigan and his wife will do likewise. I'm not sure yet if Dad's coming or not, though Harry and g.f. will stay down there; we'll need to book a room for them on Saturday night. Harry says that he's seen all the entries for the race on Saturday; most of them he's not worried about, though there are two or three unknown quantities that he'll be having a close look at."

"That sounds okay. I'll try to book us all in at the Dunraven Arms, unless you have other suggestions? If I can't get us in there, I'll skirmish around for somewhere else. Oh, one thing I forgot; please could you ask your brother that, if it's not too late, could he increase my investment on Saturday to 150 euros?"

"Certainly I will. I hope he wins; it'll be an expensive weekend otherwise. I've been to the Dunraven Arms before, though I've never stayed a night there with *anybody* so, yes please, missing you so much, can't wait for tomorrow."

Home alone that evening Will called his mother, "Mum, sorry I haven't rung you much this week. It's been very hectic with the ghastly accident and everything; how are you all?"

"Hello darling, lovely to talk to you. We're all fine though we're thinking about you having to deal with this frightful affair. Is it all over now?"

"Well, the funeral was yesterday. Fred flew over and Siobhan came with me, but it was very sad and emotional, as you can imagine. No, it's not all over; I am expecting the report from the Garda on all the details of the accident, including the roadworthy condition of the vehicles. From what I've heard, off the record, there may have been problems with the lorry but we shall see.

Now there is something else I want to talk to you about; I think the time has come that I must write to Lucille. I took to heart very much what you said over Christmas about Siobhan and my being sure etc, and she has already shown to me, particularly over the past week, how loyal she is.

It was the big New Year Festival meeting at Leopardstown. Her brother's stable, where she operates as his right hand, had several runners – and two winners – with owners and hangers on there and she gave up all that to come and help me, including breaking the news to the poor man's widow, over the whole New Year period. She has, I think, passed any test that there may have been. Tomorrow she is coming with me down to Limerick, where I have a day booked at our office and depot. We are staying the night and going to Limerick races on Saturday where the stable has a fancied runner."

"Well, darling, if you're sure that the time is right, you must follow your instincts. She sounds a really lovely girl and I can't wait to meet her. You must bring her over one weekend soon.

I feel sorry for Lucille, as I'm sure you do, though I agree, it's not fair on her if that is your joint agreement that if anything like this happened, to let each other know. Maybe, as you suggest, she feels the same way, in which case all well and good. It is much better to remain friends rather than fall out if she finds out from a third party. The world is a small place, sometimes."

"Thanks, Mum. Even though it will be a horrid and difficult letter to write, I must do it now. I'll talk to you again after the weekend."

Will sat down there and then to write the letter.

They left early on Friday morning for the drive down to Limerick. Siobhan had arrived, happy and beaming like a ray of sunshine, on a cold winter's evening on Thursday in time for a takeaway supper that Will had ordered.

"You're going to have to come over to Cheshire with me for a family grilling soon," Will said on the way.

"Oh my God, I'll have to go into training for that; I'll appoint you as my trainer. I hope it won't be like the Grand National."

"No, more like the King's Stand at Ascot, short but flat out all the way."

As they drove passed the signpost to Roscrea, Will said, "It was somewhere around here that the accident happened, you know. I wonder what was going through the poor chap's mind, driving along. It doesn't bear thinking about."

"You can leave me here," Siobhan said as they drove into Limerick, "I've got my book, knitting, your office telephone number, and a 'For Sale' sign to hang round my neck, so you don't have to worry about me."

"Okay, lovely one. Call me at the office around 5 o'clock and I'll tell you how I'm getting on."

It was a good move to spend some time at the depot. Will had a lengthy meeting with Jim McDonald, the young manager he had appointed two months previously. He had not been there since mid-December. Christmas and New Year more so had been frantically busy and successful in spite of the Connor O'Neill tragedy. What's more, they had held their own against the competition. They discussed together about acquiring or renting larger premises to accommodate more permanent cars in time for the summer season; Will asked Jim to put feelers out and to do a costing exercise for another (a) 12 and (b) 24 more cars split into different categories.

"Whatever we do, I'll guarantee to keep you supplied from Santry in the meantime," he said.

He spent time with the office staff, thanking those who had come up for the funeral and then drove out to Shannon to talk to those on the desk, coming away pleased with performance and morale.

Back in the depot office, Jim said, "There's been a lady on the telephone for you. Said she'd call back in half an hour."

Will looked at his watch. It was a quarter past five, "God, I didn't realise the time. Unless there's anything else that we need to talk about, I'll be on my way. I'll be in Santry on Monday if you want me – otherwise, I'll be down again in a month or before if you see anything with a bit more space. Well done, by the way; I'm excited about progress here, just let me know how you get on."

He found Siobhan in the comfortable drawing room of Perry's Hotel with a cup of tea, a plate with two scones, butter and jam.

"Oh, good," he said, "you won't be wanting any dinner tonight, will you?"

"Listen, I was about to ask for something a bit stronger. I've been so busy shopping; I've had no lunch, but look what I've found for you."

Out of a designer box, she produced a tumbler-size cut glass with W engraved on it.

"This is to remind you if you're having a drink without me," she said.

"You are my beautiful, lovely Princess. Thank you and I hope I never have to use it. Come on, give me a kiss and let's go."

Adare, a very pretty and old, typically Irish, small town, was only about fifteen miles from Limerick and they arrived at the Dunraven Arms in good time. A young porter boy took their luggage, consisting of Will's smart new suitcase and Siobhan's not so smart holdall type bag, up to their very elegant, well-furnished room with a huge poster bed.

"Mother of God, I'll get lost in that!"

"Not with me on your tail, you won't. Do you realise, this is our first proper away time together? Let's take our time, go down to the bar, have a drink, and choose a table in a corner of the dining room where, in our own world, we'll be entirely alone. Later we'll come back up and be the best lovers this bed has ever accommodated. I love you, Princess."

It had taken him a long time to say those words.

"I love you, 007."

In the morning, daylight dimly showing through the curtained windows, Will stirred first. Siobhan opened first one sleepy eye, then the other. She adored what she saw. He reached for her; she responded immediately, their bodies melding together, making slow, passionate love until the moment came when the sun, moon and stars converged in a silent explosion of ecstasy.

At 9 o'clock, a knock on the door; in came breakfast, wheeled in on a trolley with the Irish Examiner on top.

"Please could you put the breakfast over there on the table by the window, and I'll have the paper here," said Siobhan, from under the bed covers.

"Oh no, you won't," said Will, grabbing it out of her hand.

"Let's have a look now. We're in the fourth race at 2.30. Twelve runners, number 9 Small Talk; H. Kennedy, J. Maguire. Not featured in the betting forecast. Five quoted at odds of 7/4, 5/2, 4/1, 8/1 and 100/8, 20/1 others. Splendid. The first race is at 1 p.m.; Harry suggested we get there on the early side. The course is only five miles away; we have masses of time, though if we leave soon after 12, I wouldn't mind having a good look at the track, never having been there before."

"I think I could be ready by then," said Siobhan, stretching her arms above her head and naked body.

"God don't do that or we'll never get out of here. Go and wash your face or something."

"It's not just my face that needs washing."

The new Limerick racecourse is right-handed with a steep climb on the far side, followed by a downhill section leading to the straight on a slight incline. It lies outside the small town of Patrickswell. Will went for a quick walk around part of the course, reporting that the going was just on the soft side of good. First to arrive after them were Harry and his girlfriend.

"Hi both of you, had a good night, I hope? Dad rang last night, Siobhan; he is coming today and has managed to get a room at the hotel; he will be with us for dinner tonight. Now Siobhan, you remember Georgie, *don't you*?" and to Will, "Will, this is Georgie Sullivan, Georgie, Will Carpenter."

Georgie, tall, light brown hair tied in a ponytail, widely spaced blue eyes and dressed in designer jeans and a mock suede three-quarter length coat, a proper good looker, Will thought, though he never expected anything else.

"Hello Will," she said.

"Hello Georgie," he said.

"Right, to business. Half the field in our race you can discount. Two others, like ours, haven't had a run before; we need to have a good look at them in the paddock. One of these two, I suspect can be overlooked, knowing his trainer but, of course, you can never be exactly sure. The other could be a danger, that leaves four including Small Talk, so in effect, three.

One, Robony, has been placed 3rd once but beaten a long way. Two, Namib, who has been second but the form of that race hasn't worked out well in that the winner was beaten out of sight the next time it ran. Leaving one other: Village Boy, this horse has been second and third, but on all known form, he wouldn't get to within fifty yards of Pelican Point, who won that descent race at Leopardstown last week.

We already know that Small Talk beat Pelican Point on our home gallop. A gallop is not a race though in my view we should win. However there are eight flights of hurdles to be jumped, and all sorts of things can go wrong in the course of a race. Joe has schooled our horse twice himself and is happy with his jumping and Will, here, has ridden him in all his recent serious work, what do you think, Will?"

"I've told you before, Harry, I've never ridden a horse on which I have felt so happy and confident. I've been out on the track; the going is near perfect."

Harry saw Tim and Vicky Kerrigan arriving and beckoned them over. Introductions made, he outlined what he had just been saying and that it was all systems go.

"Tim and Vicky have a big dairy farm in Co. Carlow," Harry explained to Will. "We first met when I was at Willie Moore's. He was the first person to send me a horse when I set up on my own, for which I am very grateful."

"Harry says that you've been riding Small Talk in his work," Tim said.

"Yes, that's right. He's a smashing horse; I really love him. I can usually only get to Lostock at weekends as, unfortunately, I have a proper day job."

"Oh, what's that?"

"I manage the Supercar car rental business in Ireland," Will said.

"Gosh, you're a big cheese. Did I not read something in the papers the other day involving a car from your company?"

"Yes, I am afraid you did. One of our drivers was killed in an accident with an articulated lorry. Terrible business and we are waiting for the official Garda report on the incident. I am no big cheese, by the way."

In the crowd, Will suddenly caught sight of Jim McDonald, his Limerick depot manager with whom had spent much of the previous day.

He wandered over to him, "Well, fancy seeing you here, Jim."

"I could say the same to you, Will. I am a local man and, as you may already know, there's not a man in Co Limerick who'll want to miss a day at the races, but why are you here?"

"Just with a party of friends, We stayed last night near here. Look, Jim, there's a horse in the 4th race, Small Talk. I've been riding this horse on Saturday mornings. He should start at long odds and has a fair each-way chance. I wouldn't put you off having a small bet on him, but if you want to, please on the Tote only – not with the bookies. I'll tell you why later."

"That's our local depot manager, I was with yesterday," he told Siobhan, going back to the others, now joined by Garech who had just arrived.

Joe Maguire had a busy day coming with three other rides plus Small Talk. Both Harry and Will watched him closely in the race before theirs; it would be a disaster if he had a fall and was hurt. All was well; he finished a respectable third.

It was time. Harry collected the saddle; Joe having weighed out. Will went with him to help him saddle up.

"Come into the paddock with us Will. I'd like to have you there."

Watching the horses walk round, Harry said, "I've seen nothing to change my mind on what I was saying earlier."

The jockeys came out, Joe touching his cap to the assembled little group.

"You've schooled the horse and know him," Harry said to him.

"Will, you've ridden him in all his work, got anything that might help Joe?"

"No, the only thing I'd say is, don't disappoint him. He likes being in company and settles fine with other horses around him. He doesn't like being left behind."

Jockeys mounted; they left the paddock to canter down to the start.

"My job's done now. Can't do anymore; it's up to the pair of them," Harry said.

The race itself was something of an anti-climax. Joe settled Small Talk well in mid-division, the horse lobbing along happily. Possibly the only problem being at the first flight of hurdles which came only 150 yards after the start and was a bit crowded. Joe got a good stride however and all was well. From about halfway he moved steadily through the field to lead between the last two flights, made a good jump at the last and drew away to win comfortably, never off the bridle, by four lengths. No more, it seemed, than an exercise gallop. Harry and Will remained outwardly silent throughout the race. It was the suspense after all the planning and work at home that had born fruit, as well as the trainer's advice to the owner to have a decent bet. Race over, they boiled over. Lots of hugs and kisses. Out of the corner of his eye, Will saw a small party of Irishmen jumping up and down, shouting, arms waving; in the centre was Jim McDonald.

Joe Maguire steered Small Talk led by his lad, Vince, into the winners' enclosure.

"It was easy like you said. He's very intelligent and competitive. Likes to be in front when it matters. He'll stay further than two miles if necessary, but this trip's fine for him at the moment. Should go far, this one."

The champagne flowed. Harry, overcome and delighted with the win, accepted the congratulations from Tim and Vicky, plus the family.

"I am very proud of my brother and," turning to Will, "my lover," Siobhan said.

"I am a bit surprised Fergy isn't here. He seems to have been present each time I've been racing recently," Will said.

"I forgot to tell you; he rang yesterday having seen the overnight declarations for today. He said he had a very bad cold and couldn't come today. I told him that the horse was in good form, well, and I hoped he'd run well. Actually, it may sound unkind but I'm glad in a way that he's not here. I expect he had a little bit on him, though."

Still on a high, they were five for dinner at the hotel that night, the Kerrigans having left to go back home on the Carlow/Wicklow border.

"I hope they're not spotted by the Garda on the way home," Harry said, as they left the course.

They were shown to a round table in the centre of the dining room; Will seated on Georgie's right between her and Garech, Harry with Georgie next to him, with Siobhan on his left next to her father.

Garech said, "Will, sorry not to have brought it up this afternoon; I was very sad that you couldn't come to Leopardstown and the reason for it. An awful thing to have happened and dreadful for you having to deal with it all. I'm very sorry. Has everything been sorted out now?"

"Yeah thanks, it was a bad business. No. it hasn't been sorted yet. We've had the funeral and all that, which Siobhan very sweetly came to with me, though we have not yet had the report from the Garda and the longer it takes, the more I think there's a problem. Not with our vehicle, I'm certain of that, however, the gist of the off the records comments I've had from the Garda superintendent I've been speaking to is that there is or are problems with the artic."

"No business or mine but if you find you need legal advice, do call me. Your company in England may well have connections here through their own lawyers, otherwise, I do know all the top people here."

"Thanks, Garech, very much for that. When we set up the company here, we engaged Fitzsimmons and Maitland, who did a fine job for us."

"I know Bob Maitland well. They are an excellent firm on corporate and property matters; probably good otherwise as well, though, as I say, do let me know if I can help."

"I certainly will and thanks again."

"So glad you've come back from wherever you've been and to meet you," Will said, turning to Georgie.

"You too. It's been quite a long trip, this one, but Harry's quite capable of looking after himself – or so he tells me."

"I'm not sure about that. He'll be getting cross with me for taking too much of his housekeeper's time. Where is it you've been and what for? Gosh, sorry, that sounds frightfully nosey."

"No it doesn't; Harry's not cross at all with you; says you've helped a lot with the horses. I work for an upmarket travel company in Merrion Square. It's called Global, sounds rather pompous, though I suppose it is pretty global now. We look after and advise clients on houses, villas, chalets, yachts, in all sorts of exotic places, as well as recommending hotels. We fix up and make reservations, bookings etc for individual clients, as well as some corporate work. That's how I met Harry, Garech being a number one type client. I've just been on a trip round all our main ski resorts in Europe, checking on chalets we manage on behalf of the owners, as well as being on the lookout for new ones.

"That's exciting. Hope you managed to get in some skiing as well."

"Certainly I did. You can lead me to the water and I'll drink it."

"Do you concentrate on Europe or take in other areas as well?"

"No, I go all over really. There are three of us at the moment and we cover everywhere that the firm has an active interest. We all write our experiences and recommendations for our company brochure and magazine, which is published twice a year. I'm off to the eastern Caribbean in a few weeks' time, which will be a new venture for me. I'm sure Garech will be able to mark my card there."

"Yes, I'm sure he will," said Will.

Upstairs and getting ready for bed, Siobhan said, "I saw you having a good chat to the girlfriend. What do you make of her?"

"She's bloody attractive – don't be an arse and look at me like that – I got the faint impression that she's quite keen on herself and maybe thinks that Harry is quite a catch, and might suit her nicely, thank you. Were you joking when you said you didn't remember her?"

"I think she may have come with others who were staying the night after a party we'd all been to, though whether she was number one girlfriend that night I can't remember."

"She works for a travel company called Global in Dublin, has just returned from a trip round European ski resorts and is off to the West Indies in a few weeks. She told me that your father would 'mark her card'. "

"Did you tell her about your connection there?"

"No."

"Why not?"

"She didn't ask me – or if I'd ever been skiing."

They all agreed to have breakfast together in the morning at about 9 ish. Both Harry and Will had seen their Sunday paper by then. Small Talk had been returned at 100/6 Starting Price,

"That's about 16 ½ to 1," Will said. "I wonder what price Harry's team got us?"

He didn't have to wait long. Harry rang on the hotel's internal room-to-room telephone.

"We averaged 28 to 1," he said. "The bookies woke up very late to what was going on, so there was a flood of money coming back to the course seven minutes before the race. Very few bets on the course, though the odds came tumbling down from about 25/1 to 16/1 in the last few minutes. What are your plans for today? Dad has kindly said he'll take Georgie back to Dublin."

"We haven't worked it out yet, I'll let you know at breakfast. Very good news about the SP and well done you for fixing it all."

"What do you want to do, Honey Bunch?"

"The bugger of it is that my car's at your place, so I suppose I'd better come with you and cry all the way home on my own."

"Or, I could take you home and we could both leave early tomorrow, and you could collect your car then. It would be good to have a weekend post-mortem with Harry. I must be in my office, though, by 9 at the latest."

"Please let's do that. I can't bear to be without you."

Goodbyes all round after breakfast though not before Georgie had come rushing up to Will, "You rotten so and so. You never told me you were half West Indian."

"Probably because I'm not. I do have a very old ancestral connection and have been to a number of the islands as a deckhand on a banana boat, but that's about all."

"But surely you must have met people you could tell me about and been to many of the hotels etc?"

"Deckhands don't normally get invited to smart hotels, though if I can think of anybody who could be useful to you, of course, I'll let you know. Harry will know how to contact you."

"Oh, thank you so much," she said, with a kiss on both cheeks.

"Goodbye, you two," said Garech, "good seeing you again, Will, and don't forget what I told you. A very successful and great fun weekend, hope to see you both again soon."

"We're coming back to Lostock," Siobhan called out to Harry.

"I'm so glad that you're getting on well with Dad. He can be a tricky old bugger, though I can tell that he likes you."

"I had a good conversation with him last night at dinner. He very kindly offered to help with any advice needed over any complications on the O'Neill case."

"Oh Will, my lovely man, you're making me so happy," she said, snuggling as close to him as possible in the car with her hand stroking his thigh.

"Careful, sweetheart, we don't want to end up in a ditch. I think my little bet on our horse yesterday has won me over 4,000 euros."

"Aren't you a clever boy, I'm thrilled for you."

Harry had got back to Lostock just before them, he was checking his mail and the answering machine. Not much in the mail, just a string of messages, the main one from Fergy offering congratulations to what he called "the Kennedy clan", who, he had been told, "were present in force".

"Fergy has spies everywhere," Will said. "He's probably miffed, but if I can't help that. I'll give him a sweetener to keep him happy. He's a good man to have on our side and a very good judge of a young horse."

The letter and report from the Garda arrived in Monday's mail addressed by name to William Carpenter, Manager of Supercar (Ireland) Ltd. The covering letter, written and signed by Micheal Keegan, Superintendent, explained that the Supercar vehicle, although catastrophically damaged, showed no abnormalities contrary to a certificate of roadworthiness and was exonerated from any blame for the accident. A post-mortem examination of the driver, the late Connor O'Neill, showed no alcohol or prohibited substances. On the other hand, the articulated lorry owned by Crossway Transport of Cork showed a number of irregularities including four of the eight rear tyres and one of the two front tyres having below the legal amount of tread and faults in the braking system. Two of the tyres on the tractor also had insufficient tread and the tachograph system was faulty and well passed its service date. The driver tested clear. The letter went on to say that the report was being forwarded to a higher authority with the recommendation that the owners should be prosecuted for a number of charges including manslaughter.

Will read the full ten page report, complete with photographs – some of them gruesome and terrible in the extreme, detailed analyses, columns of figures with test results, and a very thorough and factual document.

He called Pat Byrne on the intercom, "Pat, please will you do a thorough search on anything you can find about Crossway Transport in Cork. Check in all directories, registered company statements, advertisements, transport associations, plus anything you can find through any local sourcer that you have. It's to do with the accident. I've received a pretty damning report though I'm glad to say we are in the clear."

He rang Fred, "I've got the report and covering letter on the accident. We are completely clear, however, it's damning to put it mildly on the lorry and its owners, Crossway Transport in Cork. I'll fax it to you. Give me a call when you've read it. I haven't told the old man yet as I think it's best coming from me when we've had a chat."

"Aye, I'll do that and call you back. Sounds bad. Why don't I send it on to the old man and say that you'll be calling him later. Forewarned is forearmed. Now you asked me to speak to you today about what you suggested I did to ruin my Saturday afternoon's golf game. I am sorry to say I made a stupid mistake: instead of £5, I wrote £10. Didn't like the shop much; stank of cigarette smoke with all the walls covered with sheets of newspapers with lists and rows of figures."

"How very careless of you. Big smack, though it may have not done you any harm. Go back to the dirty, smelly shop. Give the copy of the piece of paper to the shop assistant; he or she should count out two hundred and fifty smackers, maybe a bit more, to put into your clammy hands. Carefully conceal it on your person so that none of the unwashed scoundrels in the shop can nick any of it while you make your escape. Okay, perhaps you're right about the OM."

CHAPTER 14

That same Monday the sun had started to lower towards the western horizon as Lucille left the office in Holetown to drive home to Uplands. She saw the letter in Will's handwriting that she knew so well amongst the mail that Sherry had put on the silver tray on the hall table, five days after Will had posted it in his office mailbox in Santry.

Sometimes, she said to herself, When you are really looking forward to something, when it happens you worry about it.

It was the first letter that she had received from Will since their Christmas telephone call, three weeks previously. As always, she took it to "their" room, sat down and opened it.

A while later, having dried her eyes and calmed down, she replaced the letter in the envelope.

I suppose, this is what I've half been expecting, she said, again to herself.

She went downstairs; her father was out on the plantation and her mother was sitting down reading the newspaper.

"Will's got a new girlfriend," she said, holding out the letter.

Harriet Todd rose from her chair, came to her daughter, and drew her to herself, holding her tight, letting the tears flow.

"You poor darling, I'm so sorry. After such a long time, I suppose it was inevitable."

"He's kept his word maybe better than I have though he's the one I really love. I didn't say too much at Christmas as I had a sort of feeling about this. I suspect that he's known the girl, Siobhan she's called, for a while and didn't want to write until he was absolutely sure."

"In some ways, my darling, it's better this way. You can now draw a line. I'm not saying you should forget and there is nothing to forgive; you have both behaved honourably to each other and, I feel, you will remain lifelong best friends. I am sure he'll be back in Barbados, you know, sometime. Now, if you want to, you can go forward with Josh with a clear conscience and open mind. He's a lovely chap; Dad and I like him. Of course we liked Will hugely, however, all we want is the best for you."

Two days later Lucille went up to the same room and wrote to Will. 'My dearest, darling Will,' she started, thinking that's how she always addressed him so why should I stop now?

'Your lovely, sweetest letter is in front of me as I write. Typical of you to be so kind and thoughtful as always. You have kept your word and I am sure that you would not have written until you were absolutely sure. I wish you and your lovely sounding girlfriend all the very best in every way, I hope you will bring her to Barbados sometime soon and that we can meet up and be friends. You will always occupy a very large piece of my heart, come what may.

I can tell you I have made a friend, and I mean friend, with a young lawyer. He's a Bajan and has been living in Canada training to be a lawyer for several years, however, he's now back in Barbados and practising. He's called Josh Taylor; thought you would like to know. The parents like him. On other matters, I am no longer working for Max in his office in Bridgetown. I felt I needed a change and have got a super job working as administrator and PA to the partners of The Real Estate Company in Holetown. It is the oldest and most successful property company on the island and really good people to work for. Max, needless to say, has a small interest in the business and is on the Board and I do see him from time to time. On the horse front, Fawn Princess is the best race mare in Barbados and keeps winning races. I think, from what Max says, this will be her last season. She'll make a fabulous broodmare. May Go Twice's racing career is almost certainly over. He has won five or six races though he had a minor injury a few months ago and has lost some of his pace. Max is thinking of giving him to Tony Knowles to make him into a Polo Pony. Your 'friend' Frank Doune still works for Tony, I think, however, he seems to pop up in different places as well. I avoid him like the plague.

Do keep in touch, darling Will.

Your ever, ever loving

Lucille.'

Will's first reaction on reading her letter was one of guilt. Had he let her down? Then, what would she have done under similar circumstances? The same, surely? Should I call her on the telephone? No, he thought, it might make it worse for her. We are best, best friends for life. Let's leave it at that for now. Which is exactly what he did. Sending in note form what he had written down: reaction, thoughts and all, signing it:

'*Love you always,*
Will'

Sven Goran, of Danish/Jewish extraction though born and bred in Barbados, his father having arrived as a young man from Canada to which country the family had fled just before the outbreak of WW2. From small beginnings his father progressed to owning three hotels along the south coast. Sven, ambitious and academically bright, was expected by his father to go into the hotel business, however, he decided it wasn't for him. He foresaw the expansion of Barbados as an international tourist destination; owning three small hotels was fine though the big money was in property and real estate.

"Daddy, I'm sorry but the hotel business is not for me long-term. There are opportunities out there and I want to branch out on my own. Bjorn is much more suited to this life than I am and, being six years younger than me, will fit in with you very well. It's not as if I am leaving the island; there is a great deal happening here and I want to be a part of it."

His father was disappointed and said, "Okay, if that's what you want to do, I'm not going to stand in your way and there'll always be a place for you if it doesn't work out."

Sven already had a plan in his mind; there was only one properly managed company engaged in real estate and property management on the island, The Real Estate Company Ltd owned by a Barbadian family. There was room for another. The accountant for the Goran hotels, a partner in the local branch of one of the international big five companies, Stuart Foulds, in his late fifties, shared Sven's views. Sven and Stuart formed a new estate management company. They looked for one other partner to join them, Stuart taking early retirement yet keeping his pension, to avoid conflict of interest.

Johnny Arthur, a fun-loving, popular gay bachelor who, on the death of his father, had sold the family plantation, fitted the bill; he agreed to come in as the third partner as long as he didn't have to do much work. This suited the other two; Johnny already had a share in the sophisticated Alexandra's nightclub, Barbados' equivalent of Annabel's and, not being flauntingly gay, was a good 'spare' man at dinner parties, proving an excellent ambassador for the real estate business.

With a smart office in Fitts Village on the west coast about halfway between Bridgetown and Holetown, the new company flourished. Named Foulds, Arthur & Goran, commonly known as FAG, it made successful inroads into the fast-expanding tourist and up-market residential property development on the island, proving that Sven's farsighted view of such was 100% correct. Maybe his European, Jewish background, okay a generation ago, helped to hone his shrewd mind. The speed at which it was happening was startling. Not only projects like the Robert Trent Jones golf course and luxury villas at Westmoreland, now up and running, but also, Sven had seen plans submitted by a consortium of Barbadian businesses for the development and construction of a Port Grimaud style marina, luxury houses and condominiums of even greater opulence at a site north of Speightstown. It irked him considerably that he had not been a part of the original consortium.

An idea came to him as to how an extension of the project could work to the advantage of both FAG and the consortium, his late aunt's husband, Henrik Hansen, had founded a small property investment company in Denmark in the 1930s. Not being on the Jewish side of Sven's family, he had stuck it out during the war, the rumour being that he became more than a little friendly with the occupying German forces after the annexation in December 1939. The company, Mandrik A/S certainly grew rapidly. After the war, it expanded more into blocks of flats and offices, two hotels in Copenhagen, another in Paris and a small up-market one in Venice, just off the Grand Canal. In the 1960s they spread into the Mediterranean operating luxury yachts based in Turkey and Split, Croatia for cruises in the Adriatic. It was the cruising part of the business that interested Sven.

He asked Johnny Arthur to come to the office. The three partners discussed Sven's plan, following which Sven called his cousin Vagn, who now headed up the business in Copenhagen.

"Vagn", he said after the usual hellos, how are you. "I have an idea that might just interest you. If it does, I suggest coming to see you in Copenhagen to discuss it."

He went on to describe his plan for building and operating a luxury motor yacht to accommodate a maximum of twenty passengers for cruises to the southern Windward Islands as far as Tobago, out of the new marina being constructed by the Barbadian consortium at Port St. Charles.

"Sounds an interesting one, Sven. Send me a detailed plan, excluding the cost of the vessel – I have knowledge and contacts who can supply this. I will examine everything, talk to those here on the cruise operations side and come back to you shortly. If it looks positive, I look forward to seeing you in Copenhagen."

A month later, Vagn on the telephone to Sven, "Looks good. You better come."

He came away with a deal that, subject to a favourable feasibility study by an internationally known firm, Mandrik would put up enough of the equity with a maximum of 35% provided that FAG contributed at least enough to ensure a controlling interest.

Johnny Arthur agreed to put in 5% of his own money. Meetings with the firm's bankers resulted in a guarantee of 17% for FAG's contribution spread between the firm and a bank loan, leaving a further 43% to be found.

Sven called Max Geary who he knew to be the coordinator of the consortium for the marina project, "Hi, Max, Sven Goran here."

"Hello, Sven, I hear good things about FAG going well?"

"Okay though not in your league, man."

"That's bullshit, I'm just a tiny ripple in a big pond. What can I do for you today?"

"We have a plan. Can I come and show you?"

"Sure, you do that."

"Seems a terrific idea, Sven," Max said at their meeting. "Very well thought out and enterprising of you. You'll forgive me for saying that I need to examine it very carefully and say to you that I will have to discuss it with my financial and legal advisors. You will also be aware that I am the coordinator for the marina development project consortium."

"Yes, of course I am and that ground has been broken which is great news. Our project is dependent upon the main one though it will be a significant contributor to its success.

Max took his time over the next few days examining the plan in great detail. From both his lawyers and accountants he received the thumbs up, subject to the regulation risk proviso. Max made his decision.

He called Sven, "Hello Sven. This is Max. I've had a good look at your plan and discussed all eventualities with my financial and legal advisors who have raised no objections other than the obvious. It is an excellent and innovative project and I hope very much that it works for you. I am, as you know, very heavily involved with the main development project at Port St. Charles which is of greater risk than yours. I also have to say that your project is dependent on the success of the other one. This brings in a double risk assessment for me. Therefore, I cannot, at this stage become an active participant. Should an opportunity occur at a future date please do contact me, although I realise I shall have missed the founding partners' metaphorical boat. Thanks, indeed, for thinking of me."

"That's okay, Max. Thanks for calling and I quite understand. I'll keep you informed of progress. I and the others are most optimistic, however, I quite see where you're coming from. We both need a little luck so here's hoping."

'Damn and shit,' he said to himself, having put down the telephone.

Sven had better luck with Tom Canon employing the same tactics. Tom's first reaction, Sven having gone through the project at their first meeting was, "Okay, Sven, supposing I like the idea in principle, what's in it for me and my company."

"Not sure what you mean by that, Tom."

"What I mean is, if I, on behalf of my business, agreed to participate, I would require a guarantee of supplying 100% of all the f & b on board the yacht or yachts for a period of at least five years, with a renewal for a further period provided we had maintained our high standard of all our products."

"I see no reason why that should not be possible," said Sven. "Knowing your company, I would think that you could supply all that is needed in those areas, subject to detailed examination by the experts and, yes, I think we could agree in principle to that."

"Good", replied Tom. "The other lot, on the main development, have approached me but would give no such guarantee, saying that all requirements would go out to tender on a regular basis, leaving it open for suppliers to submit excessively low prices to suit their cash flow and disrupt order flow. We are very price and quality sensitive and know we are highly competitive at all times. I will be back to you as soon as my team and I have thoroughly examined all your documents."

"Thank you, Tom. I wait to hear from you."

He did, a week later. Canon & Co came in for 20%.

Trevor Chapman was rich and English. He had always been the latter but not the former. Born and brought up in Stepney, his father had been a railway porter; his mother worked shifts at Covent Garden market. Trevor was a bright child, did well at school and developed a phenomenal memory. Sports and games wise he became an avid follower, though not a participator, in most major sports. He had a most unathletic appearance. Leaving school at sixteen, he decided to become a London taxi driver to make use of his memory. He took a three-year training and driving course, surviving multiple tests and written examinations, which he funded with a little help from his parents; mainly he earned it from taking any form of casual work he could find. By the age of twenty, he was fully qualified and on the road – or rather, street. He worked very long hours, first leasing, then buying his taxi, then another which he, in turn, leased out. Ten years later he owned large fleets of black cabs, a servicing garage and a wife, Cynthia.

After another ten years passed. He owned the largest fleet of black cabs in the city, three garages servicing private cars as well as taxis, the same wife and a daughter, Tracey.

A decade after that, he owned no black cabs, no garages, the same wife and daughter, many millions in his bank account, a house on the Thames near Henley and a membership of Sunningdale golf club, a game that suited his frame. Years of wedging his body behind the wheel of a London taxi followed by many more years behind his desk at his South Kensington HQ had seen to that. Football – soccer and rugby – racing, tennis, boxing, he followed them all with great interest. He did play golf, though, with a useful handicap of fifteen which he chose not to seek to alter; having taken a series of lessons with the pro at Sunningdale, this became his main hobby.

A photograph, occupying pride of place in the Henley house of him receiving a golf trophy with Cynthia by his side, demonstrated that poor Tracey, the daughter, stood no chance of growing into a lithe, tall fashion model. Their only child, the apple of especially her father's eye, a sweet-natured, friendly girl just turned seventeen of average intelligence, had not excelled on the games field, apart from becoming goalkeeper for the hockey second eleven at her expensive private girl's boarding school.

Each year, to kick off the winter season and to celebrate Christmas, FAG hosted a cocktail party in the ballroom at Sandy Lane hotel – also used for conferences, seminars, prizegiving's and wedding receptions, the hotel guests were invited together with notables from the world of business on the island, sportsmen both local and overseas, plus celebrities from the entertainment world. Johnny Arthur played the flamboyant host part, Sven the ferret one.

Trevor, Cynthia and Tracey were on their second Christmas holiday at Sandy Lane. Sven had spotted them the previous year and had made a point of introducing himself and the services of FAG, if and when required.

The following year he moved in again; he said, "Hello Mr Chapman, Mrs Chapman and how are you, young Tracey looking so pretty this evening? How good to see you all here again."

The conversation continued building up to, "I just thought I ought to let you know before anyone else gets to hear and, in case you might possibly be interested, that my firm has managed to acquire one of the most desirable plots of land on the Royal Westmoreland Golf Course with, naturally private access and space on Mullins Beach."

"Ooh, that sounds nice, Mr Goran," enthused Cynthia Chapman.

"Please call me Sven," he replied.

"Perhaps we could take a look?" asked Trevor.

The land upon which the house was subsequently built and given the name of Palm Heart, became the result of Sven Goran's endeavours.

In December the following year, it was nearly ready for occupancy. Trevor and Cynthia plus Tracey of course, decided to spend Christmas at Sandy Lane and move into Palm Heart in the New Year, once they had settled the placing of the new furniture and decorative items.

"We'll stay until at least March," Trevor said, at the FAG party.

"Ooh, can't tell you how excited we are, aren't we Tracey darling? Trevor can't wait to get on the golf course. Thank you Sven, for introducing him to the pro – such a nice man," burbled Cynthia.

Sven said, "I am very happy that it's all finished and that you are all so pleased. By way of a little thank you, I would like to take all three of you to dinner at The Cliff one night this week to suit you."

"Ooh, that would be lovely, wouldn't it Trev?"

Trevor said that it would be and suggested Thursday.

"Fine, I'll leave you to talk to all the others here tonight and I'll see you on Thursday," then catching hold of Sheila Griffiths, he asked, "Have you met Sheila Griffiths and her husband Bruce. Bruce is the top orthopaedic surgeon on the island and Sheila runs her own super riding school close by here at their lovely home in St. Thomas. Bruce and Sheila please meet Trevor and Cynthia with their daughter Tracey. Trevor and Cynthia are just about to move into their fabulous new house at Westmoreland."

"Did he say you have a riding school?" asked Cynthia.

"Yes, that's right," replied Sheila, with a smile, though inwardly groaning with a glance towards Tracey.

"Ooh, Tracey would love to learn to ride, wouldn't you darling?"

"Yes, Mummy, I really would."

"Well then, send her along to me. I have a novice class at 9 o'clock most mornings. If she's coming in a taxi, all local drivers know where we live."

"That would be lovely then."

As the Griffiths moved on, Sheila whispered to her husband, "God, as if I haven't enough problems. What on earth am I going to put her on?"

At The Cliff restaurant, seated at a super table overlooking the sea, dinner ordered, all pleasantries over, Sven said, "I am so very pleased that you could come; as I said, this is to say thank you on behalf of Stuart and myself, not to mention Johnny who you've met each year at the party, for the trust and faith you've given to us. I can tell you with all sincerity and many years of experience that we'll not let you down.

Now, there is something else that I would like you to know about; I have seen plans of a major up-market development where the present Heywood's hotel stands, north of Speightstown.

Heywood's was built in a hurry without proper thought and needs to be knocked down even quicker. The new plan incorporates private residencies, luxury condominiums and, most importantly, a Port Grimaud style marina, able to take ocean going super-duper motor and sailing yachts. Government approval has been granted and the construction has started. Me and a few others have in mind a project to make use of the marina and its facilities; we plan to order, to our own specification, a luxury motor yacht to accommodate up to twenty passengers and to operate serious top market cruises to the southern windward islands as far as Tobago. There is no other service operating at this scale on this route from any other island in the Caribbean.

We are already in negotiations with yacht builders on both sides of the Atlantic, capable of building what we require. Of course it is expensive; there is money around on the island and, as I said earlier, considerable interest. You are the first people I have talked to about it other than our original co-founders. I have not brought any papers or plans with me, however, if the project appeals to you, I can come back with the whole prospectus, including a Feasibility Study that we have already financed by an internationally known company in this field."

"Fascinating, Sven, thank you for telling us about it. It's good of you to give me this advance information and the opportunity to be involved. I have spent all of my adult life working very hard until the last couple of years and am now enjoying my retirement. Let me see all the bumf; I'll read through it and we'll have another chat after that."

"Thanks Trevor. In the meantime, this is totally confidential. I will arrange for the prospectus to be sent up to you tomorrow."

"Thanks. I shan't tell a soul."

A few days later, after another meeting during which Trevor asked a number of questions, including, most importantly, who were the founding and already committed investors, he agreed to becoming a 20% shareholder.

Frank Doune had left home probably for the last time, several months before; now he lived in a room rented from an elderly widow in Bagatelle Terrace, St Thomas, only a ten minute ride on his newly acquired motorbike from the Knowles yard at Glendale.

His daily routine was to work from 7 a.m. to 10 a.m. with the ponies. On practise and match days, he was on duty at the ground at Holders. All other times, he worked for Walton on the water. Frank had matured physically and developed mentally. He had woken up enough to realise that he was not going to achieve his goals by showing off the tree trunks that rested on his shoulders. He had to conceal them. He was now an accomplished rider, had played several chukkas of polo, had learnt a lot from Knowles' head man, Joel, and from riding the home-bred, superbly trained Argentinean imports. A red letter day happened when Tony had a fall in practise the day before a match just after Christmas and twisted his knee; Frank was promoted to take his place in the team. From mid-morning to 4 p.m. he worked with Walton and Lucky on the water.

Residents of all the houses on Westmoreland estate and golf course had exclusive use of a private cabana on Mullins Beach, a facility of which the family Chapman made full use. Frank, on his daily tours by boat of all the beaches looking for water or jet ski clients, spotted the new family occupying one of the cabanas. The next day, dressed in brightly coloured shorts and a yellow shirt with the top three buttons unfastened, he walked along the beach to the Chapman cabana.

"Good morning," he said. "I not bother you but as a resident of Royal Westmoreland, I hope you are enjoying your time in Barbados.

"Thank you for asking," said Trevor. "We do have a house on the golf course and like it very much here."

"Glad to hear that. My name, Frank; I professional instructor of water sports and boat operator. Please, I like to help with ski or cruise. I have jet ski, too."

"Thank you, Frank. My wife and I might well like to take a trip on one of your boats and Tracey, our daughter perhaps would like to learn to ski. Would you, darling?"

"I don't know, Daddy, it looks a bit dangerous."

"No more than riding a pony and you like that?"

"Well, maybe I can try."

Frank said, "I go now. Here my phone number. I come personally wi' my boat here at time to suit you. Full insurance."

"What did you think of that bloke that came to the cabana this morning?" Trevor asked during supper at Palm Heart that evening.

"Quite dishy, I thought," said Cynthia.

"Don't know, seemed all right," said Tracey. "Not sure about the water skiing, looks quite scary."

"Come on Trace, love. Give it a go. You see lots of other people doing it. He's a proper pro, like I have with my golf. Mummy and I'll come in the boat with you, you'll be alright. Shall we give him a call?"

"Oh, okay then," she said, without much enthusiasm.

Frank turned into Mullins beach the next morning bringing Lucky with him as driver and assistant, all the skiing gear, life jackets and a cooler packed with cold Banks beer and soft drinks.

"Good morning Mr Chapman, Mrs Chapman, hello Tracey, lookin' forward to ski, are you?"

The look on her face was not encouraging.

"No worry, no fright. I be in the water with you. Lucky here, he very good instructor so you have two of us today to look after you."

Half an hour later, a near exhausted Tracey rose out of the water, more like a pile of washing out of the machine than Aphrodite, for about twenty yards before collapsing like a quivering blancmange.

"Enough," shouted Frank. "You done good."

Frank congratulated himself on his morning's work. Took $100 off the fat Brit for the lesson and cruise; glad that he had got that lump of a girl up on her skis if only for a short distance.

He praised her highly in front of her parents on the cruise down the coast, telling her how brave and strong she'd been.

"... so much better than other first time skiers," he'd told her.

She smiled at him and said, "It was fantastic."

Sheila and Bruce Griffiths liked to go to Holders for the polo on match days. Bruce, along with his old pal Keith Melville, having been former players in the national team. They were pleased with the way the game had progressed, with talk of another one or even two grounds under consideration.

Chatting to them one day in the Club House, Tony said, "You know that bolshie guy you sent me a couple of years ago, he's come on a ton in the last few months. Like a different character, polite, does his job and, what's more, he rides bloody well."

"You mean Frank – can't remember his other name even if I ever knew it. Nasty piece of work, I thought, though he is a natural rider. Picked it up very quickly, glad he's working out for you."

"I only have him part-time now, mornings until ten, match days and evening practises. He works with Walton Dailing on the water during the day. He'll be here now on the lines."

"I might go and have a look – might, I said."

Curiosity got the better of her. "Want to come?" she said to her husband.

"Not much, though I'll be your bodyguard," said Bruce.

Frank saw them coming.

"Good afternoon Mrs Griffiths, Mr Griffiths. Remember me, Frank?"

"Hello, Frank. Of course I remember you."

How could I forget, she thought.

"You still with Mr Knowles? That's a good-looking pony."

"A home bred. I think Mr Knowles play him in first chukka. I work wi' him and wi' Walton on de water."

"Seems you're keeping busy, then?"

"Yes, please. Mrs Griffiths, I thank you for teachin' me."

"Well, what a transformation. I never heard him say 'thank you' before," Sheila remarked on their way back to the Club House.

Harriet answered the telephone at Uplands.

"Hello Harriet, Josh here. Is your lovely daughter around?"

"Hi Josh, I think she's just got back from work. Hang on, I'll give her a shout…"

"Just got out of the car. How are you today?"

"Hi, Luce, pretty good, thanks. Look, would you like to come for a sail at the weekend? Johnny Arthur has asked me and a few others to go on his boat."

"Yeah, certainly. A great idea would love to. What's the form?"

"We'll start from the Yacht Club. As there's no racing on Saturday Peter and Becky Geary are coming, and I think Tony and Sue Knowles, making seven of us altogether including Johnny to entertain us. I do have a case on, however, the judge is summing up on Friday morning and I'll be very surprised and pissed off if it's not all over by mid-afternoon. The plan is to leave the yacht club at about 9.30, probably sail up the west coast, drop off somewhere for lunch, maybe Mullins, and then sail back later in the afternoon. We may party a bit in the evening so bring something to change into."

"Lovely, Josh, sounds great, look forward to seeing you on Saturday."

"That sounds nice, darling?" Harriet said.

Next morning in the office her telephone rang. "Lucille, there's a lady on the line. Says she's from St Merrion Travel in Dublin; wants to talk to someone about houses, hotels and events in Barbados. Name Georgina Sullivan."

"Put her through."

CHAPTER 15

Bernard Hogan, the owner of Garritty Transport, put down the telephone after speaking to his lawyer in Cork, sitting at his ramshackle desk running a hand through his thinning hair. The company, consisting of himself, his wife and his brother, had been charged with many offences to do with the accident, the worst being, together with his driver Mick Hendrick, manslaughter. The advice he had just received was overwhelmingly damning. The articulated lorry, one of three owned by the company, had come off the Holyhead to Dun Laoghaire ferry on a regular journey bringing machine parts to an assembly plant in Cork.

Bernard and his wife, Colleen owned 65%, and his brother Keiron the other 35% of the company. Both brothers were at fault; Keiron who managed the mechanical maintenance of the vehicles, and Bernard who ran the sales and commercial aspects, which included insurance and legal necessities, like tachometers. The vehicles were insured third party only.

Mick, the driver, suffered deep shock and trauma following the accident, the knowledge that he had killed someone haunted him despite him knowing and having been told by his doctor and family that he was blameless. The Hogans and the business were in deep trouble; both vehicles had been impounded. Financial and social ruin faced them.

Towards the end of the month, Mallory summoned Will and Fred to Solihull for a meeting to discuss the situation.

Will called Siobhan from his office, "Are you sitting comfortably?" he asked.

"I was on my hands and knees in the scullery scrubbing filthy dirty horse blankets and between washes, if you really want to know, but if you give me a minute, I'll put on the war paint, brush my hair and be all yours. What is it?"

"Sit up and listen; Fred and I have to go to Solihull for a meeting with the boss about the O'Neill accident affair. The meeting's on Friday so I thought it would be a good idea if you flew over to

Manchester in the afternoon sometime. Fred could bring me back to the airport from Solihull; I'll meet you there, we'll drive to Ayshford where you can be barbecued by the family for the weekend. We'll fly back Sunday evening."

"Oh, Will, my darling. Suppose they don't like me?"

"In that case, I'll take you to the bus stop and you can find your own way home. Don't be such an arse. They're not stupid and they almost know you already; anyway I want to see the look on my little sister's face when she meets you."

"Okay, of course I will. I'll go and paint my nails. Fuck the horse blankets."

Will caught an early plane to Birmingham on Friday. Mallory sent a car to meet him so he arrived at the office shortly before 10 o'clock to be greeted by the ever-present Aggers.

"How very good to see you, Will, looking so well in grotty old Brummie land. Ireland must be suiting you."

"I love it there. It's good to be in on a new baby and see it grow."

"Which may be on the cards, I hear."

"Gawd – what is this place, GCHbloodyQ?"

She grinned, "Fred's not arrived yet, should be here any moment. I'll get you a cup of coffee while we wait for him. Terrible business, that ghastly accident."

In the meeting, Mallory got straight to the point, "First, if I read it correctly, we, as a company have suffered no ill effects having been complexly exonerated by the Garda report?"

"That's right," Will said. "I put out two press statements, one immediately after the incident and the other after we received the report. In both, I made reference to Connor O'Neill's family and the request for privacy. The press were considerate about this; apart from some small gutter section, there wasn't too much to complain about."

Mallory continued, "Second, since prosecutions have been issued, it is not for us to press any further charges. It would be pointless anyway as the company Garritty is bankrupt and the two main directors are quite likely to face a prison sentence. Our main concern is to safeguard our late drivers' family."

"You mean against the insurance company?" said Fred.

"Precisely. Garritty had third party cover only. That means a paltry sum for our car though a massive claim for our driver's life. I want to make sure that O'Neill's family have the best possible legal representation. I've spoken to our people who have agent connections in Dublin but I don't want any stone left unturned. Will, what about the firm that operated for us in setting the business up?"

"I was going to raise this one myself," said Will. "Our people, Fitzsimmon and Maitland, did a first-class job and their reputation in the commercial field is second to none. Knowing about this meeting today, I have deliberately not contacted them, however, I do know someone at the highest level of business dealings in Dublin. He just happens to be my girlfriend's father, Garech Kennedy. He told me recently, talking about this case, that if we were looking for a top man, he knew him. Check Garech out wherever you can; don't just take my word for it."

"I'll certainly do that Will. You'll hear from me on Monday or Tuesday at the latest.

On another matter, Fred, I've taken note on what you have been saying about modernising our communication system in regard to these new-fangled mobile telephones. I've asked Jim Briscoe to make a detailed examination of this, so you'll be hearing more from me when I have received his report.

Now, this other crazy, damn fool idea that's come from one or both of you about Supercar staging a mammoth glorified piss up using a golf competition as an excuse to spend company money; it remains in the bottommost of bottom drawers."

He had a sip of his coffee and then carried on.

"Now that you're both here – and Fred knows what I am going to say - Will, I and the board are pleased with the progress being made so far with our first foreign branch company. Congratulations to you both. I must tell you, Will, that in another year's time you will have completed four years with us and if you want to stay with the company, I will be looking for you to continue this expansion maybe in a new area. I haven't made an exact decision; though it will be a senior role. Fred, you old bugger, you won't leave your beloved, rainy Manchester, however, Will, you're young but not so foolish and I hope you will take this opportunity when it comes."

"Thank you very much, Sir. I don't think of Ireland as a foreign country and I certainly would be most interested in any job or project that you may have in mind."

On the way up the M6 back to Manchester, Fred said, "You know, lad, he's an old softy at heart, isn't he? Happy to spend a fortune in legal fees supporting an employee, which is very right and proper, yet moaning like buggery on the idea of paying for the promotion of the company name and business."

"It's the change in the way business is conducted these days," Will said. "I am sure I would be just the same at his age. You knew what he was going to say to me didn't you, you canny old monkey?"

"Aye lad, but he told me not to say. You deserve it."

"It's all thanks to you, Fred. You've given me such support and confidence."

"So, why am I driving you up to Manchester instead of you flying back from Birmingham?"

"You are acting as my chauffeur to meet my princess. Siobhan is coming over for a family grilling during the weekend. We fly back on Sunday."

"She's a smasher, that girl. Eh, you know that betting shop you told me to go to? The bloke in there gave me two hundred and seventy quid, though with a very old-fashioned look, as he handed me the cash. He said, 'What was going on with this one?' I said I had no idea; I just liked the name of the horse. I don't think he believed me."

"We did have quite a bet on him. The horse is trained by Siobhan's brother and I had been riding him in his gallops. He had beaten one of Harry's good horses in a gallop and we knew then that he had a good chance in the race. Glad it worked for you."

"Always thought bloody racing was crooked," Fred said.

"That's complete bloody nonsense Fred. It's business; we had a superior product to the opposition and made use of it. Nothing wrong in that. The horse will be running again soon and I think he'll win again though he won't start at such long odds again. I'll tell you and you can back him again if you want to, so stop moaning. And talking business, I've got an idea."

"What is it?"

"Not going to tell you … yet."

The 'smasher' was waiting for them when Will and Fred arrived at the airport.

"Hang on a moment Fred and look after Siobhan while I dash in and pick up the car keys from our desk."

"Aye, I'll do that. Come here lass and give us a kiss."

"Guess what?" Will said, in the car. "Mallory's given me the sack."

"WHAT?" said Siobhan.

"Well, not exactly. He's given me another year in Ireland and then wants me to move on to something else in what he calls a 'Senior Role'. He's pleased with the way things are going, thinks that in a year's time somebody else can take over, leaving me free for something else."

"God, don't give me a heart attack like that. What does he want you to do?"

"Didn't say though I have an idea which I'll talk to you about when we have a quiet moment. We're very nearly at Ayshford now."

Mary Carpenter had been thrilled when Will had rung her to suggest bringing Siobhan for the weekend.

"The red carpet will be done, dusted and laid out," she had said.

"No, no frills required, she'll be quite nervous meeting you all," he had replied.

"I am a little nervous," Siobhan said in the car. "It's a bit like going for an interview."

"Don't be so bloody silly. It's like nothing of the kind and I'm looking forward to it. To me, it's like leading in the winner."

She needn't have worried. Mary greeted her son and his girlfriend with open arms.

"I'm so glad and happy that you've come, welcome to Ayshford," she said, giving Siobhan a big hug and kiss.

Angus, first shaking hands, then, "Can I give you a kiss, too?"

Will, having skirted around both his parents, took hold of Joanna, shyly hanging back, "And this is my little sister, Joanna."

It was Siobhan's turn to take the initiative, coming forward and hugging Joanna, "Hello, Joanna, Will's right, you're very lovely. I've been so much looking forward to meeting you – and you all," she added, hastily.

"So have we," said Mary. "Now Will, take your things, show Siobhan upstairs and come down and have a drink. You must be thirsty and starving."

"She's not what I expected," said Joanna.

"What did you expect, darling?"

"I don't know, but she's better."

"Give Siobhan a drink and yourself," Mary said, as they came into the drawing room.

Siobhan had a glass of wine and he poured a whisky and soda for himself.

"Tell us what you've both been doing today."

"I flew over to Birmingham this morning for a meeting with my chairman in Solihull, then hitched a lift with a colleague – you know, Fred who came to the Christmas party – to pick up Siobhan at Ringway, who has been, go on Princess you tell 'em …"

"I rode out for my brother this morning, did a bit of office work, then made a beeline for the airport to fly to my handsome prince, who met me and brought me here."

"What's this 'handsome prince' bit? He's not handsome, he's just my brother," said Joanna.

"I think he's handsome and you talk exactly the same as my brother, who I love dearly, talks about me."

"Maybe your brother should meet my sister. That would set the cat amongst the pigeons!" joked Will.

During dinner, Mary said, "Dad and I have made no special plans for the weekend. Joanna's been asked to a birthday party that the Tomkinsons are having for their son Jason tomorrow evening; he's home from school for the weekend. Is there anything that you have in mind, Will?"

"No, we want to spend time with you all here. I'd like to take Siobhan on a bit of a jaunt round, maybe we'll go over to the Platts. It was through Adam's Irish bloodstock agent's friend, Fergal Lynch, that we met. She and her brother Harry know Fergy well, as indeed do I now. I'd like Siobhan to see the Platt set-up anyway. I might show her the polo grounds; there won't be anything going on there but she's heard me banging on about it. Otherwise no plans. We'll have to leave mid after noonish for our plane to Dublin on Sunday."

"Which room are you sleeping in, Siobhan?" asked Joanna.

"The same one as Will," she replied.

"Ooh, I wouldn't want to do that. I remember having to share a room with him when we used to go skiing. It was horrid; sometimes he snored."

"Well, I'm used to it now and don't mind."

"Oh, you've had to share with him before, then?"

"That reminded me of that evening at the Bounty in Trim when we laughed so much all the other diners glared at us. She's a real character, your sister," said Siobhan, after they'd gone upstairs.

"Yes, I haven't worked out if it was sheer naivety or whether she was taking the piss. I suspect the latter. Anyway hurry up and get into bed; I've never made love before in this house, never mind this room and don't want to wait a moment longer than necessary to break my duck."

"Don't worry, I bet I'll be quicker than you, I've been three nights without you, remember."

She won the bet, lying on her back slightly propped by the pillows, her hair running down on both sides over her nakedness. He let his dressing gown slide to the floor. She put out her hand holding him, guiding him closer so that she could encircle him between her lips as he joined her in the bed. She gave her customary little gasp as he slipped inside her "shush" he said, "Joanna might hear and worry that I'm keeping you awake."

"You can keep me awake all night please. Oh, yes again and again like that – all night please. That's so fabulous, my wonderful, amazing prince Will. Don't stop, don't stop just come inside me and keep c-o-m-i-n-g."

"Sorry we're late," Will said, as they came down to see breakfast neatly laid out in the dining room.

"Don't worry, you're not and you both had a long day yesterday. Hope you slept well. JoJo's being a very good breakfast sous chef, aren't you, darling?"

"Did he snore?" she asked.

"Not really, more like heavy breathing", Siobhan replied, receiving a kick under the table from Will.

"I could say you were tossing and turning. Thank you Mum and Jo, we slept very well and hope we disturbed no one. Where's Dad this morning?"

"He got up quite early, had breakfast and has retired to his study."

"I thought I'd ring Adam Platt and suggest we go round there later in the morning if that's okay?"

"Yes, go ahead. I might ask you to pick up a few things in the shop in Tarporley on the way."

"Good to meet you Siobhan and hello stranger, Will," Adam said. "You live down the bloody road but all the news I get about you is from Fergy Lynch."

"You might just as well tune in to Radio Eireann. Come on Adam, you know I'm living and working in Ireland at the moment; I did see you here at Christmas."

"Only jokin'. Great to see you. I gather you had a bit of a touch at Limerick a week or so back."

"Yes, that was a good one. Thanks to your introduction via Fergy, I've been riding out for Harry, Siobhan's brother, and that horse, Small Talk in all his recent work. Around Christmas time he worked very well with Pelican Point, who won a decent race at Leopardstown at the New Year meeting so we knew we had a fair chance in a maiden at Limerick. How's everything going here?"

"Not bad, rough and smooth you know though I'm very pleased with North West Passage that Fergy sent over last year – I think you rode him a time or two – he's won a couple and we're thinking about Cheltenham for him."

"Yes, I remember the horse, that would be fantastic Adam."

They chatted for a while until making their exit.

"Must go Adam, Thanks so much for the drink, June. Mum's getting lunch ready. At least you've met one member of the Kennedy family. I'll be over again before too long, so see you then."

"Bye Will, look after yourself and lovely to meet you, Siobhan."

"The salt of the earth, those two; I'm very fond of them. Learnt all I know about riding racehorses from Adam," Will said, on the way back to Ayshford, having picked up the pre-ordered goodies from the shop.

"Yes, I can see that. I liked them, too, and will tell Harry. He'll be pleased I've met them."

"Now then baby sister, what time is Cinderella going to the ball tonight?" Will said later in the afternoon.

Then, turning to his mother, "Would you like us to take her and collect her after the party?"

"I'm not your baby sister; I'm your growing up sister and I'll soon have boobs as big as Siobhan's, so there."

"Stop it, you two. Why don't I take her and, if you don't mind, perhaps you could go and bring her back later? The party starts around 7 o'clock and I should think will be over at 11 ish. There will be other oldies collecting their young, so you may see a few of your friends."

"I'm happy to do both; it's no distance, Dad probably won't want to and you'll be busy getting dinner ready."

"Okay, if you're sure, thank you, darling."

Mary went to help Jo change. They both came down at about 6.30, Joanna wearing fine stockings, a pretty flowery dress, and her hair was tied back, flowing straight behind her, not in a ponytail. A white rose that Mary had bought for her at the local florist was fastened with a clip in her hair. She wore a necklace borrowed from Mary, too, with Will's Christmas gift – a charm bracelet - on her wrist. Light grey and pink shoes completed her ensemble.

Will thought she looked a treat and said so.

"Wait a moment, I'll get my camera," Mary said.

"And I'll fetch my chauffeur's cap," said Will. "Do you want to come, too, princess? You'll have to sit in the back."

"I'll let you go on your own; I'll help your mother with dinner."

It didn't take long before he was back.

"She was quite nervous. I took her in; luckily Antoinette was there in the hall to scoop her up and take her to join the party."

He looked at his parents, "Dad and Mum, now that JoJo's not here, I really think that a plan must be made for her. She's growing up every time I see her. I have mentioned this before but have you thought about the Zimbabwe idea I suggested?"

"I have and agree with it," said Mary. "Come on Angus darling. We must make up our minds. We know it will be expensive, however, it's much cheaper than all sorts of other alternatives. She loves animals and it's vital to have a change of scenery and meet new people. If she can kill two birds with one stone, as well as doing something to help conservation, it would be the perfect answer."

"I have details of an elephant and rhino conservation centre called Imire, owned and run for two generations by the Travers family," said Will. "They take teams of volunteers consisting of young men and girls of eighteen or over, for periods of three, six or nine months; longer, if required. Good shared accommodation plus three meals per day are provided, together with transport from Harare. Teams are under overall supervision and guidance of qualified game wardens though Reilly Travers does much of it himself. I have an old school friend whose sister went and absolutely adored it. The basic cost for a three-month stay inclusive of all I've just mentioned would be in the region of £4,000, with a reduced rate pro rata if she stayed longer.

Angus said, "Let me think about it overnight. I'll let you know in the morning."

"Wonderful, Dad. As Joanna doesn't know it at all, please don't say anything to her at this stage. She would be bitterly disappointed if you said no."

"Come on. Princess, get your glad rags on if you want to come with me to collect Miss World," Will said, after they had watched some rubbishy programme on television after dinner.

"I haven't got anything too smart with me so I'll just tidy up a bit. Do you want me to come?"

"Of course I do. I want to show you off."

The Tomkinson's house, a large Victorian old family house is set in parkland outside the small village of Utkington. Will and Siobhan went inside to dimmed lights, the sound of a band trying not very successfully to play *Can't Get You Out of My Head*, and a few locals on similar recovery missions.

Will saw Antoinette; she beckoned, mouthing, "Come over here."

They did and Will said, "This is Siobhan, and how's my little sister getting on?"

"Like a house on fire, she and Jason seem to be fancying each other. Hello Siobhan, I'm Antoinette. Joanne was quite shy to start with though she's learning fast. Come and have a drink in le salle privee. We've got fifty or sixty of the little horrors; they're living it up on coca cola and elderflower juice and we're going to call a halt in a few minutes; some have left, however, there seem to be plenty left over."

"Hello, Will," Richard came in. "And, what have you got here?"

"This is Siobhan, and keep your hands off her. I won her in a raffle."

"Must have been expensive tickets, you lucky bugger."

"That's one thing he's not," said Siobhan.

Angela and Robbie Huxtable came in, "What are you doing here, Will? You're much too old for this party."

"Yes, I'm afraid so; I'm collecting Joanna. This is Siobhan who's kindly come to look after me, Siobhan – Angela and Robbie Huxtable."

"Hello Siobhan, I'm sure you're doing a good job. We've come to collect our youngest Paul who's in there with the mob. Are you still in Ireland, Will?

"Yes, just over for the weekend."

The music stopped.

"We'd better go and find Joanna," Will said. "Hope to see you next time."

"Yes, we must talk polo," said Robbie, then they moved away.

Will said, "Robbie doesn't know it, but I had a little adventure with their elder daughter when I was still at Harrow."

Joanna appeared looking a little flushed, Will thought.

"Have you had a good time JoJo?"

"Marvellous. I danced with four boys; Jason was by far the best. I like him."

"Say goodbye and thank you to Mr and Mrs Tomkinson, then we must go. It's very late, you know, nearly midnight."

The outside light at Ayshford had been left on for them and a sweet 'Goodnight' note from Mary to all of them.

"Up you go now JoJo, don't forget to clean your teeth; sweet dreams."

"Of Jason, I hope," she said.

Sunday morning, a bleary-eyed Joanna made a late appearance for breakfast.

Answering her mother, she said, "Yes, it was a dreamy party, lots of fun, a real live band and danced with lots of boys, especially Jason."

Later, Angus came out of his study, "Okay, I'll agree to the Zimbabwe plan based on what you've told me, however, please will you send me all the details that you have of the property and the courses that they organise. Since you have the contacts, probably best for you to make the bookings and dates etc."

"Oh, that's great news, Dad. Of course I will and I'm quite certain it'll be brilliant for Jo. I know she'll be eternally grateful."

Siobhan was upstairs, packing, Mary said, "Darling, we love your Siobhan. Thanks for bringing her. She's lovely, such fun and very attractive. Hang on to her."

On the plane back to Dublin, Will said, "We have to talk seriously about what Mallory told me last Friday. One more year in Ireland. No idea what he will propose, though I have one."

"Whatever happens, or whatever you have in mind, I want to come, if you'll have me. I love you; you know."

"That's what I hoped you'd say," said Will, squeezing her hand. "I may have bored the pants off you, yet I do have this very strong feeling about my old ancestor Benjamin in Barbados and what he did there. It may be a pipe dream; however, I'd like to do there what we've done here - start a Supercar branch company - and I know just the man who, I think, would be attracted to the plan. Anyway, I am due for a holiday, so what do you say?"

"I say if you leave me, I'm coming with you."

Will took the call from Mallory early in the afternoon on Monday.

"You are spot on about Garech Kennedy. Top man and tough as old boots, I'm told. Get his man, talk to him and tell him to contact me."

Will dialled Garech's private line at his office.

"Garech Kennedy."

"Mr Kennedy, Will Carpenter, here."

"For God's sake, Will, call me Garech. What is it?"

"You remember when we were talking about the O'Neill accident at the Dunraven Arms and legal representation? I had a meeting with my chairman in England on Friday. We would be most grateful if you could let me have the name of the man and firm that you mentioned to me?"

"Leave it with me. I'll call you back."

Fifteen minutes later, he did.

"Call Arnold Nalder at Nalder and Partners. He is expecting your call. He's your man."

Will called the number and asked to speak to Mr Nalder.

"Nalder here, I know what you're calling about from Garech Kennedy. Please can you give me a quick run-down as you see it?"

Will did so, saying that he was acting under the instructions of his chairman, Robert Mallory, and that Mr Mallory had asked that Nalder gave him a call if he was prepared to take on the case.

He called Mallory back, "Our man is Arnold Nalder of Nalder and Partners. I've spoken to him, and told him all that I know. He's asked me to send him the Garda report, which I will do now by courier. I said that the instructions had come from you. He told me that he would call you."

"Well done, Will. Good to see you on Friday. I'll be in touch."

CHAPTER 16

Lucille saw Josh helping Johnny load two coolers on board his yacht as she drove up, still in the yellow moke which she couldn't bear to part with.

"Just to keep us going," he said to Johnny, he looked handsome in his white t-shirt with the Yacht Club logo and yachting cap, similarly embroidered.

"Hi Luce," said Josh, giving her a hug and kiss. "This is going to be fun with Captain Arthur at the wheel and Tony, Peter and me pulling on the ropes…"

"They are not *ropes*, they are *sheets*, and you don't *pull* 'em, you *tighten* or *slacken* 'em and it's not a *wheel*, it's a *helm!*" called out Johnny.

"Aye, aye, Cap'n. As I was saying, all you, Becky and Sue have to do is to look beautiful and make sure our glasses are no less than half full."

The others arrived as he was speaking.

A fresh breeze blew the few clouds scudding across the blue Caribbean sky as it sent them on their way, making good progress, past Harbour Lights nightclub, the Careenage with the hustle and bustle of central Bridgetown in the background, the Deep Water Harbour where two huge cruise ships were disgorging passengers, the lovely but now overbuilt Paradise Beach and up along the west coast. The opulence of Sandy Lane hotel, the commercial cluster of Holetown, the elegant Colony and Coral Reef hotels and the magnificent Italian façade of Heron Bay house.

Shortly afterwards, Johnny pointed out a small bay sandwiched between coral stone rocks behind which and peeking through trees, little bits of a column-fronted house could be seen.

"That's Maddox," he said. "You know, the house Oliver Messel created from an old farmhouse and where he lived. I remember going there, I must have been nineteen or twenty at the time. Oliver was designing a gazebo for my old man at the plantation; he sent me to Maddox to deliver back the plans with some comments. It was about mid-afternoon; Oliver was having a siesta on a chaise longue in the open-fronted drawing room. I tiptoed in as quietly as possible though he must have heard me. Opening his eyes, he saw me standing over him, 'Oh, I'm in love again', he said."

With no sheets to be tightened or slackened for a moment or two, Josh moved next to Lucille and put an arm around her, "Isn't this lovely, are you okay?"

"Yes, dear Josh, it is lovely. I'm very okay. Thank you for asking me; you are so sweet and kind to me. I love doing things with you."

"Maybe we should do more, and more often," he said.

"Yes, please."

Soon they arrived off Mullins Bay.

"We'll go in here. I told them we'd probably be coming," Johnny said.

Dropping anchor, they swam to the shore with anything they needed wrapped in towels held over their heads.

The place was crowded.

Gary the barman called out to them, "Ho! Mr Arthur, over here, We keep this for you."

He showed them to a round table with a parasol beyond the bar, where a pretty waitress was rearranging the chairs.

"There's quite a few of the English racing crowd here," said Lucille. "I recognize some of them as most are in houses that we manage. That thin man with dark hair over there is Barry Hills with his wife Penny. The jovial chap with him, not sure of his name but he's staying with Barry, Mc Something-or-other. Talking to them, the fat fellow is Charles Benson, a close friend and confidant of Robert Sangster, a heavy gambler, I gather. Can't see Sangster, probably playing golf. Oh, see that fellow over there with Roy Orbison type glasses? That's Lunchtime with his very pretty wife next to him; goodness knows what his real name is but he's called Lunchtime because the story goes he used to run an illegal gambling den in London and never got up before lunch."

"Talking of fat people, I can see one of my crowd sitting outside that cabana over there," said Johnny. "He's a very rich English guy who sold his business for zillions. Sven Goran collared him at our Sandy Lane bash a year or so ago and sold him a plot up above at Westmoreland on which he has built – or rather we have built and he has paid for – a super new house. That's his amply proportioned wife and pudgy daughter with him..."

"And talking to them, quite seriously, it seems, is my polo groom, Frank," said Tony. "I wonder what they're up to. Frank only works for me part-time now but he rides well, taught by Sheila Griffiths. His other job is on the water with Walton Dailing. Funny, can't imagine any of that lot on skis."

"I remember him," said Lucille. "He had just started to work for you when I brought Will Carpenter round to see you ride one of your ponies. A bit of an odd fellow, I thought."

"Yes, I don't particularly like him though he does his job well. What happened to Will, do you still keep in touch? He is or was a bloody good rider."

"Yes, we do sort of keep in touch. I was very fond of him. Then, our careers and the Atlantic Ocean got in the way. He has a good job in Ireland now – and a new girlfriend. I'm sure he'll find a way back here sometime."

"Right, now that we've sorted that lot out, let's enjoy ourselves and have lunch," said Johnny.

The sun was starting to go down by the time they arrived back at the yacht club.

"Come up to my place for a sundowner," Johnny said.

Johnny's 'place' being a smart house on Rendezvous Ridge that he had bought after selling the plantation. He had designed and cultivated a beautiful garden full of exotic Caribbean plants, shrubs and flowers, all admired out on the terrace with drinks served by Johnny's butler. As the light faded, the sunset followed for a long while with ever-changing colour afterglows.

"Okay, day games over, night time now. Saturday remember my suggestion, we go down the road to the Brown Sugar in Aquatic Gap for dinner and then, as my guest, to Alexandra's. You know I own a chunk of it so they should look after us."

"Man, you testing our stamina big time," said Peter. "Let's ask the ladies; Sue, Becky, Lucille what say y'all?"

Sue spoke first, "Dinner sounds great – why don't we play Alexandra's by ear?"

"I agree with that," said Becky. "It's been such a wonderful day; I'll go on until I drop which just may be after dinner."

Lucille looked at Josh.

"I'm game if you are," she said.

"Okay, good thing I booked a table at Brown Sugar. Off we go.

Josh, you and Lucille come with me."

The other two couples drew stumps after dinner, leaving Johnny with Lucille and Josh to go to the club together.

"We'll leave Alexandra's to you and the love birds. You can give us a blow by blow tomorrow. It's been such a fabulous day, Johnny, thanks a million and see you very soon. We'll have a rematch."

"Give my love to your father, Peter," Lucille called out.

"Take no notice of me," Johnny said, entering Alexandra's. "I'll find a comfortable place for you and leave you on your own. I've got a bit of 'front man' work to do; just tell me when you want to go."

Alexandra's was softly furnished and lit, with sofas, armchairs and side tables, and a separate discreet dance floor for the disco music. Not overcrowded, though enough well-dressed twenty-five to fifty year olds to make Lucille and Josh feel unnoticed. Lucille felt happier than for a long time with Josh, a man she could be at one with, could trust and maybe could fall in love with. They had been going out together for about three months, Josh had always been attentive, interested in her and what she had been doing. He had a good brain and sense of humour. They danced to one of Lucille's favourite songs, the Gary Shearston version of *I Get a Kick out of You.*

I wonder, she thought.

"You don't want to drive all the way back to Uplands at this time of night do you, Lucille?" Johnny said as they were leaving. "I've a lovely spare room. Fits two, own bathroom."

Lucille called her mother in the morning, "Mum, so sorry I didn't call you last night. We had a lovely day then it got so late that Johnny Arthur kindly said I could stay at his place. I'm spending the day with Josh and I will be home later. All news then."

"That's fine darling, glad you're alright and that you had a good day. See you later."

Why is it, Lucille said to herself as she drove home to Uplands that Sunday evening, *that when I should be deliriously happy, I am feeling sad?'*

A mile further on, *Come on Lucille Todd, stop living in the past. No two relationships are ever the same. You have a man who you like or love enough to go to bed with and who thinks the world of you so go for it.*

Monday morning, Johnny Arthur called Sven in his office, "Sven, Johnny here. Look, there's a young guy knocking around that I think might be worth taking a look at. He's a red leg called Frank – don't know his surname. I sailed up the coast yesterday with some friends – Lucille Todd was with us – and stopped at Mullins for lunch. Saw this chap deep into conversation with the Chapmans. Tony and Sue Knowles were also with us and Tony told me that this same guy, whose name is Frank, is also his polo groom. Later, at dinner at the Brown Sugar, the Chapmans were there with Ron Pickering and his wife. I gather that he's also involved with Walton Dailing's water sports operation. Could be useful to us as a sort of scout?"

"Thanks, Johnny. I'll check him out and let you know."

Sven knew Walton well; differing backgrounds but the same age, fortyish, Sven, an academic with a shrewd business brain though a non-participant in any sport or game; Walton, tall, lithe, brilliant water skier, useful tennis player and a ladies' man. Their common interest: self-promotion and success. Sven knew the kind of place to find Walton; he spotted him with an attractive lady on the Sandy Lane tennis courts playing mixed doubles against a middle-aged couple. He waited, unobserved, until they came off the court walking in his direction.

"Hi there, Walton, how?" Bajans have a habit of omitting unnecessary words.

"Good, man. This Felicity. I took her skiing this morning. She say she lookin' for a tennis player so here I am. Lucky, yes?"

"I'd say. Watch him Felicity – he not safe in the dark. Hey, Walton you wanna pass by my office?"

"Sure, Sven, I comin' that way soon. See you."

"Yeah – and good luck Felicity."

Sven's 'coming by soon' materialised two days later when he turned at the then FAG office.

"It's not that important," said Sven. "However, we at FAG are always looking at ways to make our hotel and private house guests' holidays as good as we can, and to promote local businesses. How's your water sports operation going? Your reputation for reliability and quality is the best along the west coast."

"Good, man, good. I not taking back seat, but I have a good young kid doin' more on the water leavin' more time to look after guests on shore, like you see me at Sandy Lane."

"Tell me about your young kid?"

"He come to me two, maybe three years ago in Speightstown, rough, y'know, very rough. Know nothin', no speak proper, no money. He want jet ski; I say, you work, clean jet ski, boat, boathouse, no pay. I teach you. He a natural wi' jet ski and later wi' ski. I tell him 'look, me like you twenty years ago, look at me now. I talk to all white folk. No chip. Have fun, man, that's what life about'. He learnin', has brain but still way to go."

"Okay, Walton, thanks for that. We want to put out a flyer in all the houses that we manage, suggesting that our guests contact your outfit for all water sports with your contact details. Maybe a good idea for you to send your young guy to see me – what's his name?"

"Sound good. He called Frank, Frank Doune. He a redleg. I send him to you. He and Lucky, my other boat driver, ski man, have side line; I not know, ganja. spliffs, maybe little coke. I watch, no big supply."

Frank came, not two days later, like Walton, but that same afternoon. Dressed in khaki shorts and clean, sober shirt he was shown into Sven's office.

"Good afternoon Mr Goran, Walton say you ask to see me?"

"Yes, it's Frank isn't it? Come, sit down. Walton Dailing tells me that you are doing good work for him on the water. I want to talk to you as FAG sends many clients to Walton and we take an interest in our suppliers and those who work for them. Therefore it is good to know you personally, then I can mention you by name to clients."

"Yes, Mr Goran, I understand. I do other work, too. I work for Mr Knowles, look after and help train polo ponies. I help him on match day at Holders."

"I believe, Frank, that you've met our clients Mr and Mrs Chapman. How you meet them?"

"I go see them at Mullins cabana, see if they want ski or jet ski. They have daughter, Tracey, I teach her ski."

"That's all fine, Frank. I like to know who's in contact with clients of FAG. Come to see me for anything you want to talk about."

"Thank you, Mr Goran, I do that."

That same day, a mile away from the FAG office, Georgie Sullivan entered Lucille's office at The Real Estate Company.

"Very good to meet you in person, after our telephone conversations from Dublin," she said.

"Certainly," Lucille replied. "I remember you saying that this would be your first visit to Barbados?"

"Yes, and indeed to the West Indies. St Merrion Travel, quite a young company, is certainly starting to live up to its name. We operate at the top end of the market; one of our best clients came several times to Barbados; he gave me your company name as you arranged his accommodation here."

"I've only been working here for the last nine months; I may not know him. What is your client's name and I can check what we did for him?"

"He's called Garech Kennedy."

"Hang on a moment," Lucille picked up her telephone. "Eustine, please check our client list for Mr Garech Kennedy and let me know what we fixed for him."

"How long are you here for and what would you like us to do for you?"

There was a knock on the door. Eustine came in and handed a sheet of paper to Lucille.

"Ah, yes, Mr and Mrs Kennedy stayed at Cobblers Cove hotel three years running a few years back and I see we planned various things for them to do while they were here. They haven't been back since; I hope we didn't do anything to upset them or maybe they wanted to explore other places in the world."

"No, it wasn't either of those. Mrs Kennedy died of breast cancer and Mr Kennedy hasn't felt like going abroad since. I believe, though, that he might start travelling again soon. I know the family quite well. What I would like to do, if it's okay with you, is to have a look at some of your best houses and hotels, beaches etc. I'm here for a week from today."

"We would be most interested in looking after any of your clients that you can send to us. We are the oldest – and best of course – estate and property agents on the island. I would be very happy to take you round the island, show you the sights and all that you require. If I'm not available at any time, I have a most capable deputy who can stand in for me."

"I'm sure you'll understand most of our houses are occupied at this time of the year," Lucille said, having picked up Georgie the next day from the Colony where she was staying. "You will only able to see them from the outside due to that, though there are a few empty between guests and we can have a good look at those. I have made arrangements with the managers of the best hotels to give us a tour. What do you think of the Colony?"

"It's very good mostly, one or two bits of tiredness showing, though the staff are friendly and helpful."

Later, as they were leaving St Nicholas Abbey in St Peter and driving over Cherry Tree Hill, Georgie said, "You know I spoke about Garech Kennedy? His son, Harry, is a good friend of mine. His sister's boyfriend told me he'd been out here a few times; something about an old family connection."

Lucille gripped the steering wheel of the yellow moke very hard.

With a sinking feeling in her heart she said, "Oh, what's the boyfriend's name?"

"William Carpenter."

Looking straight ahead, she answered, "I remember; I did meet him. He was a friend of my former boss, who also happens to be a director of TRECO."

"Hello, my breath of fresh air, vision of loveliness and sex bomb."

"Cut the crap and give me a kiss or I'll explode," Siobhan said, in greeting to Will on arrival at Lostock on Friday evening.

"It's been quite a week. Conference calls between Mallory, your father's man, Nalder and me over the O'Neill case, Jim McDonald pushing me about a larger site he's found for our depot in Limerick – I've got to go and look at it next week – and general business higher than I anticipated for February. Bloody glad to be here; and to see you, of course."

Usually, Siobhan managed to come to Will on one weekday night, however, this week it didn't fit in. She'd been away racing for Harry one day and Will had an evening meeting with Nalder on another, it had been just a telephone call only. On the family and Joanna front, after he had tied his father down for her to go to Imire, he discovered that Imire had a fax number, used it and had a reply from Reilly Travers. Joanna was booked in for three months from mid-April, with an option of a further three months.

"I've got you on Small Talk again in the morning, Will," Harry said, while they were having supper. "He had a lay off after his race though has been cantering again and Joe schooled him a few days ago, so it'll be his first decent gallop since his race. Planning ahead, there's a race for him at Fairyhouse a week tomorrow. It's a class higher, therefore stronger opposition than Limerick. I've been talking to Tim Kerrigan; I think – and he agreed – that we should run him there. Depending on the outcome, we will know for sure whether we should pursue any hope of taking him to Cheltenham in March for the Supreme Novice. He'll have to win and win well to stand any chance of taking on the big boys."

Next morning, pulling out from the yard, Harry said, "I want this to be a proper test this morning, that's why I've put young Padraig on Spring Garden. He's nice and light and the old horse can jump off and enjoy himself. Ro, you and Will just sit in behind him and make your moves independently when you feel it's right to go. It's a repeat for Pelican Point and Small talk; both are due to run at Fairyhouse next week. I'm going up to watch at the six furlong pole. Hands and heels only, mind, but I want them to feel hungry at lunchtime."

Will could tell Small Talk was getting excited a hundred yards short of the start, not in the least nervous with ears pricked, a bit of jig jogging, eager to get on with it.

"Okay, let's go," said Ronan, Spring Garden shot off in front, Padraig just a passenger. Small Talk beautifully settled two lengths behind, with the more experienced Pelican Point upsides him. Ro made his move as soon as he saw Spring Garden begin to slacken. Will went with him on a tight rein, half a length behind. He watched Ro crouching a bit lower, whereas he had made no move.

Just short of the six pole, he spoke to his horse, "Right, go for it."

He let out a couple of inches, while maintaining his own position. The acceleration came instantaneously. Pulling up and glancing behind, he couldn't believe how far in front he had finished, a good six lengths or more. Small Talk had a bit of a blow though horse and jockey walked round happy as Larry.

Harry came up, "So?" he asked.

Ronan said, "My horse worked very well. Pleased with him but Will just left me standing. He's some tool that fella. I could have found a bit more; my horse wasn't stopping; he was just done for pace."

"Will?"

"Spot on, that'll just put him right. God, was he having fun; he absolutely loved it."

No runners that Saturday so the three of them, Harry, Siobhan and Will, rode out second lot after breakfast. Two groups doing half-speed work up the main gallop, Will and Siobhan in the first group, after which they moved a little down the side of the track to watch Harry come up with the second one. Listening to the cheerful chat and banter between the lads and girls, Padraig having been full of his account of the morning's gallop, raising stable morale, which was pretty high anyway owing to recent successes, to a new level.

"They left me for dead", he said.

"So good to see a happy bunch enjoying their work," Will said to Siobhan.

"I'm so pleased for Harry" she replied. "He works bloody hard; had a great grounding with Willie Moore and it's paying off."

"Anything I can help you with this afternoon?" Will asked.

"No, put your feet up and relax. I might watch some of the racing on the telly, otherwise make the most of a Saturday off. Thanks for this morning, Will; it's good having you around any day that you can manage. For what it's worth Ronan and the lads like you, and I value your comments. I remember when I was riding, I was shit scared, not of getting hurt, but of making an arse of myself by falling off. Also of what the pro jockeys might think of 'this toff amateur bumping around'. However, as soon as they realised that I was reasonably competent, they treated me as one of them. The camaraderie in the jockeys' changing room, jokes, banter is second to none. Incidentally, that's where the word 'bumper' came from, meaning a race for amateurs only. Sis, you're off duty tonight too, so let's go and annoy people at the Bounty."

In the pub later, Will said: "You know there's only one thing better than a sip of the first drink of the day and that's the second."

"You know, Will, that sounds terribly Irish."

"If you can't beat 'em, join 'em."

"Georgie told me she was off to the West Indies a few days ago," Harry said. "I think she's probably in Barbados right now. Said she's made an appointment with a firm of estate and property agents recommended by Dad."

"Oh shit," said Will. "She didn't say which one or give a name, I suppose?"

"No, why?"

"Because Lucille, my old girlfriend, is PA to the partners of the main estate and property agents; more than likely to have been the one your father dealt with."

"I could always ask him," Harry said.

"No, don't bother. It was bound to happen sooner or later anyway."

"Have you found a replacement for Georgie, Harry?" Siobhan asked.

"I'm casting."

Later, in bed, Siobhan said, "You're worried about what Georgie might have said to Lucille, aren't you?"

"Well yes, a bit. I suppose it's only natural; I hate to think of people being hurt. Thank God I told her about us. It would have been wrong and awful if I hadn't. As I told you, I had the sweetest and kindest reply back from her."

She cuddled up to him. "This is the second of four nights on the trot, I've got you all to myself," she said.

Jim McDonald had done a good job. He had found a disused warehouse with plenty of spare space just out of Limerick town. Part of the warehouse could be converted into office space with the remainder for servicing, cleaning and washing down cars, as well as some interior garaging. Outside, enough space for holding a fleet of cars. A fair bit to be done and a security fence needed but the ultimate saving to the company by ceasing to have all the servicing and constant flow of cars backwards and forwards from Santry would more than cover the alteration expenses. Jim had all the structural plans and areas mapped out, plus local searches and the contact details of the agent handling the sale.

"Do you know of any other interested party?" he asked.

"No, but you know agent's talk. They're always full of bullshit.

My guess is that there's nobody in front of us. I've hedged saying that I'll report to my manager etc, but haven't told them that you've come down here."

"Well done, that's fine. I'll take all the stuff here that you've got and submit an urgent report and recommendation to Head Office. I'll keep you posted."

As he was getting in the car Will said to Jim, "By the way, Small Talk runs again at Fairyhouse on Saturday. I rode him in a piece of work last Saturday and he went like a bomb. He won't be 16/1 anymore but it's a higher class race."

"I've got the runners for tomorrow," Harry said, when Will arrived on Friday evening. "It's a hot race. Take a look."

Harry was right; horses in the race from many of the top listed trainers in Ireland.

"I've been through it very carefully; I reckon the main dangers are Red Emperor, March Hare, Tumbaga, Good Timing and Grandma Betty. There's also Morgan's Head, but we've beaten him once and I see no reason why we shouldn't again, twelve in all. It's the second race, Fergy's been on the line; he's coming, of course; reckons that Good Timing is the one to beat, an impressive winner at Thurles last time. Dad's coming, says he'll meet us there. Pelican Point's in the 4th; pity it's not the other way round."

The preliminaries over, Small Talk saddled and looking magnificent, having a good look round as he was led round the paddock by Vince, his lad. A solid 4/1, third favourite behind Good Timing in the betting ring. The Kerrigans, Harry and Will, in the middle of the paddock, all on edge, Siobhan keeping her father company from the outside. Joe, calm as usual said, "Same plan as before, Guvnor?"

"Yes, you know the horse. Ride him as you find him."

"They're off," broadcast the commentator.

Red Emperor, a normal front runner, led the field over the first three flights of hurdles. Going to the fourth with half the distance covered, Small Talk neatly settled in about 6th place.

"March Hare has fallen," the commentator said in an excited voice. "He's down and badly interfered with Betty's Grandma and Small Talk."

Harry put down his glasses, "Fuck it," he said. "That's it, he's got no chance now."

Joe Maguire who had made a superb balancing act recovery to keep the partnership intact, took his time.

"We've got a lot to do now so let's see what you're made of."

They jumped the next, the third from home brilliantly, making two lengths up on the horse in front of them, then narrowed the gap to jump the second last in fourth place, Red Emperor still leading but only just from Tumbaga and Good Timing pressing him hard, still a good 10 lengths in front of them. Between the last two, they overtook the tiring Red Emperor but still half that distance behind the leaders going to the last.

"Now, I want a real big one from you and we are in with a squeak. Yes, that's my boy, now go for it."

Joe picked up his stick and gave him a smack on the backside, the first he had ever received. Small Talk flew; a hundred yards to go and they were level.

"Go, my beauty, you can do it!"

It was close but Joe was sure that he had won.

The judge agreed, "First no 7, Small Talk, 2nd no 3, Good Timing, 3rd no 9, Tumbaga," came over the tannoy. "Distances, a head and the same."

The whole Lostock team, hoarse from shouting, for a few moments were speechless, eventually Harry saying, "I can't believe it. You can't come from so far behind in a good class race over 2 miles and win."

Joe and Small Talk received a huge cheer from the crowd in the winner's enclosure when Vince, smiling from ear to ear, led in his horse with, "Well done, Joe", ringing out from all sides.

"Some horse this. Guvnor, I was in two minds whether to pull him up, you know, but he took hold of his bit and set off after them; didn't want to be left behind. Got all the guts in the world. Thought I was going to fall off him but he kept his head up which saved me."

Fergy joined them and said, "Congratulations all round, to the owner and Lostock team, all here in force, I see."

"Thanks and well done you for finding him," said Tim Kerrigan. "Come and join us in the bar."

"That, I will. It was in this bar that my pal Tom Kearns knocked Will's drink and lunch to the floor, how long ago, Will? That's how we met."

"I'll join you a bit later," said Harry. "I've got a runner in the next and need to put the saddle on the right way round."

"I'll come with you," said Will. "Do you know I almost forgot to back him. Remembered just in time and had 50 euros on him."

Pelican Point also stood out in looks to the two biased onlookers, joined by Garech.

"After Small Talk's heroics, this horse must have some sort of a chance. We know he's fit and well and the extra half mile will suit him," Harry said, watching him walk round the paddock. "Certainly good each way value at 8/1, I'd say."

Joe employed different tactics this time, making his move forward to join the leaders a good half mile from home. He was certain the horse would stay the 2 ½ miles and wanted to make his stamina pay. He kicked for home between the last two hurdles and went into the last with a two length lead. It was head down and flat out after that, but he held on well to win by a length. Guts and great jockeyship won it for them.

"He's very brave," Joe told Harry and Garech in the winner's enclosure for the second time. "He jumps super and stays well. My advice is go chasing with him. 2 ½ miles is good but he'll stay 3 miles over fences."

To the Kerrigans, back in the bar, Harry said, "What do you think now about Small Talk and Cheltenham for the Supreme Novice?"

"After that performance today, I think we should have a crack. Opportunities like this don't come along too often."

"Well, we've got a month which is just about perfect timing, so let's go."

Headlines in the sporting press next morning screamed:

'KENNEDY AT THE DOUBLE

Rising young trainer scores twice at Fairyhouse'

CHAPTER 17

Three weeks later, Will put a call through to Mallory.

"I wonder Sir, if, apropos our last meeting with Fred, I could come and see you next Monday. I'm probably spending part of the previous weekend with my parents?"

"I should think that will be okay, Will. I'll check with Aggers and she'll call you if there's a problem. About 11 o'clock okay? What you want to talk about?"

"Just an idea Sir, sort of longer-term thoughts now that we've done the deal on the new larger premises in Limerick."

"Hmm, better be good ones."

"That's wonderful," Mary had said when Will rang to suggest coming. "Anything special?"

"Of course it's special," he replied. "But yes in two other ways as well. Robert Mallory has told me that after another year in Ireland he will want me to do something else and I want to talk to him about it, so I have a meeting with him on Monday. Also, the horse I've been riding for Siobhan's brother which has won his last two races, is running at Cheltenham on Tuesday and after the weekend we'll go first to see Mallory, then on to Cheltenham, so you'd better dust off the television screen."

Saturday morning, Will woke first, looking across at the lovely sleeping beauty next to him, a faint smile playing at the corners of her mouth, tousled hair framing her face. He hadn't slept well – butterflies in his tummy.

Blimey, he said to himself. *If I'm feeling like this, I wonder what kind of shape Harry's in.*

Siobhan's eyes opened, the smile stretched, her arms reached up to pull his mouth down to hers.

"I put too much garlic in the sauce last night," she said.

Joanna bubbled over in excitement when she greeted Will and Siobhan.

"I'm off to Zimbabwe in two weeks, you know. My new passport arrived yesterday. Jason is very envious; I had a letter from him at school; he's travelled lots but never been to Africa."

"Yes, I do know JoJo. I have arranged it all for you. Reilly Travers or maybe his wife Candace will meet you at the airport in Harare and take you to the farm. It's only about an hour and a half's drive. Reilly is the third generation of Travers to manage the farm, which his grandfather started in 1948. You'll have a great time. Now, Mum, how are you and Dad? Sorry this is such a short visit but I have this important meeting with Mallory tomorrow morning. He may have something he wants me to do, but I want to get in first with my idea."

"Good, tell me your idea later. I'm afraid your father's not so good. He has occasional bursts of enthusiasm but generally, his memory is fading and he'll sit at his desk for hours not doing anything. I've had Dr Craw round ostensibly for a drink, but really to give him the once over. His view is as I feared; he has prescribed some pills and recommended a neurologist in Chester to see him. It's not going to be easy and just as well that JoJo is going to Zimbabwe; at least you're not too far away. Still, I'll put him in front of the telly next week and try to get him to concentrate on the racing."

"There's a grotty hotel close to the office where I'll drop you while I have my meeting. You can have a cup of coffee or something stronger if you feel like getting into training for Cheltenham."

"No, coffee and *The Racing Post* will do fine for me," she replied. "While I wait for Sir Galahad to return."

"Hello, Aggers, how good to see you. I hope his nibs is in good form this morning?"

"I'll tell him you said that."

"Don't you dare!"

"Will Carpenter is here," she spoke into the intercom, with a wink at Will.

"Come in Will and sit down. Like a cup of coffee?"

"Gosh, yes please Sir."

"With or without the arsenic, Mr Mallory?" Aggers asked.

She closed the door behind her.

"Right Will, what is it?"

"It's about our last meeting Sir. You kindly virtually gave me a year's notice on the Irish job, I don't know if there is anybody that you have in mind to take over from me but if not, I would certainly recommend Pat Byrne. He's intelligent, ambitious, I think loyal and above all, interested in the company. Also, I'm very impressed with Jim McDonald in Limerick. You may even think that Jim, being more experienced, could take over the main job from me and send Pat down to Limerick. Fred gets on very well with both of them."

"Okay, is that all you've come to tell me?"

"No, Sir. You kindly said that you might have what you styled as a senior role to do with the expansion of the company. With this in mind, I have an idea and suggestion."

"And what might that be?"

"To set up a Supercar branch company in Barbados, Sir."

"What? You've come all this way at the company's expense to waste my time on some fucking pie in the sky bollocksy idea in fucking fairyland?"

"Actually, Sir, I haven't come at the company's expense. I'm taking two days holiday and this is one of them. I thought it better to put it to you in person, in order to save you breaking the telephone in anger."

"If I didn't know you better, I'd have you thrown out on the street now with a P45 in your hand. As it is, I suppose you better waste more company time and send me a detailed proposal though I can tell you know what the answer will be. What are you doing for your other day's holiday?"

"I'm going to the races, Sir."

"The races?"

"Yessir. I used to have a part-time job riding for a racehorse trainer close to home. In Ireland, I've been riding for a trainer on Saturdays and one of the horses I've been riding runs in the first race at Cheltenham tomorrow. He's called Small Talk, Sir. It's on the telly, Sir."

"God, the sooner we get you out of bloody Ireland the better."

Aggers met him on the stairs on the way down. "You look as though you've been dragged through a thorn bush backwards," she said.

"No more than I expected," Will replied. "But I've come out the other side with only a few scratches."

"Here," she said. "This will cheer you up." She handed him a square-shaped wrapped parcel. "All senior and relevant staff members are being given one."

There it was complete with instructions; his mobile telephone.

As soon as Will had left, Robert Mallory told Aggers to get Fred on the line.

"I've just had young Carpenter here," he said.

"Yes, I knew he was coming over."

"He's got some bloody stupid idiotic idea of starting a Supercar company in Barbados. What the hell does he fucking know about Barbados?"

"Quite a lot, as a matter of fact."

"He's also got mixed up with a racehorse trainer in Ireland. We better get him out of there pretty sharpish."

"You should see his girlfriend – an absolute corker and the sister of the trainer he's been riding for. They've a horse running at Cheltenham tomorrow; asked me to go with them."

"Are you going?"

"No, too many bloody people. I'll watch it on the box though."

"Well, what did he say?" Siobhan asked.

"Almost word for word what I expected," Will replied. "But he didn't sack me yet and asked me to write a proposal document. Which will take me a while and in the meantime we can plan our little holiday. You've heard me talk about my old school chum Jimmy van Duren? Just a thought and no need for any immediate decision, but I wondered what you might think if we ask him and his current girlfriend to come with us; you'd get on with him very well, he's a bit like Harry – always has a pretty girl in tow."

"Will, darling, all I want is you by my side night and day but, yes, sounds a super idea."

Will had arranged to pick up Harry and Garech at Bristol airport to save having two cars, then to go on to the Lygon Arms in Broadway. The Kerrigans came in their own car on the ferry from Rosslare to Pembroke, thence to meet up at the hotel.

"There were more shamrocks on that plane than in a nursery. Nearly all the passengers were on their way to Cheltenham," Harry said, at the airport.

In the car, he said, "As expected, it's a hell of a hot race. Not only are there the best young hurdlers in Ireland but those from all the top English trainers, Henderson, O'Neill. Pipe, Hobbs, Nicholls, they're all there; eighteen runners and not a bad one among them."

Later, in the bar in the hotel before dinner, Tim Kerrigan said, "Look, this is quite amazing - here we all are together. I never thought I would have a horse good enough to bring over here. Win, lose or draw, let's just make the most of it and have fun, which is what all it's about. Thank you Harry for making it happen, and you Siobhan, and you Will, for the parts you have played. We'll leave it now to Small Talk and Joe to do the best they can, let's all relax and be happy."

"Thanks Tim," replied Harry. "I never thought we'd be here either. I don't know about the 'relaxing' bit but – happy, certainly, and thank you for having faith in me and my team."

Harry, Will and Siobhan arrived at the course by 11 o'clock on Tuesday morning, leaving Garech to come with the Kerrigans. It was a good early Spring morning with glimpses of sun poking through scudding clouds in a stiff breeze. All well with horse and jockey, the course looked immaculate in a natural, undulating amphitheatre under the backdrop of Cleeve Hill in the distance.

Scouring through the racing and national press, Will found one interesting piece summing up the Supreme which ran, *'a possible dark horse among the Irish contingent for the Supreme Hurdle is the lightly raced Small Talk from up and coming trainer Harry Kennedy. The unbeaten winner of a maiden at Limerick, he won his next race at Fairyhouse narrowly having been badly hampered during the race.'*

"Ride him as if it's just another race, Joe," Harry said in the paddock. "I don't have to tell you, the pace will be fast all the way with no prisoners being taken. Keep him interested but don't go with the front runners who'll be flat out from the start. Remember his great turn of foot and that the hill up to the winning post will find out any non-stayers. Don't knock him about if he's obviously got no chance late in the race."

The buzz of excitement of the 50,000 strong crowd intensified as the horses started to line up at the start, erupting into the traditional tumultuous roar as the tapes went, the commentator announcing, "They're off."

Joe had no problem in settling Small Talk in behind a wall of horses and enough daylight to have a good sight of the first hurdle, which Small Talk stepped over neatly with the minimum of effort.

Passing the stands and swinging left-handed away after the second, *I'm happy here,* he thought, towards the rear of the main division, about 25 lengths behind the leaders.

Without the noise of the crowd, everything became much quieter, just the sound of the horses hooves, the clatter made jumping the hurdles and the comments, mostly unrepeatable, by the jockeys.

Along the far side of the course, Joe spoke quietly, "We'll just ease up a few places and see what's going on up front. Okay, that'll do for now."

At the top of the hill, directly opposite the stands, with three more flights of hurdles to be jumped and a downhill section in front of them, he repeated the plan, noting that some of the other jockeys were getting busy.

Jumping the hurdle halfway down the hill, an awful clatter and shouting came from behind. *At least one, maybe two must have fallen,* he thought.

Approaching the turn into the straight with two to jump. *We've got eight in front of us, time to get a move on. Yeah, what a jump, down to six to beat now.*

Going to the last, *Only four in front,* Joe said. *Come on my beauty, remember Fairyhouse.*

One crack of the whip on the take off stride gained a fabulous response, landing running with three horses and as many lengths to make up. *We'll take this gap between two of them.*

The one on his right could go no faster and dropped away. *Just the two now, both on the inside of us.*

Giving him another crack, Small Talk stuck his head out, giving everything he'd got; Joe, using his own rhythmic balance, his whip as a rudder and yelling, "Come on, you can do it, just a bit more, GO ON!"

They surged forward for the line, reaching it just before the other two.

"YESSSS, YOU'VE DONE IT!"

Standing up in his stirrups, waving his whip in the air in a moment of triumph, Joe lowered himself back on the saddle as Small Talk pulled up, leaning forward and clasping his arms around the horse's neck.

"You are wonderful, wonderful, and so brave a star," he said, as a delighted and equally overcome Vince, his lad, dashed onto the course to greet his hero and lead him on the long trek through the thousands of people in the cheering crowd, to the winner's enclosure at the far end of the paddock, where an emotional and deliriously happy group consisting of the Kerrigans, the Kennedys and Will were waiting.

Much hugging, kissing and back slapping, among tears of emotion and relief. Nicky Henderson, who trained the second horse ridden by Mick Fitzgerald, was among the first of those to come over to them to offer congratulations. Small Talk, the real hero of the race, stood among the crowd of well-wishers, ears pricked, taking it all in, having a huge drink of water out of a bucket held in front of him by Vince, knowing, as horses certainly do, that he had done well.

The rest of the day passed in a bit of a blur. Brough Scott interviewed Harry on Channel 4 television, during which Harry paid tribute to Joe Maguire, his dedicated staff at Lostock and to "My sister's boyfriend who has ridden Small Talk in all his serious work and provided most helpful advice."

Will heard his name being called out as he and Siobhan were leaving the winner's enclosure. It was Jimmy van Duren.

"Will," he said. "What are you doing here and why are you in there with the nobs?"

"Jimmy, wonderful to see you. I ride out for Harry Kennedy whenever I can and have been riding Small Talk in his work; this is Siobhan, Harry's sister."

"Fantastic, this is Sarah by the way," he said, introducing a very pretty tall girl. "Let's go and have a drink in the Turf Club."

He led the way.

"I've seen that girl somewhere before," Will said to Siobhan, as they made their way to the tented village beyond the paddock.

Entering the Turf Club tent and while Jimmy was arranging with the Secretary to bring in two guests, Sarah turned to Will.

"I'm Sarah Whatcombe," she said. "We have met before under very sad circumstances, at James' funeral."

"Yes, of course, I remember now. I just said to Siobhan that

I was sure that we had met before. Please forgive me for not remembering immediately. It was a very sad and traumatic day. James and I were very close indeed. He was a wonderful brother."

All four chatted away, full of the excitement of the day and Small Talk's victory.

Suddenly Will said, "Hey Jimmy, remember you helped me get that job on the banana boat to the West Indies? Siobhan and I are planning a holiday there in June. Why don't you come with us?"

"What an idea. Love to, but let me think about it in the cold light of day."

"I hope you didn't mind me suggesting he and the girlfriend came to Barbados with us?" Will said to Siobhan later.

"Of course not, darling one. We've already discussed it; it would be nice for me to have some company if you have to do some work while we're there as I won't know anybody."

CHAPTER 18

The telephone rang in Max Geary's office. He picked it up.

"There's a Mr Carpenter calling from Ireland."

"Oh, put him through."

"Max, this is Will Carpenter, remember me?"

"Of course, man, I remember you. I hear little bits about you now and again. What you doin' and how goes it?"

Will filled him in about his job with Supercar and the start-up company in Ireland.

Then he said, "The boss and owner of Supercar, who I met originally as his cabin boy on the *Star*, is pleased with the success in Ireland. He'd given me another year here before moving me onto something else. I had a meeting with him last Monday and suggested a branch company in Barbados. He blew his top as I expected, but he's asked me to prepare a proposal document."

"Will, things here have exploded even more since you were last here as regards the tourist industry, including many new, upmarket projects. The car rental sector has changed, too. It used to be confined to local operators but now the big international boys, Hertz, Avis and the like are here operating under concession agreements. Most of their business comes from overseas customers booking from their respective countries. Off the cuff, it would be my opinion that there is room for an independent car rental company to be set up here; the one proviso, however, and subject to some checking on my end, is that the company would have to be at least 40% owned in Barbados. Let me do some work to establish how this can be done satisfactorily and look into the project generally."

"Thank you, Max. I'd love you to be involved in any way possible. There's another thing: it's an excuse for me to come out for a holiday and for you and me to meet up. I am thinking of round about June time. On a personal matter, you know how very fond I was – and still am – of Lucille Todd, but I am afraid that distance and the passage of time has taken its toll. I have a new and lovely girlfriend, and I know that Lucille is spending time with her new boyfriend. We remain, however, the very best of friends. If we come in, say, June, there would be 4 of us, 2 couples. If possible, and depending on cost, we would like to rent a house on the west coast. I know Lucille is now working at TRECO and of course I would like to rent through her company, but I don't want to upset her."

"I know about all this, Will, and quite understand. I also know that Lucille harbours no ill feelings towards you. She has a very nice young Barbadian lawyer friend called Josh Taylor. Leave it to me to sort something out house wise and I can't tell you how good it will be to have you back in Barbados. You'll be hearing from me very soon on both counts."

"Thanks, Max. I can't wait – it's been far too long. Oh, by the way – had a bit of excitement last week: my girlfriend's brother, Harry Kennedy, is a trainer in Ireland and I ride out for him whenever I can. A horse that I've been riding in all his work won at the big Cheltenham Festival."

"Fantastic, Well done. We'll talk again soon"

The adrenalin of the Cheltenham win had taken a while to subside. Fergy Lynch thought it was Christmas, Easter and St Patrick's Day all in one; the press reports were ecstatic, Mary, Angus and Joanna had combined in a long message on Will's telephone, Fred expressed more emotion than Will thought he was capable of, and had become the hero of his golf club having told many of them to back Small Talk; even Robert Mallory sent a message of congratulations to the office, adding that he hoped Will was now safely back at work.

The following Saturday Harry booked the local pub for a lads and girls party, which Will and Siobhan attended and to which Harry brought an old flame called Jane, who Siobhan described as *'any port in a storm'*, which Will thought was a little unfair.

"Will, darling," Siobhan said, giving him an enormous hug and long, tender kiss back at Lostock after the party. "I haven't told you today how much I love you. We've hardly touched down after Cheltenham and you've been back at work for the last two days. I've missed you so much."

"Thanks, Princess. It's been the best and certainly the most exciting week of my life and you are the icing on the cake. I miss you every second we are not together. Forgot to tell you, Jimmy called yesterday and asked if I, sorry, we, were serious about him and Sarah coming to Barbados. I said certainly we were; he said Sarah just had to clear it with her boss – evidently, she is PA to some bigwig – but it looks as though they're coming. I wasn't sure at Cheltenham how much of an 'item' they were, but that definitely seems to be the case. Glad you like my friend Jimmy. Strange meeting Sarah again: she told me at James' funeral how much she had loved him. Now, come on, it's bedtime – I'm going to dream about you, then wake up and find it wasn't a dream at all."

"D'you know, you're getting more Irish than I am. And I'm not letting you go to sleep just yet."

"There're a lot of sore heads in the yard this morning," Harry remarked, coming in for breakfast. "Even Ronan looks like the tail end of a bad dream. Lucky it's a Sunday."

"Come on, let's get out and shake the cobwebs away," Siobhan said, after clearing up the breakfast things.

"Yeah, good idea," said Will. "You coming Harry?"

"No, don't think so; I've got a lot of telephoning to do, entries to make etc. Maybe go to the Bounty for a pint before lunch?"

"Okay, see you there."

"I've got heavy couple of weeks' work ahead," Will said on their walk. "I've spoken to my friend in Barbados, Max Geary. He's going to find us a house to rent and also smooth things over with Lucille who, he says, fully understands and has a nice new boyfriend. It will be best if we meet her and the boyfriend as soon as possible after we get there. I am writing my feasibility proposal for Mallory: already jotted down the main headings and I'll probably stay late in the office most evenings to get it done. A bit easier to concentrate then after everyone's gone home; still a lot of research to be done. I'll be talking a lot to Max as well – the time difference works well as it will be during his normal office hours."

"I'll come and soothe your worried brow on some evenings, my darling one, and cook you a late dinner," Siobhan said, giving his hand a squeeze. "And be the sugar to help the medicine go down?"

Two weeks later, it was done and sent by courier to Mallory with a copy to Fred. Also, Max had confirmed a house for them which he described as, "Bang on Gibbes Beach, St Peter, plenty of room for two couples, very comfortable with staff and a cook". June in Barbados is not high season and Max secured a sizeable discount from the British owner.

Towards the end of April, the jump racing season began to wind down, so all of Harry's best horses had finished for the season. Some owners, if they have suitable facilities at home, as the Kerrigans have for Small Talk on their farm, take their horses home for a couple of months rest. The remainder stayed at Lostock, though on a more relaxed regime, spending time out in post and rail fenced paddocks for several hours in the daytime, weather permitting. A few remained in full training and Will continued to ride out on Saturdays, being treated now as part of the family. Also, due to connections of Harry's and Julian Shannon's in Cheshire, Will received an invitation from the Phoenix Park Polo Club to exercise ponies at weekends and on the weekday evenings as the daylight lengthened.

In early May, Mallory called, "I've read it. It is an impressive, well put together, extremely well researched and comprehensive proposal. Congratulations. Quite out of the question of course, like I knew it would be. You go off and have a good holiday; you've deserved it. Come and see me when you get back."

Will called Fred, "I thought you'd be on the line pretty quick, lad. I'm not saying take no notice of what the old fart says, but my guess is he's playing for time. He's a canny old bugger as you know; he's looking into this, take my word. He'll be doing plenty research of his own. He's taken with the idea but won't admit it – not now, anyway. He's taken risks before, as you know, but they've been risks coming from his own ideas. It's very good that you are going out there anyway. You'll come back with a lot of stuff that you can't discover at the end of a telephone line. Let's hope it's good stuff."

"Thanks, Fred. Good advice as usual. It's still a few weeks before we go and I'll be talking to my man out there who I trust implicitly and a trail will be laid. Talk again soon."

A few days later Will rang Garech Kennedy, "Garech, I wondered if you are around in Dublin and if so, there are a couple things I would like to talk to you about?"

"Yes of course, Will. Can you make lunch? If so, how about Wednesday at the Troc?"

"That would be marvellous. I'd love to."

Garech greeted Will, "So glad that you called. We haven't caught up since Cheltenham so come and sit down."

Louis, the head waiter, showed them to Garech's favourite table, placed a glass of champagne in front of each of them and left the menu, departing with the words, "Never mind the month, the oysters are just fantastic."

"Now then Will, what's your news? Things a little quieter at Lostock now, I suppose?"

"Yes, you could say that, though Harry's very upbeat about the future. With the success of Small Talk, Pelican Point and quite a few others, things are looking good with a number of new owners coming his way. I think he's got a several orders for Goff's summer sales in July and August. They're a very happy bunch there – the staff I mean and Ronan's a bloody good head lad."

"That's good to hear and I'm proud of him. Now what about these oysters?"

"I'm game, if you are."

"Okay Louis," he called. "You've sold the oysters. A dozen each please and what do you want afterwards, Will?"

"What do you recommend Louis? How's the calves liver?"

"Couldn't do better, Sir."

"That's for me then."

"I'll have rack of lamb – pink as you know. Oh and bring us a bottle of that excellent Burgundy I had last week."

"Thank you Mr Kennedy."

"That's that, then. Now what's your news, Will?"

"Well – er," Will coughed mildly, clasping his hands together tightly under the table. "Er, I want to ask your daughter to marry me," he got out eventually. "And I hope you won't mind if I do?"

"Mind? I would be absolutely delighted if you did. Thrilled to bits, in fact. I just wondered in the back of my mind if this might be the case. Have you asked her yet?"

"No, I haven't. She may say no."

"Bloody fool if she does and I'm sure she won't. Have you said anything to Harry?"

"No, not yet and I don't think I will until afterwards."

"This is marvellous news, Will, you go ahead and pronto."

The oysters were approaching. "Bring us another glass of champagne; we've got something to celebrate," Garech called out to Louis.

"On that, I've something else I want to ask you. Who would you recommend as jewellers in Dublin where I could look for the engagement ring?"

"I use McDowell's in Upper O'Connell Street and have always found them very good. Speak to Nikki McDowell, who happens to be married to one of the Coolmore team. Have you anything in particular in mind?"

"Thanks, Garech, I shall go there this very afternoon. Emerald, I think but would need advice. What I have in mind is this, I'll have to take a chance that she'll say yes. Our first proper date was in this restaurant. Just a few days before we go off for our holiday in Barbados, I want to bring her here for dinner and I thought it might be rather romantic if the box containing her engagement ring was positioned on her place at the table when we arrived for dinner. We'd have to bring Louis into the plot; I could bring the ring here earlier in the day, or maybe the day before."

"Oh that's a brilliant idea and I'll fix it all up with Louis nearer the time. Now, finish these oysters and let's hope they don't kill us."

Will entered the door of McDowell's at 3 Upper O'Connell Street later that afternoon and asked to see Nikki McDowell, saying that Garech Kennedy had suggested that he did so. The mention of Garech's name clearly meant something to the receptionist because Nikki appeared quite swiftly.

"Hello," Will said. "My name's William Carpenter; Garech Kennedy suggested that I came to see you. Garech and I have just had lunch together; I am hoping that he will soon become my father-in-law, since I am about to ask his daughter to marry me … So I am looking for an engagement ring."

"Oh, that's wonderful news and you've come to the right place. Congratulations, come with me and let's have a look at what we have. Have you any ideas of your own?"

"Yes, I have. I would like the ring to be emerald based."

"I'll show you what we have, but we can always make alterations or, indeed, make one from scratch to your own design."

With a small amount of alteration they came up with a ring of three emeralds mounted vertically, the centre one being the largest with a rectangular shoulder diamond on either side and a cluster of small diamonds forming a frame around the remainder.

"That will look wonderful, I'm sure; thank you so much for being so patient and attentive. I hope Siobhan will love it. Could you give me a call when it's ready and I'll come and collect it rather than you send it by post?"

"Yes of course and if any changes are to be made, I'm sure we will be able to manage that."

The Friday evening before Will's last full week at work before their holiday, he arrived at Lostock at around 7.30. Siobhan heard his car arrive and rushed out to greet him.

"Hello, gorgeous," he said, climbing out of his car. "That's a pretty pinny."

"Well, I'm cooking a sumptuous supper," she replied, laughing as they went into the house.

"I've got a little plan," Will continued. "A week to tomorrow we're off on our travels so I thought we might have a little pre-holiday treat on either Wednesday or Thursday. Remember our first proper date at the Troc? Well, I thought we might play it again. What do you think?"

"Oh, Will, you are a darling. That would be quite fantastic; I'd love to do that. And please may I stay the night again with you?"

"I'll have to think about that one," he said. "Now, is this a dry house or is there a drink for a hard-working boy?"

They fixed it for the Wednesday so as to leave Thursday and Friday clear for Will to finalise working arrangements at the office while he was away, and for Siobhan to do likewise for Harry at Lostock and to do her packing.

"Just a few bikinis and a couple of floaty jobs – that's all you'll need," Will had said.

Monday afternoon, Max Geary called, "Don't want to spoil your holiday but I'm fixing up a few meetings with interested parties while you're here. Wouldn't be doing this without some degree of optimism. The fact that you'll be here yourself is a bonus. Don't forget to bring a hard copy of your feasibility proposal. I know I've got one but people like to see originals and to quiz the promoter and his experience. I've arranged for a large taxi to collect you all at the airport and take you to the house; the driver will have your name on a placard. Also, a hire car will come to the house soon afterwards. It might be best to have two cars, what do you think?"

"Yes, Max, two cars so that I'm free to come to meetings."

"Okay, I'll do that. I told Peter a while back about your visit; he sends all best and much looks forward to seeing you. Also, Tony Knowles is very excited on the polo front. Says you can ride May Go Twice and there may even be a chance of a match. Socially, I think you'll be in demand."

On Tuesday, having called Nikki McDowell, Will came to the shop just before closing time.

"There," she said, showing him the ring beautifully packed in a very smart leather jewellery box.

"Fabulous," Will said. "If that doesn't work, nothing will."

Nikki laughed, "I'm sure she'll love it. My husband's in the racing world; he's part of the Coolmore team. Not sure if he knows Siobhan's brother; they don't see so much of the jumping boys but I must ask him."

"Harry's a smashing fellow. We get on very well and I couldn't ask for a better brother-in-law to be."

Will took his parcel straight round to the Tocadero.

"Here you are, Louis," he said. "Look after it for me won't you?"

"It'll go straight into the safe, Mr Carpenter and will be on Miss Siobhan's place when you arrive tomorrow."

"Please can we have the same table that we had the last time? I'll show you which one."

"No need, Mr Carpenter; I remember which it was and it's already arranged."

Siobhan was already in the flat when Will got back from his office the next evening.

"Thought I'd get here early in plenty of time to have a bath and change, so that you can do the same," she said, wrapped in a bath towel.

"Marvellous, we might as well start as we did before," he replied, opening a bottle of champagne out of the fridge.

"Here's to us, my lovely one," he said, handing her a glass and pouring one for himself. "Now, bring it with you and chat to me in the bath."

Soon they were ready, Siobhan wearing a three-quarter length close fitting green dress showing a fair amount of cleavage and decorated with a small, well-spaced-out pattern of emotive flowers.

"You look amazing."

"I'm trying to live up to my man."

Louis, himself greeted them at the door, "Good evening, Mr Carpenter, Miss Siobhan. Very good to see you here again, let me show you to your table."

He led the way across the dining room and pulled out the chair for Siobhan to sit down. Gift wrapped; the square box sat neatly on a plate between the laid out cutlery.

"What's this?" asked Siobhan.

"Open it and you'll find out," answered Will.

Siobhan sat down, slowly untied the blue and gold ribbon and removed the wrapping to reveal the leather box. She opened it; the ring, firmly positioned in a specially designed cushion looked up at her.

Siobhan's eyes opened wide as she looked across at Will and said very quietly, "Does this mean what I think it means?"

He nodded.

She leapt to her feet, dashed round the table to Will, who had risen as well.

"YES, YES PLEASE!" she shouted, grabbing him round his neck, kissing him passionately.

All the other diners from nearby tables, realising what was going on, rose to their feet clapping and hollering messages of support and happiness. Will, in the meantime, extracted the ring from the box and slipped it onto Siobhan's finger to further applause from the whole room.

Siobhan sat down, reaching across with her left hand with the ringed finger to the fore, taking hold of Will's outstretched hand, murmuring, "Will, Will, my darling Will, I love you so, so much and will never cease to do so. Thank you for coming into my life and please never leave it."

"Don't worry darling Siobhan, I never will. I love you far too much."

Louis, who had been hovering about all this time, took out of his inside breast pocket an envelope which he placed on the table. It was addressed to 'Siobhan and Will'.

"You open it," Siobhan said.

Inside was a lovely card with a caricature of two young people swinging from a branch of a tree. The handwritten inscription read:

'To Will and Siobhan – well done I'm so happy and thrilled for

you both and I know, Siobhan, that your mother would have been, too. With love, Dad/Garech.'

Underneath there was a PS:

'Hope this will pay for your dinner and help a bit with your holiday'.

Attached was a cheque made out to Will for E5,000.

Later, back at Will's flat, he said to Siobhan, "Do you realise that this is the second time since we have known each other that you have captivated and brought all other diners in a restaurant to their feet by what you are offering me?"

Hugging him, she said, "Will, my darling, lead me to our bedroom and let's make love until we fall asleep in each other's arms. You've made me the happiest girl in the world."

They were woken by sunlight streaming in through the open window, having forgotten to draw any curtains.

"Just as well," Will murmured, their bodies still intertwined. "We've only got today and tomorrow before we go."

They had agreed that Siobhan should go back to Lostock today, finish all she had to do and come back to Will's the next day, Friday. On Saturday they were leaving on an early flight to Gatwick where they would meet up with Jimmy and Sarah and catch the midday BA flight to Bridgetown.

"How will you tell Harry?" Will asked.

"Flash him," Siobhan answered, waving her left arm in the air.

"I feel bad not to see him myself. I hope he won't think I'm being rude, but I'll give you time to get home before I ring him."

"I'm sure he won't. He likes you very much indeed and I know he will be so happy for us both."

They left after breakfast at the same time, Siobhan to Lostock and Will to his office.

His first call was to his parents. Mary, as usual, answered the telephone.

"Hello, Mum, guess what?"

"You and Siobhan have got engaged."

"How the bloody hell did you guess that?"

"Mother's intuition," she replied. "Absolutely brilliant news. I'm so very, very happy for you both. She's a really super, lovely girl and I'm so happy for you both. Let me call your Dad ---- Angus, come here; Will's got something to tell you..."

"Hello, Dad, Siobhan and I are engaged."

"Oh, good, I'm so pleased, Now have you got everything ready for your holiday – you know, tickets, money, passport and don't forget your driving license; you never know you might need it. Have a good time, I'll pass you back to Mum."

"Wow, Mum, romance with a capital R."

"Yes, well you know your father. Believe me, he's just as happy and pleased as I am. Had a lovely long letter from JoJo yesterday; she's having an amazing time, absolutely loving it and everybody being very nice to her."

"That's great, Mum. Of course I understand about Dad. Listen, I've got a hell of a lot to do so must crack on. Just wanted you to be first to know. We're leaving sparrow fart on Saturday. I'll send you my friend Max Geary's telephone number just in case you need to contact me urgently."

Next he called Garech, thanking him profusely on the telephone and filling him in on the events and reaction at the Trocadero, and what a good job Louis had done. Most of all for his most generous cheque.

Will also sat down and wrote him a long and appreciative letter, emphasising how grateful he was for all the parts and enthusiasm he had played so far, and how he hoped to be a good son-in-law to him and husband to his daughter.

Then he rang Fred.

"Well done, lad, you lucky bugger. Can't say I'm surprised. She's terrific. Hope all goes well on all fronts in Barbados. Shall I tell the old man?"

"What do you think? He's not met Siobhan yet, so maybe I'll send him a postcard to remind him of Barbados."

"Yes, that'll do well. I'll probably mention it to him en passant."

"I'll keep you posted with events and progress there. All very best to you."

Finally, he called Harry.

"One doesn't need to be the brain of Britain – or even Ireland – to be surprised which, of course, I'm not. Delighted however, and thrilled for you both. Thank God she's chosen someone I like and, for that matter, respect. I hope you make a better job of training her than I have! Have an absolutely marvellous holiday. We'll have quite a celebration when you get back."

CHAPTER 19

Siobhan looked radiant and very chic in her designer jeans and white T-shirt, cashmere cardigan and slip-on slightly raised pale pink shoes as they departed from the flat at 5.30 on Saturday morning.

"Oh Will, darling, I'm so excited - our first real adventure together."

They'd been out for an early dinner at their local in Dunboyne the night before, but were both too full of anticipation to sleep well.

Will checked their luggage through to Bridgetown, they were issued with boarding cards to Gatwick and Bridgetown so all they had to do at Gatwick was go through the in transit passport control.

"There they are," Will shouted, spotting Jimmy and Sarah heading in the same direction. Much waving, kissing and hugging before Siobhan could wait no longer to say, holding up her left hand, "Look what I've got!!"

"Oh, that's just amazing, fabulous, game changing and brilliant," Jimmy said, kissing Siobhan and hugging again Will, his great pal and old school friend.

Sarah joined with equal enthusiasm, "Quick, where's the nearest bar? We've got time and we need to start where we are about to continue."

"A bottle of champagne and four glasses for my just engaged best friend and his beautiful future wife," Jimmy called out to the barman.

On the plane they had selected two seats, window and aisle, in rows one behind the other, rather than four together in the central section of the wide-bodied jumbo jet.

Before take-off, Jimmy sought out the cabin stewardess for their section and whispered something in her ear.

"Leave it to me," she said.

Lo and behold along came a bottle of champagne wrapped in a linen napkin on a tray with four glasses.

"Nicked it from first class while no one was looking," she said.

Just under nine hours later, the tip of North Point, Barbados, came into view, waves crashing onto the coral stone cliffs sending cascades of spray into the air. They made a wide sweep to approach the runway of Grantley Adams airport from the south east and made a smooth landing. A warm tropical breeze greeted the happy foursome as they descended the steps of the plane and made their way into the airport building.

Half an hour later they emerged into the afternoon sunshine where Will spotted his name on a placard being held by a grinning taxi driver.

"Mr Carpenter?"

"Yes, that's me."

"You wait here. Me, Austin – I go fetch car."

Soon they were installed in a large 6 seater Mercedes and subjected to a long chatter from Austin, "This your first time in Barbados? How long you stay? You like cricket? Here my card, call me when you want taxi," and so on and on.

Forty minutes later, Austin took a left turn off Highway 2A, downhill along a narrow lane until hitting the coast road. A right turn onto it, almost immediately followed by turning into a narrow opening which revealed a short distance away, a low, attractive-looking white painted house. In a small turning circle in front of the house stood a yellow moke. Seeing it, Will took a sharp intake of breath.

"That's Lucille's car," he said quietly to Siobhan.

Lucille, her long blonde hair streaming behind her, wearing a brightly coloured dress, came out of the house, ran towards Will, flung her arms around his neck, kissed him and said, "Will, hello and how wonderful it is to see you again; you haven't changed a bit."

Then, turning to his fiancé, "You must be Siobhan. It is so lovely to meet you and for you to come to Barbados. Will's told me a bit about you – you look terrific but must be tired after your long journey."

"Lucille, sweetheart, you look great too. It's so kind of you to come and meet us. This is Jimmy and Sarah and I can't tell you how marvellous it is to be back in Barbados."

"Come on in all of you and I'll give you a quick tour of the house. Austin, please will you bring in all the luggage and put it in the entrance hall."

"Yes, Miss Lucille."

Just then two cars rolled into view. Their hired cars. Formalities such as driving licenses to be examined, local visitor permits to be issued, forms to the signed, all speeded up by Lucille and quickly disposed of.

They followed Lucille. Inside the front door stood three ladies.

"Now, let me introduce you to Elaine, Misha and Naomi. Elaine and Misha look after the house and Naomi is a just fabulous cook," said Lucille.

All three of them smiled and said how much they hoped to help make sure that they had a good time.

"I've laid on enough supplies – food and drink – to tide you over for tonight and maybe tomorrow, but all the tips about what to do and where, is in the house brochure on the hall table. Perhaps you'd like a drink now? Elaine makes a wicked rum punch if you'd like one?"

"I certainly would," said Will.

"So would I," said Siobhan.

"Make that four then," said Jimmy.

Lucille took them through to the big drawing room which opened via large sliding glass doors straight onto a coral stone terrace, then the golden white sand of beautiful Gibbes Beach.

"Wow," they said, practically in unison.

"Take your pick of the bedrooms," Lucille said. "There are actually four to choose from – three on the ground floor and one up a small staircase – all with their own bathrooms."

Austin had gone, having left the luggage in the hall, as requested. The four of them sipped at their rum punches in the drawing room, joined by Lucille who just had a fruit juice.

"Mine will come later," she said.

Siobhan, who had been uncharacteristically quiet and lost in admiration, spoke up, "Lucille, please forgive me for saying so, but I've heard so much about you from Will over many, many months. All I can say is that what I see before me is even better and more beautiful than what he described. You are so lovely and very brave to come and face us all. Thank you and I hope we will be long and lasting very best of friends."

She went over to Lucille; the two girls hugged with tears running down both their faces.

"I'm sure we will," Lucille said, wiping hers away. "Now, I am going to leave you to get sorted out. The girls know how to contact me, but I'll leave the TRECO card and telephone number on the table in the hall. I'm sure we'll be seeing a lot of each other, but do call me if you need anything."

Will escorted her to the moke, giving her hand a squeeze.

"She's lovely. Well done. See you."

She drove away waving her hand on high.

"What about a swim?" Will said.

Siobhan and Sarah had agreed on which bedrooms to occupy, they all stripped off their travelling clothes, slipped into swimmers and tore off across the sand and plunged into the calm, clear Caribbean Sea.

As it was a Saturday afternoon, TRECO office in Holetown was closed but Lucille had her own key.

She called Josh, "What time are we meeting? I'm feeling a bit emotional. Will and his friends arrived this afternoon and I've just got back from showing them round Westscape where they're staying."

"Sure, sweetheart. I'm just back from the golf course but why don't you pop round here as soon as you like and we'll go from there?"

"I'll do that. See you soon."

Next, she called Max at home, "Hi, Max, Lucille here. Just to say Will and his friends have arrived safely and I've showed them round Westscape."

"Well done – what's the girlfriend like?"

"Gorgeous and really nice. It was quite emotional, as you can guess, but I thought it best to get it over with quickly. She was so nice to me and so was he. He looks fine, hasn't really changed at all so I mustn't let it get to me. Going round to Josh's now. Talk soon."

"Hello, Dad, you okay?"

"Sure, and you?"

"Okay, a bit emotional. Just met Will and his friends and showed them round their house."

"Yes, I can guess – here's Mum."

"Darling, well done. Very brave of you."

"That's what his girlfriend said. She's lovely and was so sweet and kind to me. We had a big hug. It was wonderful to see Will, but I mustn't hark on it. I'm going round to Josh's now. Not sure if I'll be back this evening but will call you in the morning if not."

The light was starting to fade as they came out of the water.

"And that's just for starters," said Will.

They all went in. Unpacking didn't take long; soon they were ready for another rum punch prepared by Elaine in the drawing room.

Naomi came in. "What time you like dinner?" she asked.

"What time do you normally suggest?" asked Will.

"Around 8 o'clock. That okay?"

"Yes, fine but maybe a little earlier tonight. We'll be getting tired soon after the journey. It's about 11 o'clock at night now, our time."

"I make it 7.15/7.30 then. Okay?"

"Okay."

The telephone rang. Misha answered it.

"For you Mr. Carpenter."

"Will, how are you after your journey? Max here."

"Max, great to speak to you and in the same time zone."

"A little bird told me you'd all arrived."

"I wonder what particular tune your little bird was whistling."

"Don't worry – a happy one. Look, I won't bother you now and I expect you'll all want to crash out and be tourists tomorrow, so I'll give you a call on Monday morning and we can make a plan. I just wanted to say hi and welcome. It's great to have you back in Barbados."

"Shan't be doing much touring," Will said. "This place is just heaven, so I doubt if we'll move very far tomorrow."

The elegant round carved coral stone dining table at the other end of the drawing room could seat up to eight people, so they were well spaced out in great comfort for dinner. Naomi produced a superb mushroom and asparagus salad with parmesan and vinaigrette to start with and a Caribbean-style chicken dish to follow, along with a perfectly drinkable Chilean white wine.

"I've been thinking about the series of coincidences that have brought us all together here," said Jimmy.

"I wouldn't have come in the first place if it were not for your introduction to the shipping company operating the banana boats," replied Will. "Then I met the owner of Supercar through being his cabin boy and then I got my subsequent job in Ireland where guess who, sitting here, came into the picture."

"There's more," went on Jimmy. "How did I meet Sarah, also sitting here? Through your wonderful and dearly loved late brother James."

"I was going out with James," Sarah said. "You've got to meet my best friend, Jimmy, he told me. Jimmy was so kind and supportive to me after your James was killed. I remember distinctly meeting you, Will, at his funeral. Our romance – Jimmy's and mine – started slowly quite a while later; Jimmy got through girlfriends like water going through a sieve; for ages, I thought of him only as James' best friend. A bit different now, I'm glad to say."

"And then we all met together on that fabulous day at Cheltenham when Small Talk, trained by Siobhan's brother Harry won," Will said. "You haven't met Harry yet but soon will do; a star man."

"A toast then," Jimmy said. "To absent friends, James and Harry."

Tiredness and bed came swiftly and welcoming. Covered only by the single sheet and cuddled together like two peas in a snug pod, Will cast his mind through the events of the day from leaving his flat in Dunboyne to arriving at this lovely house in Barbados and Jimmy's touching words at dinner. What twists of fate had brought them all together.

He woke early – about 6 o'clock, Barbados time – to see, on opening his eyes, Siobhan's deep brown ones looking at him. His reaction was instantaneous; she reached for him, gently pulling and guiding him over her, lifting her head to receive the kiss that he gave her already parted lips and through which she gave her involuntary little gasp as their bodies became as one together. Soon she ran a hand stroking down his body to grasp the shaft of joy that was exploring deep inside her.

"I want to feel you coming" she whispered. "Please now, I can't wait any longer."

"Neither can I, my darling," he just managed to say, as they plunged into ecstatic oblivion.

They lay, side by side, hand by hand. The only sounds being the lapping of the sea on the shore and the cooing of doves in the trees surrounding the house.

"Love you, precious; I think the sea beckons," Will said eventually. "So show me your bikini collection."

"Right, you saw the quite modest one yesterday and I'm not producing the thong just yet so it's one of these three."

"That one," said Will, choosing a vermillion colour bottom half with a curious heart shape design in the front and matching vermillion top half.

"Very saucy," he said, "I like the target."

There were sounds of movement from Jimmy and Sarah's room as Will opened the sliding doors onto the front terrace and beach. A minute or two later they appeared, Sarah also wearing a sexy bikini.

"Gosh, I like that one," said Jimmy, looking at Siobhan. "What's that funny-looking decoration supposed to be?"

"Don't mention it. I've already had a very crude comment about it from Will," she retorted. "Something about a target."

They wandered towards the sea; the sun well up by now, getting on for 7.30, the temperature climbing. Sarah, lovely long legs and slender body with fair rather than blonde hair falling just short of her shoulders; quite tall, maybe even a shade taller than Jimmy, good looking with an athletic perhaps slightly stocky figure, they made a very attractive couple.

Swim over followed by a delicious breakfast of fresh orange juice, pawpaw, eggs cooked as preferred, toast and coffee laid out by Elaine and Misha on a breakfast table under a sun umbrella on the terrace.

"Busy day so far," commented Jimmy. "What shall we do next?"

"I suggest you go for a run and collect the Sunday papers," said Will. "Me, my future missus and Sarah are going to bring out our books, take on a little sun on the day beds that I see are thoughtfully being wheeled out onto the terrace by Elaine and Misha and watch the world go by."

Around 10 o'clock a few locals started to appear along the beach, some with families laughing and swimming in the sea. Their joint attention was drawn, however, by the antics of a youngish local man doing athletic cartwheels on the beach and edge of the sea. He also performed acrobatic somersaults over the mini waves. Gradually he made his way towards Westscape at the southern end of the beach. He carried with him a large plastic bag which he dumped on the sand when in the sea. Seeing that Westscape was occupied he approached the house and the four of them on the terrace.

"Yo takin' de sun?" he said. "De sun very good for you – that why I am this colour – all day in de sun. Where you from?"

"England and Ireland," Will said.

"Know people there. Come in winter. Look here," he delved into his bag and produced a T-shirt with a caricature drawing of a black man with a goatee beard and Rastafarian dreadlocks like his, with the name Natty Ned emblazoned on it.

"Dat me, Natty Ned. I make T-shirt for yo wid whatever yo want – message, drawing, name? Very good. Yo like?"

"Maybe, we're here for two weeks so perhaps come again one day soon and we'll think about it."

"Fine w'me. I live up de hill, very near. Have other stuff – make you feel good." Here he gave a little demonstration of 'feeling good' dancing a few steps blowing imaginary smoke into the air. "You like music? I reborn Bob Marley. I go now but come back."

"Well, not too many guesses required as to what the 'other stuff' may be. Did you see the colour of his eyes? Bright red," said Will.

"Probably grows his own," Jimmy said.

A short while later a ski boat zoomed into the bay looking for punters. None appeared but the driver evidently knew Natty Ned, who had reached the other end of the beach. They had a chat before the boat sped away seeking better luck elsewhere.

Frank Doune finished his Sunday morning stint at Tony Knowles' about mid-morning; Sunday was always busy because Tony himself had more time available to spend with the polo ponies. There was no game scheduled this Sunday although Frank knew there was a match on the fixture list between two local teams at Holders the following one. June, usually a quiet month on the water, Walton only had one boat operating, two others being under repair and servicing at the boathouse in Speightstown. Mid-June, July and August, despite the threat of hurricanes is the main summer season; then quiet again until livening up in December through to April. Frank headed down to Holetown beach where he knew Lucky would be based. He wasn't there.

Good, thought Frank. *Maybe he's picked up some business.*

He was in no hurry and grabbed a coke at the beach bar to drink while he waited.

An hour later Lucky tied up at the pontoon. "How-dee?" he

called out.

"Nah, very quiet. Found two at Mullins but no more. See Ned on Gibbes, he tell me people at Westscape – smart people, young, bettypretty."

"I go take a look, maybe tomorrow."

"That ski boat," Jimmy said. "Anybody want to have a go if we see it again? I've done it once or twice, it's good fun."

"Yeah, why not?" Will replied. "I've done a little in France also snow skiing in the Christmas holidays. Love to see these two nymphs skimming over the water."

"Let's have a go," said Sarah.

"I'm in," agreed Siobhan.

"Right. If we see Druggy Ned again, we'll tell him to fix it up with his pal. Shall we go for a stroll along the beach and another swim in order to work up a thirst before lunch?"

The walk along the beach, swim, sun, rum punch or two for some, and lunch, took their toll with long afternoon siestas providing very satisfactory answers. Surfacing again, it was to the knowledge that they had been on the island for the first 24 hours of their stay.

"Come on Will, one more quick swim, don't want to miss out on anything. Heaven can't be better than this," Siobhan said.

Together, under the powerful shower afterwards, they let the warm water run over their bodies washing away all the salt from the sea, rubbing shampoo into their scalps and following it all the way down, missing nothing out. Then, coming out of the shower into the warm evening fading sunshine, wrapped in their bath towels they stood on the terrace gazing trancelike at the peaceful scene of the sea gently lapping onto the sand.

"Hope we're not interrupting anything," Jimmy said walking up behind.

"No, certainly not," Siobhan answered. "We were just thinking how lovely it all is and how lucky we are."

"Yes, we feel exactly the same."

A little later, dressed and sitting on the terrace with a glass of wine brought by Elaine, Will said, "I've probably got to go into Bridgetown for a meeting with my man Max in the morning. He's going to ring quite early to confirm. I suggest that maybe you two girls make a list of what we need and do a bit of a shop. I'll call Lucille before I go but I think the best place would be in Holetown, a couple of miles south of here on the coast road. There's a big shopping centre and supermarket there with an ATM in the complex. On the financial front, there's the bill Lucille left for the supplies put in the house and I think the best thing for us to do is to keep any receipts for housekeeping expenses that we pay for so that we can do a reckoning near the end of the trip. All good shops etc take credit cards and there's also the ATMs. Remember that $1 Barbados equals 50 cents US. How does that seem?

"Fine by me," Jimmy said.

Misha came out of the house, "De phone want you," she said to Will.

He went inside, "Hi, Will. Tony Knowles here. Max said you were here which is great news. How you doin?"

"Just fine, Tony. We arrived yesterday, me, my girlfriend, who is also my future wife I am delighted to say, and two other friends. We're here for two weeks; it is so lovely to be back in Barbados and this house which Max found for us is fabulous."

"That's very good and congratulations, hope we can meet your lovely lady which brings me on to say two things. One, how are you on the polo front?"

"Not bad, most of my riding in the last year has been for Siobhan's brother who is a successful trainer in Ireland where I am living and working at the moment, but I have kept up my contacts with Cheshire polo and have been exercising and practising with Phoenix Park Polo Club near Dublin, so I am pretty well up to speed there."

"Good, listen would you like to come up to Holders on Wednesday afternoon and ride a practice chukka? I have a little surprise for you."

"I'd love that and I may possibly know what that surprise may be from what Max has told me."

"Ah, the cat's out of the bag then. The other thing is that Sue and I are having a few people to drinks on Tuesday evening at our place and would love it if you could come and, of course, bring your friends?"

"I'm sure we would love to do that. Thanks so much for asking us."

"Wonderful – see you on Tuesday. Bye for now."

"Look forward to it, Bye now."

"That was my polo friend, Tony Knowles," he told the others. "He asked me to come for polo practise on Wednesday afternoon and for us all to go for drinks at his house on Tuesday evening."

"Sounds lovely, the social drums are beating," Jimmy said.

Soon after 8 o'clock on Monday morning, Max rang, "Will, could you make it here in my office later this morning, say around 11?"

"Certainly Max and I'll bring all my stuff."

"Good, remember how to get here?"

"How could I ever forget? See you later."

He called Lucille at TRECO, "Hi, Luce, love, thanks again for being here when we arrived on Saturday. Very difficult and brave of you. I was most apprehensive, but you handled it brilliantly. Enough said. I'm off to Bridgetown this morning for a meeting with Max. I think the girls are going shopping and I've suggested the Super Centre in Holetown."

"Will, you are still my pin up and always will be. I think your Siobhan is fantastic and lovely; put her on the line now, I'll mark her card about shopping etc. I know we'll be great friends. I've got my memories that will never leave me."

"Thanks, sweetheart. My thoughts entirely. Hang on, I'll give her a shout ... Siobhan, darling, come and talk to Lucille; she's going to give you some shopping tips."

They talked for some time.

Having hung up Siobhan came back to the others, "She's so sweet, that Lucille, she gave me lots of hints, do's and don'ts. Two important things: she can order for us, wholesale, all meaty things like whole fillets of steak etc and, boys, all booze – wine and spirits, so give me a quick list of what you want and I'll call her back."

"Jimmy, I have to go in a minute or two, so could you do that. I suggest a gallon of Doorly's rum and, if you like it, at least one 12 bottle case of that white wine we've been drinking and a case of equivalent red. Order more if you like and whatever else you want. I'm off to work so have fun in the sun."

Siobhan came out to the car with him, "Kiss, please. Hope you have a good meeting."

Will remembered the last time he had driven along this

section of the coast road. It was when Max was driving him back to the Deep Water Harbour after showing where him where his ancestor's old plantation used to be. After a little further he passed the Bamboo Beach Bar which stirred different memories, then past the entrance to the harbour and all that went with it. Soon he was in Bridgetown proper, halfway along Broad Street, turn left, one block back, the small private car park. Through the doors, two receptionists were sitting at the counter.

"I have an appointment with Mr Geary," Will said.

"You must be Mr Carpenter?"

"I am indeed."

"One moment, please," one said, with a big smile.

The inner door opened; there was Max holding his arms outstretched in greeting.

"Will, my dear friend, how truly great to see you back in Barbados, come on in."

Entering his private office, he said, "Sit down here now. What can I get you – a cup of coffee, glass of water?"

"Coffee, just black would be marvellous. Super to see you Max."

For the next 10 minutes or so they talked non-stop about many things that had happened jointly since they last met, having a good catch up.

"So, you've got your lovely Siobhan with you?"

"Yes, and two other friends. It was very brave and kind of Lucille to meet us at the house when we arrived. The house is fabulous, by the way. I've had a couple of chats with her, one this morning and it's all fine and happy. I hope we'll meet her boyfriend while we're here."

"I'm sure you will. He's a good chap and a fine young lawyer with a kind heart. Now to business: there's a good chance of getting your plan off the ground based on the information and financial calculations in your proposal. The one potential sticking point is that the company must be registered here with a 40% foreign investment. How do you think your Mr Mallory will react to that?"

"Mallory and his family are the owners of the entire company including the Irish one, so the answer is I don't know, but until the Irish company started, he refused to have any overseas branches. It was me, aided by one of Mallory's most trusted branch managers who managed to get that show on the road. Luckily, it is turning out well though he's already thrown this proposal out of the window twice. My 'mole' however has told me not to give up. Mallory knows I am here and what I am doing."

Max continued, "The way I see it is that I am pretty sure I can raise what is required under Barbados law, including a contribution by myself. This could be useful in two ways: one, to show my interest based on my knowledge of you and your track record in Ireland and, two, because I believe that part of my investment could be used as a nominee amount held by me but on behalf of the parent company. It would all have to be put into legal language but I know the man who could do it. It could also work as a stick to dangle in front of Mr Mallory."

"Mallory is a stickler for honesty and legality. He wouldn't tolerate anything that he considers 'shady'. Every document would be investigated by his own lawyers with a toothcomb."

"Naturally, and I appreciate that. Provided we can make progress in principle, I would certainly fly to England for a meeting with him and his advisors, at which I assume you would be present."

"Of course I would."

"I have told you that the big boys of the car rental world, Hertz, Avis and the rest are all here and you must have faced this when you started the Irish company?"

"Certainly I did though what I tried to do, I think reasonably successfully, was to instil in the local market that this was an Irish company under Irish management, and to induce Irish travel agents, hotel managers and the like to come to us and recommend their clients to do likewise. We could and should do the same thing here."

Max said, "I've told you in our telephone conversations that there have been many developments since you were last here. Probably the biggest, the construction of which had already started, has been the Fort St Charles project north of Speightstown. That's now up and running and you must go and have a look at it while you are here. I can arrange this for you. There is another project in the pipeline which will be separate from, but dependent upon, Port St Charles. I am not involved with it though have access to the management and founders. It consists of first one and possibly a second ultra-smart small high speed luxury cruise vessel with a maximum of 20 passengers, operating cruises to the southern windward islands as far as Tobago. I understand that the first vessel is well under construction. Once we are successfully launched this company could become a client. The lead man of the project is Sven Goran and the company is Foulds, Archer and Goran or FAG for short. They are a rival company of TRECO. You are bound to come across Sven; he's a smart business man, Danish by extraction."

"Okay Max, so where do we go from here?"

"Would you be willing to leave your feasibility study with me? There are people I would like to show you off to while you are here."

"Certainly, here it is," Will opened his briefcase and passed the document to Max.

"Tony Knowles rang last night," Will said.

"You know he's got May Go Twice as a polo pony?"

"Yes, I think you told me that a little while ago. He's asked me to come up to Holders on Wednesday so I expect I'll ride him. We are all going for a drink with him and Sue tomorrow evening."

"Oh good, Eileen and I are going so I'll be able to meet Siobhan!"

"Yes you will and my very good friend Jimmy van Duren and his most attractive girlfriend, Sarah. What's your news on the horse front?"

"Fawn Princess is probably the best filly/mare in Barbados. She has won several top-class races. I think, though, I'll probably retire her from racing this year and keep her as a broodmare which, both on her breeding and race record, should be good. Other than that, I've got a couple of nice-looking home breds that are starting to show form, so I'm hopeful that at least one of them will be successful. If I come to England on our Supercar project, I may take the opportunity to have a scout round for a successor or two for the ones you looked after on your ship, but we can talk about that when and if the time comes."

"That's about it for today then, Max. It's all very exciting and I'm thrilled that you think so too. As you know, I have a reason for me and my family to be reconnected with Barbados. See you tomorrow; you can have a look at my filly and not just as a potential broodmare!"

Will was back at Westscape in time for a late lunch.

"How was it?" Siobhan asked

"Positive and encouraging enough for an opener but a long way to go yet. How was your shopping?"

"Pretty good, thanks to Lucille. We got enough to keep us going for a day or two. Buying fruit was the best part: there was a row of ladies in the square outside the supermarket, each with their own stalls clamouring for business and arguing amongst themselves, *'don't buy from she: her pawpaw bad, some here … see, see'*; hilarious."

Jimmy said, "A young man walked up to the house from the beach. A Bajan but light-skinned and with straight black hair. Said he was a water and jet ski instructor and operator and were we interested? I said we might be and provisionally fixed for him to come at 10.30 tomorrow morning. He left his telephone number; said his name was Frank. Quite respectful in a sort of way, but a bit cocky maybe."

"I think I know him. If it's the Frank I've met, he's a redleg and I met him two or three times when I was on day shore leave from my ship. I think he also works part-time for Tony exercising his polo ponies. A surly chippy bugger. Lucille told me his name and can't stand him."

"Well, we can cancel him?" said Jimmy.

"No, let him come. I may have got it wrong."

"If we're going out to drinks with your polo friend tomorrow why don't we go on to dinner somewhere afterwards? Lucille told Siobhan about a restaurant not far from here called the Carambola or something like that. Said she went with her boyfriend recently and that it was very good. Do you know it?"

"That's a great idea Jimmy and it means that we would not have to rush back in time for dinner here, and gives the girls here the night off. No, I don't know the Carambola, but look it up in the telephone book and give them a call – about 8.30 ish I should think."

Half past ten the next morning a boat swooped round the point into the bay and pointed towards their end of the beach.

"That looks like the same boat that was here on Sunday," Jimmy said. A fuzzy-haired but clean-shaven black driver stood up and waved at them before nosing into the shore. Chucking out an anchor, jumped into the shallow water and came towards them.

"Hi, me Lucky," he said with a broad, cheerful grin. "Frank send me, Yo want ski? I teach you. Frank, he come soon. We have good time."

"I think we saw you here on Sunday?"

"Yes, man I here, talk wi' Ned. He my friend. You buy T-shirt from him?"

"No, but we might. My name's Jimmy, this is Will, Siobhan and Sarah."

"Okay, let's go. You ski before? One ski, two ski?"

"The girls haven't skied before but Will and I have a few time, but better start with two skis."

They all clambered into the boat and moved about 50 yards from the shore.

"Go on Jim-boy, show us how it's done," Will said.

Jimmy did so, getting up at the second attempt and making two slightly wobbly circuits of the bay before coming a cropper trying to cross the wake. Will next, rather better, cris crossing several times. Claps from boat, praise from Lucky, "Yo great, man; one ski next time. Now we have fun wi' two lovely girls. Why do I love this job so much? Oh, yes man. Which go first?"

Sarah said, "Go on Siobhan, you go."

"Okay, come on Lucky teach me."

Luck adjusted the skis to fit her. Lifted her bodily up and gently lowering her into the water.

"See why I like this job? Now, Seaborn – dat a nice name, born in de sea like mermaid, yeah? You do what I say; here, take de rope, lie back in water, think of nice things. When de rope come tight, hold de bar, keep knees bent, look to front; don't try to stand until de water strong nuff. Keep arms straight in front. Do not bend arms. Okay? Here we go."

Siobhan rose like the proverbial mermaid, looked at Will with his hands raised in salute, pulled at the rope and flipped over backwards into the water.

"You not do what I say," called out Lucky, bringing the boat back to her. "I say do not bend de arms. You pull and de sea gobble you up."

Next time she obeyed, looked straight in front of her and made a complete circle of the bay.

"Well done Seaborn," said Will, putting himself in front of Lucky to help her into the boat, "You were brilliant."

"I loved it. Can I have another go tomorrow?"

Despite Sarah having been captain of her old school netball team and her wish to succeed, her lithe body, slender model-type figure did not go hand in hand with water skiing. Lucky, under Jimmy's watchful and steely eyes, did his best to achieve success but their combined efforts ended in a tangle of arms, legs, torso, skis and rope similar to the game of spillikins. The last straw came when, to Lucky's enjoyment and everyone else's amusement, the top half of her bikini became dislodged amongst the chaos.

"That's it. I'm going to stick to bungee jumping."

"You've never bungee jumped."

"No, but I'm thinking about it".

"You know," Will said later to Siobhan, while they were changing before going to the Knowles drinks party, "I've worked out why we were better than the others water-skiing."

"Tell me."

"It's because there is a huge similarity with riding. The same muscles, legs, arms and back muscles and the same balance. For skiing and riding, we use our arms and back to hold or pull against something and our legs to adjust or balance while in motion, like we ski over waves or the wash of the boat by adjusting and moving our knees and thighs just like when trotting, cantering or jumping a fence."

"You're probably right, though I don't think we need draw Jimmy and Sarah's attention to this interesting theory, certainly not Sarah's, I hope she'll have another go; we don't want to put her off."

Sue Knowles greeted them on arrival, "Hello Will, so good to see you again. Come on in, Tony's in there somewhere."

"Great to see you too, Sue, and for asking all four us. Let me introduce you first to my lovely Siobhan and to my great friend Jimmy van Duren and to Sarah Whatcombe, – Sue Knowles, our hostess."

Hellos all round and they followed Sue into the house. Tony saw them, and gave a hug to Will.

"Hi Tony, this is Siobhan and meet my friends Jimmy and Sarah. Lovely to be here and back in Barbados."

Lucille appeared, kissed Will and Siobhan, grabbed Sarah and Jimmy and said, "I am going to separate you lot. Come with me you two and I'll introduce you to a few locals. First, meet my boyfriend

Josh Taylor," she said, putting her arm firmly round him.

"Josh, here are Jimmy and Sarah who have taken Westscape with Will and Siobhan."

Max came up to Will, "I knew any lady friend of Will's would be something very special and I'm right. You must be Siobhan; I am Max Geary."

"Oh, Max, it's so good to meet you properly. I've heard non-stop about you from Will for so long." She leant towards him and gave him a kiss. "I feel I've known you long enough to do that."

"I'm flattered you think that. Here's my son Peter and his wife Becky. Peter trains my horses at the Garrison."

"Hi Will and Siobhan. Great to see you Will and to meet you Siobhan. I believe your brother is a trainer in Ireland?"

"Yes, and Will is his work jockey, as well as having a proper job."

"Speaking of Ireland," Max said, beckoning to a couple nearby, "Here is a genuine Irish couple, although they've lived here for long enough, Caira and Dermot Delaney. Caira owns and runs a very successful travel agency. Will Carpenter and Siobhan Kennedy. I'll leave you for a moment – I've got to see that fellow over there talking to Eileen."

"What brings you to Barbados?" Dermot asked, in a strong Irish accent.

"Well ostensibly for a holiday but Max and I are doing a little business as well. I manage a car rental business out of Santry and Siobhan's brother trains horses near Trim. She is his secretary, housekeeper and gofer, and I ride out for him whenever I can. I came to Barbados a several times a few years ago as a cabin boy on a banana boat and was lucky enough to meet Max on my first trip, He very kindly took me to see the land where an ancestor of mine called Benjamin Carpenter had a plantation in the old days."

"Oh my God, Ben Carpenter is well known in Bajan folklore. What was the ship you worked on."

"The *Star*."

"I don't believe that! I came here on the Star to marry Caira, here, having got engaged to her in Ireland all those years ago and we have never left."

"Yet!" said Caira. "We both come from County Cork but are now almost more Bajan than the Bajans."

"What are you lot gassing about? Ireland, I suppose." Then, to

Will, "I'm Sheila Griffiths and that's my husband Bruce over there" she said, pointing to a tall, lean figure talking to another group. "We haven't met, I don't think but I've heard a lot about you round and about."

"Oh dear, nothing too bad, I hope. Will Carpenter, and here's my Irish connection, Siobhan."

Caira said, "Sheila runs a wonderful riding school. English by birth, she's another old established ex-pat. Bruce, a Bajan, although listening to him you wouldn't think so, is the top orthopaedic surgeon in the Eastern Caribbean."

A moment later a tall, elegantly dressed man formed up to them, "Hi, Johnny, how are things?" Caira said. "Johnny, this is Will Carpenter and his beautiful Irish girlfriend Siobhan. Johnny is the Man about Town of Barbados who knows everybody and what they are doing tomorrow. He's also a director of one of the leading estate and property agents on the island."

"Johnny Arthur, good to meet you and what do you mean, Caira 'one of' the leading agents? We are THE leading agents."

"Don't let Max Geary of TRECO hear you say that."

"Joking of course, we are get along very well together. You here for a holiday?"

"Yes, plus maybe a bit of business. We're staying at a house on Gibbes Beach, found for us, I'm afraid to say, by TRECO."

"Oh, well, you can't win them all. Glad to meet you anyway and have a lovely holiday and I hope the business bit goes well too."

They chatted away to a few others and when Sarah and Jimmy hove into view, Will said that it was probably time they left. Just as they were about to go, Max came back.

"We're off now but I'm on the case, Will, a bit of positive feedback from more than one source. I'll give you a call to arrange a meeting with interested parties."

"Good, Max we're about off too. Speak soon."

They made their way over to where Tony and Sue were talking.

"We must be on our way both of you so thank you very much. It's been good to see friends made when I was last here and, I hope, to make new ones. We have a table booked at the Carambola."

"You'll love it there, have a good evening. See you tomorrow afternoon; you can have a sit on May Go so see how you get on; we'll probably play a practice chukka."

"Well, what did you think of all that?" Will asked, as they drove away.

"Everyone was so friendly," Sarah said. "Happy and carefree. Lucille was sweet to introduce us to several people, can't remember most of their names though. We talked a bit to her boyfriend, Josh."

"What did you make of him," asked Will.

"He's obviously very intelligent," Sarah answered. "Quite quiet, very pleasant to talk to and clearly very struck with Lucille. Socially I think she probably leads the way. The highlight, however, was a youngish man, dressed you might say, casually, in a white open-necked shirt and very loose-fitting baggy silk trousers. He was hilarious, making the most amusing and highly indiscreet comments about everybody he could see. Clearly very popular though. Everybody he was being rude about greeted him with great affection.

His name is Simon and he said to me, *'I make ladies' dresses; You must come to my workplace – I can't call it a salon that's far too pretentious, though I'd like you to take a dress and model it. I might even give it to you. Not far from here, ask anybody in Holetown.'*

We've got to go Siobhan, he's an absolute hoot. Lucille says he's very well known internationally, permanently broke notwithstanding all the nobs flocking to him in the winter season and asking him to their smart parties."

"Can't wait. Let's go tomorrow. Do you think he'll lend me one too?"

The party mood continued at the Carambola. In a beautiful setting close to Paynes Bay, a mile or so south of Holetown, raised about 20 feet above the sea, which it overlooked. Candle lit under a coloured canvas-type roof that was open to the sea. Excellent service, very good food, highly romantic and great fun. They drove home, all very happy. The Westscape girls had left the door lights on for them and the light over the beach terrace.

"There's no one about; do you think we can go for a skinny," Siobhan said. "We can take a towel each in case anybody comes along the beach."

The boys needed no second bidding, stripping off, they grabbed towels and hoofed it across the sand, then discarding the towels, plunged into the sea, swimming out a few yards before forming a circle and holding hands as they played *ring-a-ring-a-roses*.

"We've got a little bit of shopping to do, so why don't we go on to Simon's place afterwards and have a look?" Sarah asked Siobhan.

"Yeah, super idea, let's do that. It shouldn't take too long."

The fruit ladies giggled when they asked for directions to Simon's establishment.

"Oh, you go to Simon? He funny-up." With arm waving movements to help, one said, "You go there, short distance, swing so, chattel house, big sign, okay."

They found it without difficulty. It was, indeed, a white-painted chattel house standing a few yards back from the road. The name 'Simon' painted vertically with a tropical flowered background stood tall by the roadside. Simon, wearing what seemed to be identical clothes to the evening before, greeted them.

"Oh my – two darlings for the price of one?"

"Yes, I've brought my friend, Siobhan, who I don't think you met last night," said Sarah.

Inside were multi-coloured gowns, dresses, trouser suits, silk scarves and a few shorts, hung on hangers and displayed haphazardly.

"Come through to the back and I'll show you how it's all done."

Two local ladies were amongst the total chaos of pieces of material, pots of paint and dyes, clothes frames and other paraphernalia, making the 'showroom' look neat and tidy.

"This is a slack time of year. You've no idea of how untidy and disorderly it gets in the winter. Ladies, mostly very rich from many different countries want me to make them look beautiful. It's very difficult. Many are Italian countesses; well, who'd marry an Italian unless he was a count – in some cases, the 'o' should be dropped. I've one, hugely rich, who makes Edith Piaf look like Marilyn Monroe. I have to insert all manner of things inside the dresses to try to make her look normal. Then there are the opposites: the amount of material I need to cover them up and hide what lies beneath is beyond imagination. But you two darlings – please may I marry both of you; we could all live happily ever after and become immensely rich on the proceeds of the dresses you would model for me. Come and try on any that you can see. If you would like other colours or designs, I can make them for you. Where are you staying?"

"In a house called Westscape on Gibbes Beach."

"I know it very well and the owner, a fabulously rich English lady who I've known for years. She spends most of the winter here but her gentleman friends do change relatively frequently. She probably has a cupboard full of my dresses locked away at the house."

With a bit of tweaking and minor alterations done on the spot, they came away with a dress each on approval.

The fashion parade certainly met with approval – not just with Will and Jimmy, as well as with Naomi, Misha and Elaine, "Oh, we know where yo' bin," they said. "Mr Simon, he come here often. The Lady have many, many like dat."

"I'll have to leave for the polo ground soon after three," Will said at lunch the next day,

"Seaborn here says she wants to come with me."

"Can we all come?" asked Jimmy,

"It'll probably be quite boring – just a bit of practice, that's all."

"Well, let's go anyway," said Sarah.

There was quite a lot of activity on the ground. Tony saw them coming and waved at them.

"That was a great party last night; thank you and Sue so much. We went on and had a super dinner at the Carambola. Hope it's okay for us all to be here. Siobhan and the others will keep well out of the way."

"Of course it's okay and I'm glad you enjoyed the party. Come with me Will, I've got some kit for you in the Clubhouse."

On the way there he said, "I've got some news for you: there's a Club match on Sunday, my team The Hawks against Bill Phillips' team, The Eagles. My number 2 player, David Fields, is off the island so would you like to take his place?"

"Tony, for God's sake, of course I' d love to, but haven't you got someone else better qualified than me?"

"You're only here for a short time and I'd really like you to play so come on and see if some of this kit will fit you: we are not too different in size and shape. I'll see you back at the lines in a minute. There are two ponies I want you to ride; one, as you have guessed, is May Go Twice and the other, a home-bred brown that's been around for a while and knows his way – not the fastest in the book though reliable."

Will saw Jimmy, Sarah and Siobhan standing a bit apart from

the small army of players and grooms milling around the ponies.

"I'm sorry to desert you. Why don't you go and have a look in the Clubhouse and maybe walk round the ground, Guess what, Tony has asked me to play in his team in the match on Sunday."

"Oh, Will darling, that's fantastic. How exciting for you."

"Yes, one of his team regulars is away off the island. I must go now. He's asked me to ride two now. I'll tell you about them later."

Approaching the lines, Will spotted Frank; their eyes crossed.

Will thought, *I must try my best with this chap. He works for Tony; I'm not supposed to know anything about his other work on the water.*

He walked over to where Frank was tending to a pony.

"Hello," he said. "My name's Will Carpenter. I recognize you from when I was last here a few years ago."

"Yes, I remember too, Mr Carpenter. My name, Frank. I work part-time for Mr Knowles but also assistant to Walton Dailing wi' water sports. I think you stay at Westscape. I sent my driver Lucky to you. You like him to come again?"

Cool but careful, Will thought.

"Yes, I think so. The others in my party are just over there, but I think tomorrow morning would be good."

Will recognized May Go Twice as soon as he saw him hitched to a bar.

"Hello, old friend," he said, walking up to him and giving him a pat on his neck and a hug. "You won't remember me though we shared many moments together on the high seas and a few times at the Garrison."

"Catching up on old times, are you?" asked Tony, who had followed Will over.

"Yes, it's quite nostalgic really."

"I can believe it. The brown one I was talking about is the pony next to May Go here. Would you take the brown first as Frank has him ready. Give him on a steady canter round and then help yourself to the balls dotted around and have a bit of practice to get your eye in. After that Frank will have May Go ready, then you can repeat the exercise on him."

Will did as he was told on the brown pony though he was itching to have a go on May Go. It was like changing from a Ford Popular to a Porsche. Tony had done a good job in retraining him from a racehorse to a polo pony. He took a fair grip yet was nimble enough to turn sharply and knew exactly that the ball was there to be chased.

"Well done. I was watching you; you got on fine with him," Tony said, afterwards.

"It was like sitting on a canon. Light the fuse and hit the target," Will replied.

"Go and find the others, bring them into the Clubhouse for a drink."

Siobhan rushed up to him. "How's my hero? It's the first time I've seen you ride a polo pony. You looked just as professional as on a racehorse."

"Flattery will get you everywhere but I'm glad I fooled you. I wasn't nearly as much in control as you thought. Did that young man Frank find you?"

"Yes, and we fixed for Lucky to come round mid-morning tomorrow."

"Bit of an odd ball I thought," said Jimmy. "Too smooth for my liking."

"Yes, I'll tell you about him later."

Frank Doune made his way to his lodgings after taking the ponies back to Knowles' yard and settling them down for the night.

He said to himself, *I remember that Carpenter gringo. Remember him talking to Geary and Chally Jones at the Garrison. And then again up at Knowles' place with that blonde Todd girl in tow, riding the ponies, then talking to the smart people in the pony lines at Holders. Now he's back, stick and balling on the ground for Knowles. Should be me, doing that.*

A mixture of anticipation and apprehension greeted Lucky the next morning when he arrived, waving his arms in salute as he approached the shore. This time he brought an extra crew member to help him.

"Man, this my lucky day," he exclaimed in welcome. "Dat's why my name Lucky. I always so but today, special so. Let's go."

They followed the same order as before; Jimmy first, much more confident than the previous time, crossing the boat wake several times, he made two big circuits of the bay and indicated when he'd had enough, sinking gratefully into the water.

"Terrific," he said. "Thanks Lucky. That's my exercise for the day, bring on the rum."

Will was next.

Lucky said, "Wi' yo, put on monoski on one leg and an ordinary ski wi' loose fit on other leg. Here, de boy show you. He name, Nipper; careful now, I say Nipper. When yo 'goin' good, look straight in front wi' arms no bend. Ease foot wi 'ordinary ski and let go. Place foot carefully into back fitting of monoski. No look down. Place more weight on back leg and see how yo' go. Okay?

"I'll give it a try," said Will.

All went well to start with. He had difficulty in maintaining his balance while fiddling to extract his leg from the ski to be discarded but with a bit of wobbling, managed it. However, he lost his balance and crashed into the water as he was trying to transfer his weight onto the monoski.

"Dat good, very good," said Lucky, after having collected the discarded ski. "Try one more time."

This time he was successful and completed a whole circuit and more on the monoski.

"Hey, yo' have de will, Will. Good man. Next time yo' cross the wake and the time after, I teach yo' go backwards," Lucky laughed.

"Now, we come to happy time. Seaborn yo 'show 'em how. Nipper, fit skis on lovely lady."

Siobhan skied happily and confidently, raising her hand to wave to the clapping and encouragement coming from the boat.

"Good, next time yo' and Jim on monoski," called out Lucky.

"Now," he said. "Lucky get more lucky; Dis why I bring Nipper: he drive boat. I go in water wi' Sarah."

Having checked her skis, he lifted her into the sea, followed with a dive that hardly disturbed the water, coming up by her side.

"Now I hold you. Take the rope handle." He held her round her waist, treading water as he did so, "Now, knees bent, arms straight, keep so, look up in front."

The boat moved slowly forward; Lucky swam with it; as the speed increased.

He shouted, "Stay same position."

Then, "Now, stand up, arms straight, look ahead."

Sarah rose out of the water.

"There, a mermaid," Lucky yelled from behind her. "YEAH, YO' DONE IT!"

"Thank you, Lucky," said Sarah, back on the shore. "That was marvellous and all thanks to you – here," she said, planting a kiss on Lucky's cheek.

"Ah, yes, my lucky day," he said boarding the boat. "Hey, Nipper, you drive de boat – I go dreamin.'"

"There goes a happy Black Sambo," said Jimmy.

"Sh – you can't say that," said Will.

CHAPTER 20

Thursday afternoon, Max called.

"Will can you make a meeting tomorrow morning? I've been talking to two sets of people and they'd both like to meet you. We could do it all together – the two of them representing their organisations, me with my import, and you as the brainchild representing the promoting company."

"Certainly I can. Your office?"

"Yes. 10.30."

"I'll be there."

Will arrived early at 10.15. Max took him straight into the boardroom.

"Right," he said. "One of the two men is Mike Williams, a Bajan, been in the hotel business all his working life and now Regional director of the company that owns four West Coast hotels, plus two in Grenada and one in St Lucia.

The other is Martin Jackson, the majority shareholder of Jackson Motors, probably the largest importer and distributor of motor cars and vans in Barbados. Their separate interests are obvious: Williams to rent the cars to their clients and Jackson to supply the cars."

His internal telephone rang. "They are both here. Gwen is bringing them."

Max opened the door. "Come in gentlemen, please. Coffee anybody?" Both indicated that would be most welcome.

"Now, I would like you to meet William Carpenter – known as Will, of Supercar, England and Ireland, where he is presently working as boss of the Irish company which he set up two and a half years ago. You have all read Will's feasibility report that he wrote with the approval of the Chairman and owner of Supercar, Robert Mallory. Will knows that I am an interested potential investor in the company which we hope to set up in Barbados. So gentlemen, please grill Will here with all the questions which, at this stage, you would like answered or commented upon."

For the next hour that was exactly what they did. Williams,

ultra-polite as to be expected of a hotelier, though he was direct too and penetrating as to the experience Will had in dealings of rental sales to clients of hotels in Ireland and also his initial training with Supercar at the head and branch offices in England.

Jackson was more interested in the supply of the vehicles themselves making it clear that his company would require an exclusive deal regarding this.

To Jackson, Will replied that he saw no problem. He excused his lack of knowledge of the Barbados motor trade and said that he would be most keen to come to Jackson Motors to learn more in this respect.

To Williams, he was able to satisfactorily answer his questions, stating his experiences with hotels in Ireland, the Manchester area and Solihull in England.

Max said his bit about having known Will for a considerable period before and during his employment by Supercar.

Will raised one question himself.

"Gentlemen," he said. "The company that we hope to set up will be a Barbados company, the details of which Max has discussed with me. It has occurred to me and, in view of your knowledge of the whole of the Eastern Caribbean, is there any reason why, in due course, we could not expand, under license, to other Caribbean states that have a thriving tourist industry?"

Max said, "This is a very forward-thinking and intriguing question which is more than worthy of investigation however, don't let's get too far ahead of ourselves, and get this show on the road first."

The meeting broke up in a most friendly manner with both Williams and Jackson thanking Will and hoping to meet again soon and to keep in touch. Will agreed, saying he would be on the island for another ten days and that Max had all his contact details both here and in Ireland.

"How did that go, do you think?" Will asked, after both men had left.

"You fielded their questions extremely well," Max replied. "There is no doubt that you made a favourable impression on both of them. Both now have two alternatives; they can either say 'thanks but no thanks', or can come back asking for further information having discussed the plan with their co-directors and/

or professional advisors. My guess, knowing them both as I do, is that it will be the latter. But, you never know; I've been wrong before. Rest assured, I'll call you as soon as I hear anything, which probably now won't be until after the weekend so go and have a good one with Siobhan – she's a real star, by the way – and your other two friends."

"Thanks and I hope you will, too. Oh – how about this – Tony has asked me to play in his team in the match on Sunday. I'll be riding May Go Twice in at least one chukka."

"Brilliant, not sure if Eileen has laid on anything for Sunday, and if not, we'll try to come up."

Sunday morning dawned, a mild, warm breeze drifting through the wide open window of their room. Siobhan stirred sleepily. Will opened an eye and glanced across at her, a flicker of a smile floating over her lips.

"Do you realise we've been here for a week?" she said. "I wish we could turn the clock back and start all over again. I wouldn't want to change anything."

They all spent a lazy morning on the beach, swimming, sunbathing and watching the world go by. Will said he ought to leave for Holders at about 2 o'clock to get ready for the match.

"It doesn't start until 3.30," he said. "Why don't I go ahead in one car and you all can come on later – gives you longer to enjoy the sunshine?"

When he arrived, there was already quite a lot of activity – ponies being unloaded from trailers and tethered in order of play for each team, tack, hay nets and all manner of gear laid out, players from both teams greeting each other. Soon, Will spotted Tony and went over to him.

"Hi, Will, all set for today?"

"Yes, and the butterflies are buzzing."

"They'll buzz off as soon as the game starts. I'd like you to start on the brown pony you rode on Wednesday – we call him Tom, as in Brown, get it? Then May Go in the second chukka and the same again for chukkas 3 and 4."

Will moved off, said hello to Frank who was unloading Tom, receiving a muttered monosyllabic reply as he walked past. Just then he saw someone come up to Tony and talk urgently and earnestly to him with a bit of arm waving and gesticulation in the direction of the pony lines. Tony came back to where Will was standing.

"That was Bill Phillips, the captain of the Eagles. There's a problem: the son of his no. 4 player, Fred Harris, has been on a dive, came up too quickly and has the bends. Fred has had to rush him off to the hospital where they have a decompression chamber; Bill has asked if I can 'lend' him Frank to play on his side. It leaves me short-handed, but I'll have to agree. Frank did have a game as a stand in once before."

"That's okay, the rest of us can muck in between chukkas. I'm sure we'll manage."

People were starting to arrive, some wandering down to the lines. Will saw a dapper-looking man dressed in a smart blue suit.

He thought, *I remember him from somewhere, but where?*

Suddenly it dawned on him; it was Keith Melville, the president of the Club.

"Good afternoon Mr Melville," said. "You won't remember but you very kindly gave me a visitors pass when I was first here a few years ago. I'm Will Carpenter."

"Oh, of course I remember now. It was Max Geary who told me about you. So you're back again and playing today, it looks like?"

"Yes, Tony Knowles has asked me to stand in for one of his team who is away."

"Well, the best of luck and no doubt see you in the bar after the match."

Jimmy, Sarah and Siobhan hove into view. Siobhan couldn't resist kissing him.

"How's my ace polo player feeling?"

"Nervous as hell. I wish we could get going."

"Well you look the part, anyway," said Jimmy. "Please may I have your autograph?"

"Piss off. No, wait. I can see Lucille with her parents and it must be Josh approaching, so don't go away."

George and Harriet Todd plus Lucille and Josh came up.

"My God, Will, you're not playing are you?" asked Lucille.

"I wouldn't be dressed like this otherwise. Tony's asked to stand in for somebody who's away."

George Todd held out his hand, "Hello Will. Lucille told us you were back here. Delighted to see you."

"… and so am I," said Harriet.

"Very good to see you both as well. This is Siobhan Kennedy, Jimmy van Duren and Sarah Whatcombe. George and Harriet Todd, Lucille's parents, who most kindly had me to stay in their lovely plantation house when I was last here."

"Hi Will, I'm Josh Taylor. I don't think we've met properly until now."

"No, but very glad we're doing so now. I think you met Jimmy and Sarah the other evening. Look, see you all later but I think I'd better go and meet my other team members."

Siobhan gripped him. "Good luck, 007, I love you," she whispered.

As he left them he saw the Irish couple, the Delaneys, come up to Siobhan and start talking to her.

Soon all was ready. Tony explained that there was to be a parade of the teams in front of the stand with each team member introduced by the commentator over the tannoy.

Preceded by the two mounted umpires, the teams led out from the lines onto the ground mallets held high in the air, the Hawks in blue and the Eagles in red. The Eagles were named first.

When it came to Will, the commentator said, "And here, all the way from England via Ireland we have the Star Wars Invader, Will Carpenter."

A few claps and a hooray, from a tiny section of the crowd.

One of the umpires tossed a ball and the game started. From the ensuing melee, Will managed to hook the ball backwards to his number 3 who hit it forwards, however, Tom didn't have the pace to get anywhere near it. The chukka ranged backwards and forwards. Will held his own but was not able to make any serious impression, the chukka ending at one goal apiece. Without Frank to help there was plenty of scurrying around to make all the necessary changes for the second chukka, but when Will rode out on May Go Twice he was on a big high.

Now let's see what we can do, shall we, my old pal? Will whispered to the horse.

He could feel by his quivering and champing at his bit that May Go was as excited as Will himself. He liked to think that there was an inkling of memory at the back of the horse's mind. They were off; the ball went forward but was well cleared by the Hawk's defence, deep into the Eagle's half. Collected by the no. 4 who passed to Tony, who sent a long one upfront.

"This is for us so come on May Go, after it," Will said to the horse.

No second biding was necessary; May Go showed the burst of acceleration he used to produce on the racecourse.

Will saw a defender coming on his left but he told the horse, "With your speed, May Go, we'll get there first and he'll have to give way."

With his mallet held high he was on the stride before striking the ball. Out of the corner of his eye, he could see the defender still coming with his mallet thrust forward horizontally. Will had started the downward spiral of his mallet to strike the ball when there was an almighty collision of horse and human with a polo mallet smashed like a matchstick between May Go Twice's legs.

As if in slow motion, the whole combination fell to the ground, but not before Will caught the look of hatred in the defender's eyes. A look he had seen before and remembered. As they hit the ground he felt an excruciating pain in his right leg – then bang. Nothing.

A fuddled, muddled group of people stood over him. He had never felt pain like this, *What was happening?*

He heard a sharp crack like a firework and a voice that he vaguely recognized saying, "Sorry, Tony, there was no other option."

Will's eyes started to focus. Siobhan was standing above him, tears streaming down her face. He raised his arm; she took it, gripping it hard.

A tall man bent down over him. "I'm going to give you an injection. It will ease the pain."

Will hardly felt the prick of the needle.

The crowd had gasped with fright and astonishment when the accident happened. A few rushed onto the ground.

"My God, it's Will," Siobhan had screamed, running as fast as she could, Jimmy and Sarah with her.

Lucille had made an involuntary move forward as she, too, realised that it was Will.

Harriet, her mother, put out a restraining hand. "No, darling, I think you should stay here for the moment."

Some men arrived with a stretcher. The siren of an ambulance could be heard approaching. Bruce Griffiths, who had administered the injection, was now knelt down beside Will, looking closely at his eyes.

"Can you hear me properly?" he asked.

"Yes," said Will. "What's happened?"

"You've had a bang on your head and I'm afraid your right leg is broken. I'm Bruce Griffiths. You've met my wife Sheila. I'm a doctor and am going to look after you. First I may need to give you another pain-deadening injection while we get you into the ambulance and to the hospital."

"Okay. Is Siobhan there?"

"Of course I'm here, darling. I'm staying with you. Jimmy and Sarah are here too," she said.

"Good. It's bloody agony."

"Before we move you, I'm giving you the injection now. It will make you a bit woozy."

Standing up, Bruce said to Siobhan, Jimmy and Sarah, "He was unconscious for nearly four minutes – that's quite a long time so he has concussion. The leg is definitely broken, how badly I shan't know until I've seen the X-ray, but I fear it's quite a bad one, probably tibia and fibula – that's the big and little bones. The good news is that I think and hope it's below the knee. I need to wait until the second injection takes effect, because moving him will be painful despite all the stretcher aids we can put on. I've already alerted the Bayview Hospital and arranged a private room for him. Depending on the X-ray I may need to operate to set the leg. This is best done as soon as possible, which may be tonight."

"Please may I go in the ambulance with him?" asked Siobhan.

"Yes, my dear, I don't see why not."

Tony Knowles came to them, "What a terrible thing to have happened. I'm so sorry for you all. I blame myself for letting them have Frank to play. Crossing like that is the worst foul in polo. He will have to face the consequences and an official enquiry. What can I do for you now?"

"You're most kind Tony, you mustn't blame yourself in any way," Jimmy said. "Anybody would have done the same. I think Siobhan will go with Will in the ambulance now and then depending on what Bruce Griffiths says, Sarah and I will follow on later. One thing perhaps, please could you possibly ask Lucille to let the staff at Westscape know what's happened and to leave some food out for us?"

"Yes, of course I'll do that."

Jimmy said, "I'm desperately sorry about the horse and I know Will shall feel the same as me. I hope he doesn't know yet. He was so much looking forward to riding him. I'm sure you know about the connection he had."

"Yes, I do. He was a lovely horse to have anything to do with. It was very fortunate that Will Huey, the vet, was on the ground. There was no alternative other than putting him down. The off side shoulder was broken. It was very lucky the other pony only suffered minor injuries."

Max Geary appeared. "Siobhan, I'm so sorry. What a terrible thing to have happened. Eileen and I were out to lunch and only arrived just as the match was starting. I am on hand for anything that you need; you only have to ask. The good news is that Will could not be in better hands. He squeezed her hand, then moved to bend over Will.

"You poor chap. I'm so sorry but don't worry about anything. Bruce is brilliant and will soon fix you up. I'm taking care of all our matters and will come to see you as soon as you're up to it."

"Thanks, Max, I'm feeling a bit swimmy at the moment and the leg's bloody sore."

Siobhan travelled in the ambulance with Will and a medical orderly; she held his hand all of the half-hour journey to Bayfield hospital, as Will winced with pain as the van went over each bump in the road. A team of doctors, nurses and orderlies greeted the ambulance and wheeled Will straight to the X-ray department where a doctor cut away his riding boot and breeches. He was X-rayed from every angle, and then taken to a private room on the ground floor equipped with all medical needs. Jimmy and Sarah followed the ambulance and were shown into a waiting room.

Bruce arrived and went straight to the X-ray department. Soon he had the results downloaded onto a large screen, plus photocopies. He beckoned to Siobhan to come and look at them.

"There's good news and bad news," he said. "The good news is that the fracture is below the knee. The thigh bone area is badly bruised but no more. The bad news is that it's a complicated fracture. Both bones are broken and the big one, the tibia, in two places, leaving a piece of bone between 2 and 3 inches long completely separated. Here, I'll show you. Also, the piece of separated bone has become displaced and therefore out of line. It is very fortunate that this section didn't break through the outer skin and become a compound fracture. However, it does mean that I shall have to operate to straighten the leg and join up the pieces. Luckily Will is a fit young man and quite able to undergo such an operation. The best option under these circumstances is for the operation to be done immediately. Therefore I propose doing it as soon as the theatre etc can be prepared this evening. As you are, so I understand, his nearest and dearest available, I would need you to sign one of these stupid forms authorising me to proceed."

"Of course I will sign the form. Shall I tell him or will you?"

"From a professional point of view, it's best that I do, though please stay with me and do your best to comfort him when I've left to make the arrangements."

"Okay, you go on in to him. I'll be with you in a minute; I just want nip along to tell Jimmy and Sarah what's happening. Is it alright if they pop in to see him when you've finished?"

"Yes, but not for long."

She was back in Will's room in a couple of minutes, Bruce had gone through most of what was to take place.

"Don't worry, darling, everything's going to be fine. Just as well to get this operation over with now. It had to be done anyway, so the sooner the better. Jimmy and Sarah are here and want to see you very briefly."

"I'm about done for now," said Bruce. "The anaesthetist will come and give you a pre-med, probably in about half an hour's time. You'll feel much more comfortable afterwards so I'll leave you now."

Jimmy and Sarah came in, "You poor old bugger, Will. I wish I could give you a rum punch," said Jimmy.

"Funnily enough I don't want one, except perhaps as a pain killer. It bloody hurts. That fucking bastard, Frank, I never did trust or like him."

"Yeah but he's got his comeuppance on its way. I doubt whether you'll ever see him on a polo ground again. Listen, we've been told not to stay long, what would you like us to do for you?"

"I don't think there is anything else you can do though it's so good that you are here to help Siobhan. She'll bring anything I need, so off you go and have an evening swim."

"Hang on a moment, I'll come out and see you in a second," Siobhan said.

Outside his door Siobhan said, "You two go home now. I'm going to stay here at least until he comes round after the operation."

"Okay, we'll go via Holders and pick up the other car so that we're more mobile again. You ring us at Westscape – doesn't matter whatever the time and I'll come for you. Tell us what I can bring – pyjamas, washing kit etc. Don't forget, ring us for anything,"

"He doesn't have any pyjamas."

"You should have gone with them," Will said, when Siobhan came back into his room.

"Darling, I want to be here – with you, now and always. I love you, okay?"

He squeezed her hand. "I suppose we'd better let a few people know what's happened. Tomorrow please will you call Fred in his office, also my parents – don't dramatise, just be factual. I'll call them myself as soon as I can. Don't forget the time difference – they are five hours in front of us."

A knock on the door and a medical army arrived. A nice-looking black anaesthetist and a team of nurses wheeling a trolley with all sorts of medical gadgets.

"Can I stay or do you want me to go?" Siobhan the team.

"No, you stay – just sit on chair by window," said a very pretty nurse.

"He's going to feel very dopey in a minute," said the anaesthetist, holding up a syringe.

A last squeeze, a kiss on his forehead and Siobhan retired to her chair.

Three hours later, the door to Will's room opened. He was wheeled in on his bed looking the same as when he had been wheeled out in a semi-conscious state, except that both his legs were protected by a large semi-circular cage so that the single sheet did not rest on his legs. The hospital staff had been most kind and courteous to Siobhan bringing her a light supper, soft drinks and reading material from the waiting room. She hurried over to his bedside, took hold of his hand and whispered to him. His hand responded and a smile of recognition crossed his face.

Bruce came in, still scrubbed up from the operating theatre. He took Siobhan over to the window and spoke quietly.

"All well, but took longer than I thought. It was quite messy around the fractures but I'm happy with the result. He's in plaster from toe to hip; for the next few days, it is very important that all movements are kept to the bare minimum. He will be under constant watch by the nursing staff; this one down from intensive care. He will also receive strong pain killing drugs and a certain amount of sedation to stop him wanting to move. I'll be in to see him in the morning, though my guess is that he should remain here in the hospital for a good week and preferably on the island for at least another week or so after, before he flies home. When that time comes, I know the local BA manager, who I am sure will be very helpful."

"Thank you Bruce, you are being marvellous. I'll talk to Lucille Todd at TRECO in the morning and see if we can extend our stay at Westscape. I'll stay here now with him a little longer. Jimmy van Duren kindly said he would come and collect me, but from tomorrow I will have my own transport."

She called the Westscape number. Jimmy answered.

"All well," Siobhan said.

"I'm on my way," he replied.

She didn't sleep much. Even though it was well after midnight when she and Jimmy got back to Westscape, Sarah had waited up for them. They had a glass or two of wine to wind down before going to bed. She couldn't help worrying and fearing for Will and the pain he was suffering; eventually, she drifted off into a disturbed sleep.

Frank Doune made good his Houdini-like ability of escaping. All attention being focused on the two ponies and Will lying on the ground by players of both teams, the umpires and members of the crowd, nobody noticed him slipping away into the cover of the trees on the far side of the ground. He had no feelings of guilt or remorse, calculating that he would have time to cover the distance of about one and a half miles taking a cross country route to the Knowles' stables at Gendale before anybody arrived back from Holders, he made his way there to retrieve his motorbike.

First thing in the morning Siobhan called Lucille.

"Oh, Siobhan, I hoped you would call. How is he?"

She gave a full run down on everything that had happened after Will had been taken from the ground in the ambulance.

"As you know, the match was abandoned. Frank scarpered somehow without being seen. The umpires had an emergency meeting with the Club chairman and officials. A statement was later put out saying that the incident was being investigated and a report will be made 'in due course'. Poor Will, please give him my love and a fond message. Would you mind if I went to see him when he's feeling a bit better?"

"Of course I wouldn't mind, he would love to see you. Bruce Griffiths wants him to stay in the hospital for at least a week and not to fly for at least another week afterwards. We are due to leave next weekend; I'm sure Jimmy and Sarah will have to go then, but could you possibly sound out if we can extend our stay at Westscape?"

"Certainly I will. There is no one booked to come and I'll speak to my boss. Then I'll bring Max up to speed as well. He will certainly be worried; I know how fond he is of Will."

All three girls, Naomi, Elaine and Misha formed up to Siobhan, "Oh, Miss Seaborn, we so sorry 'bout Mr Will; please to tell him so and wish him good soon."

"Thank you all. I will pass on your lovely message. When he's a bit better, I hope he will come here and we can all look after him."

It had been a dull, rainy June morning in Manchester though the sun was just poking through when the telephone rang in Fred's office.

"There's a lady on the line for you. Couldn't pick up her name: sounds like Shorn Kennedy."

"Put her through, please."

"Fred, Siobhan here, speaking from Barbados. Very bad news, I'm afraid; Will's had a serious accident playing polo and is in hospital with a badly broken leg and concussion."

"Oh dear, the poor lad – and poor you, as well. When did this happen?"

"Yesterday afternoon. He had an emergency operation on the leg last night. I'm going back to see him after this call. It's 9 o'clock in the morning here."

"Okay, Siobhan, don't worry. Just give me your local telephone number and that of the hospital. I'll handle everything necessary at this end."

"Thanks, Fred, you're a star man. The doctor, who is the top man here and well known to Will's business connections, says he shouldn't fly for at least another two weeks."

She gave him both numbers requested and hung up.

An hour and a half away, Mary Carpenter was just settling down to watch an afternoon's racing from the Royal Meeting at Ascot on the television. The Royal Procession with the Queen and the Duke of Edinburgh in the leading carriage was about halfway down the course when the telephone rang.

"Damn," she said, and then, "Hello," rather brusquely.

"Mary, it's Siobhan here."

Instantly Mary's attention was drawn away from the television. Siobhan told her chapter and verse what had happened.

"You poor, poor things," she said, when Siobhan had finished.

"I'm off to the hospital now and will keep you posted on everything," she continued. "It's comforting to know that the doctor is a good friend of all Will's contacts here and is the very top man."

Siobhan also rang Harry, who had come in for lunch and also to watch Ascot.

"Bugger!" he said. "What am I going to do for a work jockey? Good thing it's at the end of the season. Tell him to sharpen up and get mended quick." He did wish him all the best as well.

Will was sitting propped up in bed when Siobhan arrived back at Bayview Hospital, well named as it was stood on a slight rise on St. Paul's Avenue overlooking Carlisle Bay and close to Harbour Lights nightclub.

His eyes and face lit up when Siobhan walked in. "Hello, darling one," he said, his arms reaching out for her kiss.

"How does it feel this morning?"

"Well, I think I'm drugged up to the eyeballs because when they wear off, it's bloody painful. Bruce Griffiths has been in already; said he was pleased with everything but that it would remain painful for some days. Something about the bones being pissed off for being broken."

"I've spoken to Fred and your mother. Both very solicitous, sending love etc, etc. Fred said he'll deal with everything his end. Also spoke to Lucille about staying on at Westscape; she thought no problem there; she's going to update Max. She wants to come and see you; I told her that would be okay as long as she didn't climb into bed with you."

"You didn't really say that?"

"Of course not, stupid! Spoke to my brother who was furious about you being so careless and what was he going to do for a work jockey. Oh, and very touching message from the girls at Westscape; very upset, they are and asked me to say so, and how sad and sorry they are."

"How kind of them; please say thank you."

"I will. I did tell them that they can help me look after you when we get you back to Westscape, which I'm sure they will."

The pretty nurse who had brought the trolley the evening before came in, "Time for your next dose, Will. How you feelin'?"

"A bit sore," he said.

She made him lean forward while she adjusted and puffed up his pillows and gave him his pills.

He added, "And I need a pee."

"Oh. wait I bring bottle."

She fetched it and approached the bed.

Siobhan took it out of her hands, "I can help him with that."

"Okay, but I show you how."

"If you two don't mind, I think I can manage it myself; just give me the wretched thing."

"She's very sweet, that one," he said, after she left the room clutching the bottle now wrapped in a napkin. "She's called Greta."

"Don't make me jealous, darling."

Soon Will's eyes started to close.

"You have a snooze, darling Will. I love you so, so much. I'll go now and come back later in the afternoon."

Max came mid-afternoon. "I hope I'm not disturbing you, Will. How goes it?"

"God no. I've just had a bit of a snooze. Siobhan was here this morning and the darling thing is coming back later. I'm fine – well pissed off, but Bruce Griffiths is happy with everything. The good news is that I shall be staying on the island a bit longer; Bruce says that I shouldn't fly for a couple of weeks or so, which means we'll be able to meet and make progress maybe."

"Glad to see your brain is functioning okay; I agree with all you say. We can make daily contact. Will, I don't want to add to your distress, however, I have to tell you that May Go Twice had to be put down."

"Oh no Max, that's terrible, oh dear, oh dear, I'm so sorry. Stupidly I never thought to ask, just assumed I suppose that he was okay. What about the other pony?"

"He's okay, thank God, just a few lumps and bumps, however, poor May Go broke his near side shoulder when hitting the ground in a twisting motion. He tried to get up then fell back, obviously in pain. Luckily the vet, Will Huey, was there and did the necessary."

"Max, I'm so sad. I know how much that horse meant to you and to me, too. I never dreamt in a million years that the horse I looked after on a ship across the Atlantic would result in meeting you and riding him in a polo match in Barbados – sadly, with such tragic results."

"Will, look on the positive side. We met, are alive, very good friends with much to look forward to. I've brought you copies of today's papers, the Advocate and the Nation; both carry a piece on yesterday, which you can have a look at in a minute."

Max left soon afterwards and bumped into Siobhan who was returning.

"I feel I know you well enough already to give you a kiss in return," he said. "Will looking good. He's very brave. I've had to tell him about May Go. All fixed for Westscape; you can stay as long as you want to. I'll keep in daily touch, so I'll say goodbye for now; you go on in and see him."

Will was reading the piece in *The Advocate* when Siobhan came into his room. He gave it to her to read too.

'SERIOUS ACCIDENT ON POLO FIELD

A match at Holders polo ground on Sunday was abandoned following an incident in which a player was seriously injured. A source has alleged that a player made a foul challenge resulting in both polo ponies being brought to the ground. One pony, the former racehorse MAY GO TWICE, was fatally injured and his rider suffered a broken leg and concussion. He was taken by ambulance to Bayview Hospital where his condition is described as stable. It is understood that the injured player is Mr William Carpenter, who is from England, and was playing as guest of the Barbados Polo Club. The source stated that Mr Carpenter was not the perpetrator of the foul and that the Club is undertaking an enquiry into the matter.'

"That sums it up quite well, I think," Will said. "I imagine the club will hush it up as much as possible, largely because of Frank, a groom, only being brought in as a last-minute substitute."

"I hope Max didn't wake you up. I've just saw him outside; he told me that we can stay at Westscape for as long as we want to, which is great news. Jimmy and Sarah are coming to see you tomorrow; they send lots and lots of love. They are lovely, both of them and I do hope they'll follow our example."

"So do I, but Jimmy's a crafty old trout about taking a fly. I can't believe all this happened only yesterday. I do hope they'll let me out of here soon, so that we can be properly together again. I hate you to be missing the sea and sun."

Siobhan said, "I am here because I want to be with the man I love. Bruce will let you out as soon as he considers it's safe to do so."

Going into Will's room the next morning was like entering a florists shop. Flowers and plants were everywhere; one with a card saying, *'From Pat, Jim and all the staff of Supercar (Ireland) and wishing you a speedy recovery'*, another *'From Fred and all the staff in the Manchester Office, get better soon, Lad, we're missing you'*, a huge bouquet of heliconia and hibiscus *'From Robert and Kathleen Mallory with all our best wishes'* and a lovely one, *'With much love from Mum, Dad and Zimbabwe JoJo'*.

"They're all so touching, darling, aren't they?" said Siobhan, wiping away a tear of happiness. "How was your night?"

"Better than the previous one, thanks, but a sore bottom."

"That's great news. If your bottom's sore, your leg must be getting better."

"Don't see the logic in that one."

"Because it means you're thinking more about your bottom than your leg."

"Come over here, I want a kiss."

She did and received a severe tweak on her own bottom as she leaned over him.

Jimmy and Sarah arrived soon afterwards.

"Christ, what is this, the Chelsea Flower show or what? How are you, old fruit?" Jimmy said.

"Well, apart from a slight headache and a broken leg, tip-top thanks," said Will. "But better for seeing you and the vision of loveliness you've brought with you."

"Hmm, must be feeling better, then. At least you haven't lost your sense of humour. Fred, from your office, called this morning. Asked after you of course and told me to tell you that since you're supposed to be here on business, the company insurance will pick up the tab for all your medical expenses, including any extra cost of getting you home."

"Blimey, that's good news, thanks for telling me," said Will.

"Yes and let's have a think about a few other 'extras' that we can include," Jimmy said.

"What we're going to do now, is that I am going to let Jimmy bore your non-existent pants off you, while I take the head girl here for a girlie lunch and lie on the beach and bring her back later," said Sarah.

"Bless you, Sarah love. That's really kind of you; I keep on telling her not to miss out on things. Be careful though: I bet you'll find Lucky and his mates sniffing around in no time. They can suss out a couple of gorgeous twist and curls from two miles away."

"Hey, I didn't plan this ...." Siobhan started to say.

"Never mind, just do it and have a nice time. Jimmy and I have lots to talk about anyway," Will told her.

It was two days before Frank left the house in Bagatelle Terrace. Avoiding the coast road, he took Highway 2A before dropping down to Speightstown and Walton Dailing's boathouse. Walton was there.

"Where yo' bin?" he asked.

"I bin sick."

"Yo 'no bin sick. Yo' think me a fool? I see people, I read de Nation. I know what yo' done. Yo' fuckin' nigger, yo' in deep shit, man. I help yo' how long? Four, five years? I try to help now, but yo' listen what I say. Yo' go to Polo Club, yo' say sorry, big sorry, yo' grovel. Mr Knowles, he sack yo' but yo' still say sorry to he. His horse die, y'know? Mr Carpenter hurt bad, broken leg, in hospital. Next, yo' go see Lucky; he know what yo' done. Yo' work on water wi' him. Ski, jet ski. No tourist, hotel guest know yo' or what yo' done. Keep that way. I tell Lucky yo' comin'. Yo' work wi' him. He your boss."

Sven Goran called Walton, "What's all this I've heard about yer man, Frank?"

"It so. He caused the accident at Holders on Sunday. He frightened and ran away. I see him today, told him to own up and go to Polo Club, Better than police picking him up. He bloody fool. Tony Knowles will sack him and right so. I tell him work under me and my assistant Lucky on water; keep head down. No tourist will know him or what he done. He still useful, has brain. I keep strong watch on him, okay?"

"If you say so. I'll give it a week or two and then have a word with him. Keep me informed. Thanks, Walton."

Tony Knowles came to see Will. Jimmy was still there.

"Hi, Will, sorry, I won't disturb you now, I'll come back another time."

"No do come in, you know Jimmy; you kindly allowed me to bring him and his lovely girlfriend to your party."

"Of course I do and I saw you both briefly that dreadful day on Sunday. How are you, my dear chap."

"Going on fine, thanks. Bruce is quite happy but I'll probably be in here for a week or so. Listen, I am so dreadfully sorry about May Go; Max came in yesterday to tell me, I feel awful about it all; I loved that horse as I know you did."

"Will, don't even think about it. You did what any competent player would have done. I got a huge thrill when I saw you chase my pass up field, May Go's racecourse acceleration made it obvious that you were going to get there. I saw that bloody Frank coming at you, but he had no chance or enough speed to take the ball cleanly in front of you. He knew that too and the way he slunk off the field speaks even worse of him; he didn't turn up yesterday and hasn't been seen since. I shall sack him of course, but he will have to face the Club enquiry. I wouldn't want to be in his shoes."

"Thanks Tony, I'm so sad about it all."

Jimmy said, "Sarah and I were, and still are, despite last Sunday's disaster, absolutely loving our time here. Will has been ecstatic about it for ages and it's even better than we expected. To actually meet some of the people that he has talked about makes it even better. I hope we will become regular visitors."

"Good to hear that. Some people think we are too laid back, but that is an unfair judgement. Safe to say that we work hard and play hard. Life would be a trifle boring otherwise. Will, I must be going now though I'll be in touch with you and Siobhan regarding your progress and plans over the next few days. Jimmy, hope to see you before you leave us but, if not – here's to the next time."

"Definitely and all the very best to you."

Sven Goran was in a good mood. He had just concluded a conference call with his cousin Vagn in Denmark and the shipbuilders in Holland.

The first sea trials of Genevieve One had been completed with success in every department. The plan now was that the final trials would take place during the next two weeks, not just to check the few minor modifications but also for crew training. Sven had negotiated work permits for the senior crew on the basis that no such technical knowledge was available on the island. Vagn had engaged the Captain in Denmark, Engineers and navigation staff had been recruited and had been working with the shipbuilders in the final stages of construction in Holland. Deckhands, cabin and catering staff, Sven had raised locally with the help of Tom Canon and his team from T.F Canon & Co.

Sven's internal telephone rang. "There's a young man wishes to see you Mr Goran, says you know him, name of Frank."

"Bring him in please."

"Mr Goran, I come to see you because I make big mistake."

"Yes, Frank, I know about it but why have you come to see me?"

"You say last time if I had problem to come to you."

"Frank, I know nothing about polo though I understand that you committed a serious foul, which caused the death of a horse and serious injuries to a rider. Furthermore, you left the scene saying nothing and without any expression of regret."

"Yes, Mr Goran."

"You will certainly lose your job with Mr Knowles and what is more, your name and reputation among the echelons of people of influence in Barbados is mud, to put it politely. I have spoken to Walton Dailing; he has advised you what to do – so go and DO IT. Look, you know you did wrong. You learn. Keep your head down, work with Walton and Lucky. Count yourself very fortunate that you still have a job with Walton."

Frank's thoughts were circling round his head as he made his way back to Bagatelle Terrace.

I say sorry but I not sorry. Should be me on May Go; I make him polo pony. Why he ride him? Money. Why he here? Money.

Six o'clock Wednesday evening, a knock on the door. "I'll go," said Tony. "Wonder who this can be."

He opened the door. Frank said, "I come say sorry."

"You've taken your time. I am very disappointed in you, Frank; you've let me down but, much more important than that, you've caused the death of a horse, a favourite horse who, as always, was trying his best to win; you've caused very serious injury to someone who was trying his best to win by legitimate means and you've brought the game and the Polo Club into disrepute. Needless to say, I can no longer employ you. I shall tell the Chairman of the Club that you have been to see me, that you have apologised for your actions and that I have told you to present yourself at the Club's Headquarters at Holders Hill to account for yourself. Goodnight."

Tony closed the door.

8 o'clock Thursday morning, Bruce came into Will's room.

"How goes it, Will?"

"It's certainly less painful. I only had one painkiller yesterday."

"What about headaches?"

"Gone, none for a couple of days."

"Good. On Saturday, we'll take another series of X-rays, which will show what progress we've made. Depending on what we find, will determine when you can go back to Westscape."

No sooner had he left than Max appeared.

"Have I got news for you?" he said. "But, first of all, what's yours?"

"Bruce just been in. He's going to take another X-ray on Saturday. We'll know more then. Now, yours please."

"Both Williams and Jackson have more or less committed themselves. They read the papers, of course, and asked me to pass on condolences etc. Those guys keep their eyes and ears open; news like last Sunday flashes around the island like a forest fire. I've had meetings with them separately, they've done their own homework, posed some more questions, but I'm as sure as dammit that they'll both come in. Apart from anything else, they know each other businesswise, which is a help. I've got one or two others sniffing around as well. As soon as possible when we get you out of here, we must talk to your main contact at Supercar – not the Chairman at this stage, but the experienced chap that has an ear to him."

"You mean Fred."

"Yes, he's the man I would talk to."

"I'd like to be with you when you talk to him. We don't want to find ourselves in a strong position here, only to have it blown away by the boss."

The door opened, and Siobhan came in.

"Morning darling one, it's like rush hour here this morning."

"Oh, should I go away if you're having a business meeting?"

"No, certainly not. We're just discussing tactics."

"Good morning Siobhan," Max said. "Your man here is as bright as a button this morning and looking so much better. We've about finished but we'll plan that Will?"

"Yes, certainly. I'll be good to bring Fred into the picture and for you talk to him."

When he'd gone, Will filled her in with the events of the morning.

"That's good news on both fronts, darling. So sad that Jimmy and Sarah have to go. It's been wonderful having them here; they've become really great friends, lifelong ones I do hope. It's their last night tomorrow, they've asked me to go out to dinner with them, which is lovely. I said wouldn't they like to be on their own, but they insisted. Lucille recommended a restaurant called The Cliff; very smart, she said. Evidently, you have to book weeks in advance in the winter, though Jimmy managed to get us a good table when he booked yesterday. The plan is that we'll come to see you first and go on from here."

"That's a splendid idea and I'm so glad you are going with them."

"Lucille asked if she could come and see you after she finishes work this afternoon about 5.30 ish, she said."

"Yes. Tell her that would be fine."

"Would you like to see her on your own or would you like me to be here."

"I don't know. What do you think? There are no secrets between us."

"I get the feeling that she would like to see you alone. We get along fine and I promise I won't be in the least bit jealous. I've got you for the rest of my life. I know she still has a very soft spot for you."

"Okay, if that's what you think and if you don't mind. I'll give you chapter and verse anyway. Come here, 'I want to go on a kissing spree' – that was an Eartha Kitt song, – 'with nobody else but you.'"

Lucille arrived, as planned, straight from her office. She smiled at Will and sat down on the chair which she pulled next to the bed.

"How are you getting on?" she asked. Will sensed that she was nervous, a bit apprehensive and determined to retain her self control. In turn he wanted to put her at ease.

"Pretty good, I think. It's not so painful and Bruce is coming to take another X-ray on Saturday. So sweet of you to come. This is the first time we've been able to see each other on our own."

"Yes, I know. I wondered if we'd ever get the chance so your accident played into our hands in that respect. I hope Siobhan doesn't mind me coming?"

"No, not a bit. She likes you very much and both of us are so grateful for all you've done to help since the accident and, indeed, all the time we've been here."

"Will, just want you to know that I feel no rancour at all; Siobhan is really lovely and very beautiful. I like her too; you are very lucky to have found each other. Maybe I held a pipe dream for too long, though all I can say is that when I saw you again, I would have behaved in exactly the same way as before. What we had will never leave me and I am grateful and lucky to have experienced it."

"Lucille, sweetheart, I feel exactly the same. I want you to know that. I'm so glad, too, that you've found someone else. We only met very briefly, so tell me about him."

"Josh is a really, nice, kind, thoughtful, highly intelligent man. He is being so attentive and loving towards me. I admire and respect him; the trouble is that I don't love him – well not enough anyway."

"I feared that might be the case and I feel guilty in a way."

"You mustn't, because you're not. I am a grown-up lady. I have a blissful home life with devoted parents and a super job which I enjoy very much."

"You know or maybe you don't, so I'm telling you this in

confidence, that Max and I are planning a business venture that I put to him a while ago. If it comes off, it means that I shall be spending quite a lot of time here. I hope that doesn't bother you?"

"Will, don't be silly. It will be marvellous to see you, always, as two long time great friends and former lovers which is what we are."

"It's good to be able to talk this way, Luce. As you know Jimmy and Sarah leave on Saturday. If my X-ray on the same day turns out well, I'm hoping that Bruce will let me go back to Westscape but I doubt if that will be until Monday at the earliest. I'm a bit worried about Siobhan being there on her own. Do you think she'll be okay? She's a good strong Irish girl and not one to make a fuss though to be on her own in a strange, to her, land – what do you think?"

"I'm sure she will be okay, but if she's nervous, I don't mind keeping her company and staying overnight for the weekend. A bit of sea and sun would be rather good. I've nothing planned that can't be changed a little.

Would you like me to suggest it to her?"

"Yes please, if you really can, and I won't say a word unless she tells me."

They chatted on about this and that, both were trying not to become sentimental. When she left, Lucille bent over Will, gave him a quick kiss, a squeeze of the hand and was out of the door. In the privacy of the yellow moke, she let herself go, tears running unchecked down her face, She couldn't help reminding herself of a similar journey she made having said goodbye to Will the last time at the entrance to the Deep Water Harbour.

She had recovered by the time she arrived at Uplands.

"Had a good day, darling?" Harriet said.

"Yes, thank you."

"Anything the matter?" asked Harriet, sensing that something was wrong.

"I've just been to see Will in hospital," she said, breaking down again and hugging her mother.

Frank left the Committee Room at the Polo Club clutching a letter in his hand, which he tore into shreds before leaving the parking area, where he had left his motorbike. His appearance before the

Committee had been a short one. The Chairman read out to him a resume of the foul play and the resulting fatality of a pony and serious injury to a player. He asked Frank if he had anything to say. Frank said that he regretted the incident but was only asked to play half an hour before the match.

He was asked to wait outside.

Fifteen minutes later he was summoned in again. The Chairman told him that the Committee took account of the short notice to play he had been given owing to the sudden indisposition of another player, however, Frank had two years employment with a prominent playing member of the Club and had shown himself to be a competent rider and fully versed in the rules of polo.

The Chairman told him, "Until further notice, you are barred from attending any polo ground under the auspices of the Barbados Polo Club."

"How did it go with Lucille?" Siobhan asked, the next morning.

"Very well really. We had good chat, sort of cleared the air. She was very sweet, said how much she liked you. It was a good thing to see her on her own; she probably thought she could open up a bit more without having to make an effort. I told her that if the Max deal comes off we'll be spending quite a lot of time here – at least I hope it's a 'we' ?"

"Try and keep me away!!"

"... so, it will be good to have her as a close friend to us both. I know that's what she'd like. I'm sure next time she'll ask us to Uplands, the plantation."

"Good, darling, I'm glad, and I love you to bits."

Jimmy had arranged for Lucky to come in the afternoon for a last ski. Siobhan left Will to have a sleep and joined them.

"Hey, Seaborn," Lucky said. "I hear 'bout yo' friend, but why he not here? He good skier, only need one leg."

It was a good finale: Jimmy succeeded on a monoski, Sarah, more relaxed and confident crossed the wake several times really enjoying herself, while Siobhan, remembering what Will had told her, looked so elegant as she crisscrossed time and time again, standing up straight, using her knees as shock absorbers when riding the waves and wake.

Six o'clock that evening, Jimmy, Sarah and Siobhan came into

Will's room, carrying a basket containing a large thermos, a freezer bag of ice and four glasses.

"Look what Elaine has prepared especially for you and with fond messages from all the girls," Jimmy said, opening the thermos, putting ice in each glass and filling them all with homemade rum punch. "She says she'll have plenty more for you next week."

"D'you know, I was only thinking this afternoon that I was more than ready for one of these, so well done and thanks to Elaine."

"Must be telepathy," said Sarah. "When you have your next one, think of us huddling under umbrellas in a thunderstorm, walking along the King's Road."

Siobhan said, "Thinking about tomorrow, I'll come in the morning to find out about the X-rays, but later what we've planned is that Jimmy and Sarah's plane leaves at 7 o'clock and we have to be at the airport by about 5. We will all come via here for them to say goodbye, then I'll take them on to the airport and come back to say goodnight to you. Guess what, that lovely Lucille rang to offer to come and stay over Saturday and Sunday nights to keep me company. Isn't that kind of her?"

"Yes, I'm so glad she's done that," said Will. "We did speak about it when she was here."

"Oh, was it your idea?"

"I didn't say that. I just said that I was a little concerned about you being on your own and she offered. Speaking of which, are you okay to find your way to the airport and back on your own?"

"If I can find my way across the bogs of Ireland to Listowel racecourse and back in the dark when the bar closed two hours after the last race, I think I can manage to find Grantley Adams airport in Barbados."

The rumbo thermos finished, Jimmy said that they'd better be on their way.

"Hope you have a smashing evening. It's so kind of you to take Siobhan," Will said.

"Good night, darling one. So, so sorry that you can't come, but you'll soon be out of here and we'll have lots of time to make up."

Siobhan had just arrived the following morning when Bruce came in with the X-ray photos.

"It's good news tempered with cautious news," he said. "The good news is that the bones have set in the right order and position.

Take a look here and you'll see what I mean. The cautious news is that it is still not a week since the accident. I know how much you want to get out of here and under normal circumstances, I would advise against it for probably another week. However, I also know where you are intending to go and, if I read you correctly, Siobhan, I think you'll make a good nursemaid because that is what Will needs. Given all that, you haven't been out of this room, Will, and only out of bed with help from two nurses onto that ghastly commode thing that they bring in to you. You haven't stood up straight yet, for instance. You will need teaching how to walk with crutches and have to get used to them. Therefore, I am suggesting that you stay here to do all these things until Monday at the earliest, probably Tuesday. What say you?"

Siobhan spoke first, "Let me reassure you that Will shall have my undivided attention day and, I'm delighted to say, night."

Will said, "When can I start my crutchery lessons?"

Bruce laughed, "As soon as I'm out of your room but something I must drum into your head - you have had a very serious accident and have a badly broken leg, which is going to take months, if not a year, to mend properly. The more you overdo things, the longer it will take and, be sure to know and think of this: the bones are still in a fragile situation and any mistake you make by being over ambitious or careless will put you back weeks, if not months. I don't want you to consider flying until I give you the okay, which will be after another X-ray and new plaster."

"Thanks, Bruce. Yes of course I want to go back to the house, but everybody's been fantastic here; I couldn't have asked for more."

"That's good to hear. Right, I'll go and sort out some crutches. To start with, two nurses will help and show you. Siobhan, you watch and don't let him do too much; just round the room today. Tomorrow he can start moving down the corridor and to the loo etc, but he'll get tired quite quickly so make him stop."

Siobhan returned later in the afternoon with Jimmy and Sarah to find Will sitting on a chair with his leg propped up on a stool, a pair of elbow crutches lying by his side.

"Good to see you out of that bed; care for a run round the car park?" Jimmy said.

"Don't encourage him," Siobhan begged him. "I have to put a double bridle on him as it is."

"Did Siobhan tell you about last night?" Sarah asked.

"Gosh, no, I was just starting to when Bruce Griffiths came in. You tell him Jimmy."

"It was really good, fabulous place perched just above the sea, great food, not surprised it gets booked up, though it was bloody expensive, real arm and a leg stuff – sorry – but listen: the table next to us was occupied by a fat Brit, a bit of a Philip Green lookalike, his blonde, bubbly wife and daughter who, sadly for her, has taken more of her father's looks than her mother's, plus another couple. They were talking about last Sunday: the fat Brit, his wife and daughter were at the game. 'I've heard that the bloke who caused the accident was Frank –you know the one that taught you, Tracey, to ride and who took you water skiing.' His wife said she didn't believe it, as Frank was 'such a nice young man, very polite. You liked him, didn't you Tracey darling?' 'Oh, yes Mummy,' she replied. The other man, also a Brit who seemed to be involved with horses, said, 'He's not a nice young man at all, at least that's what another trainer guy I know well at the Garrison says. Dead shifty and a branch of a tree on his shoulders. Been warned off all the polo grounds by the Club.' "

"That's interesting. I wonder who the other couple were? I'm sure Max'll know. I'll ask him."

Jimmy said, "Come on Sarah, sweetheart, we've got to go if we're going to catch this plane, so goodbye, old fruit. Sorry it ended like this for you, but it's been fantastic and we're really hooked. Hope you'll be out of here soon, keep us in the loop and let us know when you're coming back. Best of luck with your deal too, really hope that comes off."

"So do I, fabulous that you came and thanks for looking after this Irish she-wolf in my enforced absence. Siobhan darling, don't bother to come back again. I'll see you in the morning on a training run."

"Couldn't resist popping in to say goodnight. Love you, darling, see you in the morning."

By the time Siobhan arrived on Sunday morning, Will had already done several laps of his room and had found a lavatory at the end of the corridor with all sorts of handles, gadgets and wall brackets, including a moveable V-shaped stool that he could fit his leg onto.

Might try and borrow this, he thought.

Siobhan had brought him a pair of shorts and a couple of shirts during the week so when she came in, he was ready for a walk around the little garden.

"Darling I really do want to go back to the house tomorrow. I'm getting itchy feet – sorry, an itchy foot. I promise to be careful but I need to get on the telephone and start making plans. I want to talk to Max and arrange for him to come to Westscape so that we can talk to Fred."

Will left Bayview mid-morning on Monday with prolonged goodbyes and thanks to all the nursing and hospital staff. Siobhan had come with a huge box of chocolates to be shared out among them all. Bruce had agreed amid renewed severe warnings and arranged for an ambulance to take him back to Westscape, with Siobhan following behind with all his stuff and a prescription from Bruce for painkillers, 'only to be taken in emergency,' he had said.

A touching sight awaited them; all three house staff, Naomi, Elaine and Misha lined up on the doorstep to welcome him, as he was lifted on a wheelchair out of the ambulance by two orderlies, "Oh, Mr Will, welcome back, so good to see you!" they said.

"Thank you all," he replied, being helped out of the wheelchair and given his crutches. "Now then Elaine, how about some of your medicine."

"Already waiting for you inside, Mr. Will."

Will turned to the ambulance crew saying, "Thanks to all of you and I hope I shan't bother you again!"

Inside an armchair had been placed at a good angle for him in the drawing room near the telephone and on the terrace, a day bed had been made ready under the parasol, with a rum punch on a table beside it.

Siobhan followed him, and said, "Thank you, girls, for making it look so good for him."

"Anything you want. Miss Seaborn, you just aks." Bajan dialect doesn't ask, it aks.

Will dialled the Manchester office number, "Hello, it's Will Carpenter here, is Fred there?"

"Oh Will, is it really you, how's the leg?"

"A bit fragile, but in one piece now. Thank you all for the beautiful flowers."

"It's the least we could do; wait I'll put you through."

"Now then, Lad, how are you?"

"Lying in the sunshine, having a rum punch, thanks. Seriously, I'm fresh out of hospital half an hour ago. How's yourself?"

"Well, I wouldn't mind changing places with you, but not too bad otherwise. What's your news?"

"In some ways, it's lucky that I'm still here. I've got my main man, Max Geary, coming to see me and I want to make sure that you are available so that we can talk while he's with me. Things have progressed here. We have two serious investors with whom Max and I had a very good meeting two days before my accident. Max feels, and I agree with him, that we can't go any further without the tacit understanding that the boss is taking this matter seriously. Max is a proper big wig here; I've known him for four to five years and these other two guys are for real. One is the Caribbean director for a hotel chain with four luxury hotels here in Barbados and others in different islands, and the other is the top man and joint owner of the largest distributor of cars and vans on the island. Max and I have agreed that it would be best for me to talk to you in his presence, saying very much what I'm saying now. In other words, I'm asking you, as his long-standing confidant, to have a word with him before my meeting with Max tomorrow. If he tells you to fuck off, I will have to cancel Max and call off the deal without causing serious embarrassment. I'm not saying he has to agree anything – merely for you to tell me that it is in order to proceed to the next stage which I will talk about in detail with him and preferably you as well as soon as I can come back."

"Okay Lad, I get the picture. Can't promise anything, but I'll do as you ask. Any idea when you'll be able to travel?"

"Don't know for sure though I hope in about ten days or so. My doctor here is a top man, British trained, and he's very streetwise and sensible. I could call you at about the same time tomorrow?"

"Okay Lad, look after yourself. Have you got Miss Ireland on the job?"

"I can't imagine what kind of a job you're thinking about, but she's being brilliant. If you get a definite no-no, please will you call me back so that I can start organising my immigration papers."

He rang Max, "Max, I'm back at Westscape."

"Delighted to hear it."

"I've just had a long chat with my man Fred in Manchester. He's going to talk to Robert Mallory today. Would you be able to come here tomorrow morning about this time or a little earlier, then we could both talk to Fred? He is probably the closest business friend and confidant to Mallory outside the boardroom. It would be very good if you could talk to him as well. I trust him implicitly and he's been very good to me ever since I joined the company."

"Yes, I can manage that and would welcome talking to your colleague in Manchester; we can take it forward from there."

"Hi Siobhan," Max said, arriving at the house the following morning. "How's the patient?"

"Like a cat on a hot tin roof but it's lovely to have him back. He's doing fine and longing to see you so come on in. Would you like a cup of coffee or anything?"

"A glass of iced water would be great."

"Morning Max," Will called from the drawing room. "Thanks for coming. Let's hope we can make some progress. I'll call Fred Ogden now, he's a typical gruff Lancastrian but a real good, solid sort with a lively sense of humour."

He picked up the telephone and dialled the number, "Fred, I suppose you're sheltering from the rain in Manchester but I've got Max Geary here and he's looking forward to talking to you… so here's Max."

"Hello, Max Geary here. Will's told me a good deal about you and how much he values your opinion and appreciates the help and encouragement you've given him. First, may I say that I first met Will on a chance encounter on board a ship when he was a deckhand, with the responsibility of looking after two racehorses I was importing to Barbados. I was most impressed with him then and more so when we met again on subsequent visits on the same ship when calling in Barbados. We have kept in contact ever since and I was delighted to welcome him and his friends this time. His accident on the polo field was a major tragedy for which he was in no way to blame. However, before the accident, I had already had two meetings with him about the project which he had outlined to me before he arrived.

I have to say that the project to launch a Barbados car rental company under the Supercar banner has great merit. There are still many details to discuss and hopefully finalise, but I have secured the definite interest of two major players to form part of the local interest of which Will has informed you, i.e. that the parent company will have a controlling interest. We have got to the stage where it has become necessary to know the interest in principle of your chairman in order to take the matter to the next level."

"Thanks, Mr Geary or may I call you Max?"

"By all means."

"Will has discussed his proposal with me during the last few months and also with my Chairman, Robert Mallory, who owns Supercar, together with his family. You may be aware that Will met Mr Mallory on the same ship that you were talking about. Mr Mallory was impressed with the young Will and his attitude to life.

Following his call to me yesterday, I spoke to my Chairman; all I can say is that he has authorised me to confirm that the project has the interest of Supercar and that negotiations should proceed to what you describe as the next level. Whatever that may be, I can confirm that you and Will should go as far as you can with it, so that he can take it straight to Mr Mallory on his return to the UK. It would help enormously if you could submit to Will your side of the project, including details of the prospective investors and the companies they represent and details regarding your own company and possible investment. If this could be in the form of a report, that would be best."

"That makes complete sense to me and I will certainly do so. I'm so pleased we've had this opportunity to talk this matter over and I'll hand you back to Will."

"I got the gist of all that, Fred. Glad the Old Man's advanced a bit out of his corner. Please pass on my best wishes to him and also please pass my thanks to him, you and all in Manchester so much for sending me those fabulous flowers in hospital. As one of my visitors said, coming into my room was like going to the Chelsea Flower Show. Goodbye Fred and I expect we'll talk again during the next few days."

"Aye, and you take good care, Lad. Lucky you having that gorgeous Siobhan to look after you. All best."

The next few days passed in an almost dreamlike trance. Nothing more to do on the work front; just the two of them together. They didn't want or need to go anywhere, Siobhan went to do the bits of necessary shopping, the rest of the time they lay or sat under the terrace parasol, talking or reading as there was a plentiful supply of books in the house. Sometimes, Siobhan went for a swim as Will watched her nymph-like figure crossing the sand and plunging into the water, then rising like a dolphin with an outstretched arm in the air, waving to him. Afterwards, she'd return to him with a loving, watery kiss. Lucky came zooming in one morning and Siobhan made his day by going for a long ski, looking very much the glamour girl as she weaved backwards and forwards behind the boat.

At night they just lay together, nothing physical – two and a half feet of plaster of Paris made sure of that – but just blissfully happy whether they were asleep or awake.

A week later Bruce called. "Time for another X-ray. Depending on what it shows, I should be able to advise you re travel plans."

Siobhan had taken the call.

Will called out, "Tell him not to send an ambulance, I'm sure I'll be okay in the car with the seat pushed right back."

The appointment was fixed for the next day.

Max also rang, "How's he doing?"

"He's right here so can tell you himself."

"Hi, Max, we've had the most wonderful and quiet few days. All going well, I'm sure. Bruce just called; I'm going for another X-ray tomorrow. If he's satisfied I can make travel plans."

"That's good news Will, though we will be sorry to lose you. Listen, before you go I think you should meet the lawyer who has been advising me and I think should act for the new company, which he will set up. Can I bring him out to see you?"

"Max, better than that, Siobhan is taking me to Bayview tomorrow for the X-ray, so why don't we come straight on to your office? Save you coming all the way out here."

"If you can manage that, yes great."

"As you're going on from here to Max's office, I'll have a look at these here when the radiologist has finished and call you later" Bruce said.

"Okay, good, fingers crossed," said Will.

Going along Broad Street, Will said turn right here, "Now, see that little opening on your right – that's Max's office car park."

"Oh, Mr Carpenter, how you doin'? I tell Mr Geary you're here,"

Gwen, the receptionist, said.

Max appeared straightaway, "Hi Will, come this way. No steps. Hello Siobhan, welcome."

He led the way into his office, "Are you best on a sofa or armchair?"

"Probably the sofa is best, if you can give me a hand up from it. I hope you don't mind me bringing my chauffeuse."

"She's a damn sight more than that and of course not. Let me introduce you both to Nile Winters, the Rumpole of Barbados."

"Come on Max, I'm much better looking than Rumpole. Very good to meet you, Will."

He turned towards Siobhan, "You too. You must be Irish with a name like that."

"Right first time, from the Emerald Isle."

Will looked at Nile as they spoke. A little above medium height, a tinge of red in his curly hair, blue eyes and a slightly ruddy complexion, probably mid-fifties. He thought, *I've seen him somewhere before. I know I have.*

"Very good to meet you," he said. "Particularly as Max has been singing your praises so I'm looking forward to working with you to get this project moving."

"I hear about you too – and I read the papers. How the leg coming on?" Nile said.

"The leg is mending, I hope. Actually, I've just come from having a new X-ray. If it's okay, Bruce Griffiths says I can go home."

They sat down and talked the whole project through for half an hour or so. Nothing that Will didn't already know came to light, but it was a good move to meet and discuss in person. "My Chairman is a real stickler for detail, accuracy and legality. You can bet your bottom dollar that his own lawyers will go through all clauses, agreements and the like with a fine tooth comb," Will said.

"I am sure he will from what I hear about him, but I am happy and confidant that, from a Barbados perspective, all is in order, legal and correct."

Listening to Nile, Will remembered where he had seen him.

When they rose to leave, he said, "We have met before. I've been trying to remember when and where. It was at the Bamboo Beach Bar, about four years ago. I was having lunch with Lucille Todd and you came and said hello to her."

"Oh, I know Lucille and her family well, man. If I may say so, you a good judge of a pretty lady."

"Nile, just you keep your hands and mind away from this one," broke in Max. "She well spoken for."

Bruce called.

Will answered himself.

"I'm sorry to have to tell you but your X-rays are fine so you can go home. I need to fix it up with the local BA manager, so when would suit you?"

"I am afraid to say as soon as you can conveniently make it. I've got to make arrangements the other end, so what about in a couple of days?"

"Leave it with me, I'll see what I can do. I'm going to give you a full report which you'll need to give to your doctor in England or Ireland and I strongly recommend that you see an orthopaedic surgeon to guide you through the next few months. You will need a lot of physiotherapy on your knee and ankle to get the movement working in both joints when the plaster comes off. I'll call you when I have more news."

"Thanks Bruce, yet again."

"You heard all that? We're okay to go. How do you want to play this one? I shall obviously have to stay in England for a little while to see Mallory before he goes cold on the deal. I'm sure Fred will arrange a comfortable car and driver to take us up to Cheshire, but do you want to go straight on to Dublin?

"Will darling, of course I don't want to do that. I want to stay with you; however, I suppose I better speak to Harry and see how he's coping. We will have been away for nearly a month."

"Yes and I must call my parents to tell them the good news. I want to be back in Ireland a.s.a.p. There's no point in contacting an English doctor. Ask Harry when you speak to him about orthopaedic guys in Dublin. Tell you who'll know a good one - Joe Maguire."

Later, having spoken to Harry, Siobhan said, "Darling, I think it's probably best for me to go straight on to Dublin. Harry will meet me. There are things I need to do, the first being I must make sure everything in the flat is okay, like no obstacles that you might fall over, enough food there for us both when you do get back and

I will talk to Harry and Joe about a doctor for you etc, etc. You'll be fine at Ayshford, Mummy will fuss over you and, as you say, you've got to go to Solihull. By the time we've both done all these things, I'll be ready to meet you as soon as you can come. It's only a short flight and I insist that you book a business class seat. Fred will do it for you."

"Perhaps you're right. I'll get Fred to take me to see Mallory; I want him there anyway."

"I've fixed you up for Friday," Bruce said, on the telephone the next morning. "Best that you give David Locke, the BA manager a call. He'll give you all details. He's laid on a wheelchair both here and at Heathrow, and a forklift truck here to get you on the plane because there's no loading ramp."

"Christ, Bruce you're not only my doctor but my travel agent as well. I'll call him right away. Thanks again and hope it won't be too long before we're back here again."

"Darling, would you like to ring Lucille and tell her that we're leaving on Friday, or do you think I should?"

"I think it's better coming from you. We don't want her to think that you are avoiding speaking to her. Remember she still thinks you are the bees knees – like I do, by the way!"

"Okay. I'll tell her about collecting the car and ask her to book us a taxi to the airport as well."

Will called his parents to expect him on Saturday. Mother fussed like an old hen but Will declined any 'special needs' and promised to conclude all his news on arrival.

When Will spoke to Fred, he asked if Fred could arrange a car and driver to take him from Heathrow to Ayshford and, "I'm bringing with me a full dossier from Max Geary under his business letter heading. It would be great if you would liaise with the Old Man and fix up a meeting with him as soon as you can – say next Monday. I hope we can go together. You could pick me up at Ayshford and we could go through everything in the car on the way?"

Siobhan and Will had the rest of the day, all the following one and Friday morning to themselves. Packing would take hardly any time. Siobhan had a minimal amount of shopping to do. Will gave her his card and asked her to draw some money from the ATM.

"We should give a good tip to the girls; they've looked after us so well. Jimmy left me a contribution to give them."

Friday morning came.

"Happy, darling?" said Will softly, as the sun streamed in through their bedroom window.

"Blissfully," Siobhan murmured.

Max called, "Just to wish you both bon voyage and to say two things: first, there's a driver on his way to you with the Supercar dossier as prepared by myself, setting out the prospectus from the Barbados end, including Nile Winters' legal opinion, and second, I expect to see you both again as soon as possible."

"Thanks, Max for all the help and support through everything and I hope your second wish comes true. I'll call you as soon as I have any news."

Mid-morning Lucille drove up.

"Come to say goodbye to you both. The taxi will be here at 4 o'clock, Will." She kissed them both, Siobhan first, then Will.

Siobhan said, "Thank you Lucille, for all you have done for us and especially for being so kind to me by staying here those two nights after Jimmy and Sarah left. It's been so lovely meeting you and I can't wait to be back again."

Lucille drove away, knowing she mustn't look back.

The three girls, Misha, Elaine and Naomi, said a fond farewell to them both.

Siobhan gave them all a hug and a kiss and, "Thank you all for helping me with this invalid."

"Oh, he no invalid for long. Goodbye, Mr Will, Miss Seaborn. Hope you come back soon."

"D'you know, darling," said Siobhan, as they drove away in the taxi. "This has been like a honeymoon, slightly interrupted maybe, but if the real one is anything like as good as this one, then I shall remain the happiest and luckiest girl in the world."

CHAPTER 21

Fourteen hours later Will's driver drove through the gates of Ayshford.

"Thank you Syd and well driven."

"Thank you Sir and I hope you soon make a full recovery. Always thought 'orses was dangerous."

Mary Carpenter came out of the house pushing an old-fashioned wheelchair.

"Where did you get that thing from Mum and I don't want it so take it away," said Will, heaving himself out of the car and reaching for his crutches.

"I borrowed it from Tarporley hospital. I said you'd got a newly broken leg, 'Oh, you'll need this then' they said – and a commode, which is up in your bedroom."

"Oh! Mum, you are brilliant and thank you, but I'm past that stage," he said, giving her a big hug and a kiss.

"Come on in; I bet you're starving."

"Well, I wouldn't mind a sandwich or something – and a stiff drink. Breakfast on the plane seems a long time ago. How's Dad?"

"Not brilliant, I have to say. I'm afraid his memory is fading, but never mind that now, come and say hello to him while I get you something to eat and drink."

Will hobbled on his crutches into the drawing room, "Hello Dad," he said.

"My goodness, hello Will, where have you sprung from and what have you done to yourself?"

"I've come from Barbados and I broke my leg playing polo," Will replied.

"Hmm, polo indeed. A dangerous game, I've always thought. Barbados, eh, that's a long way away. What were you doing there?"

"Part holiday and part work Dad, but never mind me, it's great to see you and how are you?"

"I'm fine but quite busy, you know."

Mary came in with a ham sandwich and a whisky and soda.

"Tell us about your journey, how did you manage on the 'plane?"

"It was quite funny really. They lifted me on a forklift truck into the inside of the plane where I had a complete row of five seats with the armrests down, on which I lay, with lots of cushions under the leg. Siobhan had a seat on the other side of the aisle just behind my head. I could prop myself up to drink but she virtually fed me as I was at the wrong angle. She was brilliant though I managed to sleep quite a bit with the aid of a pill that my wonderful doctor in Barbados had given me. Siobhan's gone straight on to Dublin to see her brother and make a few arrangements before I go back, probably next Tuesday or Wednesday. Now, what news of JoJo?"

"She's having an unbelievable time she says, but is due back in a couple of weeks or so, I think."

"Right, well we must think of the next step for her. Without being rude, she mustn't procrastinate here for any length of time."

"No, I agree," said Mary. "Let's have a talk about it tomorrow. Now, what are your plans?"

"Well, Mum, the main object of going back to Barbados apart from a holiday of course, was to suss out a project I'm working on to start up a Barbadian registered car rental company under the Supercar banner. I am very pleased to say that the idea has been favourably received. There are all sorts of problems which I won't bore you with, but I have brought back with me a very detailed and concise document written by my main contact, would be investor and colleague to discuss with Robert Mallory. I have been talking to Fred Ogden, who you have met and have asked him to arrange a meeting with Mallory as soon as possible, hopefully this coming Monday. I am expecting Fred to ring me here over the weekend. As soon as we have had the meeting, I must get back to Ireland."

"Well darling, that does sound exciting. I'm not going to question you anymore for now; you must be dog tired. How will you manage the stairs?"

"I don't know, haven't needed to climb any yet, though I'll have to get used to them and I suppose I'd better try now."

"I'll come with you and get your father to come too.

It was slow going and difficult, even more so coming down.

"Bloody hell, I wouldn't want to do this more than once a day," he said.

Siobhan called while he was upstairs. Mary answered and transferred the call to Will. They had parted when she had to follow the 'In transit' sign, with Will being wheeled to immigration.

"How was it, darling – the car journey, I mean?"

"Oh, fine – a jolly, cockney driver, no problems at all."

He told her about mother and her wheelchair and the commode, though he didn't mention the stairs. "How about you, darling one?"

"Fine, too. Harry met me; filled me in on things here. Nothing disastrous I'm glad to say. I think he's been partying a bit. Various pieces of female evidence about the place. He says no problem about getting a good orthopaedic man. There are a number to choose from and he or I will speak to Joe Maguire tomorrow. Love you darling and missing you terribly."

Fred rang quite early for a Sunday. Will was still upstairs so Mary transferred the call.

"Glad you're back, Lad, safe but not sound, I imagine. Sorry to ring so early but this work is getting in the way of my golf. We're on for tomorrow, however, the old man is very grumpy. Doesn't like being put in a corner, everything has to be his idea, remember. We must be very careful not to present this as a *fait accompli*. It's his money and company that we're playing with, all with the best of intentions though he hates the idea of not being in complete control. He's old-fashioned, we know and he knows, but he doesn't care about that. I know how much work and effort you've put into this and the success you've made in Ireland though we're on a knife edge on this one. I'll pick you up around 9.30 in the morning, if that's okay?"

"Yeah, that's fine Fred. We can talk more in the car."

This was disappointing news for Will. After the highs in all senses and the physical low during the past month, he hoped for a better reaction from Mallory, however, Fred knows him better than anyone except perhaps for his wife, and Will was sure that Fred's attitude and advice were the best ones to follow.

Downstairs after breakfast, he called Jimmy, "Jimmy, Will here, I'm back."

"Will, good, that's great news - tell me all."

Will spent five minutes doing just that, "… so here I am, staying few days with my parents as I have an important meeting with my Chairman in Solihull tomorrow. Siobhan went straight on to Dublin to get a few things fixed for my return which will probably be on Tuesday. What's your news?"

"My/our news is – wait for it – Sarah and I have joined your club."

"Jimmy that's just fabulous news, I can't wait to tell Siobhan, she'll be as delighted as I am. What swung it for you, you old fox?"

"Well, apart from the obvious one, that we quite like each other, I thought and do think that I've never seen two people so happy and in love than you two, so I thought that I should do the same. Luckily Sarah agreed, so here we are, an engaged couple and it's ALL YOUR FAULT if it goes wrong."

"Okay, blame me if you want to, though it's brilliant news and well done you. Can't say that I'm surprised; Siobhan and I said several times that we hoped this might happen. We took to Sarah in a big way; I know Siobhan will be in touch, but a big kiss to Sarah from us both."

Will went on to talk to Jimmy about Joanna and the need to find something good for her to do once she was back from Zimbabwe, as well as the need for her to widen her outlook and to have something worthwhile to do. In other words, a stint in London with someone to watch over her. Jimmy said that he'd talk to Sarah and that both would cast about.

Next day Fred and Will arrived at Supercar HQ around 11.30, having planned their strategy. Aggers appeared, "Hello, Fred and oh my God, Hopalong, how are we going to get you up the stairs?"

"With difficulty, Aggers, but you know my motto, 'Climb every mountain'."

Robert Mallory met them at the top, "You'll need a large brandy after that Will."

"No Sir, though a cup of black coffee would go down a treat."

Mallory had arranged for a comfortable armchair and a stool for Will to put his leg on.

"Glad to see you back, Will; sorry about the leg, but tell me what you've been doing apart from playing polo?"

Will let that one go.

"Thank you Sir, it goes back to the early days when I met the owner of those two horses I was looking after on the Star. His name is Max Geary; it turns out that he is a serious big wig business wise in Barbados and I have kept in touch with him ever since. A few months ago I told him that my girlfriend and I plus two other friends would like to come back to Barbados for a holiday.

In answer to his question, I told him that I worked for Supercar and that I had been instrumental in helping to set up a Supercar branch in Ireland. He told me that he had heard about Supercar being a progressive and efficient company with a human touch and said if a branch company could be set up in Ireland, why couldn't the same be done in Barbados? In his view, there is room for a locally based and registered car rental company to take on the big international boys which, after all, is what we've done in Ireland.

You may remember, Sir, I mentioned it to you a while ago but at that time neither I nor probably you, Sir, took it seriously. However, Max Geary collared me almost as soon as we arrived in Barbados and said words to the effect of, 'what about a Barbados Supercar?'

I've had a series of meetings with him and a couple of interested investors and a prominent lawyer both before and subsequent to my accident. The result is the dossier that Fred is holding in his hand now.

You said in my very early days with the company that if I ever heard anything of company interest, I should bring it to your attention, so here we are. Incidentally, Fred is the only employee of the company that has any knowledge that we had met before I joined and that only because we have worked very closely, not just in the Manchester area, but in Ireland as well. Fred has been my mentor and advisor in chief and I'm very grateful to him."

"I think that what Will is saying is that the approach has come from the other side, if you understand what I mean," said Fred.

"I'll have to read this document very carefully and have it run through by legal and accounting teams," responded Mallory.

"I understand that," said Fred. "However, if you look at the legal Opinion, you'll see that a company registered in Barbados must have at least 40% of the equity locally owned. As I understand it from Will, the two interested participants, plus Max Geary himself, will make up at least the necessary 40%. Also one has to observe that the two main Barbados shareholders will have the best interest of the company very much at heart: one, the hotel will direct all their guests in four hotels to hire Supercar vehicles and two, the other will supply all the cars for the fleet. Both of the above will give the company an advantage over the international big boys who only operate under license."

They continued talking for a further period of time until

Mallory said, "I don't think we can do any more until I've read the whole blooming dossier thing and got the experts to pick holes in it."

They stopped for a sandwich on the motorway on the way back, which Fred brought out to the car.

"What do you think, Fred?"

"He's biting. Great move that the approach has come from them. To be wanted is very good for his ego; makes him feel in control. He'll make a fuss; however, I think he'll go for it. For what it's worth I think it's a good plan. You'll have to handle it Lad, though I'll support you."

"I want to go back to Ireland tomorrow, Fred. When you get back tonight do you think you could have a word with your pals at Ringway? Siobhan says I should have a business class seat with more legroom and I'll need a wheelchair both ends. Doesn't matter much about flight times; I'll ask my mother to take me to Ringway, so not too early in the morning. Siobhan will meet me at the other end."

"Aye, I'll do that Lad. Call you as soon as I've fixed it."

"Come in for a cup of tea Fred," said Will, as they arrived back at Ayshford.

"Okay, just a quick one, thanks."

"Mum, are you there? I've brought Fred in for a cup of tea."

Mary came in from the garden. "Hello Fred, how nice to see you again; did you have a good meeting?"

"You never know with the old boy. Wouldn't want to play poker with him though we think it went okay. It's a great project Will's got hold of."

He didn't stay long. "Thanks for the tea and the biscuits Mrs Carpenter and all the best to you. Call you later Lad, or first thing in the morning."

"He's such a nice chap," she said as Fred drove away.

"Yes, I'm devoted to him in so many ways. A solid but fun head on his shoulders without the semblance of any kind of chip."

"Wedding bells in the air," Will said to Siobhan on the telephone.

"Yes darling, I know, but I don't want you hobbling up the aisle on crutches."

"Not us, stupid."

Silence for a few seconds, then, "Don't tell me the Barbados air has worked, oh that's fantastic, brilliant news, just as we hoped. Give me Sarah's telephone number."

"Don't know hers, though she's probably with Jimmy, so here's his."

He gave it to her.

"I'll be back tomorrow, not sure what time yet. Fred's going to call me later or first thing in the morning. Would you possibly be able to meet me?"

"I'll have to look in my diary to see if I can fit it in – you bloody idiot, I'd be waiting all day for you."

Mary drove him to Ringway to catch a late morning plane.

"What are we going to do about Dad, Mum?"

"I've spoken at length to Dr Craw. I'm afraid it's the start of Alzheimer's. He's sort of okay at the moment though Craw has referred him to a neurologist in Chester and I'm going to take him for a thorough all round check-up."

"Good. Let me know how it goes. I've spoken to Jimmy van Duren about JoJo. You know him - he and his girlfriend were with us in Barbados – they've just got engaged by the way soon after they came back. Life's circle is a funny old thing: she was James' girlfriend, came to the funeral with her parents, introduced herself to me and told me how much she loved James. She and Jimmy got together quite a long time later though Jimmy met her originally with James. By the way, we all raised our glasses to James one evening in Barbados. Anyway, both of them are going to scout around for ideas for JoJo in London."

Will was easy to spot being the only one on a wheelchair with a leg stuck out like a giant carrot. Siobhan rushed forward and bent over him with an embrace as romantic as she could make it.

"Oh, so you know each other then?" remarked the lady wheelchair attendant.

"Yes but I haven't seen him for two and a half days."

"What do you want to do darling?"

"Well, it depends on how you are fixed but I really ought to call by the office, have a catch up with Pat Byrne and see what's going on etc. I'm sure he could run me back to the flat a bit later."

"Have you gone stark raving barmy?" Siobhan asked. "If you think I'm going to let you out of my sight, think again. We'll go to the office, you do what you have to do, I'll do my knitting and then when Sir is ready I'll take him home and smother him with the kind of love that I cannot display in public."

A week later Robert Mallory came home from his office and said to Kathleen, his wife, "You better start packing your bags. We are going for a holiday."

"… going for a WHAT?" she exclaimed. "We don't 'do' holidays."

"You heard; we're going for a holiday to Barbados to see what that young rascal Carpenter's been up to."

That same afternoon, Aggers had rung Will. "The boss wants to go to Barbados and has asked you to fix it up for him. I'll do all his flights etc, however, he wants you to arrange a programme for him to meet all the relevant contacts and see all that he needs to see."

"That's good news, Aggers. Tell him I'm on the case. When does he want to go?"

"As soon as you've fixed it all."

Will relayed this to Siobhan, then called Max's office, "Could I speak to Mr Geary please?"

"Mr Geary not here, Who speakin' please?"

"William Carpenter. Could you please ask him to call me in my office. Please tell him it's quite important."

"Oh, Mr Carpenter, I tell him; yes, please."

Half an hour later Max rang.

"Hi Will, glad you're back and hope all's well your end. What news?"

"Yeah, now back in Ireland. Fred and I had a meeting with Robert Mallory while I was in England. Must have gone well because he wants to come out."

"Holy Smoke, that's good news. When?"

"Now, or as soon as we can fix it up. Wants to meet you, Williams, Jackson, Nile, have a tour round everywhere, see anything important, you know – the works. It'll all hang on this trip, I guess. His wife's coming too, so where do you think we should put them to stay? Must be good. We should not offer to pay his accommodation; he would consider that bribery, however, it might be an idea to give him a car plus guide for his island tour over one or maybe two days."

"Leave that with me, Will. I'll give you a call back tomorrow. How's the leg?"

"Going on okay, I think, Siobhan's being brilliant driving me around, and her brother's retained jockey, Joe Maguire, has recommended a very good orthopaedic man in Dublin to take over from Bruce."

Max called back the next morning, Irish time.

"I've spoken to all concerned. No problem with Martin Jackson but Mike Williams has to go to the States in a couple of weeks. He won't be away for long so I'm sure we'll be able to fit something in. I suggest we recommend the Coral Reef hotel. You may know it by now, bang in the middle of the Golden Mile so to speak, along the west coast. Owned and run by the O'Hara brothers; their father, Budge O'Hara, arrived here, some say on a sailing boat, in 1947 shortly after the end of the war and never left. He and his wife, Cynthia, founded the Coral Reef and it's held its place among the top hotels ever since. It's right next to the Colony which is one under Mike Williams' management so he could show it to your man Mallory. What would you say to Lucille being the tour guide? I could easily arrange this with TRECO."

"Sounds good, Max. I'll pass it on. Coral Reef would be perfect, I think. Poor Lucille, though she's an excellent choice. If she agrees, I'll fill her in regarding Mallory and I think you and I should have another chat or two before he and Kathleen arrive. I'll keep you posted but let's hope we are on our way."

Will relayed all this to Aggers, especially about William's USA trip coming up in two weeks' time.

"You know Mr Mallory, Will. Once he's made up his mind about something, it needs to be put in place by yesterday."

Will had arranged for one of the office juniors to fetch him from the flat in the morning and take him home in the evening, which left Siobhan to come and go as she pleased to fit in with her jobs at Lostock.

"I'm getting mightily pissed off with this bloody leg," he said, when he returned home that evening. "Not being able to drive is the worst – well nearly the worst," he corrected himself with a sheepish grin.

"Come here, you idiot. Don't you know I'd go to the ends of the world to be with you if only for a solitary moment, so stop fussing. It won't be for too much longer and as soon as you have the plaster above the knee removed, you'll be much freer. In the meantime, having found you, I'm not letting you go. Come on, here's your drink ready for you."

"You're a saint in wolf's clothing and I'm the luckiest man alive. Mallory's probably going to Barbados in less than a week's time."

"He is? That's fantastic news!"

Five days later Robert and Kathleen Mallory took their seats in the First Class cabin for their British Airways flight to Barbados. There, they were met and driven to the Coral Reef Hotel where they were shown to their beachfront ground floor suite in the early evening.

"Now, let's have a look at what Will's planned for us: Day 1, that's tomorrow: nothing much, just pottering about the hotel here."

"That'll be good, especially after our journey. Get you into the sea," said Kathleen. "Followed by lunch on the terrace and bit of a siesta in the afternoon."

"Hmm – wasting time, more like."

He continued, "Day 2 - Meeting in Bridgetown with Max Geary. He's Will's man so that's okay. Day 3 - Meeting at Colony Hotel - next door evidently - with Mike Williams, the Regional Director and potential investor. Day 4 - Tour of Northern section of the island, seeing other new developments and sights etc. That'll be bloody boring - you'll have to keep me awake. Day 5 - East and centre of island and lunch with Geary on south coast. Dunno about that, will have had enough by then."

"Don't be such a misery. I'm really looking forward to it."

He read the rest of the itinerary, "Day 6 - Meeting with Martin Jackson, boss of Jackson Motors. A potential investor who will supply all the cars etc. Well, at least you won't need to come to that and can visit the hairdresser or something. Days 7 and 8 - Wind up days - sure we won't need them so can book our return flights now."

"No, Robert, we've come all this way, don't be so hasty."

Next day, No 1 on the itinerary, Robert and Kathleen were actually quite content to have their day of rest consisting mainly of making use of their private terrace and plunge pool with a couple of longer swims in the sea. Lunch taken on the covered beach terrace, a siesta in the afternoon, a wander round the hotel and immaculately tended tropical gardens, a drink at the bar and lo and behold, it was time for dinner. Kathleen thought it was absolutely marvellous.

Day 2, Max sent a car to collect Robert in time for their meeting at 10.30, "You stay here, my dear, and enjoy the sunshine."

Entering the smart entrance foyer to be greeted by one of two attractive receptionists from behind a curve-shaped table cum desk, Mallory's mind flicked to the entrance of the Supercar head office in Solihull.

"I've come to see Mr Geary," he said.

"Yes, please. You are Mr Mallory?" the receptionist queried, lifting her telephone.

"I am."

In no more than a moment, Max appeared through the side door.

"Mr Mallory, welcome to Barbados. Do come with me."

He led him through the waiting area and straight into his own office, gesturing to him to sit on one of two armchairs, with a small round table between them.

"I've been looking forward and hoping that we would meet for a while, but the speed at which you made your decision to come has been remarkable."

"I needed to see with my own eyes what that young rascal Carpenter's been doing."

"I don't know about the young rascal bit but I don't think that a man at the head of a company like yours would have come all this way just on a whim."

"Right, let's get down to it. Give me chapter and verse, and I'll let you know if I'm to go home tomorrow or stay another few days."

For the next hour, that's exactly what Max did, with some but not many interventions and questions from Mallory.

At the end, it was on first name terms of Max and Robert, with the latter announcing, "I'm not going home tomorrow."

By way of a departure question, Mallory asked, "How did you meet Will Carpenter?"

Max told him.

"Hmm, he was me and my wife's cabin boy on that ship. His job title was 'Cabin Steward' though he really was no more than a boy. There was something there in him that I wanted to find out. I think he's answered that question."

"I hope so", replied Max. "Let me run you back to your hotel.

I've got go up that way in any case; I'm a director of a real estate company in Holetown and there's someone I need to see there."

In the car, Mallory said, "A pity about Will's accident. What happened?"

"It was a tragedy. Will is a good player and was asked to play as a guest by the captain of one of the teams, a good friend of mine." He went on to describe in detail what happened, emphasising that Will was in no way to blame.

"How did it go?" Kathleen asked.

"Knows his onions, this guy Geary. Very switched on, so far so good. Didn't like his office – more like a hotel than a place of business."

"Oh, go on, you're just old-fashioned," said his wife.

"I may be old-fashioned but I know where to keep my money."

"Under the bedroom floorboards, more like. Speaking of hotels, a Mr Williams called to speak to you. About the meeting tomorrow; he said just turn right and walk along the beach for a few yards. It's the next hotel, the Colony. He'll expect you any time after ten, not smart, you don't have to dress up. Asked me to come too, if I liked."

She did like. *Why not*, she thought, *it's not often I get the chance of being with Robert on any sort of business and it's good to do things together.*

Mike Williams, tall and good-looking with dark hair, wearing a smart short-sleeved shirt and dark tie, met them in the hotel foyer.

"Hey, Kathleen said I wasn't to dress up."

"She's right, you're a guest. I'm not only the Manager but Regional Director in charge of four hotels so I'm on duty and I have to look neat and tidy and expect my staff to be the same. Welcome to the Colony, come into my office for a short time; I'll tell you a bit about myself, the company I work for and the policy of our hotels. Then I'll take you on a quick tour round the hotel during which please tell me anything you don't like or if you spot something wrong."

Like Max Geary the day before, Mike, very affable and informal like good hotel managers should be, went through the reasons why he thought and approved of the proposed project.

"I'm a Bajan born and bred, I went to school here, my father was a sugar planter but foresaw the end of Barbados as a major source of sugar on the world market owing to geographical production costs. He saw tourism as taking over as the number one source of revenue and the export of Barbadian products with the USA being the nearest country to find top quality training, so here I am back at home with my wife and family in a job I really enjoy."

The hotel tour, Mallory regarded as a bit of a drag; all very plush as a hotel of this standard should be. Kathleen found it much more interesting; she loved all the bathroom and shower fittings and gadgets, bed linen and spotless furniture. What impressed Robert Mallory was the staff's attitude and attention to detail. *A good team,* he thought.

Mike Williams saw them off. "Anything that you've forgotten to ask or need to know, just pop back anytime. I'm off to Miami in two days but only for a short week, so if you're still here when I get back, do let me know. It's been great meeting you and I hope we'll do so again soon."

"I liked him," said Kathleen.

"Bit of a grease ball but runs a tight ship, give him that, and that is what we're after. Bloody hell, I wouldn't be in the hotel business for all the tea in China."

"No, and I wouldn't like to be one of your guests."

"Probably so. Now, let's have a look at Master Carpenter's programme for us tomorrow, Day 4. We seem to have a lady guide to show us some of the sights on the northern section of the island. I'm not the greatest sightseer as you know, so I hope she's got a comfortable car; prod me if I go to sleep."

Whatever Robert Mallory was expecting, it certainly wasn't the vivacious blonde that greeted him and Kathleen in the entrance lobby of the hotel.

"Mr and Mrs Mallory? I am Lucille Todd, your guide to see some of our beautiful island today so, if you are ready, shall we go?"

She led them to a spanking clean Toyota SUV. The driver emerged.

"This is our driver today, Austin, who knows pretty well every nook, cranny and pothole on the whole island."

Austin grinned, "Yes please," he said.

Taking the coast road northwards, Lucille pointed out

landmarks of interest such as Heron Bay, the Barbados home of Lord and Lady Bamford, the opulent Royal Pavilion Hotel, on and past the very lovely Gibbes Beach, then the more touristy Mullins Beach with its bar and restaurant. Just short of Speightstown they passed a smart entrance gate.

Lucille said, "In there is a really nice, top-class hotel called Cobblers' Cove. English owned, not too big, with a lovely beach just to its right. Very popular with British guests. Max said not to put you there as he thought for the main purpose of this trip, the Coral Reef was a better alternative."

Through the town of Speightstown, 'the main town in the north', complete with a variety of restaurants, elegant clothes shops, banks and a small quayside off which lay fishing and small boats for hire.

"I want to show you now, probably the largest and most important development of our time," she said. "Until three years ago the area that we are approaching was a rather dull and unattractive piece of land. As you can see, we now have a manmade lagoon surrounded by separate and different condominium buildings, all having been awarded the highest and best architectural designs, plus individual waterside private homes and hotels. A marina designed to accommodate up to the largest private and commercial motor yachts, with direct access to the sea, is included in the development. The grand opening of the whole complex is scheduled in approximately three months' time."

"Can we have a look round?" asked Mallory.

"I thought you might ask that and I have special permission," Lucille said, showing a cellophane pass with her name and photograph, which she hung around her neck.

"This is most impressive," Mallory said. "A more modern and very well-designed version of Port Grimaud in the South of France."

"Yes, I believe the original designing company of Port Grimaud was professionally consulted here," Lucille said. "Max Geary and his associates have an interest in the development consortium."

Moving on, they took a right turn through the old village of Mile and a Quarter and on, stopping to see, from the outside, the Jacobean house of St Nicholas Abbey.

"It isn't an Abbey at all," Lucille said. "However, this house built in 1658 is one of three houses of similar construction in, to use a

British expression, The Colonies, the other two being Drax Hall also in Barbados and Bacons Castle in Virginia, USA. These days it is a much-visited tourist attraction, with a miniature steam railway running round the original plantation."

They drove on to one of the best island viewpoints, Cherry Tree Hill, with fabulous views along the wild Atlantic east coast.

"What's the sugar cane situation in Barbados now?" Mallory asked.

"It's been in serious decline for many years. Barbadian plantations are small in area with very little flat land. We can't compete with huge flat areas and modern machinery. My father and our family have been sugar planters for many generations. We pass close by our plantation. Would you like to have a look?"

"Well, if it doesn't take you far out of the way, that would be most interesting. What do you think, my dear?" Robert said to his wife.

Lucille picked up her cell phone, "Hi. Mum. Listen I'm doing an island trip with business associates of Max's, just wondered if we could pop into Uplands on our way?"

"Yes, course, darling. Where are you now?"

"We're up at Cherry Tree so could be with you in about half an hour. Actually, the people I have with me are the owner and his wife of the company in England that Will works for."

"So you know Will do you?" Mallory asked.

"Yes, I've known him since he first came here on a banana boat."

"Will was our cabin steward on that ship," Kathleen said.

"What a coincidence. He was looking after two racehorses on the ship belonging to my boss at the time, Max Geary. Max took him with the horses to the stables at the racecourse and asked me to take him back to his ship. When he was here recently I arranged for the house he rented with his friends. We passed by it this morning at Gibbes Beach. You remember Mr Carpenter, Austin, don't you? I think you collected him and his friends at the airport."

"Yes please, Miss Lucille. Dey keep fun talk. He had accident; how he leg?"

"Oh, you know about Will's accident?"

"The whole of Barbados knows. Certainly; it was terrible. My parents and I were at the match; I saw it all. I went to see him in hospital; he was very brave. One of the saddest parts about it all was that the horse he was riding was the same horse, turned into polo pony, that he had looked after on the ship; he broke his shoulder in the accident and had to be put down. Tragic."

"What do you do now, Lucille if you don't work for Mr Geary?" asked Kathleen.

"Actually, I still do, in a way. I had been one of Max's receptionists, PA, secretary for a number of years but decided I needed a change. He is a director and part owner of what I consider the best firm of real estate and property management firms on the island, The Real Estate Company Ltd, known for short as TRECO. They were looking for an office manager and admin supervisor. I applied for the job and got it; this was about 18 months ago. I am very happy there; the office is in Holetown, very near your hotel. Now, here we are welcome to Uplands."

They came up the gravelled drive, past the fork to the farm buildings, to the sweep in front of the house. As they were getting out of the car, Harriet Todd emerged through the front door.

"Hi Mum, you didn't expect to see me so soon did you? May I introduce you to Robert and Kathleen Mallory – my mother, Harriet Todd."

"This is a pleasant surprise – do come in and see an old Barbadian plantation house with a few modern additions like electricity and hot and cold running water"

They went inside just as George Todd appeared. "Sorry I'm a bit scruffy; I was out on the farm when I had a message from Harriet that you were coming."

"So sorry to intrude, but..."

"You're not; far from it. Delighted to meet you, especially as you're a friend of Max Geary and, I gather, Will Carpenter's boss."

"Having been on the island for all of four days, I'm not sure if Will isn't my boss. We are here to look at what he's been doing with the possibility of forming a joint company here."

Sherry came in with a tray of coffee cups and saucers. "Or would you like something stronger? We have our own Uplands rum?" George asked.

"Not just now, thank you; otherwise we'll go to sleep in the car."

"Thank you, Sherry, that's just fine."

They chatted for a few minutes until Harriet said to Kathleen, "Would you like to have a quick look round the house? Come on

Lucille darling, let's leave the men here and show Kathleen how we live."

"We've heard from your daughter today and from others that sugar, for a long time Barbados' premier export, is no longer so," Robert said.

"Yes, only about one-third of our crop these days is sugar. We have switched everything else into vegetables, fruit and potatoes with very small margins throughout. Long gone are the days of rich sugar planters. Did you know that Will had an ancestor called Benjamin Carpenter, who was one of the most successful and philanthropic of all the early settlers? He arrived here about forty years before my own great grandfather."

"No, I was not aware of that. I knew there was some family connection, but Will has never told me the details. That speaks well of him. We told Lucille in the car that he was our cabin steward on a banana boat, the *Star*, on his first trip here. My wife and I took a shine to him and he started work with my company about a year later."

"Yes, I believe Will and Lucille met somehow through Max Geary. Something to do with a racehorse. They met again each time Will was here on his ship; one weekend she brought him to stay here. We liked him very much and I think they became very attached to each other but they were both very young at the time. As you know, Will was here recently and he introduced us to his new girlfriend, an absolutely charming and pretty Irish girl, who we also took to. I believe they are engaged."

"I believe so too, although I have not been told officially."

"Come on, Robert, we must get out of these lovely peoples' hair. Had a fascinating tour of house and learnt a lot," said Kathleen coming back into the drawing room with Harriet and Lucille.

"I do so much hope we can meet again," said Harriet.

"If things go well on the negotiating table, we certainly will," replied Robert.

"Had enough for today?" asked Lucille, back in the car.

"I think so dear but, gosh you've been so good to us and we are loving it," said Kathleen.

"Okay, Austin, back to the Coral Reef."

"Yes, Miss Lucille."

At dinner that night, Robert said, "Do you know, my dear, I'm quite enjoying this."

"So am I for many different reasons – the main one being that we're doing it together. From what Lucille was sort of intimating, I think there had been something going on between her and Will," Kathleen said.

"There was. Her father told me but I understand they are both behaving in a grown-up way and remain very best of friends. Lucille has another boyfriend though her father doesn't think he's forever."

Lucille and Austin were ready waiting the next morning. Day 5.

"Good morning Lucille; thank you so much for yesterday" Kathleen greeted them.

"Good morning to you both. I had a call from Max earlier. He's suggesting we do a run down the rest of the east coast, after which he's invited you to lunch with him at a very good restaurant called Champers in the Bridgetown suburb of Hastings. Would that be okay for you? I know he's arranged a meeting for you with Martin Jackson tomorrow morning and that's at Warrens Industrial Park, on your side of the island which is not too far from your hotel."

She looked at Robert, "That would be perfect for us, don't you think dearest?" asked Kathleen, getting the nod from her husband.

"Much of the east coast is barren and windswept as we saw yesterday though a lot of Bajans have weekend cottages there to escape from the urban conurbation of Bridgetown. Two-thirds of the local population live on one-third of the island. Say if you don't want to, but I suggest making a brief stop at St John's Church, not just from a religious angle as it's also lovely to see as it is one of the most beautiful structures in Barbados with fabulous views, built in 1645, although rebuilt and repaired a number of times following severe damage by fire and hurricanes. In the cemetery is a headstone over the grave of Ferdinand Paleologus, a descendent of Constantine the Great, who came to Barbados as prospective sugar planter. He died in 1670. The main religion in Barbados is Anglican under various denominations though there is a strong Roman Catholic presence and a recently renovated Jewish synagogue."

"Yes of course, we'd like to have a look," said Robert.

From St John's they made their way southerly, passing Sam

Lord's Castle, Lucille telling the story of the English buccaneer who hung lanterns on coconut trees to lure ships onto the reef off the beach by his property. Then past the airport and the steady increase of residential and commercial property. Soon they arrive at Champers Restaurant overlooking Rockley Beach in the district known as Worthing.

Max was there already. "Hello, you travellers, I should think that you are ready for a Barbados cocktail – a rum punch. They make a very good one here."

"Hello Max. You know I might just break a rule and say yes, please."

"And I'll join him," said Kathleen. "I have to say that we have had a most fascinating two days learning about and seeing your wonderful island. Lucille here, and Austin too, have made it so enjoyable with lots of lovely stories and places we've been to and seen."

"That's very good to hear. Lucille, would you like to come and join us for lunch?"

"Max, that's a lovely idea and I'd love to, however, having been out of the office for the best part of two days, I've a lot to do. Sadly I must say no –but thank you. Mr and Mrs Mallory, I've really enjoyed taking you round to see part of the island. There's plenty more left for another time. Austin will come and pick you up tomorrow and take you to meet Martin Jackson. If I don't see you again, I hope to do so next time; please pass on my best wishes to Will when you see or meet him next, and tell him I hope his leg is getting better fast."

They went inside and to their table on which were two rum punches.

"You not having one?" Kathleen asked.

"I try not to during the week. The trouble is that if I have one, I can't resist another and it's goodbye afternoon," Max said.

"You're like me at home. Usually gasping for a whisky and soda as soon as I get back from the office."

"Anyway, how did you get on?"

"I'm not joking, it's been really great…"

"And Lucille is such nice girl. So thoughtful and amusing," butted in Kathleen.

"Will called me only just before you arrived asking how it was all going. I wanted to wait until she'd gone before telling you. They were - and I'm sure still are - very fond of each other, but it's a different situation now. I met Siobhan, his Irish girlfriend, and I believe fiancée. She is really delightful, kind and loving towards him. Spent hours and hours with him in hospital."

"Good; I'm looking forward to meeting her," said Mallory.

They had lunch chatting about not only what they had been doing, but touching on business plans.

"I have to say, I was most, most sceptical about the idea as put to me by Will, but so was I about the Irish business, which is working out very well. Speaking off the record as this is not a defining moment or occasion, I am hopeful that we will proceed. Naturally, I will send Will, and I presume Siobhan will come with him, out here for a lengthy period to set up the business as he has done in Ireland, though he and I will expect and need your expert 'put in'."

"That goes without saying" responded Max. "After all, I will have my own investment to look after. As I see it, I am expecting Williams and Jackson to contribute 15 to 20% each. I will encourage them to put in identical sums. This eliminates either of them being considered minority shareholders. I am prepared to invest 7½ to 10%. Either way that reaches to the 40% required in Barbados law owned by shareholders in a Barbados registered company with a majority shareholding being held by a foreign company."

"That makes sense to me," said Mallory. "I would propose myself as non-executive chairman. Despite his young age, what do you think of Will being managing director and you, Williams and Jackson as executive directors, with the emphasis on the latter two looking after the management of their respective and quite different interests, but available for advice and inclusion on all company matters?"

"Let me think about that one. Will shall need a work permit, but I'm sure Nile Winters will be able to swing that one. At this stage we have to bear in mind that there will be a hell of a lot of work to be done before the company starts trading, like setting up the company, acquiring suitable premises relatively close to the airport for housing, care and maintenance of the fleet, and for office space.

I have known Will on and off for what – four or five years – but the other two have only met him once. I know that he set up everything in Ireland, however, this is Barbados. I might prefer to suggest myself as managing director with Will's position as a director, manager and managing director designate when we start trading. How about that?"

"That, too, makes a great deal of sense. You know the score here backwards, Will knows about the car rental business. Let me mull that one over."

"I'd love to be a fly on the wall in Champers restaurant in Barbados right now. Max, Robert and Kathleen Mallory are having lunch together," Will said, on his return from the office.

"I wonder what they're eating, kingfish or red snapper do you think?" said Siobhan, wearing an apron, coming out of the kitchen.

"Bugger what they're eating, it's what are they're bloody talking about that concerns me. However, the news is reasonably good. No one has fallen out with the boss so far."

"Darling, I don't want to nag but don't you think you should make an appointment to see the guy Joe Maguire has recommended? We've been back over two weeks now."

"Yes, you're quite right. I'll do it tomorrow. His name's Sean O'Hehir. Joe told me he'd fixed him up and many of the other 'lads' as he calls them, several times."

"I'll go on my own tomorrow. You don't want to sit through a boring meeting with this chap Jackson and see his car assembly factory," Mallory said, back at the Coral Reef.

"Not much, I must say, though I have enjoyed watching and listening to your chat with Max Geary at lunch today; didn't realise you could be so diplomatic."

"My goodness, Austin, I didn't think it was going to be such a big plant," Mallory said as they drew up to the forecourt of a large, well-designed steel-fronted factory cum showroom. The ground floor was taken up by countless spotlessly clean-looking models of new cars of all shapes, sizes and manufacture.

"I wait for you here," said Austin. "Dis place, very good, very expensive. Best on island."

Mallory walked in on a shining off-white metallic painted floor with not an item of dust or dirt to be seen. A row of ladies and good-looking young men, all smartly dressed, engaged with service reception on the right hand end and sales on the other.

Mallory chose 'Sales'.

"I have an appointment with Mr Jackson; my name is Robert Mallory."

"Would that be Mr Martin Jackson, Sir."

"Yes."

"One moment Sir."

An attractive young lady appeared, "Please come with me Sir, Mr Jackson is expecting you."

She led him to a lift door concealed in the décor, pressed a button, and the door slid to one side. They entered, another button pressed and at lightning speed, they reached the third floor. The door opened; Martin Jackson stood facing them.

His office was as modern and immaculate as the showrooms downstairs. Although the difference between Mallory's Solihull premises and Jackson's were like chalk and cheese, the two men had many similar characteristics. Both were bosses in their own land and this was Jackson's.

"Max Geary is not only a very good business and personal friend of mine, he is someone whose advice and recommendations, I ignore at my peril. Since meeting him recently to discuss the project under consideration, I have obtained enough information about Supercar and you personally, together with my own judgement on the matter, to think that the project to have a joint company based and registered in Barbados would be good for my country and, more important, good for my company. I can supply the company with as many cars of whatever size and manufacture that are required. Some makes we assemble here, others we buy in ready made. Our servicemen are trained for every single vehicle that is supplied by us. You have my word on that and my company's investment to prove it. I met your young man who was here recently. He is someone with whom I can do business. So, are we in agreement?"

"Yes, Mr Jackson, we are. I have another meeting with Max Geary and shall instruct him to proceed. The young man you were kindly complimentary about will be in overall charge though he will work closely with you all. I will arrange for him to come to Barbados as soon as his present job for me in Ireland is completed, which I estimate will be in three or four months, by which time I believe that the necessary preliminary work and legal documentation by

Max and his lawyer, Nile Winters, will also be completed. Are we in agreement on that as well?"

"We are. Now, I expect you would like to have a look round here to see what we do behind the scenes. If you don't mind, I'll ask my works manager, Glen, to take you. He probably knows more of the ins and outs than I do."

Half an hour later Mallory was back in the car and soon back at the Coral Reef, just in time for lunch.

"We've done, I think. One more meeting with Max Geary to tie things up, which I hope can take place here, then we can go home," Mallory informed his long-suffering wife.

"Oh come on Robert, surely we can have a couple more days of peace and quiet?"

"Umph, don't know what you want to do but if you insist, okay, I suppose."

Will picked up the ringing telephone in his office.

"Will, I've got Mr Mallory on the line for you."

"Right, put him through."

"Will, Mallory here. I've got a new job for you. How's the leg?"

"The leg's going on fine, I think. I've got an appointment with the orthopaedic man in Dublin tomorrow. What's the job, Sir."

"I've done the deal here, so you'd better start packing if you're interested."

Silence for a moment, then, "That's brilliant news Sir, I can hardly believe it, the best I've ever heard. Interested? I'll say, please don't look any further. Well done, Sir. When do we start?"

"I'll be back in a few days, can you come over to see me then? There's a lot of formalities to be completed, some of which don't concern you, but probably about the turn of the New Year. Fix when you are coming with Aggers."

"Is it okay if I ask Fred to drive me?"

"Yes, I want him there anyway."

"Darling, darling, have I got news for you? Hope you haven't packed your bikinis away. I've just had Mallory on the line from Barbados. He's done the deal and wants me to run it. Can't tell you any more just now, but I have to go over to see him after he gets back in a few days. Isn't it fantastic?"

"Will, my treasure, I am so thrilled, thrilled to bits. How exciting

– when, where, how?"

"Probably in the New Year."

"Oh, darling Will, what a start it will be to our married life. Can you come back a little earlier this evening so we can celebrate?"

Next call to Fred. "Do you know, Fred, our wonderful chairman and boss has come up with a fabulous idea of forming a Supercar company in Barbados, together with some local investors? Isn't that clever of him? Furthermore, he wants me to go out and run it. He's back in a few days and wants to see us both as a.s.a.p. Told me to fix it with Aggers; can you give me a few days to choose from and can you collect me from Ringway and drive me?"

"What a surprise and, well done, lad. Give me a moment and I'll be back to you. Yes, of course I'll take you."

Siobhan was ready with a chilled bottle of champagne to welcome Will when he got home.

She said, "Well done 007, I'm so proud of you; I've booked a table and am taking you out to dinner at the castle tonight so let's drink this while we get ready."

"That's lovely of you, darling, but there's no need."

"Be quiet and do as you're told."

Will and Siobhan pitched up at Mr Sean O'Hehir's private practice the following day.

As they were shown into his consulting room, he greeted them enthusiastically, "If Joe Maguire sent you to me, you must have something to do with racing."

"Joe told me that you had mended him several times. I did this playing polo in Barbados and my lovely girlfriend here Siobhan, is Harry Kennedy's sister. I ride out for Harry as a work jockey though I have a proper job as well."

"Right, when did you break the leg and do you have X-rays?"

"A month ago and here they are."

O'Hehir put them on his screen, "Wow, you made a proper mess of it, didn't you? By the looks of it, yer man out there's done an excellent job. What's his name?"

"Bruce Griffiths."

"Hmm, that name rings a bell. I must look him up."

New X-rays were taken and a new plaster fitted.

"Yer goin' on just fine though it's only a month. You must have this on for at least another month before I can reduce the size of the plaster. You'll not be riding for several months yet."

"Can you give me an approximate time scale? You see we want to get married and she doesn't want me going down the aisle on crutches. Also, I have a new job to go back to in Barbados in the New Year."

"Normally I would say that you will not be totally out of plaster for another four to five months and that it depends on how much effort you put in yourself. If you're like most of the other mad jockeys that I look after, we can knock a good month off that time. You can start putting a bit of weight on the leg when I next change the plaster. Hopefully, then it will only be from the knee down which means that you can start intensive physiotherapy on the knee joint. This is vital. So, if we're lucky you should be out of plaster by Christmas. That does not mean that you can go jumping on a horse then. There is huge muscle wastage which will have to be built up and also the knee and ankle joints to be freed up. All of this depends on you taking the exercises I will prescribe and working hard at it."

CHAPTER 22

Fred met Will at Ringway.

"What swung it?" he asked.

"I worked on Max as we discussed and it worked. We'll see when we get there but what with that, my former girlfriend taking him to her parents' plantation, him being made very welcome and treated exceptionally well everywhere he went, he came away feeling really wanted and gradually he came round to the project being a good one. I'm certain he would never have done it if he hadn't gone to see the setup himself."

The next three months flew by. With Fred's agreement, Pat Byrne was promoted to Manager Designate to take over from Will. Jim McDonald had done a great job with the new premises in Limerick, now nearing completion; he was made Area Manager reporting to Pat Byrne but with more responsibility than heretofore, since he would be in charge of a larger fleet and not reliant on vehicles being sent from Santry.

Will's plaster was reduced at his next appointment with Sean O'Hehir, and Will was extremely shocked to see his naked leg. It looked like a matchstick with knobbles.

"Does this mean I can drive?"

"I'm not saying you can drive; I'm not saying you can't drive. I am saying you shouldn't drive. I will narrow the plaster over your foot and heel so that you will be able to fit a surgical boot over it. I will recommend an excellent physiotherapist in the Santry area. It is up to you to contact her. You should arrange daily visits from her at your office where she will treat you and instruct you how to do the exercises that I will prescribe to you with a copy to her. I cannot overemphasise the importance of this. Come and see me again in a month's time."

A family wedding meeting took place at Lostock, consisting of Garech, Harry and the two principals. Garech insistent that it should take place at his own family home where Harry and Siobhan were brought up, which they all wanted anyway.

Picking a date was not so easy.

"If I'm mobile which I am determined to be, I expect to go to Barbados as soon as possible after Christmas. Naturally, I want Siobhan to come too. Apart from anything else, we've got to find somewhere to live."

A date thrown around was 15th February, a Saturday.

"That's only about six weeks after the New Year," said Garech.

Will said, "This is just a thought but if Siobhan came out with me at the beginning of January and stayed for a month, would that give you time, bride to be, to come back and complete everything? I could come about a week later."

Siobhan answered, "Dad and I can start making all arrangements right now – marquee, catering, invitations etc – even my wedding dress, Daddy, darling. I am sure two weeks before would be okay."

The meeting had been thirsty work so, with general agreement, they sought to repair it.

"Now then, my darling one, what about our honeymoon: do you want it to be a surprise packet or do you want us to plan it together?"

"Well, seeing as we plan to remain together 'until death us do part', I think we should kick off on that foot."

"Right, that's settled then. My thinking is that it shouldn't be in Barbados. We'll probably be sick of the place by then. On the other hand, February is a marvellous time of year to be in the Caribbean, so maybe somewhere not too far away might be a good idea. What do you think about that?"

"Agreed."

"Right, now, as regards help and advice about where, although Lucille is very much in that sort of business, I don't think it would be fair or kind to ask her to fix up our honeymoon."

"I'd be mighty pissed off if I were in her position," Siobhan said.

A few minutes later, she continued, "Hey, I've an idea. Remember that Irish couple we met and I had a long chat to about Ireland and everything, while you were getting changed for the polo match? I'm sure she said she had a travel business. Why don't we ask her? She gave me her name and telephone number."

"Why not?" agreed Will.

"Well go on, ask her."

"You ask her – you're the one who spoke to her."

"You call her and hand her over to me if you like."

"How do you pronounce 'Ciara'?"

"Kay-ra."

Will picked up the telephone, "Is that Mrs Delaney?" he asked.

"Nuh. I fetch her."

"Ciara Delaney," a voice came on the line.

"Umm, er, this is Will Carpenter speaking from Ireland. We met briefly at Holders' polo ground a few months back with my now fiancé, Siobhan, er she's with me now and would like to talk to you…" he said, thrusting the telephone into Siobhan's hand.

In the early evening of 28th November, the telephone was ringing as Will came into the flat.

"Will…"

"Yes, Mum, how are you?"

"It's Dad. I think he's had a heart attack and has just been taken by ambulance to Chester Hospital. I'm about to follow by car and I wanted to let you know immediately."

"Oh my God, no, Mum. I can't bear it for you. I'll take the first plane that I can in the morning and go straight to the hospital. I know where it is but will you ring me later – doesn't matter whatever the time is. Thank Heavens Jo is back so you're not alone. Poor Dad. I'll be there as soon as I can."

He put down the telephone just as Siobhan came through the door.

"Sorry I'm late, was held up helping Harry with……..", she broke off seeing the look on Will's face, "… Will, what's happened, you look terrible?"

She ran towards him.

He told her, clinging onto her outstretched arms.

"Oh, Will, darling darling Will, what are you going to do?"

"I shall go over first thing in the morning. Mum's going to call later when she knows more. Will you call the Supercar desk at the airport, ask them to get me the earliest possible flight in the morning. Also, call Pat Byrne, tell him what's happened and to cancel or change all my appointments for the next few days. Tell him I'll ring him myself when I can."

Later, much later, around midnight, Mary called again, "He's in intensive care, unconscious with breathing difficulties. It is a heart attack. The surgeon, a terribly nice and caring man, I'm afraid is not optimistic."

"I'm on a plane at 7 a.m., at Ringway about 8, so should be at the hospital around 9 ish. How are you feeling, Mum?"

"Rather numb; I don't think it has sunk in yet. JoJo's being wonderful; she'll come with me in the morning."

Will gave his name on arrival at the hospital and was directed straight to the intensive care section. Mary and Jo, already there, saw him come in.

"It's not good news but come in and see him; he looks so peaceful; the breathing is better but they think he has little or no movement. He did open his eyes for short time but his brain clearly was not taking anything in."

Will went in, saw his father with tubes and wires connected from different his body to dials, instruments and scanners. Approaching the bed, he took hold of his father's nearest hand, the left one. It was warm but without any semblance of grip.

"How did it happen, Mum?"

"I was in the garden, about 4 o'clock, the light was going and I was just about to come in. I had a wheelbarrow with a few empty pots and some weeds that I had picked up. Dad came towards me telling me to come in as it was getting dark. He picked up the handles of the wheelbarrow, walked no more than a dozen yards and collapsed. I shouted for Jo; she came running. We managed to get him through the garden door and onto the sofa in the drawing room, where he collapsed again and was obviously in pain, clutching his chest. I dialled 999, the ambulance and paramedics from Tarporley came within twenty minutes and said they would take him straight here. That's when I rang you."

The doctor, a Mr Priestly, came in with a senior Sister. Mary introduced Will and Joanna.

"Could you wait outside for a few minutes. There are some checks and examinations that I need to do; I'll be with you shortly," the doctor said.

Ten minutes later he came out to them. "I'm terribly sorry to have to tell you that, barring a miracle, we're not going to win this one. His body is just not strong enough to withstand what's happening to him. I cannot tell you how long, however, my view is that it could be a matter of hours or perhaps a few days."

Mary took it all so bravely, Jo burst into floods of tears; Will held onto her and his mother.

"We've been here before, Mum, but we had Dad to help us then," he said.

A while later, Mary said, "I'm going to stay here with Dad, but there are some household things that need doing. Will, would you be angel, take JoJo, and do this for me?"

They returned an hour and a half later. A nurse came forward as they entered the intensive care section.

"I am sorry to have to tell you, your father died fifteen minutes ago."

They went in. All the medical paraphernalia had been removed. Mary was sitting by his bedside holding his hand. She had been crying but had dried her eyes and she looked up as Will and Joanna came in.

"It was marvellous," she said. "He rallied, opened his eyes, I'm certain he recognized me, possibly the flicker of a smile. Then, quite suddenly, he was gone."

Will took charge.

The senior intensive care sister who had come in with the doctor earlier said, "I'm so sorry; there was nothing more we could do. We'll take care of everything here. If you could telephone me to tell me the name of the undertakers or, if you like, we can arrange that as well."

"Thank you, I know Mannings in Tarporley, we'll use them."

"Yes, I know them too. They're very good. When you think the time is ripe, I think you should take your mother and sister home. It will make it worse for them to stay here too long."

Forty-five minutes later they all left, Mary insisting that she drove her own car with Will following on behind. As soon as they were home, Will rang David Hatch.

"I'll come right away," he said.

Will had told Siobhan to stay at Lostock so he rang there next. She answered the telephone.

"Oh Will darling, I don't know what to say that has not already been said and thought except that I wish I was with you. When would you like me to come? I can be ready in an hour. How's your mother taking it?"

"Immensely bravely. You know I almost think that she half

expected something like this to happen as if it had been lodged in her mind. Of course I want you here. I'll speak to Mum and call you back."

David Hatch came, said all the right comforting things, and read a few prayers to the three of them. Jo made some tea while they talked together for nearly an hour.

"Think how much worse it would have been if Angus had remained a virtual cabbage. There's no knowing what confused, unhappy and muddled thoughts might possibly have been going on his mind."

"You are quite right, David. Much better for him and us."

After he had left, Will told his mother that he'd spoken to Siobhan and would she like her to come.

"Of course I would; in fact, I'd be disappointed if she didn't. She's part of our family or just about to be."

Will picked her up at Ringway the next morning and they were back at Ayshford by lunchtime. He had been driving for about three weeks, only short distances to and from the office. He managed fine with an automatic car: a bit jerky on the accelerator with his clumsy surgical boot, though pretty nifty on the brake pedal using his left foot.

Because of the relative closeness to Christmas, the family led by Will arranged with David Hatch for the funeral to be a week later, 5th December. Mannings brought Angus to Ayshford two days beforehand, laying him on his own desk with the same crimson rug on which James had rested just a few years before. They had a lovely, simple service, well attended by many of Angus and Mary's friends, dating back to the old Dower House time, with a fair smattering of young. Will and Siobhan were most touched that Jimmy and Sarah came up by train there and back in the day. Will had already asked Jimmy to be his best man at the wedding. Julian Shannon gave a moving address in which he emphasised Angus' younger life and how well he had coped in his later years. Both Will and Joanna gave readings.

After the service, most of the congregation came back to Ayshford where Will had arranged for Jo's school friend's mother to take care of the wake. Champagne, white wine and sort of elderflower non-alcoholic cocktail were served and sandwiches handed round. Will thanked Julian Shannon for his address. All seemed to have heard about Will's broken leg with many of the polo players hoping he would be back in action the next season. Will replied to many of them that he hoped so too, though that it might be a long way away from Cheshire, telling them about his new job.

He noticed Joanna in earnest conversation with young Jason Tomkinson. At the church, Will and Siobhan had a quick chat to Jimmy and Sarah; Jimmy apologised that they couldn't come back to Ayshford because they had to catch their train.

"But," he said, "Sarah's on the case for Joanna. A friend of hers runs a small charity and may want a sort of girl Friday to do some donkey work. I or she will talk on the telephone."

"Mum, I want you to know that you have and are being absolutely brilliant."

"Oh, I don't think so, darling. I have so, so many happy memories of your father – enough to keep me going for the rest of my life. I'm desperate that he's no longer here but, you know, I believe he is in spirit. Now you will come back for Christmas, the two of you, won't you? I am so excited and thrilled about your new job, though of course sad that you'll be so far away. Not quite the same as popping over from Ireland for the weekend."

"Don't worry Mum: the world is getting smaller by the day and anyway we want you to come and visit us as soon as possible. We can talk about all that at Christmas."

On the way back to Ireland, Will said, "Darling, I hope you didn't mind me saying we'd go for Christmas. I know we hadn't quite decided but that was before all this and she'd have been so disappointed if we didn't."

"Of course I understand. Of course we must go."

"Thank you sweetheart. Can we stay in the flat tonight and go on to Lostock in the morning? I've got a mountain of work to do this afternoon."

"I was thinking along the same lines. I left my car at the flat anyway; when I came, Pat Byrne kindly collected me there and took me to the airport. He was going to the desk anyway and it fitted in well. I'll cook us a cosy dinner at home."

Harry's new season had started well. Last season successes by the two principals, Small Talk and Pelican Point had been well backed up by good, solid victories a little way down the scale, which had attracted new owners. He now had a median of 65 horses in the yard – up 15 from the previous year. Small Talk had won his first race of the season, a conditions race at Fairyhouse, quite comfortably and starting at odds on. He had a good blow after the race but Joe said it was just what he needed and enjoyed himself. Siobhan spent much of November interviewing and finally selecting a secretary, housekeeper and general gofer to replace her. It wasn't an easy task though not unpleasant, as she pointed out to all applicants. Eventually, she appointed a buxom girl from a family in Trim whose elder brother was a married lad working for Dermot Weld on the Curragh. *Probably not future sister-in-law material,* she thought, to which Harry agreed.

Harry hadn't been in long when Will and Siobhan arrived back at Lostock.

"Now that you're a bit more mobile, why don't you come with me down to the yard and we'll have a look at some of the new ones."

Ronan met them at the gate, "Sorry to hear about your father but good to see you walking again, Will."

"Thanks, Ro. I'm hoping to get rid of this sodding plaster in a couple of weeks. How's my champion after his race?"

"Come and have a look. Never left an oath. He's brilliant; any fool could train him."

"Thanks Ro," said Harry.

Garech came over for lunch on Sunday, saying how sorry he was about Angus, "Great shame I never got to meet him. I was so looking forward to doing that at the wedding. I would be delighted if your mother and sister would like to stay with me."

CHAPTER 23

Sven Goran's Genevieve plans were hotting up. In early November he had taken an extra-large space on the Barbados stand at the World Travel Market, held annually over five days at the 100 acre Excel Centre in London's dockland area, attended by the world's leading travel and travel associated companies. The FAG section on the stand featured an artist's impression of Genevieve, the planned mini cruise destinations and airbrushed photographs of Genevieve on her sea trials. Sven attended himself and went on to see his cousin Vagn in Copenhagen. He also made an inspection of Genevieve in Holland.

The vessel herself was due to arrive in Barbados before Christmas to undergo a settling in period for the locally trained hospitality and catering crew. Sven sent a message via Walton Dailing for Frank to come and see him.

"I've been talking to Walton about you. He tells me that since that appalling incident last June, for which you were entirely responsible, you have been of assistance to him and Lucky in his water sport business and he has received favourable reports from his clients. What have you got to say?"

"Mr Goran, I make big mistake. I lose my job wi' horses. I sorry."

"Frank, you will have heard about the imminent arrival of the small luxury cruise boat to be called Genevieve to be based in the new marina at Port St Charles?"

"Yes, Mr Goran."

"And are you aware that myself and my company here are the chief promoters of this vessel?"

"Yes, Mr Goran."

"Frank, I'm going to discuss with you a possible position for you on board Genevieve. I must tell you that in view of your record I am taking a huge risk on you. Should you abuse your position or let me down, there will be no way back for you."

"I no let you down, Mr Goran."

"Right: on Genevieve there will be a permanent small day boat, similar to a ski boat, that can be launched from a derrick on the deck into the sea and used for taking passengers from the mother ship for snorkelling expeditions, close up sightseeing of rock or coral formations or, maybe water skiing. Do you understand?"

"Yes, Mr Goran."

"I am offering you the chance of being the operator of this craft and in charge of its overall maintenance and onboard equipment. You will report directly to the purser – the person in charge of all the hospitality and administrative crew – and also assist him with any matters with which he may require in connection with the passengers. This is a very responsible position and you must observe extreme tact and politeness at all times."

"Yes, please, Mr Goran."

"Genevieve will be arriving in about 3 to 4 weeks' time. Close to then you will receive a full list of the crew members from the Captain downwards. There will be a series of crew meetings and hospitality training, first on land and then on board, some crew trials close to Barbados followed by a dummy run on the route before the proper maiden voyage scheduled for near the end of January. In the meantime, you will continue to work with Walton and Lucky. Do you understand?"

"Yes, Mr Goran, I understand good. I not make mistake again."

Max Geary had also been busy. Now that the deal had been agreed and after consultation with Will and Mallory, he issued a Press Release:

'NEW CAR RENTAL BUSINESS IN BARBADOS!

A Barbados registered company has been formed in conjunction with the international car rental British company, Supercar Ltd, and a consortium of Barbados investors. The company will be located in premises close to and operate from the Grantley Adams International airport. In command will be Director and Manager, Mr William Carpenter, currently Manager of Supercar (Ireland) Ltd.

Further news to be issued in due course.

Signed: Max Geary

Managing Director, Supercar (Caribbean) Ltd.'

In no time, it seemed, Will and Siobhan were back at Ayshford for Christmas. Will officially handed over control of Santry to Pat Byrne, who had arranged a Christmas farewell party for him at Santry. Jim McDonald plus some of the Limerick crew came to join their counterparts at the office and airport desk. Pat spoke of the work Will had done in setting it all up in the first place, how successful it had been and, above all, such a happy work environment.

He wished Will and Siobhan all success and equal happiness in his next assignment, of which he said, "Of course I'm not in the least bit jealous," after which Three Cheers rang out.

Will replied briefly saying how much he had enjoyed working with the entire team, how he had learnt so much from the job and workmates.

"I haven't gone yet" he concluded. "I'll be around for a few days after Christmas and again for a little matter in the middle of February"

Next morning was PM – Plaster Morning, the day Will had in capital letters in his diary. Siobhan came with him to Sean O'Hehir's consulting rooms.

"Now, let's have a look," he said.

"I want more than a look," Will replied. "I want you to get cracking with those bloody shears."

"I have to congratulate you," O'Hehir said, feeling and manipulating the knee and ankle. "You've done your stuff with the exercises."

"It's not me, it's that Amazonian ogress, Bernice, who's been descending on me practically every day for the last month, terrifying the wits out of me. Talk about the Lumberjack song, that's a nursery ditty compared to Bernice."

"Well, it's done the trick. You can go, leaving the plaster behind you."

Turning to Siobhan, he said, "Glad Joe did the business for your brother the other day at Fairyhouse."

"Yes, he was delighted. You know your patient here was that horse's work jockey all of last season."

Will grabbed his hand, "Thank you, miracle man."

O'Hehir said, "And yer man Griffiths. Looked him up. Top man, Would have taken much longer if it were not for him."

Back at the flat, they packed up the remainder of what was left and turned the key for the last time, heading back to Lostock where Harry had kindly said they could store a few things. Going up to bed later, Siobhan turned to face Will, "I seem to remember you saying something like Normal Service being resumed," she said.

"Come here, you beautiful, adorable, ravishing sex-starved kitten. It's the Happy Hour."

Next day, 22nd December, they left for Ayshford.

That Christmas would be an effort, there was no doubting.

Will said to Siobhan, "You are like bubbles popping up from a lake of champagne."

On their second night, Will asked their landlords, John and Helen Blackford, to join Mary, Jo, Siobhan and himself at the Swan in Tarporley for dinner. He wanted to get his mother out of the house for an evening – it was her first outing since Angus had died. They had not previously met Siobhan and Will put her next to John Blackford and himself next to Helen.

Earlier in the day, Will buttonholed Jo, "We've hardly had time for a proper chat since you came back from Zim. Now tell, tell me please?"

"It was just amazing; thank you for ever and ever for fixing it. Lovely, kind and wonderful family, the Travers. What they've done for animal conservation and husbandry in often difficult and dangerous conditions is nobody's business. You must go one day; made such good friends with the others like me; we've all sorts of plans for reunions and future travel. Just marvellous but I'm glad I came back when I did. It would have been too awful if Dad had died with none of us here."

"Yes, it would," agreed Will. "I hope my next plan for you will be as good though in a different way. My great chum Jimmy and his lovely bride to be, Sarah, have got something in mind which sounds interesting. Sarah has a friend, a lady about her own age, who runs a charity in London that provides support for displaced families, black and white – believe me, there are far too many of both – mainly in Zim, but also other African countries. She, this friend of Sarah's, is looking for someone young like you to help. No qualifications needed except a willingness to be useful, do any form of quite menial tasks – stuff envelopes, stick on stamps, wash the floor, make the tea – for very little money, but in a fun team. So how about that, after spending about three weeks here with Mum? They'll find you a place – a flat probably to share with other girls, or maybe have you to p.g with them until either they or you find somewhere yourself."

"Yes, I'll go for that. You were absolutely right some time ago;

going to Zim has been such an eye-opener. I'm a bit different now."

"Yes and London's a bit different too. Instead of rhinos with horns, you'll find other kinds of horns that you'll have to fend off or otherwise, if you so desire. You are a very attractive young lady, sister, as young Master Tomkinson has woken up to but he's chicken feed compared to the lecherous louts and lounge lizards of London. However, you will have the guidance of a major player in that league, Jimmy van Duran, as a mentor and, for once, he'll be on your side of the fence. Anyway, before all that you've got a very important part to play on 15th February, haven't you?"

"Yes, I know; I'm having kittens about it already. How many bridesmaids is Siobhan having?"

"Four I think including you. You and Mum are staying with Siobhan's Dad. He's really good news, quite a lady's man, he'll look after you very well. Siobhan is having the dress material and design sent over to Mum, whose promised to her dressmaker friend to make it for you. She will also have the name and telephone number in Dublin of the lady making the other girl's dresses in case of any problems, and to make sure they are all the same."

It was a rather sombre Christmas day – no getting away from it. Jo, Will and Siobhan did as good a job as possible with the tree, decorations and spirit of Christmas, however, poor Mary, brave as she had been during the week of the funeral, struggled.

CHAPTER 24

On January 3rd, coming out into the hot afternoon sunshine at Grantley Adams airport amid bustling crowds of arriving holidaymakers with the sound of a steel band in the background, Max was there to greet Will and Siobhan to the start of their new life. Discussions with Max had convinced them that taking an apartment in a condominium block in Oistins, on the south coast and conveniently close to the airport on a temporary basis, was a better option than staying in a hotel, the more so as Max owned the block.

"It won't be like Westscape; you know darling one. Oistins is very much the residential, commercial and mass tourist area with lots of bars, shops, snacky restaurants and a large fish market, though it's where we need to be for the time being."

The one-bedroom apartment on the first floor had a decent-sized sitting room, bathroom, kitchen and open veranda overlooking the sea. Daily maid service provided.

"Max, this is perfect for us," Siobhan exclaimed. "I can't tell you how excited we both are to be actually here. When we left, what six months ago, it was all still up in the air and poor Will was encased in plaster of Paris. He only had it removed two or three days before Christmas and still has to be careful, though he's so much better."

"Thank you my dear and welcome back to Barbados. I've put in enough basic supplies to keep you going and your maid, Pearl, who I've known for a long time will tell you all the best places locally from which to buy what you need. Will, as we discussed, I've made a temporary office available for you in my suite where you'll have the use of all secretarial and office services. I suggest you come along tomorrow morning and I'll introduce you and show you round. Also, I've fixed with Martin Jackson for you to have a car each – probably ex demo models. They will be owned by Jackson Motors but leased to the new company and fully insured; they are in the parking lot downstairs and here are the keys," he said, putting them on a table.

"In due course, I'll arrange for you both to have Barbados

licenses, in the meantime I'll get you tourist ones like you had last summer. I also think you should open Barbados bank accounts. Will, you can do this right away as your work permit has come through. Siobhan, it would be easier and less hassle for you to wait until after your wedding in February. In both cases, if you will allow me, I'll arrange this with my bank – again less hassle. How does that suit y'all?"

"I don't know what to say, Max; it's all too good to be true," said Will.

"I'm sure we'll both have plenty of things to worry about, don't let's anticipate them now. I'll leave you now to get sorted out and see you in the morning. Will, around 9.00 suit you?"

Will's small air-conditioned office had a window plus all mod cons. Peter Geary, Max's son was there.

"You've met Peter, haven't you?" Max said.

"Certainly I have. How are you, Peter, great to be back here?"

"Peter has a proper day job. Training a few horses for me at the Garrison is not a full-time occupation – not like Newmarket or The Curragh, you know. Peter is a qualified Chartered Surveyor and we'll need his services. Come into the Boardroom and I'll show you."

On the table was laid out an Ordnance Survey map of the parish of Christ Church, the largest parish on the island, which included the airport. Peter had marked in red several possible sites.

"We need an area with enough space for the servicing and housing of the fleet plus office and administration, good access from a road, within preferably no more than 10/15 minutes drive from the airport. If possible we want to use existing buildings that can be accommodated to suit our purpose, rather than build from scratch. This to save what could be interminable delays arguing about planning permission – the same here as it is in other countries. I am going to suggest that Peter takes you for a drive round the whole area, take the map with you and come up with your first three in order of preference. There's no better time to start than now so…?"

"This is exactly what I did in Ireland," Will said. "It took over a month and I'll try to improve on that."

He did. In two days, three properties consisting of a disused sugar factory and two derelict farmhouses that, owing to the farmland, had been bought and amalgamated into a larger farm, were shortlisted.

"Peter and I are in full agreement about these," he said, back in Max's office. "Let's go for the most commercially suitable." Turning to Peter, he said, "Peter, whatever our choice, we're going to need an architect. Any ideas?"

"There's a young man I've been watching and done some work with for a while; fully qualified for two or three years now. Jack Stoner is his name, a Bajan, from a respectable black family, done stints in England and the States. I think he would be ideal for this job. The firm he works for, Emmerson Symonds and Partners, are well regarded on residential and commercial levels."

"I have no problem with that," said Max. "So why don't you give Pete Symonds a call and fix a meeting with him, Will and yourself?"

"There's one other thing, more on a personal level," Will said. "Siobhan and I need somewhere to rent on a medium to long-term basis. We are fine where we are at the moment but long term we want a bit more space. I don't mind commuting for, say half an hour each way, to find the right place. Ideally, we'd love to find somewhere before she leaves to prepare herself for the wedding."

"If it's okay with the two of you, Lucille's the person who can help you there," said Max. "I've spoken to her already and she's more than willing to do this."

"Wonderful, I'll give her a call," Will said.

"Darling, Pearl is a hoot. Definitely my NBF; stands no nonsense from the local traders, 'I tell yo, do Miss Seaborn good', I'm afraid that name's going to stick, I'll be Miss Seaborn for life. She's crazy about cricket, a game you know I know nothing about. She thinks this guy called Sobers – who he? – is God's right-hand man. Mind you, racing comes pretty high on her list as well. She rattled off all Max's horses by name. When I told her my brother was a racehorse trainer, I thought she was having an orgasm in the car."

"Sir Garfield Sobers, to give him his full name and title, is arguably the greatest cricketer the West Indies and maybe the world has ever known. He's a Bajan of course and been retired for a long time though still hero worshipped. Became a scratch golfer as well, oh and by the way, he's left-handed. What have you got for supper?"

"Flying fish, straight from the market, christophines and sweet potatoes. And some super ice cream for the deep freeze."

"Max says he's got Lucille on the case looking for a house for us. Shall we give her a call and ask her to come for supper one night?"

"Yes, of course, love to see her. Go on, ring her."

"No, much better if you do. She'll have gone home now anyway. Call her at TRECO in the morning."

"Max, what's this I see in the Advocate about a new luxury small cruise boat that's just arrived in the island?" Will asked Max the next day.

"Oh, yes, I meant to tell you about that. Might be useful for us."

He filled Will in with the story so far as he knew it. "The main man behind the project, a guy called Sven Goran who heads up probably TRECO's main competitor Foulds, Archer and Goran, known as FAG, asked me, probably two years ago now, to come in on it. I thought about it but eventually said No for a number of reasons, the main one being that the success of Genevieve – the name of the boat – depends entirely upon the success of the marina at Port St Charles which, as you know, I'm pretty deep into. If that fails so does the Genevieve project. I hope both are successful though I didn't want to run the risk of losing out twice in one go. I'm very optimistic about the marina and if Genevieve succeeds too, that will boost the marina so maybe it will be a win-win situation."

"Max, I can't wait for you to meet my man Fred. That's exactly the way his mind would be thinking."

"Welcome to the first meeting of the Executive Directors of Supercar (Caribbean) Ltd," Max Geary's opening remarks from the Chair in his Boardroom. "And especially to our new Bajan resident, director and project Manager, Will Carpenter."

The meeting confirmed the choice of one of the derelict farm houses and buildings, selected above the old sugar factory. Peter's advice on this was that the costs of dismantling and removing the abandoned machinery outweighed those of clearing out and pulling down the old farm buildings. Also, the outer walls of the farmhouse were sound enough to do a complete revamp of the inside to turn it into a good office building.

The choice of the youngish though well-established architect recommended by Peter was approved with instructions to prepare plans to be submitted for tender to selected construction companies.

"Hi, Luce, love, come on in; really great to see you," said Will, giving her a hug.

"You, too. Good to see you upright again. Let's have a look."

He held out his leg.

"Can I touch it?" she asked, bending down and doing so, before Will could answer.

"Wow, quite knobbly isn't it. They're not a pair, are they? The legs, I mean."

"Neither would yours be if one had been in as many pieces, though my man in Dublin was so full of praise for what Bruce did here in the first place. Said he shortened the recovery by at least a couple of months."

As Siobhan came out of the kitchen, Lucille said, "Just making an inspection – hope you don't mind."

Siobhan laughed, "Of course not. Hello and lovely to see you and to be back again," joining her in a fond embrace.

"Well, Mr Barbados Businessman, how's it going?"

"We had our first board meeting this afternoon and nobody fell out. We've chosen the site, made some plans and now all we have to do is carry them out."

"Max says you want somewhere to live?"

"Yes, this is perfect to kick off from, however, we'd like a house up in the country somewhere, ideally not more than thirty minutes from the airport."

"I've a long list of properties for sale or rent. Most of them you can scrub out as either too expensive, in bad area, or plain not nice enough. What I might suggest is that I take Siobhan to have a look at some of them. Then I'll get the gist of what you are looking for, we can narrow down to a short list and start getting serious."

"I'll be here for another 2 to 2 ½ weeks before I have to go back to Ireland to get ready for the big day," she gave a little twirl round.

"We can certainly get things moving by that stage. Look, why don't you come to the TRECO office in Holetown tomorrow morning and we'll start the ball rolling?"

They spent most of the day – Lucille and Siobhan – looking at properties. None of them hit the right spot: either too grand and in the 'holiday house' bracket, or without character and dull. There was one, designed by a well-known Barbadian architect, Ian Morrison, though it was up in northern St Joseph and too far away.

On the way back from there, Lucille said, "I've got an idea. There's a house, not far from Uplands, I don't think it's actually on the market and it belongs to the manager of one of the big Canadian banks. Originally it was the overseers house on a plantation and he bought it, spent a lot of money on it, putting in a good swimming pool etc. I know he's been transferred back to Canada; whether he wants to keep the house for holidays or for when he retires, I don't know. Let's drive past it and have a snoop from the outside."

This they did. It's set a bit back from a quiet road, on a slight rise, with a pleasant-looking garden and good views. No close neighbours, in plantation country, with a small group of palm trees and a quite small bush like brightly coloured tree.

"What's that tree called?" Siobhan asked, pointing at it.

"We call it *Pride of Barbados*," Lucille replied. "What its proper horticultural name is, I don't know."

"This is the best we've seen."

"Okay, I'll make some discreet enquiries and let you know."

"I've seen a house that would suit us perfectly," Siobhan said that evening, telling Will all that she knew and what Lucille has said.

The following weekend they took a drive past. There was a car in the driveway and they went on a little way, then turned round coming back from the opposite direction.

"Looks absolutely ideal," Will said. "Let's hope Lucille comes up with something."

In what seemed like no time, on the evening of 1st February, Siobhan and Will bid each other a tearful but, as they consoled themselves, temporary goodbye on Siobhan's final journey as a single lady. Harry met her at Dublin airport at lunchtime the next day, she having changed planes at Heathrow. On the way back to Lostock, he brought her up to date with all the wedding plans.

The day after Siobhan left, Will had a call from Jimmy van D.

"Just in case you've got any other ideas in your head, you are staying with me in London when you arrive for two nights or more, depending on your powers of recovery."

"Oh, God, I suppose you've invited Madame Claude's granddaughters as well. This spells trouble. I've got to stay a night with my Mum on the way to Ireland."

"I think you should go by train. Don't worry, I'll fix it with her."

A week later he was on the evening flight to London.

He'd seen Max in the office in the morning, "See you on the 15th," he'd said.

"Gosh, you're coming?"

"Of course we are. Eileen and I had our invitations weeks ago and we are definitely coming. I'm going to Newmarket as well. Tim Bulwer-Long is sorting out a few horses for me to have a look at."

"Just checking in, darling one. I've arrived and am at Jimmy's; how's it going your end?"

"Chaos. Everyone running round in circles and getting overworked up, no one more so than me. Harry's the only sane one; he had a double at Tramore yesterday and he's far more excited about that than any old wedding. Had a fitting for the dress yesterday; I think it's fabulous, hope you do too; good old dad. Missing you dreadfully."

"I think you look fabulous in your birthday suit, never mind a wedding dress. Ditto re the missing bit."

"Now, you watch out tomorrow night. I hope you booked your appointment at the VD clinic. I shall want to see the Clearance Certificate - don't forget to bring it."

"Well, there's no sign of Sarah here, she must have moved out. Not sure what's happening except you know Harry's coming over. Jimmy has very kindly asked him to stay here too. I think there are six of us going out for a quiet dinner."

"Who do you think I am? What bollocks."

It was not quiet. The six friends, Harry, two of Will's Cheshire polo teammates and another Harrovian school friend, were served a lethal cocktail called an eiderdown as a sharpener by two scantily clad, exceptionally nubile young ladies, chased up with a magnum of vintage Pol Roger champagne. Dinner in the private room of a fashionable restaurant in the King's Road followed. Will had hardly sat down before he became aware of movement from beneath the table - hands were stroking and feeling round his ankles, gradually moving up his calves and forcing his knees apart. Nor did it stop there; the hands kept moving higher and higher massaging his thighs, causing a certain amount of pleasurable discomfort and making him push back his chair whereupon the hands, arms, head and upper torso emerged from the region of his lower abdomen like a snake, the arms draping themselves around his neck, planting a resounding kiss on his lips followed by the rest of the body, totally bereft of any form of clothing, swivelling slightly so that her bottom jiggled gently on Will's lap, legs swinging merrily in the air to one side. He recognized the young lady as one of the pair who had been serving the drinks at Jimmy's flat.

The most sensational dinner followed though Will's recollection of the rest of the evening remained somewhat clouded. Vaguely he remembered the dinner table being cleared, it becoming a stage upon which his subterranean friend plus two companions performed lascivious acts to the accompaniment of music coming from the sound system. He thought he remembered too, his future brother-in-law giving a certain amount of assistance to the performers.

Considering everything, Will's hangover was not as bad as he'd feared it would be, which speaks very highly of the quality, not to mention the quantity of what they had consumed the night before. He took Jimmy's good advice about travelling by train and after a rather muttered goodbye and thank you to his host, plus 'see you in a few days', he took a taxi to Euston station. Harry had, some time ago, asked Jimmy and Sarah to stay at Lostock for the wedding.

Mary met him at Crewe. "Do you remember, Mum, all those times when you and Dad used to do this when I was a deckhand on the *Star*?"

"Of course I do, darling. How could I ever forget? It still feels like yesterday. How's your hangover from last night?"

"It's there, though don't ask too many questions as I may have forgotten the answers."

"It's rather sweet, Siobhan rang me last night just to say hello and told me that it was your stag night and would I look after you today? You've picked a winner in that one."

During the course of the rest of the day and evening, Will brought his mother up to date with all that had been going on in Barbados and that they had seen a house that they liked.

"Mum, have you thought yet about what you may do?"

"Darling, the Blackfords have and are being extremely kind and thoughtful. They have told me that I can stay here for as long as I want to and have guaranteed me that they will not put the rent up for as long as I stay here. However, it's too big for me really on my own, particularly with you and Siobhan being settled, and JoJo fleeing the nest, quite rightly, and only being here probably for short periods, high days and holidays. I'm going to take my time though I will look for something smaller, but I will definitely not move away from this area," she said.

"I'm still alive, I hope you're glad to hear," Will told Siobhan on the telephone.

"Good, I am glad, very, very glad and I don't want to hear all the gory details, well not yet anyway," she replied.

"Mum's taking me to Ringway for a late morning plane that arrives at 1.30. Is that okay for you?"

"I would make it okay even if it wasn't. A week without you is a week too long. I'll be there."

"Right, Harry and I have worked out the P of A for the weekend. Do you want to hear it?" Siobhan said, in the car on the way back to Lostock.

"Well, on the assumption that I might possibly have some sort of part to play, yes please," replied Will.

"I'm going to be the dutiful bride and stay the night before with Dad. You won't see me until I walk up the aisle on his arm. Your mother and Jo are staying with Dad too. I spoke to her and I know her arrival time. Dad has arranged a car to pick them up.

Jimmy and Sarah will stay at Lostock and you'll have your last night of freedom there with them and Harry, then you'll come directly to the church from there.

A car has been booked to take them home after the party. The service is at 4.30, followed by the reception, speeches by Dad, you and Jimmy – and for God's sake don't bang on about how wonderful I am etc; they all know that and I've told Dad the same.

Dinner in the adjoining marquee will be at 7.45 to 8.00 and the party will kick off around 9.30 back in the main marquee.

We will stay at Dad's for what's left of the night. You'll need to bring all your luggage with you or give it to me the day before, as we'll be going straight to the airport from Dad's on Sunday. You can leave all your wedding stuff at Dad's."

"You've been brilliant, the lot of you. It seems all I've got to do is to turn up on time – as the song goes."

The next day, February 13th, Will had a little mission to accomplish in Dublin and also went on a courtesy visit to his old office to see the team there, particularly Pat Byrne, to whom he brought up to date on progress on the new company. Both Pat and his girlfriend, and Jim McDonald and his wife, had received invitations to the wedding.

"I'm glad it's today that you've come and not tomorrow," Pat said.

"Why's that?"

"Because Fred and the boss are coming tomorrow and we have to be on our best behaviour."

On the day before the wedding, Garech invited all the Lostock contingent, which included Jimmy and Sarah at this stage, to lunch to see the house and marquee set up. They had just arrived when the car bringing Mary and Jo came up the drive. Garech opened the car door to greet Mary.

"As we are about to be joint outlaws, please may I call you Mary immediately and say how very glad I am that you are here for this absolutely marvellous occasion. It is lovely to meet you as the mother of this splendid young man, to whom I took immediately on first acquaintance."

"You certainly may and thank you for inviting me to stay with you. My feelings for your beautiful daughter echo yours for Will, so at least we've started off on the right foot. I'm only sad and sorry that Angus couldn't be here too, though I'm certain he'll be looking down from on high tomorrow."

Jo's eyes were out on stalks, never having seen such a display of fabricated elegance.

Siobhan said, "Jo darling, can I have a look at your dress? My dressmaker will be here in a minute and will give you a quick fitting."

Lunch over they all drove the short distance to St. Michael's Church at nearby Millicent, had a chat with the vicar and a quick run-through for the next day.

"This, my dearest and soon to be my nearest, is where I shall say goodbye until I see you in this very place tomorrow afternoon AND DON'T BE BLOODY LATE !!"

She looked stunningly, ethereally, ravishingly beautiful, her father's silver wedding present to her late mother's diamond tiara under her veil, her long white satin close-fitting dress falling into a narrowing train behind her, clutching a bouquet of orlaya grandiflora, calla lilies, delphiniums, orchids and gladiola, her left arm firmly linked under her father's right, she walked up the aisle of the packed church to where the man of her life waited like a horse in the starting stalls, ready and impatient for them to open. When she came back down that same aisle fifty minutes later, veil thrown back, hair let down, laughter in her face and her eyes, church bells pealing, that man now walking beside her was her husband.

Will, equally happy, in between continual glances at his beaming wife caught the eye of several guests as they made their way to the open door at the far end of the church. Fred with Robert and Kathleen Mallory, all staying at the Shelbourne Hotel in Dublin, Pat Byrne with a pretty girl next to him, Joe Maguire with Ronan next to him, Max and Eileen Geary and several more.

What he did not know was that at exactly the time he and Siobhan were exchanging their vows, Lucille was in St John's Church, Barbados, kneeling and saying a prayer for them. She had received an invitation although she had decided she couldn't quite face coming.

At Sallins, everything immaculately prepared, the church congregation soon piled into the marquee, champagne, white wine or an elderflower cocktail, offered on silver trays by well-dressed catering staff awaiting them. Somehow Fergy Lynch had discovered who Max Geary was, probably from Harry, and was after him like a greyhound after a hare. Adam and June Platt were among the first to come and congratulate the bride and groom. Jo clung close and shyly to her mother, both being well looked after by Garech, until Harry carted Jo off to introduce her to some of the young as sister of the bridegroom.

Soon it was cake cutting time followed by the speeches, starting with Garech delivering a short but impassioned speech summarising his love for his daughter and great respect and liking of his son-in-law.

Then Will, nervous internally but outwardly bold, thanking Garech for this most happy and glorious wedding and for producing his filly trained to the minute, ending up with, "I've been told by my wife not to tell you all how wonderful she is because, she said, and I quote, 'They already know that'. However, if anyone among you disagrees, I invite him – or her – to come and see me outside."

Jimmy, who had steadied Will throughout the day as a super friend and best man, spoke briefly about his long-term friendship with Will going back to Harrow days, touched briefly on the sadness of losing another very great friend in James, Will's brother, and how Will had assumed his head of the family role at a young age, cracked a couple of funnies and raised a toast to the bridesmaids, including Jo 'shortly to be coming on the market'.

A sit down dinner at round tables of ten, all individually placed, followed. In addition to the bride and groom the top table consisted of Garech and Mary, Robert and Kathleen Mallory, Max and Eileen Geary and Jimmy and Sarah. One of Ireland's premier party bands kicked off the music and dancing with a great rendering of *Feeling Hot, Hot, Hot.* Will and Siobhan, still in her wedding dress but without the train, being the first on the floor to much cheering and banter all round. Later Chris de Burgh, a guest anyway, sang his well-known hit song with a slight change of wording and retitled for the day to *Lady in White.*

It was after 3 a.m. that people started to drift away and Garech called proceedings to a halt.

CHAPTER 25

Leo Garbutt, the English owner with his Grenadian-born wife of the Calabash hotel in Grenada, stood at the entrance of the hotel when the taxi bringing Will and Siobhan the short distance from the airport drew up.

"Welcome to the Calabash and to Grenada, Mr and Mrs Carpenter," he said. "We hope your honeymoon here will be as good as you hope and expect it to be."

"Oh, God, the secret's out, but thank you so much," Will said.

Further evidence of the 'secret' being out was soon apparent. The hotel rooms, all suites and only thirty of them, are arranged in blocks of two, one above the other with plenty of space between them, in a wide half-moon-shaped row behind a very large mown lawn that led down to the lovely bay and beach, complete with beach bar and lunch dining area.

In their room on the upper floor, stood an enormous bouquet of flowers with the inscription on a card, *'Wishing you love and happiness from both families, now joined as one'*.

Another smaller bowl of flowers and a bottle of champagne in the fridge was from the Management and Staff of the Calabash hotel and a third, *'Wishing your health and happiness from Ciara and Dermot Delaney'*.

"My God, how wonderful all this is," Siobhan said.

"Yes, and I remember when we first spoke to Ciara about it from the flat, she asked if I had a work permit for Barbados. I said no and that I would have by February. 'Good,' she said. 'I can book you as a Caricom resident at an all in price, which will make a hell of a difference," Will said.

By the time they had got sorted out in their luxuriously furnished suite, the light was beginning to fade so they decided to leave the beach until the morning, opening and drinking the bottle of champagne sitting on comfortable armchairs on the balcony taking in the view, still full of reminiscences of their wedding day.

"Did you see Fergy get after Max?" Will asked. "Harry wound him up big time about Max having a string of racehorses in

Barbados."

"And Jo," said Siobhan. "She was really going for it on the dance floor, moving up ten pounds in the handicap. I'm afraid young Tomkinson in Cheshire may now be an also ran."

"It's good preparation for her life in London under Jimmy's wing," Will said. "She's going this coming week. Jimmy and Sarah have kindly said she can stay with them for a while. Sarah's friend, who runs the charity she'll be working for, says she knows another girl looking for a flatmate."

"Your father was just fantastic about everything. I know my Mum was most appreciative of the way he looked after her."

"Oh, he loves all that kind of thing and he really loved the place coming alive again for the first time since Mum died. They used to have some serious bashes there, you know."

Will and Siobhan's allocated table on the seaside of the semi-open dining room could not have been more romantic; candle lit, stars in the night sky, a pianist playing a few yards away, a gentle tropical breath of wind, what more could be asked? Dinner chosen from a quite small selection, helped by a most charming waiter, arrived and was up to the standard of the surroundings. Love between them clung like a magnet.

"We've been married now for all of two days and it seems much, much longer. I can hardly remember what it felt like not being married to you," Siobhan said.

"Well, to all intents and purposes, it has been much longer. The difference now is that there is a contract," said Will, suppressing an inward smile.

"Piss off and stop talking like a bloody businessman."

The romantic mood continued well past dinner, during the 100 yard walk under the stars back to their room and carried on for a considerable time afterwards. Indeed it was still with them when a knock on their door heralded the entrance of their allocated daily maid to put the finishing touches in their kitchenette for their pre-ordered cooked breakfast, which she prepared and laid on a linen tablecloth on the balcony table.

Soon after 10 o'clock they wandered hand in hand down to the beach where comfortable chairs, day beds, sun umbrellas and small tables were arranged haphazardly, not in Germanic straight lines. They chose one not too far yet far enough away from the round, thatched and open-sided beach bar. Towels and cushions were swiftly provided. They swam, strongly at first, then turning over on their backs, more leisurely, to look at the small number of boats lying at anchor and, further out, some more serious-looking sailing yachts and the odd motor cruiser. Back to the shore, morning exercise over, some sun to be taken. Busy morning.

Later, perched on bar stools, the excellent bar lady whose name was Felicity, not a common name for a West Indian, read their thoughts.

"How yo' like, planters punch wi' fruit and banana or no?"

"No, plain rum punch, easy on the sweet bits, quite dry please."

"Okay, comin' up."

After the second rumbo, feeling no pain, it was time for lunch under the coconut frond-covered, open-sided beach restaurant with an open air kitchen.

"We got good red snapper today, from the sea this morning," the chef said.

"Yes please – make that two," said Will, getting the nod from his wife.

The next few days drifted by following roughly the same pattern, on sort of nodding acquaintance with some of the other hotel guests, most of whom seemed quite civilised and well behaved, with quite a few Brits among them.

One evening the inevitable owner's cocktail party was held on the terrace next to the swimming pool; they thought it was rather churlish not to go.

Leo Garbutt came up to talk to them, "Where in England do you live?" he enquired.

"Actually we don't. My wife is Irish; we were married in Ireland where I've been working for the last couple of years and now we live down the road from here in Barbados."

"Really?" he asked, "What are you doing there?"

Will told him about starting up the new Supercar company and went on to say, "I came to Grenada a few times some years ago. In those days I was a deckhand on the Star banana boat and never got out of St George's harbour."

"Oh yes, sometimes we have people off those small ships coming here for lunch and a swim."

The next day Will said, "We ought to have a look at some of

the island while we are here, so that we can tell others. I never got the chance before. I know there is this spectacular lake called the Grand Etang. Maybe we should be brave, tear ourselves away from here, go and have a look – what do you think?"

"Okay, it's such heaven here, but perhaps we should."

A car with a driver picked them up for a drive of about an hour up into the hills along steep narrow roads through small mountain villages, banana, nutmeg and almond plantations. Grenada, a volcanic island is very different from limestone Barbados. Bananas are the main export fruit though Grenada is also the second largest producer of nutmeg in the world, having been introduced into the island by the Dutch from the East Indies in the mid-19th century. Grand Etang, 1750 feet above sea level, is a lake in an extinct volcanic crater. Now the crater is smothered in beautiful tropical vegetation, trees and flowers on the banks, the lake below, covering about 35 acres and very deep in the middle.

Sightseeing done, well worth it, back in time for a swim, rumbo and lunch.

The days – ten of them – came and went in a haze. Swimming was the best form of exercise possible for Will to get his leg back to 100% and each day he increased the length of time of his swims. Together they ventured out into the bay looking at close quarters some of the big yachts with ensigns of many countries, USA, Great Britain, France, Italy and more, all with stories to tell of adventures and romance, if only they could speak.

It was time to go.

Thank you room no.11, were their thoughts.

Goodbyes from Mr and Mrs Garbutt, same as the welcome on arrival.

"It's been fabulous," said Siobhan. "And the good news is that we're not going far and are sure you'll see us again before too long."

Three hours later, they were back in their apartment in Oistins, Will taking up the reins of a new business and a new marriage.

CHAPTER 26

"Welcome back – or should I say 'home,'" Max said, as Will came into the office.

"My, that was some wedding your father-in-law put on. What a hell of a guy he is; got on with him so well and most kind of him to put Eileen and me on his table for dinner. And he's bred a Classic winning filly; she's just fantastic and Eileen and I love her already. Our first time in Ireland and we spent a few days in Dublin looking around. A lovely city. Bought a horse too – not in Ireland but Tim Bulwer Long found me a nice three-year-old out of James Bethell's yard; he and James are good friends and this one, Tame Prince, only ran three times as a two-year-old, finishing second once and the owner wanted out. You must come and see him when he arrives.

Now, progress has been made on the business front; the purchase of the old farm and outbuilding is done and I have here the first draft of plans by the architect. Peter and he are coming in this morning for us to discuss them."

During the next few weeks the plans were agreed, submitted and approval granted. Tenders to selected construction companies submitted and subsequently awarded, to Will's immense delight, to Tony Knowles company with only a tiny piece of insider information from Will.

Demolition and subsequent construction started in early May with an estimated completion date prior to the final fitting out and decoration by the end of September. These dates being vital for the two main supplying partners, Jackson Motors and Mike Williams' hotel company so as to be open for business the following winter season starting in mid-December.

In between all this, in mid-March, the overwhelming highlight on the other side of the Atlantic which Will and Siobhan had to miss, was the thrilling victory of Small Talk in the Champion Hurdle at Cheltenham. They saw the full recording of the race on television specially laid on by Max with the aid of Cable and Wireless in Max's boardroom; the grin on Joe Maguire's face as he was led into the winners' enclosure by Vince, stretched from one end of Gloucestershire to the other. Harry, needless to say, had a remarkably good-looking girlfriend, even by his standards, by his side.

"Hmm, he hasn't told us about that one," Siobhan said.

They called him at Lostock the next day, much the worse for wear, and still on a huge high.

"Who's the bird?" Will asked.

"What bird?"

"Fuck off, the one that was nearly having it off with you on the telly at Cheltenham?"

"Ah well, she's the daughter of a Newmarket trainer, who's making a bit of a name for herself doing television commentaries on the horses in the paddock on race days, looking more like a fashion model as she walks round with the horses. I won't let her in the yard here because Ronan and the lads just look up at her and down tools; sorry, I've got that the wrong way round."

Six months later Will and Siobhan moved into their new home just north of the small village settlement of Jericho in St. George, the house Lucille had pointed out to them in January. Through her and TRECO, Will secured a five-year lease on the house from the Canadian owner.

In September they did manage a magical week to go over to Jimmy and Sarah's wedding at her parents' house near Hungerford.

Jimmy had explained sometime earlier, "Will, I've got to ask my younger brother to be best man, so no offence I hope."

"Don't be such an arse, of course you have, and I'm just so glad that we can come."

"You know that we've taken your advice about the honeymoon. We're going to the Calabash in Grenada though we were wondering if we could come on to you for two or three days afterwards?"

"It's in the diary and we'd be bloody pissed off if you didn't."

At the wedding reception, Will spotted Simon and Camilla Richardson, "God, fancy seeing you two!"

"My word, it's our cabin boy – look darling."

"Oh, Will how lovely to see you."

"Yes, you too, but before you drop me in the shit, this is my wife, Siobhan."

"Yes, we know, having heard all about it from Jimmy. Wonderful to meet you Siobhan. Jimmy and Sarah said what a fabulous time they had with you both last year and about all the dramas. How's the leg now?"

"Pretty well mended and I'm back in the saddle."

"Yes, that's not difficult to imagine."

They brought each other up to date with their lives and made vows to keep in touch.

Two nights at Ayshford and another two at Lostock was all they had time for. Mary was fine though rather tired looking. She had seen a house that might have done; however, she didn't like it enough to commit.

"You've got to come out to us very soon," Siobhan said. "We're properly settled in our house now, so please let's get something sorted. Any time from now on, so where's your diary? Apart from Jimmy and Sarah for a few days, we're completely free."

They provisionally arranged for two weeks in early December.

Joanna they had seen all too briefly at the wedding.

"London's a gas," was about as much as Will could get out of her so, "All must be well," he said.

Meanwhile, Sven Goran was majorly occupied with the imminent arrival of Genevieve, making several local trips to St Lucia, Grenada and specially to Tobago, setting up port and land agents to deal with berthing of the ship and shore activities for the passengers.

She arrived, docking in the marina in the early evening on the last day of October, amid much publicity engineered by Sven; floodlights, celebratory amplified music played by the Barbados Regimental Band, with a spectacular firework display lighting up the sky over Port St Charles and the marina. Frank and the rest of the Barbados trained crew, dressed in smart uniforms marched up the gangplank to meet the ship's officers, who had brought her across the Atlantic. The Prime Minister made a speech of welcome; an invited guest list proceeded on a tour of the vessel, served with champagne and goodies to eat. Max received an invitation though he declined in a personal letter to Sven, wishing him well.

Captain Pieter Doorman, his Chief Officer Herman van der Stieg, and Engineer, Jet de Vries, were the only members of the crew who had brought Genevieve across the Atlantic remaining on board for the forthcoming Barbados – Tobago – Barbados cruise programme.

The Barbados selected and trained hospitality crew, under the command of the Bajan purser, Crispin Alleyne, all, with the exception of Frank, having had previous experience on large cruise ships in the Caribbean. The day boat arrived separately a week or so earlier, shipped from Miami; a new model though it was similar to Walton Dailing's boats that Frank was used to. He and Walton had launched, tested and tried it, before it was hoisted on board Genevieve. The dummy run starting a few days later over the full cruise course, passed without mishap and included Frank's boat being lowered into the water several times in different localities, with other crew members taking the place of fare-paying passengers for practice. In the turn round port of Scarborough, Tobago, Frank did not notice the keen interest shown in him and his movements in and around the dockyard by an insignificant individual holding a small camera.

The scheduled cruise time with passengers would be seven days, the published maiden voyage set to depart on 15th December to kick the winter season off with a bang. The outward journey to Bequia, Union, Palm, Tobago Cays and Tobago and the return to Grenada, Carriacou, Canouan, Mustique and back to the marina at Port St Charles.

By mid-May, eleven months after his accident, Will started to ride again. Sheila Griffiths always had a few older horses, some former racehorses or show jumpers, that she liked to go for long cross-country rides with friends, and Will and Siobhan joined this little group for early morning rides at weekends. Frequently, particularly when Max had a horse running, he and Siobhan went to the races.

Max would take them up into the Turf Club stand; on one such day, the Chairman of the Club said, "If Max were to propose you, would you like to become a Member of the Club, now that you are a Barbados Resident?"

"It would be a great honour," Will replied. "And one I would accept with much pleasure."

"Good, in that case, with Max as your proposer and me as your seconder, it is likely that your application will be approved."

A proper old-fashioned way of doing things.

On schedule, Barbados version only a month late, in mid-

October, the fleet garage, parking area and administrative office of Supercar (Caribbean) Ltd opened its doors through the impressive metal double electric gates, set in the security fence ringing the property. Not opulent but entirely functional, at least that's what Will hoped Robert Mallory would think.

His own office on the first floor looked out through a big plate glass window down onto the parking area to his left, reception in the middle and the main covered garage to his right.

Further to his left and just out of sight behind the building, an open concreted yard had been prepared with its separate goods entrance. For his manager and right-hand man, Will hired a bright, forward-thinking, ambitious young Barbadian. Educated at Harrison College, he had trained as an accountant with one of the big five international firms, though he aspired to something with more action and enterprise and leapt at Will's advertisement in the Advocate. Will chose him from a shortlist of six. His name is Leroy Proverbs, his father works as an insurance broker in Bridgetown and his mother chief housekeeper at a west coast hotel. Will took him under his wing, spending many hours with him during the period of the construction work. He told Leroy that he himself had obtained a job with Supercar, from lowly beginnings as a deckhand and that, after initial training, had worked his way up at two branch offices before being given the job in Ireland.

"You are having your initial training with me though I never had the good fortune that you've had with your accountancy and you've got one over me there," Will said.

The basic number of staff needed for the start-up came from various sources; a driver or two from other car rental firms, two all-round mechanics on secondment from Martin Jackson, clerical staff selected with help from Max and Mike Williams, so that by the time the first batch of cars in each class and variety rolled through the gates, they were pretty well there.

In November, Will and Max drafted out the list of invitees to the opening party held at the new complex. It contained all hotel managers, airline officials, heads of businesses with travel connections and others deemed important enough by Max, including Sven Goran, Johnny Arthur and Stuart Foulds from FAG. Lucille was included representing TRECO.

Robert and Kathleen Mallory came, staying at Cobblers Cove

hotel this time. Will rang Fred to ask if he would like to come, "No, lad, I'll not come this time. Too many bloody others though I'd like to soon, when you're more settled."

"Okay Fred, don't blame you though don't forget your golf clubs when you do come," Will said.

The party, held in an open-sided marquee in the parking area included a tour of the complex, and a welcome speech by Robert Mallory introduced, just as he had been in Ireland, by Will. He paid particular tribute to the Barbadian investors who had put so much faith in his company which, he said, he had started with money borrowed from somebody who had put faith in him.

Mallory also hosted a private dinner party at Cobblers Cove for the Barbados company directors and their wives, this to emphasise his strongly held beliefs that a business such as his should resemble that of a family, in that each member plays a part in looking after one another.

He said, "In these days of instant electronic communication, this is so much easier. My telephone is never off the hook and my door never closed to you, though I could never have done this ten or fifteen years ago. I look forward to seeing any of you at any time that you come to England and I am right behind you in our joint venture."

"Ooh, I'm looking forward to this – come on Tracey, are you ready?" Cynthia Chapman said, as the car to take them to Port St Charles for the official maiden voyage of Genevieve, drew up at Palm Heart.

Trevor, wearing a yachting cap with Genevieve emblazoned on the front, a striped sailor type short-sleeved shirt, white linen trousers a touch on the tight side and white docksider shoes, preceded them into the car.

Sven Goran greeted them at the quayside and took them on board.

"Are you coming with us?" Cynthia asked.

"Oh no – there's no room for me," Sven replied. "However, as an all-important investor and part owner, you've been given the No 1 cabin, with Tracey next door to you. Johnny Arthur will look after you."

Johnny, in his capacity as a director of FAG, was the only other single occupier of a cabin. He played the host part similar to that at Alexander's nightclub.

With much hooting of the siren and waving, both from a small army of 'extras' on the quayside and the full complement of passengers on board, Genevieve slipped her moorings and headed out to sea.

Cynthia spotted Frank, "Ooh, there's Frank. Are you one of the crew, Frank? Haven't seen you recently."

"Yes, Mrs Chapman, I in charge of dayboat under the davits over there. I take you on snorkelling or close to reef trips in de Keys and others places, or to the shore if no landing quay."

"Ooh, that's nice. You look smart in your uniform."

"Wonder how he got that job," said Trevor.

At Scarborough, on turn round day, Frank busied himself helping Johnny Arthur deal with passengers' questions on the quayside about where to go and what to, introducing them to the shore agents. The last ones settled; he was just about to return on board when two men who had been watching him caught his attention.

"You Frank?" said one of them, pleasantly enough.

"Yeah, dat me."

"Me, Manuel, this my friend Tonio. You got two minute?"

"Yeah, okay."

"Come, we go have some coffee, okay?"

They led him to a café and snack bar close to the quay, speaking with a Spanish accent, very common the nearer one is to the coast of Venezuela. Sitting at a table in a corner, Tonio produced a bulky A4 size envelope from a satchel he carried. It was not sealed; Frank could see it was packed with bank notes. Tonio picked one out. $100 Barbados dollars.

"They all the same," he said. "We know you, who you are. We have friend in Barbados."

"So?" said Frank.

"We have stuff for him. You take. You keep envelope. Next trip we have more."

"Who your friend?"

"Not important you know."

"Where de 'stuff'?"

"We have, in small bag, like airline cabin bag, weigh 8/10

pounds."

Frank had never seen this amount of money – already cash. He remembered the days when he hid all his cash under the floorboards of his parents' chattel house. On Genevieve, Frank only had a bunk bed in a curtained-off cubicle and a small canvas bag for his own belongings. He would manage, somehow.

"Genevieve leave in 5 hours," he said.

"We come back in 3 hours," said Tonio. "Meet here."

"Okay."

Frank returned to his cubicle. He decided to ditch his canvas bag and fit his personal belongings into the 'new' bag. Anything that would not fit, he'd ditch. He could buy new ones now, couldn't he? Bought a new bag in the town, hadn't he?

Three hours later the two men were back at the café, Manuel carrying an ordinary, not new, airline carry-on bag. Fifteen minutes later the three of them left, this time with Frank carrying the bag in one hand and a brown envelope in the other.

"You take to Bird's Nest Hotel, say 'For John'. This time, special big envelope; next time, not so big," said Tonio.

Frank carried the bag, with the street value of its contents unknown to him being US$250,000, nonchalantly onto Genevieve and he stuffed the envelope into the pillowcase on his bunk. Then he replaced the new bag for his old, which he left on his bunk, throwing it overboard later while the passengers were having dinner at sea.

The marina harbour master and other notables watched at the quayside as Genevieve entered the marina and nestled up to her docking berth, Sven being the first up the gangplank to greet the passengers.

Johnny Arthur held both thumbs high in the air, Cynthia Chapman, the premier ambassadress ran out of 'oohs and arrhs', and the other passengers praised the crew, variety of scenery, food and drink and the efficiency of the team effort.

Never a moment's anxiety, fabulous views, amazing snorkelling, exciting, such comfortable cabins and deck areas, were the assorted accolades heaped on the Captain and Sven by the departing passengers.

Frank had never heard of the Bird's Nest Hotel though he found it easy enough, tucked some way back from the sea, close to Dover.

He handed the bag to the receptionist, saying as instructed, "For John," which she accepted without question.

The next day he walked into Jackson Motors, turning to the Sales section of the reception department. An hour later he completed the purchase of a 1.8 litre Honda car with a low mileage on the clock, including taking the advice of and paying for the insurance as recommended by the salesman – all in cash. The salesman entered the full details of the transaction in his ledger, provided a computerised invoice and receipt, said goodbye and thank you very much to Frank, who departed and drove away in his car. The day after, he sold his motorbike.

Genevieve cruises with hardly an empty cabin continued at the rate of three per month, slackening off during the summer and autumn, until increasing again towards the end of the year. Sometimes Manuel and Tonio appeared in the crowd at the quayside in Tobago, sometimes they did not. The procedure was the same each time.

CHAPTER 27

The first year of married life for Will and Siobhan passed; an immensely happy one, delighted with their new home and surroundings, Will working hard and for long hours with progressing results, together with setbacks to be faced by all new businesses in, to Will, still a comparatively foreign land with different customs. Siobhan gave him huge loving support, frequently popping into the office to see if there was anything she could to help. In this way too, she endeared herself to Will's workmates, especially Leroy who thought she was the bee's knees. Max continued to be a complete rock of support and never minded fielding all the questions Will fired at him.

On the Saturday of their first wedding anniversary, they had a housewarming party at Jericho. All their friends came for a rum punch, wine and BBQ lunch, including Simon the Frock, Siobhan wearing a typical Simon flowing dress and looking marvellous. Bruce Griffiths made a point of saying how pleased he was to see Will playing polo again and what a fine example and advertisement he was for himself. Lucille came, bringing Josh Taylor and her parents with her.

Harriet confiding to Siobhan that, "The trouble is that Josh is a hell of a nice and good fellow but he is a touch dull."

"Never mind," said Siobhan. "She knows she can always come here at any time. I'm sure she will find someone worth waiting for. She's far too good not to."

In June, Mary's visit came and went. The best possible thing for her– the first proper break for a very long time. The tiredness she showed on Will and Siobhan's lightning visit in September still there, however, when met by them both, she was so excited and eager to see where and how they lived. She loved the house, was fascinated by the garden and amazed by the countryside and tropical vegetation. For two days Siobhan let her wind down, swim in the pool and potter about. Then she started taking her on trips to different sections of the island, including to Uplands to meet George and Harriet Todd, and to see Will and the set up at the

Supercar office and depot. She took her to Gibbes Beach to see Westscape from the outside, followed by a trip along the length of the beaches and hotels of the west coast.

"Absolutely amazing and fantastic, my dear," Mary said. "Quite incredible though I think you are better off where you are."

Towards the end of her stay, they invited Max and Eileen, and Bruce and Sheila to dinner.

"I was the one who spotted your son as a deckhand looking after my horses and showed him his ancestor's plantation," Max said.

"And I was the one who found him half dead with his leg in pieces on the polo field," said Bruce.

The next day, Sunday, they took Mary to the polo ground and watched Will play in Tony Knowles' team.

She left a different lady and a happier one, ready to face her next chapter.

"Remember, Mum, we both have a telephone. Let's use it often and sensibly," Will said, seeing her off on her way home.

The British High Commission headquarters in Barbados is in Lower Collymore Rock the diplomatic quarter of Bridgetown. The Resident High Commissioner is a British diplomat appointed by the British Government to help deal with all trade and business matters and to assist whenever possible with any difficulties experienced by British nationals travelling in Barbados and other Eastern Caribbean islands. British officials at the High Commission are usually on a three to five-year assignment. Barbadian staff are employed on a long-term basis. The Commission keeps a record of all businesses with any direct connection with Great Britain, including the names of British subjects with work permits in those businesses and family members residing with them. There is also an unofficial list of certain British individuals living privately on the island normally used for social purposes. The names of William and Siobhan Carpenter are on both lists.

One day in September Will received a printed invitation, sent to the office of Supercar (Caribbean Ltd), from the Barbados High Commissioner requesting, 'Mr & Mrs William Carpenter' to attend a dinner at the High Commission in about ten days' time.

Will accepted for them both after showing it to Siobhan, and grumbling, "I suppose I've got to wear a suit."

Eleven guests assembled, greeted by the High Commissioner, a jolly man in his mid to late fifties called Peter Davies, and his rather dull-looking wife. A mixed bunch of Brits and Bajans, black and white; the others being a British couple, director of a well-known construction company engaged on a major cement plant near Maycock's Bay in St Lucy, and his wife, a most entertaining black lawyer calling himself Doctor and his Thai born wife, *really charming*, Will thought, and Tom Canon and his wife; Tom was the MD of T.F. Canon & Co, who Will had met in his early days with Max at the Garrison. It was a horse of Tom Canon's that May Go Twice had beaten that famous (to Will) day. The eleventh guest being a single man in his early thirties, who Peter Davies introduced as Kevin Singleton, Third Secretary at the Commission.

At dinner, Will was placed between Mrs High Commissioner, who lived up to her looks, and the young Third Secretary, a most interesting chap who had been on the island only for a couple of months.

"Where were you before coming here?" Will asked.

"In a very different part of the world," the young man replied. "Bahrain."

"Gosh, yes that must have been very different. How did you get there?"

"Well, I think largely because I speak Arabic which I learnt at university as I thought not too many people do, other than those who live there."

"Well, what did you think of all that?" Will asked, on their way home.

"I was fine," Siobhan said. "I had Tom Canon; all he wanted to talk about was racing, especially when I told him Harry was my brother. He said he wasn't really up to date with jump racing, but knew all about Small Talk and some of Harry's other horses. He was most impressed when I told him that you had ridden Small Talk in all his work as a young horse. He's got stacks of horses here, you know, and a stud farm at his own place. He's going to invite us to come over there. Hope he will; I'd love to go, wouldn't you? How did you get on?"

"Certainly would," said Will. "We have met him at the

Garrison though I don't suppose he remembers; such a different environment. I had an interesting chat to the Third Secretary fellow. Strange to think that a fluent Arab speaker should be sent to a place like Barbados. Don't think he'll get much practice here."

Two days later, "Mr Carpenter, a call from the British High Commission for you."

"Mr Carpenter, Kevin Singleton here. We met the other evening."

"Yes. A very good evening. So kind of the High Commissioner to ask us."

"Thank you. I enjoyed talking to you. There's something else I would like to talk to you about."

"Certainly, would you like to come here?"

"Well, if it's okay with you, do you think that it would be possible for you to come to the High Commission?"

"Er, yes, if you'd prefer it that way, certainly. When would suit you?"

"How about sometime tomorrow?"

"I'm a bit tied up early – could do about midday, how about that?"

"That would be fine. I'll expect you then."

"I wonder what he wants," Will said to Siobhan that evening, telling her about the call from Kevin Singleton. "I'm hoping that he's not offering me a lesson in Arabic."

"Good of you to come," said Singleton, taking Will into a private office at the Commission. "Peter Davies is the only person with knowledge of this meeting concerning a suspected criminal matter. My brief as Third Secretary here is to investigate that it has come to the notice of the UK security services that there has been a significant increase, at specific times, of activity in the illegal drugs trade coming into the UK, it is believed from the West Indies. Acting with my superiors and colleagues, we have strong evidence that these specific activities are centred in and around the port of Barry, south Wales. You will be aware that there is a regular shipping service between the islands of the Eastern Caribbean and Barry, exporting general cargo and importing bananas?"

"Yes, I know. I served as a deckhand on a banana boat on that actual run some years ago before joining my present company."

"I and my colleagues are aware of that, Mr Carpenter."

"Do call me Will."

"Okay, I'm Kevin. To continue, I have been making several trips wearing my Third Secretary hat to all the banana exporting islands where the ships call and have found no conclusive evidence of serious activities, such as we are talking about. Petty stuff, yes, that's always there, but not to the extent that we believe to be the case. So that leaves Barbados. How is the stuff, and we are talking about cocaine and crack cocaine in the main, getting here? And how is it getting out?"

"Obviously, I don't know and your revelations are startlingly new and bad news to me. Clearly you have a reason for talking to me about it and you have my word that this conversation will go no further, but please may I ask you where and how I come into the picture?"

"Yes, I will answer your question and before going any further, please may I check a few things with you?"

"Certainly."

"Okay. Supercar is tied up with Jackson Motors on the import of all cars, vehicles etc including spare parts, yes?"

"Yes."

"All the above are shipped to Barbados on the outward route from Barry in containers?"

"No, not necessarily. Some are, though you'd have to ask Martyn Jackson about the ports of origin of the vehicles. I am pretty certain the vast majority arrive in containers but, again, not necessarily all. The same would apply to spare parts."

"What happens to the containers after having been unloaded?"

"If we have space, the ones that come to us, stay here until required again, but if you speak to the freight agents, they'll probably be more accurate than I am about that."

"Do you know how many containers go back to the UK full?"

"No, again the freight agents will know more than me."

"How much space do you have available for empty containers?"

"Properly placed, 6 to 8."

"I think that's about as far as I can go for the moment but, if you agree, I would like to pursue this further with you."

"Of course you can. Thanks for telling me. I will keep my eyes and ears open and report anything suspicious to you, though you have not answered my question to you."

"Well I have, at least partially so but one more thing: we think we may and I repeat, may have a line on how the 'stuff' is arriving in Barbados. My task is to find out how it's getting out and who's the Mr Big."

"What did he want, your Third Secretary man?" Siobhan asked that evening.

"Oh, something about what happens to empty shipping containers and how many go back to England or wherever, full."

"Hmm, so that's what keeps the High Commission occupied; how very interesting."

Will found himself tossing over in his mind what Singleton had told him. Of course, transferring illegal hard goods by land and sea presented the best option, particularly since airline security had been so tightened following the era of hijacks and suicide bombing by air. He had read reports of drugs being found in hand luggage by X-rays at airports and actually inside the human body, though only in small quantities, not the amounts Singleton was talking about. Barbados probably has more sea trade traffic than the other islands in the eastern Caribbean; also Barbados is more or less on a direct line to the UK and Europe from ports in Colombia and Venezuela.

But how does the 'stuff' get here, he wondered.

He wanted to speak to Max, but first, he must clear it with Singleton.

"I want to talk to you re our meeting yesterday and I think it would be best if we discussed it here in my office," Will said, on calling Singleton the following morning. "Any chance you could come today?"

"I can be there in an hour," Singleton replied.

"Mr Singleton to see you, Mr Carpenter," the receptionist called to say.

"Send him up please. I'll meet him at the top of the stairs."

"Morning, Kevin, come in. I've been thinking…," he related his thoughts and that he wanted to bring Max into the picture.

"I've met Max Geary once. A very senior man here."

"I've known him since I first set foot, literally, in Barbados all those years ago. He's MD of this company and I trust him implicitly."

"Okay, go ahead."

"Right, I will but first I think it would be a good idea for you to have a tour round the place here. I'll tell you why later."

"Okay, can I do it now?"

"Certainly. In order to make it lowkey, I'm going to ask my bright young manager, Leroy Proverbs, to take you."

He called Leroy on the intercom asking him to come.

"Leroy, let me introduce you to Mr Singleton, who works with the British High Commission, He hasn't been on the island long and is finding his feet. Please would you be kind enough to give him a tour round what we do here. Show him everything – inside and out – then bring him back and have a cup of coffee with us."

"Yes, Mr Carpenter, please come with me Mr Singleton."

"Max, I met a guy at a dinner at the High Commission recently. A day or so later he came to see me and raised a serious matter. I think we should talk about; would it be okay if the three of us had a meeting at your office?"

"Sure, of course Will; just give me the subject matter."

"Drugs."

At the meeting, Kevin Singleton related to Max the story so far.

Will said, "This is not just a guy sailing in here on his yacht with a bundle of coke. This seems to be a regular drug running operation on a big scale. How's it getting here and how's it getting out?"

"Very serious, as you say," Max agreed. "I will run a check on all ships coming in and out over the past six months with ports of origin and final destination. We'll see if any clues emerge. I'll also have a chat with Errol Kirton, the Chief of Police who I know. He's a good man."

The results produced nothing of any consequence from any port of origin.

Will, on the telephone to Max, "It's a long shot but when did that luxury mega yacht, Genevieve, start running cruises down the islands?"

"About the beginning of the year, I think, so about 9 to 10 months ago."

"I received a flyer on their programme and itinerary. I think the turn round port is Scarborough, Tobago. Not a million miles from the coast of Venezuela?"

"Maybe your man from the BHC will be going there soon," Max said.

Kevin Singleton was due, anyway, to make a routine visit to Trinidad and Tobago, the two islands being linked as one country, with all the admin work being carried out in Trinidad. Kevin had never been to Tobago and arranged to do so having discussed the matter with his opposite number in Port of Spain. He timed his flip to Tobago to coincide with the day of Genevieve's next visit. Getting there early he wandered about the small town, mingled with the crowd around the dock area, saw Genevieve arrive, the passengers being directed by a senior crew member, helped by a junior, to the taxi rank or towards the town.

Passengers dealt with, they both went back on board, the junior one over to the motorised day boat on a deck davit, lifted the engine cover, made a few adjustments, replaced the cover and went on shore himself. Going to a dockside café, he emerged a while later and returned to the yacht. Later in the day, the passengers started to return and were welcomed back on board by the senior crew member as when disembarking. Genevieve departed soon afterwards. Nothing untoward to note or report.

A few days later, Singleton was at the marina to see Genevieve return at the end of the cruise. The same two crewmen plus a senior uniformed officer, presumably the Captain, were on hand to say goodbye to the passengers, with the junior one helping with luggage down the gangplank.

For the next cruise date for Genevieve in Tobago, at the request of Singleton, his opposite number in Trinidad hopped over to Tobago on a similar mission. Sure enough, there were two crewmen seeing off the passengers, the junior one going over to the café when they had gone. This time he appeared out of the café approximately half an hour later, carrying what looked like an airline cabin bag, going back to the yacht in an unhurried and casual fashion.

Singleton, taking Will with him, plus a plain clothes detective deputed by Errol Kirton, stood among the small crowd in the marina when Genevieve arrived, Will standing separately about five yards apart. The disembarking procedure was the same as before. Suddenly Will's mind went into overdrive, *That's bloody Frank,* he said to himself. The passengers gone, the crowd dispersing, the three of them went into the marina manager's office which had a good view of the yacht.

"That young crew member on the gangplank," he said to Singleton and the detective. "I know him but didn't know he was working on the Genevieve. He caused the death of a horse I was riding and bloody nearly killed me as well."

He continued, telling them the polo story and his previous encounters with Frank, "His name is Frank Doune."

Singleton said, "It's definitely the man I saw in Tobago. We don't want to nick him now. For all we know, he's got a load of dirty washing in his bag. But we do want to know where he's taking it to."

"I follow him when he come off ship," Gary, the detective said. "If he have car, I radio my colleague outside the gate to track him."

An hour later Frank came off the yacht carrying the bag, no longer in uniform, he's now in ordinary shorts and t-shirt. The light was fading fast. Gary, on his own, left the marina office a good 40 yards behind Frank. In the car park, he saw him get into a grey Honda. With Frank in the car, he moved more hurriedly and just caught the number plate as Frank accelerated out of the marina.

"S2349," he spoke into his cell phone. "Follow best you can but no stop him, no arrest."

"Got it," came the reply.

Singleton, Gary and Will drove straight to the BHC. Just as they got there, Gary's phone bleeped.

"He take 2A to Bridgetown; at Errol Barrow roundabout, south of town he swing right to Top Rock, but 4 cars 'tween me an' I lose him; it goin' home time so much traffic an' dark now."

"I'll trace the car by the number plate," said Gary.

"Yeah. thanks Gary. You've done very well," said Kevin. "I think we're on to something. It looks as though we might have our runner in our sights, now to hit the target."

"Yes but we've got to up the ante," Will said.

He called Max at his office and just missed him as he had already left. He called the home number. Eileen answered.

"Hello Eileen, Will Carpenter here, Max not home yet?"

"No, but he soon will be. Can I take a message for him?"

"Yes Eileen, could you ask him to call me on my cell phone? It's quite urgent."

Five minutes later he called, "Yes Will, what is it?"

Will filled him in on the day's events.

"Can you and Kevin Singleton come right now?"

Will rang Siobhan, "Going to be late home, darling. Got an urgent meeting with Max; I'll call you later."

Fifteen minutes later they were at Max's house.

"Detective Gary will have made his report. Our – Kevin's and mine – idea and plan is, first would you be able to check with Errol Kirton that he's seen Gary's report. We are sure that by tomorrow morning S2349 will have been traced to Frank Doune's address, though he must not suspect that we are after him. Next, I've been making informal, casual enquiries as to how empty ship containers are dealt with. It seems a fairly haphazard arrangement and not necessarily the order in which they become empty, or where they are located. Now, and this is the important bit, we are suggesting that the next empty container – all containers are listed and numbered at the Harbour Master's office – targeted to be filled with general cargo bound for Barry, is chosen from one in our yard at Supercar. At the moment, we don't know how the 'stuff' is getting out, but if we ... set a trap...?

If nothing happens the first time, there's always the next one.

There's more detail though that's the principle of the plan. Obviously it will be a police exercise. Secrecy and security is paramount; hence the importance of Errol Kirton being involved from the outset."

"How will the 'stuff' actually get inside the container?" asked Max.

"We've considered this – one idea would be via a police mole infiltrated into the Supercar payroll as a driver, storeman or some such, though first, we have to find where Frank's hideout is."

Max said, "The whole area round where the police lost him is a network of residential houses, small hotels, guest houses, shops, bars, restaurants and whatever."

"Yes but the next time, now we know roughly where he's going, he'll be followed much more closely with more than one car involved and radio contact between them," Kevin said.

"That's assuming he goes to the same place," said Max.

"And we've got to come up with a lure to ensure that it is Mr Big making the drop," added Will.

"I'll contact Errol Kirton myself in the morning. Probably best if I see him on my own in the first instance," said Max.

"Mr Geary on the line for you."

"Thanks, put him through. Hello Max, what news?"

"Can you get hold of Singleton and both of you come to Police HQ in Roebuck Street at 3 o'clock this afternoon? Call me back as soon as you can."

"Fixed," said Will, a few minutes later.

"Good. When you arrive, say you have an appointment with the Commissioner of Police."

Will picked up Kevin at the High Commission. Max, already at Roebuck Street, introduced the Commissioner of Police, Errol Kirton, to Will and Kevin.

About six foot, well-built and in uniform, he said, "Max Geary has outlined the situation and I must congratulate you gentlemen for what you have unravelled so far and for bringing the matter, via Max, to me. It seems quite an operation that you have discovered. I take it, Mr Singleton that you are in direct contact with your counterparts in the UK?"

"Yes, most definitely, and they are keeping a close eye on the situation there, including a watch on all incoming cargo. We are, I hope, all agreed that the target is whoever is heading the operation here. The relevant police forces in Venezuela and Colombia where we suspect the drugs emanate from, have been informed."

"Your plan to direct the goods to a container in the Supercar yard is a good one. A problem is to induce the head man to take the bait. I see no difficulty in the harbour master's office directing cargo to be loaded in a container already in your yard, Mr Carpenter, but in doing so we must be very careful that this does not raise any suspicion in the mind of our villain.

I am going to put a man in the harbour master's office to find out the names of anybody who has been making enquiries about which container and its location is next to be loaded with general cargo. In the meantime, a detailed watch will be made on all arrivals of the Genevieve; your man Frank's movements will be closely monitored from now on. We'll catch where he's taking the stuff to, but he won't know we are onto him, I assure you."

A week went by. Genevieve's next arrival yielded nothing. Frank was listed in the police report as having arrived home in Bagatelle Terrace at 18.48 hrs. The next time it was different; he was seen carrying an airline cabin bag on board Genevieve at Scarborough. Three days later a police observer in the dockyard at the Port St Charles marina watched Frank take the bag to his car. Three separate unmarked cars followed him for sections of the journey he took, the last one taking up the trail on the road leading off from the Errol Barrow roundabout on Tom Adams Highway in the direction of Graeme Hall and Top Rock. He turned right of that road, then left and came to a stop outside the Hotel and Guest House, The Bird's Nest. The plain clothes policeman in the passenger seat got out of the car which carried on down the road. He watched Frank take the bag inside, coming out empty-handed less than a minute later.

Kirton's man in the harbour master's office reported that it was not unusual for enquiries to be made about the next available container to be loaded, but a name that had cropped up a few times during the last six months or so was a Miss Lianne Elton, with an address in Marine Gardens, Hastings. The registered name of owner of the Bird's Nest Hotel and Guest House with six bedrooms, four bathrooms, bar and restaurant is Miss Lianne Elton with an address in Marine Gardens.

The following morning, a clerk in the harbour master's office received a call asking for the container number and location of the next container available for taking a crated packing case measuring approximately 24 inches by 16 inches by 16 inches, weight approximately 26 lbs., contents table mats and napkins, destination: Barry, South Wales.

"Moment please," the clerk replied. Then, "That would be KL6790/P4368 at premises of Supercar (Caribbean) Ltd to be shipped on SS Bonaire."

"Please book that for me."

"Yes please. Your name please?"

"Miss Elton, 12, Marine Gardens, Christchurch."

"Thank you, please. Loading times 1.00 to 9.00 p.m. next Thursday."

Errol Kirton studied the report from the harbour master's office. He called Max.

"The bait is laid and the trap set for next Thursday," he said. "One thing worries me; my policeman's mind doubts that Miss Elton is Mr Big. That she is working or associated with Mr Big may well be so. I've asked my man in the office to try to find out if, on previous occasions when she has booked space in a container, whether she delivered the packing case to the container depot herself, which personally I think is unlikely, or if someone else did it on her behalf. If so that person may be the one we are after. Most ladies don't go round hefting 26-pound crated packages."

"I take your point and agree. I'll talk to the 'lads' about it."

The 'lads' as Max called Will and Kevin, had the same doubts as Kirton. The start of a busy few days for both of them.

"You know when your young manager, Leroy, took me round your depot, I take it that the entrance round the back with newly tarmacked strip onto the main road, is for goods vehicles," Kevin said to Will.

"Yes, absolutely. We want to keep the main entrance in the front looking smart and suitable for customers collecting and returning their rental cars. Round the back is, as you say, the goods entrance and exit for stores, spare parts and the like, including containers to be off loaded by our own crane. You saw the area where we keep empty containers."

"So that when Miss Elton plus, we hope, her 'assistant' comes with her wooden crate on Thursday, she'll go to the goods entrance?"

"Yes."

Criminal drug-related activities in the UK fall under a department of HMRC. Kevin Singleton's contact, directly via the High Commission, is an agent in that department. Based on the events and history that Kevin had been able to report, a possible line was being followed. For very many years, numbered Swiss bank accounts have been safe havens for holding sums of money that are not disclosed by the account holders for whatever reason. However, more recently the Swiss government and the banks themselves have been under a great deal of pressure to relax some of the secrecy, especially when criminal activity is suspected. The agent had reported that large sums had been transmitted from another European capital city – not disclosed – to a Swiss bank and onward via New York to a bank in Bogota, Columbia. Likewise, sums had been deposited in the Swiss bank account from the same European capital. The interesting point being that these transactions followed a similar fashion, as if one was dependent on the other. The timings coincided with the drug activity in South Wales.

Next morning, Wednesday, Max called Will to say that Kirton's man in the harbour master's office had reported that Miss Elton always came with a man to help her with the package. Later that morning he and Kevin decided to take a walk to Marine Gardens, an easy distance from Kevin's office at the BHC.

What they discovered there prompted them to make a long call to Errol Kirton at the end of which, Kirton said, "Okay, I'll take care of that."

That evening, after Will had been home for a while, Siobhan said, "Will, darling, is anything the matter? You've seemed rather tense and quiet the last few days. Have I done something to upset you?"

"Come here, darling. If you had done, it would have been the first time, but no you certainly haven't. The truth is that I hate, more than anything, not being able to talk and discuss everything and all things with you. Just recently that has been and is happening, but don't worry, it's not personal and by tomorrow it should all be over and you'll know everything."

"If it's something to do with the business, I can curb my curiosity for another day, as long as you know I'm always here for you."

Thursday morning, Will checked that all was in order for the acceptance of goods through the rear entrance. He had previously put out a notice saying that deliveries would be arriving that afternoon and evening for loading the container under direction from the harbour master. Soon after 11 o'clock, the harbour master's mobile unit arrived complete with weighing machines, computerised invoice and receipt systems plus three staff members, one of whom being Kirton's man with a device to contact three unmarked police cars parked locally, but separately. By midday all was ready. The senior clerk said that he expected the container to be no more than half full. In Will's office, only Kevin was with him. Will was to call Max as soon as there was any action.

During the afternoon booked orders arrived and were dealt with in the normal way, the largest being a consignment of six thousand litres of ready-made and bottled Barbados rum punch by T .F. Canon & Co to an English pub chain to promote a rival alternative to Pimms.

By the time darkness fell, deliveries had more or less dried up, though the time stipulated was 9 p.m., so they just had to wait. The flood lights in the yard were switched on. At 7 o'clock the last Supercar permanent staff left for home. Max rang at 6.30 on Will's cell phone to say he was going home and to please ring him there.

Will and Kevin looked at each other, both with similar thoughts in their minds.

What if nobody comes? Has their plot been rumbled? Is there a mole in their midst? What the fuck's going on?

Will risked a call to Siobhan saying he was delayed and would call when he was leaving.

8.30 went by, 8.45, nothing.

8.55 Will's intercom bleeped.

"4x4 car approaching, stand by," said a voice.

It came slowly through the gate. A man wearing overalls and a thick woollen hat covering most of his face, got out as did a lady from the passenger's door. The man opened the tailgate and lifted out a wooden packing case. Carrying it, he and the lady approached the mobile unit.

"I have a package booked. I am Miss Elton."

A uniformed Police Officer formed up out of the shadows, flanked by two others, both armed. The first officer said to the man, "Sven Goran, I am arresting you on suspicion of importing and attempting to export a quantity of illegal drugs. Please will you open the packing case?"

Sven stood still, gazing at the night sky, watching his world fall down around him.

One of the officers ordered him to place his hands behind his back and fixed handcuffs over his wrists.

"Lianne Goran, I am arresting you on suspicion of receiving a quantity of illegal drugs and attempting to export same."

She too was handcuffed.

The three police cars had driven into the yard. Sven was escorted to one and Lianne Goran to another; both of them were driven away and placed in custody pending further enquiries.

At the same time, two uniformed police officers were knocking on the door of a house in Bagatelle Terrace.

Will and Kevin, who had been watching the scene from the side of the building, came forward.

Will called Max on his cell phone, "All done. Suspects arrested."

"Shall I come?" Max said.

"I think it can wait until the morning, unless you really want to."

"Okay. Well done to you all. Quite an ordeal. 9.00 in my office?"

"Fine. I'll bring Kevin."

To Siobhan, "I'm on my way, darling. Could do with a drink."

"Well, go on, how did you do it?" Max opened the conversation. Will and Kevin agreed that Will would do most of the talking.

"There were two major breakthroughs, one on each side of the Atlantic. First, we thought an examination of where Miss Elton lived was appropriate. The house in Marine Gardens is a substantial detached house in pleasant surroundings; not quite in keeping with the down market Bird's Nest Hotel and Guest House. As we were walking past a lady came out of the house, onto the road. 'Hello', we said, 'are you Miss Elton?'

'Oh no,' she said. 'No Miss Elton live here'. Then she said, 'Yo from the hotel – Bird's Nest, maybe? She marry Mr Goran five years back but keep name, Miss Elton at hotel. I de maid for Mr and Mrs Goran.'

'Mr Sven Goran?'

'No, no Mr Bjorn Goran, Mr Sven brother. Mr Bjorn own other hotels nearby here.'

Next, Kevin's contact agent in the UK succeeded in extracting the European capital city where the instructions to transfer funds to the bank in Bogota came from. It was Copenhagen. We know that Mandrik S/A is the major shareholder in the luxury yacht, Genevieve. Where are they based? Copenhagen. Who is the principle shareholder of Mandrik S/A? Mr Vagn Goran.

Next, it wasn't too difficult to work out that Sven was using his younger brother as a cover, helped by his wife keeping her maiden name at the Bird's Nest. However, it was essential that it was not Bjorn who accompanied his wife for the drop at Supercar, even though he may have done so on other occasions. Hence our call to Errol Kirton. I think you'll find that Bjorn Goran is recovering from a minor incident last night that needed medical attention, and that a Police Officer is probably questioning him as we speak. At this moment, we understand that the Danish National Police are interviewing Mr Vagn Goran, Sven's cousin, in regard to this matter."

Kevin added, "Well all that ties in with a call I received from Errol Kirton a short while ago. Sven Goran's passport has revealed that in addition to the visits he made to Tobago in respect of arrangements for Genevieve at the port, he made two separate ones to Bogota directly from here in the course of the last nine months, each lasting three to four days."

"Darling, give the Calabash in Grenada a call. Let's see if we can't sneak off there next weekend?"

EPILOGUE

Nine months to the date after their Calabash weekend, Siobhan's and Will's son was born. They named him James; Lucille, Jimmy van Duren and Max agreed to be godparents. Two years later, along came a daughter; by common consent, her name is Lucille.

Lucille herself met, fell deeply in love with and married the manager of another hotel in the same Group as that of Mike Williams. After a while, he was promoted to be manager of the luxurious Camino Real hotel in Oaxaca, southern Mexico. Three years later he applied for and was appointed manager of Cobblers Cove, back home in Barbados, where they are now, also with two children, Will being godparent of the elder and Siobhan of the younger.

Will and Fred became main board Directors of Supercar. Robert Mallory never retired; he just died quietly one night. Going to bed feeling a little under the weather, he never woke up. In his Will, having made certain that Kathleen would never have to worry financially, he provided bequests to various family members. He also left a very considerable sum to Will, to whom he referred as his 'surrogate' son in place and in memory of his own son, Allan. Fred is now Chairman of the company with himself and Will joint Managing Directors. Both the Irish and Barbados subsidiaries are going from strength to strength. Fred couldn't bear to leave his beloved Manchester, so gradually moved the HQ from Solihull to nearer home. 'Aggers' retired with her pension well supplanted by Mallory. The 'Robert Mallory Memorial Pro-Am Golf Tournament' is an annual highlight of the Irish golf scene. In Barbados, Supercar (Caribbean) have depots in St Lucia and Grenada.

Will and Siobhan divide their time between both continents. They have a nice house with a bit of land near Malpas in Cheshire, not far from where Mary lives comfortably in a small house just outside Tarporley. In Barbados, with the bequest from Mallory, Will bought the piece of land shown to him by Max all those years before, on which the remaining walls of the original Welchmans

Hall stand. Here, he and Siobhan are building their Barbados home. He plays polo in Barbados and Cheshire. Joanna lapped up the London scene and has a responsible job with her Charity supporting deprived children and families from Zimbabwe to where she makes frequent visits. She has a steady boyfriend, a Guards Officer – Irish of course – of whom the family approve and are 'hopeful' as to the outcome.

Harry met his match with Loretta, the paddock commentator and fashion model. He married her, to the delight of all, except for several others who would have liked to. Harry is now one of the top trainers in Ireland.

George and Harriet Todd wanted to retire, especially after Lucille married and returned to Barbados. Will and Max hit upon an idea to create an Agricultural College on the same lines as Cirencester in England. They formed a consortium to put the plan into operation at Uplands with George Todd much involved. Three years later the 'Uplands Benjamin Carpenter Agricultural College of the West Indies' opened to much pomp and circumstance by the Governor General with the Prime Minister and all notable business and professionals of the island present.

As the mythical tape was cut, Will turned to Siobhan, "I feel this is Redemption Time," he said.